No Better Than Beasts

ALSO BY Z. R. ELLOR

May the Best Man Win

Acting the Part

No Better Than Beasts

Z. R. ELLOR

Roaring Brook Press
New York

Published by Roaring Brook Press

Roaring Brook Press is a division of Holtzbrinck Publishing

Holdings Limited Partnership

120 Broadway, New York, NY 10271 • fiercereads.com

Our books may be purchased in bulk for promotional, educational, or business
use. Please contact your local bookseller or the Macmillan Corporate and
Premium Sales Department at (800) 221-7945 ext. 5442 or by email at
MacmillanSpecialMarkets@macmillan.com.

Library of Congress Cataloging-in-Publication Data is available.

First edition, 2024

Book design by Trisha Previte

Printed in the United States of America

ISBN 978-1-250-86699-8

1 3 5 7 9 10 8 6 4 2

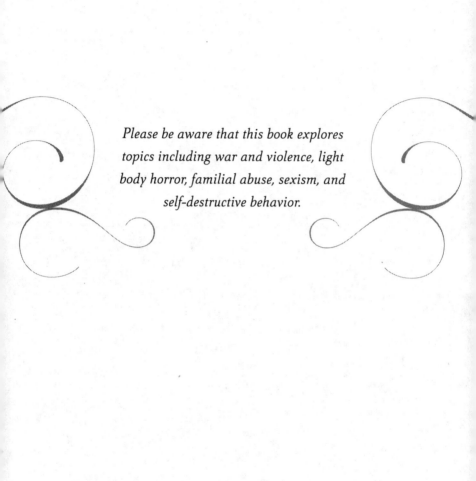

Please be aware that this book explores topics including war and violence, light body horror, familial abuse, sexism, and self-destructive behavior.

To the boys who live out someone else's wishes,
the girls denied wishes of their own, and those of us
who wish to be marvelously strange

Overture

Dangrus, capital of the Szpratzian Empire

When she was nine years old, Drakne Zolkedna traded a princess's soul for dancing shoes.

Fydir, her eldest brother, had been generously endowed with a city townhome. Its pink-painted brick and brass-lattice window tops convinced Drakne they'd moved into an enormous cake. Lacy curtains and paintings of dancing bears framed her bedroom walls, a bedroom she didn't have to share with anyone. Maids polished the wooden floors until she could slide whole hallways in her stockinged feet. After years on the streets and in crowded apartments, her new house felt as grand as a royal palace.

Best of all, Fydir hosted traditional Kolznechian balls all winter long. Aristocrats in top hats and gowns danced in circles around potted pines with branches draped in ribbons and lit with blazing electric bulbs. Footmen with crystal trays served finger cakes, chocolates, and flutes of sparkling wine. Gifts wrapped in crinkling paper were passed from hand to hand. Music and meter rose from the orchestra through the floorboards, curling around Drakne's toes and ankles. Sparking something deep inside her.

Her nursemaid always put her to bed early on those evenings.

So when the old woman retired to the kitchen, Drakne slipped down the hall, to the room everyone assumed was an unused closet. If she stood on a stool, she could, through a slit in the wall, peer down in secret at the glittering assembly. Could imagine she herself danced ballet to the sweeping sound of violins.

One evening, as she swirled her nightgown to the notes of a minuet, a man stepped into the little room.

He was small and shrunken beneath his tuxedo jacket, and he bobbed as he moved, like a pigeon. Archduke Marinus. The richest man in the Szpratzian Empire, who had made Fydir his spymaster. Who had paid for their house and its secrets.

"Hello, Your Grace," Drakne said. "How might I help you?"

He smiled, sweet enough to rot teeth. "Miss Zolkedna. Always a pleasure to meet a girl with such a unique gift."

Drakne's heart sped. "Beg pardon?" Mama Minka's dying warning echoed in her ears. *Protect your magic, Little Goose. Hide it from those who might devour you.* "I don't know what you mean."

"Don't be afraid. Your brother told me all about it. Kolznechian magic is a special interest of mine."

Fydir would never! But the truth wedged between her ribs like ice. Fydir would not refuse his patron. Every day, he left their lovely house to do the archduke's bidding. Every night, he came home sharper and colder. *I do it to feed and shelter you,* he always said. *I do it to keep you safe.*

But Drakne didn't feel safe. She felt betrayed.

"Would you like to help your family?" the archduke asked. "Will you do me a favor?"

Even at nine years old, she'd known it was a command. She

nodded. He pointed through the screen at a young woman, her hair stacked in thick ringlets beneath a gold tiara. Hunger filled his eyes as she laughed at another guest's joke.

Marinus told her what he wanted. Drakne slipped into the ballroom and took the woman's hand as music swelled.

Princess Sofiya had a soft spot for children. When Drakne begged her for a dance, Sofiya tucked a sprig of holly into Drakne's dark hair and pulled her into a waltz. As though by magic, Sofiya's friends and attendants fell into step as music wove about them. Drakne, spinning in the warm arms of a princess, could almost believe herself at the center of a fairy tale.

But the gaze of the archduke, who was watching hidden from above, prickled on her skin. If this was a fairy tale, it had no happy ending, and she was the evil fairy who beguiled maidens into the monster's den.

The next morning, a courier delivered a pair of dancing shoes. Rose pink with diamonds pinning ribbons to the toes, crafted for small feet. No note came with the package, but when Fydir quietly asked if Drakne understood the archduke's message, she nodded. She'd done well. She was to do it again. And she had to keep it a secret.

Through the long, dark winters, their iced-cake house hosted one shining soiree after the next. Guests came to take in the siblings' *authentic* Kolznechian culture and seek favors from the archduke and Princess Sofiya. By the end of the first year, tired of watching in secret, Archduke Marinus joined the melee of skirts and suit coats, circling Sofiya like a bald-pated hawk. By the end of the second, he would not dance a measure without Sofiya in his arms.

From age nine to eleven, Drakne grew like a yearling colt, knees and ankles knobby, shoulders awkwardly wide. Diamond shoe after diamond shoe arrived, as she outgrew them almost as fast as she wore down the soles. Tutors were sent to refine Drakne's footwork, but her magic, she clumsily taught herself. Only she could see the bronze threads that flowed from her toe shoes like notes on a score sheet, weaving a spell that bound Princess Sofiya in the archduke's arms until the last bell of the evening.

For each prancing step Drakne took could force others to dance as she bade them.

Wizardry, whispered gossips. *A beguiling glamour.* Some suspected the Zolkedan siblings. *All Kolznechians dabble in dark magic. They've let that fiend they call the Rat King rule their country for two hundred years.* But Sofiya earned the worst barbs. *Marinus is the richest man in the Empire and she's unmarried at thirty. She must have bargained with the snowfae to tease him into her hands.* Shame and suspicion biting at her heels, Sofiya stopped sleeping, stopped smiling—until she returned to hug Drakne to her cheek. Sofiya's affection ate through Drakne's stomach like the coals that saints fed sinners in hell, and for days after the balls, Drakne couldn't eat without tasting bile and brimstone.

"This needs to stop," Nabik said one morn after the guests had departed. The middle Zolkedan sibling, only eighteen months her senior, had discovered the eggs and porridge a nauseated Drakne had scraped out her window. "The princess hates the archduke. Whenever they dance, she wishes she was dead. I can *feel* it."

Drakne bit her lip. Nabik had the power of *true* northern wizardry. He could sense the wishes of others, make them tangible by summoning mended bootlaces or jars of candy from nothing. But fairy tales made no mention of young wizards weeping over wishes that shouldn't come true. "I have to. We're nothing without him."

"It's making you sick, too. Haven't you noticed?"

She hesitated. It sounded like such a funny thing. For guilt and shame to make you sick, like fetid water.

"Tell Fydir how bad it's gotten. Please. He'll put a stop to it."

"What if he's angry?" Her voice sounded quite timid. "What if he stops loving me?"

Nabik wrapped his arms around her, pulling her into a tight, warm hug. "No matter what he does, I'll always love you. I *promise*."

That afternoon, Drakne slipped through the heavy cedar door of Fydir's study. Orchestral music spilled from the phonograph in the corner, warming her heart. Coming around his desk, she stared at the carpet and stammered about Sofiya's plight and her own. Fydir set down his spy reports, tapped his cigar on the ashtray, and gave Drakne an encouraging smile.

Fydir was a man everyone noticed, with his strong, broad shoulders, gold-bearded chin, and red velvet dress uniform. Far too conspicuous to gather information himself, he'd assembled a vast network of informants who, supposedly, slipped in and out of the house to pass whispers behind his closed study door. Drakne had made a game of trying to pick out the spies amid their guests, but had yet to catch one.

"Marinus is an odious man," Fydir said. "He'll be most

surprised the day he bows at my feet. Would you like that? To be a princess like Sofiya?"

Drakne didn't dream of being a princess. She wanted to dance, see the circus, and always eat cupcakes. She wanted Fydir not to yell so much at Nabik, and for Mama Zolka to come home. But she nodded. She knew Fydir wanted her to say yes. "What should I do?"

"Keep at it." Fydir patted her cheek. "For now, we need to do as he asks. And don't feel guilty. Sofiya could resist your little trick if she wanted to. It's only dancing magic."

Fydir made it sound so small. Made her *feel* so small. "That's not how it works." Drakne hummed along to the phonograph music, lifting her arms into fourth position. Fydir's hands flew up to mirror hers. His cigar fell to the rug. She took three prancing steps backward. He stepped back as well, his long shadow pulling away from her. The rug began to smolder.

"Drakne!"

She jumped. The spell broke. Fydir leapt on the cigar, crushing it beneath his heel into an ash-gray smear.

"Out," he growled. "I have work to do. Out!"

The next ball was a grand occasion, held to mark Yuleheigh itself: the winter solstice, when the day was darkest and the goddess Winter bid her people to hold one another close. Drakne watched guests arrive through her bedroom window as she braided rosy ribbons in her long, dark hair and bit her lip. Soft, fresh snow tumbled down to the street. The wind blew, and a shape manifested in the flakes: a white winter owl, its chest full of flurries, its wings outlined in starlight. Drakne pressed her nose to the pane. Another gust of wind carried the owl away.

Harsh light shone through the glass as the soul-engine auto-cars of Sofiya's motorcade pulled onto their street. Drakne winced and rubbed her eyes. Turning from the window, she shook out her ruffled white skirt and ducked into the hallway. "Nabik! Where are you?"

"Here," he said, and Drakne jumped. Was he right behind her? She turned around and glimpsed his pale face peering out of her wardrobe. "I was . . . hiding."

"From Fydir?" she asked. Fydir liked to yell that Nabik wasn't a real man, that he cried too easily, that he smiled too much, and the older Nabik grew, the more Fydir shouted. Their fights often ended with Nabik curled up in bed, praying into his pillow. *Saint Kema, make me a warrior. Saint Avazane, make me a loyal brother.* "I'll hide with you."

But as she reached the wardrobe, Nabik jumped out and shut it behind him. His brow was furrowed and his fists were clenched. "No. I'm being silly." Violins warbled downstairs. He pushed her dancing shoes into her hands. "We'll both be wanted in the ballroom. Get ready."

Something's wrong. She knew it. "Wait!" But he'd already run away. Worries spiraled through her head as she laced up her slippers and went downstairs.

As she stepped into the ballroom, Princess Sofiya glided over and kissed her forehead. "Drakne! Happy Yuleheigh!"

"Happy Yuleheigh," Drakne mumbled.

"What a dear girl." Powder had painted Sofiya's cheeks a jolly red but couldn't conceal the hollowness of her eyes. "Dance with me, else—" Her eyes shot toward the archduke, who watched intently from beneath the mistletoe. "Else he will."

"I'll dance with you," Drakne promised. "I won't—"

The opening chords of Zdaski's "Melody for a Snowfae Maiden" stirred on the strings of a cello. Violins joined, and the melody filled the gilded ballroom. Heavy skirts in bright jewel tones rustled as guests took their places for the dance. Drakne's toes prickled. Excited shivers ran through every inch of her. She never felt more powerful than when she danced.

Archduke Marinus raised his voice. "Miss Drakne Zolkedna. Open the dancing with a ballet solo."

No. He was going to separate her from the princess at the very start. Drakne looked about for aid, but Fydir only smiled at her, his expression as sculpted as a bronze bust, and Nabik flinched from her gaze. Drakne crossed to the center of the floor. Her heart pressed against the top of her throat as she lifted into an arabesque.

Then she spied it: the great roaring hearth, framed in marble and topped with pine garlands, the leaping flames hot and merry. Drakne grinned. It was the perfect dancing partner for the archduke.

She swept her leg around, down, into a demi-plié. Her arms lifted into third position. Magic arced, a faint flicker of sparks leaping from the balls of her feet to the tips of her fingers. Dancers stirred. Stepped to their positions. Princess Sofiya's hands landed atop Marinus's narrow, sloping shoulders. She shot Drakne a desperate look—but then Drakne twirled a pirouette, and the music carried them both away.

Horns and violins played the legend of snowfae girls charming beauty into snowflakes and rainbows. Drakne spun the tale in steps and gestures. *Rond de jambe. Passé. Glissade.* Guests whirled and laughed, caught up in the music. Drakne focused her magic on the princess and the archduke. With each tap of her toes, she tugged at the bronze strings that bound them like a puppeteer, guiding them through the press of bodies. Past stacks of wrapped packages and presents, past pine trees draped in ribbons and shimmering foil. Closer and closer to the fireplace.

This is my power, not yours. The thought burned through her. *I want it back.* Some part of her remembered that terrible things happened to Kolznechians accused of using magic. But surely Fydir would protect her. However angry he might get, they were still family.

A spasm rolled through her feet. A blister burst where her toe shoe pinched tight. Crimson bloomed on the pink satin.

Drakne wobbled. Sofiya pulled back against the archduke's grip.

"Keep dancing," Marinus hissed, tightening his grasp. Drakne braced herself. *I'll dance till you burn.* She couldn't even blink away her tears. It took all her concentration to spin the spell. *Dance. Fight.* Everywhere the fabric of her shoes rubbed burned like fire. She tried shifting her weight. A toenail cracked in a starburst of pain. *Not just for yourself. For Sofiya. For Nabik, who feels all our wishes—*

Nabik. Who had run away from her. Who dared not meet her eyes. Who had thrust her shoes into her hands.

Who had deliberately given her an older, too-small pair.

As she pushed up en pointe, Drakne slipped in her own blood and crashed down on the polished floor. The bronze threads snapped like the strings of a violin's bow. The dancers froze, staring at the stains on her shoes. The music died, and shocked whispers took its place.

Princess Sofiya slapped the archduke and screamed.

"You little fool," Fydir hissed, seizing Drakne's wrist. She yelped, trying to pull free, and he shook her arm so hard she felt her bones twist. Tears poured down her cheeks.

"Fix this, Zolkedan!" the archduke shouted. Behind him, Sofiya gasped and sobbed. He lowered his voice. "Make her dance."

Fydir gestured at Drakne's bloody feet. "She can't, sir. I'm sorry. I'll see her punished."

By morning, three doctors had declared Sofiya hysterical and ordered her confined to a rest cure in the distant mountains. When Drakne woke, with her head aching, her feet bandaged, and the outline of Fydir's fingers on her arm, she was on a train racing across the countryside toward the boarding school that would be her home for the next seven years. The buildings there were cold gray brick, with bars on the windows and leaks in the roof. They assigned her a cramped dormitory room to share with four other girls, where her thin cot came with only a single threadbare sheet. She had never felt more alone.

But a letter waited on her pillow, the envelope sealed with the stamp of a crowned rat.

Under Soul-Fed Chimneys

CHAPTER ONE

Almond Butter Bullets

Malirmatvi, northern border of the Szpratzian Empire

The strikers sent a snowfae to deliver their demands.

The union women had piled sewing machines against the factory doors and flooded into the road, arms locked with yellow sashes tied about their waists. One woman held a club studded with sharp industrial sewing needles. They cheered and chanted as their representative climbed the snowy hill. Locks of platinum hair blew loose from her bun; her plum eyes squinted into the crisp autumn wind.

The red-uniformed soldiers in formation behind Nabik Zolkedan stared and whispered. Even his old gray gelding, nickering and pawing the ground, watched the girl approach. Fables said that Winter herself had made snowfae to fill the world with beauty, but Nabik himself never paid much heed to a woman's looks.

"Captain Zolkedan." Boris Atvidan, the factory owner, greeted Nabik with poorly disguised frustration. "Here she comes. This girl's been riling up the stitchers for weeks, convincing them to unionize." Atvidan wore a fine elk-skin coat. Embers of rage and alcohol glowed at his temples. Behind him was a cluster of women, their cheeks chapped and their eyes cast down. Strikebreakers, ready to take up the labor the others had left behind.

"I'd bet she's a Kolznechian spy." He spat. "Weakening the Empire so the Rat King can invade."

Nabik caught scent of the factory in the wafting breeze and wrinkled his nose. It was the smell of the workers' reeking latrine mixed with the fumes from the tannery. The factory's loose boards and shutters rattled noisily in the wind. *If I had to sew hats there, I'm not sure if I'd first lose a finger to frostbite or a lung to the gases.* The Kolznechian families who lived here called the neighborhood Rot Hill, and many ruder names besides.

"The Kolznechians are the poorest folk in the city, and they're treated like it," Nabik said. "Of course they're organizing strikes. A man of your means should take up a more dignified pastime than spreading baseless gossip—perhaps stamp collecting?"

"Gossip? Is that what you call it, when your own border patrols report giant rats moving in the forest?"

Tense whispers swept through the ranks of soldiers. Nabik straightened his spine. "Governor Zolkedan is investigating the sightings." Preventing Kolznechian intrusions was the chief duty of Fydir's new position. He'd given Nabik the task of calming the city. "Good day, miss," he called to the snowfae girl as she drew into earshot. "My name is—"

"I am Talzne," she said. No patronymic or matronymic. From what Nabik knew of the snowfae, they spurned such human customs and kept to themselves. That she was here at all confused him mightily. "I should like to speak first and present the complaints and demands of the hatmakers' union," she said, businesslike. "You will excuse my lack of pleasantries. This has all become more urgent since Atvidan called in the guns."

Her list of grievances was long. Women losing digits to jammed mechanical presses, fainting and vomiting from inhaling tanners' chemicals, being forced to work sixteen-hour shifts until they dropped. Atvidan had bought a mansion off his beaver hats; couldn't he pay to repair equipment and install proper ventilation? Atvidan compensated his trappers if they crossed the border and sprouted fur or feathers; shouldn't the hatmakers be compensated for their injuries too?

"These women would be freezing on the streets if it weren't for me," Atvidan huffed. Silver buttons flashed at his throat. "I let them make an honest living. Not that I expect a pagan Kolznechian girl like you to value how civilization works."

"Show some respect," Nabik growled, gray eyes narrowed beneath his black brows. Having reached six feet tall by the age of nineteen, he was imposing even without a horse beneath him. With his wide jaw, rough features, and polished medallions on his red wool uniform coat, he looked every inch a soldier. "I'm the one with the army, not you."

Talzne gave him a long, searching look. "You're Kolznechian, aren't you?"

Nabik tightened his grip on his reins. His horse shifted skittishly beneath him. In her accent, he heard echoes of Znaditin, the Kolznechian capital. He'd grown up on tales of that city and its crystal trees, the pumpkin boats that traded up the Sounding Sea, a god called Winter with silver in her veins. Stories flooded his head. Legends that would serve him no purpose save to drown out his resolve. "I serve the Szpratzian Empire."

"Why? Why are you doing this? Half the union is Kolznechian—"

"So are half the strikebreakers," Nabik said. "So is the governor who sent me. We all want the same things. Peace and prosperity, all the blessings that keep us warm in wintertime. When we have calm in the streets, we can turn our attention to other matters. Like an inspection of all factories in Rot Hill—"

"You'll inspect *us*?" Atvidan spat.

"That would be a start," Talzne said, "but inspectors alone can't make him pay better. We need something more."

Against his better judgment, Nabik reached for Talzne in his mind. His magic read her wish. *Join us. Help us.* He wanted to. Her wants and his sung in harmony.

But Fydir had given him orders to calm the city. And every lesson his brother had taught him about being a soldier had one common core: *Obey.*

"Enough." Nabik's voice came out steady, but his hands trembled. "Tell the strikers to stand down and return to work. They can trust the governor and the inspectors to resolve this."

"What? No!" said Talzne. Nabik nearly sighed in frustration. Was he the only one who understood the way of things? Workers worked, and soldiers fought.

Nabik raised an arm, waving his men forward. Talzne glared at him, sharp as frostbite, before sprinting back down the hill to link arms with her sisters. Nabik led his men in a measured, steady march, ranks locked, boot steps a steady rhythm, even the puffs of their breath rising in unison. He looked at the women and whispered a prayer. *Please, oh Winter, let them run.*

Ten yards separated the lines when the striking women scattered like starlings. Skirts flapped about their ankles as they darted away, shouting to their fellows, vanishing into a maze of ramshackle workshops and warehouses. Some tossed rude gestures back behind them.

"Hold the perimeter," Nabik told his men as they fanned out around the factory grounds. "Don't give chase. Arrest them if they jump you." He dismounted, handed his reins to a young private, and pointed to two of his men. "With me. Check the inside for stragglers."

Nabik pushed through the rattling wooden doors, gagging at the awful stench. Patches of mold and mushroom bloomed on exposed roof beams. Crumbs of food drew squeaking mice to the corners. Scrap fabric sat stacked in dusty piles; the strikers had pissed on the lot.

But what lay in the center of the floor nearly made Nabik vomit on his boots.

Soul-engines. Once, the machines had been people. They still looked it, in part. The matting apparatus resembled a blank-faced woman with iron blocks for hands. No human workers remained to deliver her the loose wool she would press into felt, and so those block hands pounded down on an empty conveyor belt. The fulling machines, three of them, were smaller, the humans inside compressed by Marinus's devious invention into a space no higher than Nabik's waist. Felt still ran in wet ribbons through the roller wheels that had once been the workers' chests, squashed down into tight mats. From there, the felt unspooled onto a table, where human workers would stitch it into hat shapes. They would then stretch the hats over wooden blocks and set them in a soul-engine shaped like a man on his knees, his head tipped back and distorted in an agonized howl, his mouth stretched large enough to breathe steam through six hats on their wooden molds at once.

Soul-engines transformed the workers bound inside into metal and gears. Powered by the soul of a single laborer, one machine could do the work of ten. Marvels of industry Nabik couldn't look upon without wanting to scream. *I could draw my gun. Force Atvidan to release them.*

But as long as the factory held their bond-contracts, the industrial codes would force them to labor out their yearslong terms—laws Archduke Marinus had spent fortunes to push through Parliament. The Empire must modernize at any cost, the archduke claimed, lest rival nations overtake them. *Soul-engines make steady work for unskilled laborers. They let poor families relieve their debts.* What he did not mention was that he held the patent on soul-engines, that his engineers built them in his workshops, that every factory or craftsman that used them paid him monthly fees. That the poorest families in the Empire had spent years torn apart from one another all to pay for the gold dust on his caviar. *He's already so rich,* Nabik had privately said to his brother. *Isn't that enough for him?*

No, Fydir had said. *You don't build a world like this for yourself unless nothing is ever enough.*

As the sun sank through the yellowed sky, Nabik marched his soldiers up from Rot Hill and into the city's bustling heart. The main avenue, newly widened to permit soul-engine autocars, bloomed with murals of red and blue wildflowers painted across freshly whitewashed buildings. The streets bustled with farmers, butchers, and fishermen hauling overstuffed barrels to market, their cries and grumbled curses mixing with the harmony of a street preacher in tattered yellow robes who was warning them that Saint Clovis would toss the wicked onto burning coals. As the soldiers approached, the crowds stilled and parted, silently, to let them pass.

The wind picked up as they climbed the hill toward the governor's manor. Nabik shivered as snowflakes caught in his collar. As if pulled by magnets, his eyes were drawn to the city's northern edge. Brick and barbed wire slunk along the Kolznechian border. Gunning turrets pointed at the foreign, silent forest.

Help me, came a faint whisper. Soft as snowfall. It might have only been a dream.

Two hundred years had passed since a power-hungry court wizard betrayed the royal family, murdering the last Kolznechian monarch and naming himself the Rat King. While Nabik's ancestors had fled south, most of their kinfolk had clung to the lands they knew, even though it meant following a king they didn't. And then a curse had crept over the kingdom, like a fog. Changing the flesh of all who remained.

Soldiers with fox fangs and ferret faces had chased fleeing peasants with mouse-round ears toward the border. The surviving nobles had warped, hairy backs growing full pelts and jaws sprouting hungry, tearing teeth, like the wolves and bears of their family sigils. The stories said terrible, twisted screams could be heard as far south as the Szpratzian capital those first nights, as backs broke, joints popped, and hands crumpled into clumsy paws. Now, in the depths of winter, Kolznechian wolves sang hunting songs in human tongues, and their prey begged for mercy in the same. Even a few hours in Kolznechian territory would raise fur on the tips of your ears—and then the howling wolves might call your name.

The governor's manor lay between the city's small cathedral and the barracks. As his soldiers marched off to their quarters, Nabik rode through the manor gate. The high windows of its two wings stared down at him like eyes. Its gabled roofs rose sharp against the gray of the clouds. The weather vane, shaped from tin into a falcon with four spinning wings, spun wildly. Nabik had lived here only two months; the Zolkedan brothers had traveled north directly after Fydir received his promotion. He was certain by now it would never feel like home.

The new military governor of Malirmatvi stood in the manor's grand, near-empty foyer, between its wide wings. Draped in a massive fox-trimmed coat, his golden beard grown thick, and his rifle case thrown over his shoulder, Fydir looked every inch a storybook lord of the wild north.

"Brother!" he boomed, throwing an arm about Nabik's shoulders. "I heard you did well—sent those union peasants fleeing." Fydir passed his coat off to a serving maid. As she staggered with its weight, he took a glass of whiskey from her tray. She then offered the tray to Nabik, who shook his head. His brother's praise had warmed him more than any liquor, thawing out each part of him the north wind touched.

Nabik waved the maid away; she curtsied and departed, allowing the brothers to speak privately.

"Fydir, I'm concerned. The mood in the city—"

"The city, the city. This muddy little city and its moods. It's all you talk about these days. You're as dull as a banker, and you don't even have money to make yourself interesting."

Nabik stiffened. For all of Fydir's cheer, he himself felt as alert as if he stood on a battlefield. "Any word on the giant rat sightings?"

"Lady Ruba assures me the Rat King has no intention of entering Malirmatvi. He's hunting a fugitive near the border."

"Can we trust her? Wasn't she exiled from his court?"

"Are you scared of a girl half your size?" Fydir laughed. "Yes, we can trust her. She tells me she's seeking a *lord*." He spoke the title even more hungrily than when he'd spoken her name.

Oh no. Whenever his brother courted a noblewoman, it ended with him drunk in bed, cursing her snobbery and prudishness, while Nabik had to do all his work for weeks. "Could you really be happy with someone you'd only married for a lordship?"

"Are you an expert on love now? Who was the last girl you kissed? Porcelain dolls don't count." It tripped off his tongue lightly, so that if Nabik asked, *Am I really that undesirable?* Fydir would answer, *I was joking—you're as sensitive as a serving maid.*

"I'm no expert, and thank Winter for that," Nabik said, like he was in on the joke. "With all my obligations, I can't exactly squeeze in a spouse." Before Fydir could push further, he changed the subject. "Say, have you heard from Drakne?" She hadn't answered his letters in months, but perhaps she'd written to congratulate Fydir on his promotion. It was only polite. Not that Drakne cared for manners.

Fydir slid the leather case holding his rifle off his shoulder and cradled it in his arms like an infant. The massive custom-made gun, a gift from the archduke, had swiftly become Fydir's

21

favorite weapon. He'd whisper to the metal as he polished the bronze stock—but only when he didn't think Nabik could hear him. He wouldn't let his brother so much as set eyes on his trophy. "We can expect her to arrive in the next week."

"I'll have the maids put the good dishes up out of reach." The last time Drakne had come home, when they were still in the capital, he'd caught her sneaking in from a dance hall through the kitchens and called Fydir downstairs to confront her. They'd shouted at each other for nearly an hour, until Fydir pushed a stack of dishes down to shatter on the floor. Both of them slunk upstairs after, quiet and ashamed, while Nabik cleaned up the debris. He had learned peacekeeping long before he'd come to Malirmatvi.

"No need to pretend you're the family's nursemaid," Fydir said. "Drakne may be slow to learn—saints, all those failed classes I paid for—but soon, she'll be as disciplined as you." He looked about for a servant; spotting none, he shoved his empty glass into Nabik's hand.

Their new staff had learned to keep well-stocked liquor cabinets and iceboxes close at hand. Nabik ducked into the salon to find the nearest. It was a dark, cold chamber, with the fire gone out and violet brocade curtains covering the windows. The gold damask accents glued to the green wallpaper glittered dully; armchairs, a chaise lounge, standing mirrors, and a grand piano packed the room wall to wall. It smelled of tallow candles and dusty books, and there was a squeaking, shuffling sound he took for mice until he pushed aside a curtain and found a small girl crouched there.

Though she wore the uniform of a house servant, she couldn't have been older than six. The red ridges of an adult's slap glistened on her cheek. She froze, staring up at Nabik with tears running silently down her cheeks. *Barely higher than my waist and already terrified of grown men.*

"It's okay," Nabik said, softening his voice and kneeling to meet her eyes. He waved his hand in a semicircle—a flutter of the fingers, like stirring a pot. Snowflakes spun out of the air and twined about his knuckles. Twig arms and coal-fleck eyes grew from two snowballs into a tiny plump figure in his palm. "Say hello. Winter's come to bring you good luck."

The girl waved shyly. The little snowman bowed in reply. She giggled. Out in the front hall, someone called, "Olga! Where are you?" The girl leapt to her feet and scampered away.

Nabik gave his creation an assessing look. *Wizardry lives on the winter wind. My power is stronger here.* Back in the capital, he'd have worked himself into a migraine from concentrating hard enough to summon and animate snow. How many sweltering summer days had he spent curled up in his bedroom, weeping with frustration over the spells he couldn't work for Fydir? Shame prickled in his cheeks at the memory. *I failed him.* After that, he'd pushed down his instincts to work magic, pretended to be just another common soldier. He'd forgotten his power could bring joy.

"Where's my drink?" Fydir shouted. "What are you doing in there?"

Nabik jumped, crushing the snowman into powder, but not before his brother saw. Fydir stormed through the doorway into the darkened salon.

"You little fool," Fydir said. "You think magic is some plaything?"

Nabik stumbled backward. His hip caught an end table. A porcelain vase tipped over and fell, cracking on the carpet. Instinct took over. He reached for his brother, and his magic did too, like a wild wind. *No.* He had stopped reading Fydir for good reasons. But it was too late. His brother's feelings swept through him, sharper than his own pain, hungry as an all-devouring fire.

Fydir *wished.* So fiercely Nabik couldn't glimpse his goal, so thoroughly perhaps the goal didn't truly matter. And Fydir *feared.* Hungry visions stalked his mind—Archduke Marinus, nobles and officers, even Nabik and Drakne, standing tall above him, plotting behind his back, weaving spells the likes of which he never could. Every thought, like a pickax, hollowed out a pit inside him, an abyss that screamed to be filled with more, more, *more*—

Nabik's shoulder slammed against a windowpane, knocking it open. The pain jolted him back to himself. "Blessed Winter," he gasped. "Brother—let me help you."

"I don't need your help." Cold coiled through the window. Puffs of white rose from Fydir's lips. "I need you to remember the way of things. Kolznechian magic terrifies the Empire. If you're not careful, everything will be ruined before it's begun."

"What are we beginning?"

"You'll know soon enough. Until then, your duty is to obey your commanding officer. And that means no magic unless I give you my express permission."

Nabik frowned. Being a proper Szpratzian officer didn't come easy to him. He had no interest in girls or gambling, no care for war, conquest, or fortunes. Yet, no matter how he struggled, Fydir was there to teach him the way. He owed his brother a great deal. Only—"It's my magic. Can't you trust me with it? I'll be careful about revealing myself, I swear it—"

"You swear it?" Fydir said, mocking. "Forgive me if I don't

trust a wizard. Isn't that what Mama Zolka said when she left? *I'll be back soon. I swear it.*"

Why must he always change the subject? "She didn't know that she wouldn't be able to return. Only that the north wind was calling her to help lift the curse on Kolznechia." Thirteen years ago, Mama Zolka had kissed Mama Minka and Drakne goodbye, pulled Fydir into a hug, and whispered *I'll be back soon, sweetheart* in Nabik's ear before she strode down the road, whistling.

On the coldest of days, she'd sent snowflake owls south with messages. Each could whisper only a few words before vanishing. Until her last, almost a year after her departure, which Nabik, Drakne, and Fydir had received together: *Winter binds every wizard who crosses the border to her service. I can't come back. I'm sorry. Keep warm. Stay together. I love you.*

"She couldn't even come back when Mama Minka died." Nabik lowered his head. "Imagine how it felt. It must have been so hard for her—"

"What's *hard* is raising two children when you're fifteen!" Fydir shouted, and though Nabik flinched at the sound, he knew the part of Fydir screaming was a child still. "Sending you two off to sort the washerwomen's rags for pennies while I went to break my back working in the noblemen's stables. What's hard is killing—killing again and again, until you make yourself *like* it because it buys you a future! What's hard is having one person, one, in all the world you trust—"

"Me?"

"Of course it's you." Fydir's fists unclenched. The salon's shadows softened on his brow. "What's hard is knowing you want to leave. Just like she did."

"Never," Nabik promised. "I'm your man. That's all I've ever wanted."

Behind him, the open window banged in the wind. Nabik turned to shut it. A squall from the north filled his nose with the tempting scent of peppermint and pine.

~

Drakne, with chaos, arrived the next morning.

Nabik was sitting in the parlor, reading books on military strategy and sipping strong black tea, when Fydir's shouts rolled up the promenade.

"Start a fire in the master bedroom!" Fydir bellowed as he burst through the doors. Servants leapt to follow his commands. "Bring broth and a bedpan—no, not the doctor, she's only weak—now, you fools!"

A pale, dark-haired figure lay curled in Fydir's arms, clad in grease-stained wool coveralls. *Engine grease. A factory worker?* She wept like her heart was broken, shivered like she'd been pulled from the ice. Nabik paused. What was his brother doing with this wounded girl?

It wasn't until Fydir swept her past him and up the stairs, until the door to a spare bedroom locked behind them, that Nabik realized. *Drakne.*

"Fydir?" he shouted, running after them. Remembering Mama Minka, coughing and white-faced as she died beneath that one thin sheet. He pounded at the door. Fear and desperation made his voice crack. "Drakne? Fydir! Is she hurt?"

The door swung open. Fydir stepped out, jaw set in a harsh

frown. Behind him, servants continued to flutter around Drakne. "Stop bawling. It's only a cough. She'll be fine."

"I want to see her." This did not look like *only a cough*. Nabik tried to duck around his brother, get a better look. Fydir shut the door.

"You're a soldier. Not a nursemaid. The servants will look after her. You will do your duty. Take some men and go to the Gorsky Bank. They're having trouble with a mob. Put an end to it."

"I will. After I make sure Drakne's well."

"That's an order." Fydir's voice dropped, low like a roll of thunder. Promising a plate-throwing storm. "It seems our sister isn't the only one who needs to learn respect. Go. Now!"

Nabik knew better than to argue with that. He ran for the barracks, barely stopping to grab his hat before he stepped out the door. But when the north wind caught his cheek, he paused and looked out from the hilltop to the border.

Dark pines and silver birches wavered, windswept, in the forest, like snowfae maidens beckoning him toward the cursed land. *I could steal a sleigh from the barracks. Pack for a long journey. No one would stop me from crossing if I said it was on Fydir's orders.* He could use his magic freely, train with other wizards, find his mother. But he could never come back. *And my family needs me.*

He gathered up his men and marched them down into the heart of the city. The bank glittered in the thin sunlight. Its white plaster facade, pillars, and plinth were carved with frolicking milkmaids and prancing cows. The third-story clock bore the metal-plated face of a smiling full moon.

The crowd of fishermen gathered by its brass-barred doors were much less merry in comparison.

"Burn the papers," they shouted. Some were ancient, with white hair and beards hanging ropy with salt. Younger folk ringed them, holding clubs, gutting knives, and meat hooks. Children flocked about, waving signs that read *Bank Theft* and *The Bank Stole Our Boats.* "Burn! The! Papers!"

"What's going on?" Nabik demanded as he approached, soldiers flanking him.

"Imperial bloodsucker!" A grizzled old fisherman spat on his boots.

The woman beside him shook her head and turned to Nabik. "In the fish drought three years back, Lord Gorsky offered us relief loans with our boats as collateral. But the interest is too steep. His men have taken over thirty vessels."

Nabik gritted his teeth. He knew all about loans and debt. After Mama Minka died, the landlord had shoved a heap of unpaid bills in his seven-year-old arms and said, *Lazy runts get the boot.* Lord Gorsky could forgive all the mortgages and never miss a cent. *If he crossed the border, how long before the curse turned him into a spineless sucking leech?*

"At least there's no snowfae today," grunted a soldier.

"Snowfae might be the least of our problems," said another. "I've heard there's a wizard in the woods. A woman wizard, who charms goodwives to dance naked under the full moon."

"Bad enough we've got the Rat King as a neighbor."

"And now the Kolznechians are meddling with unions. Between their spells and these marches, they'll put half the Empire out of business. If the governor let us teach those fur-faced bastards a lesson—"

"Magic is rare," Nabik said, cutting off the soldier before his talk veered closer to violence, "even among Kolznechians. And most of these fisherfolk are Szpratzians anyhow." He squared his chest and pressed his hands to his hips, as Fydir had taught him, hoping it would make him look older and more authoritative. "In the interest of public safety," he shouted, "I order you all to disperse. Leave freely, before we use force. You can bring your complaints to the open city council meeting in a fortnight."

"We'll lose more boats in a fortnight!" shouted a one-armed woman with a thick knit cap. "Tell Lord Gorsky to stop collecting."

I wish that would work. The lord would likely laugh in his face. "Maybe," Nabik stuttered, "maybe the priests will give you alms, or—hey! Stop!"

Two of his soldiers had drawn their guns and were poking at an old man in a salt-stained coat. They knocked his cane away. It clattered against the bank steps. A younger man grabbed the graybeard's arm before he fell.

"What are you doing?" Nabik demanded.

"He threatened us!" whined one soldier. "He's got a knife!"

"It's a paring knife!" Nabik said, taking one look at the short, dull blade on the fisherman's belt. "Put the guns down, now!"

"Guns?" gasped a voice in the crowd, then "Guns!" bellowed another. Lightning quick, fear swept through the gathering. Children fled, darting into alleys and behind their mothers' skirts. Older protestors ducked behind the plaster pillars; younger ones hoisted clubs and hooks aloft.

"Don't worry!" Nabik shouted. "All's well!" His men surged forward. They grabbed the protestors' signs, brandished bayonets in their faces, kicked mud at the women and children. Some of the younger protesters linked elbows to form a wall. Soldiers yelled and cursed at them. Nabik raised his voice. "Step back! That's an order!" But his words vanished amid the noise of the seething crowd.

And then the north wind blew.

The protestors' wishes swept through him like the tide. They craved relief from red fear and muddy confusion, the stabbing pain of hunger and a million little aches. They wanted the scent of anchovies from a day's catch, not the sting of tears as bank officials turned them from their own boats. And hope, bright and fragile, burned in their hearts as they joined arms and demanded justice.

"Get back!" barked a lieutenant, lifting his rifle. A dozen enlisted men followed suit. "Back, or I'll shoot!"

Nabik's breath stopped. His heart hammered double-time in his chest. He couldn't tell the wind's howl from his own panic. All he felt was the crowd's sudden, desperate wish to *live*. If he acted—if he dared—

A muzzle flashed.

"No!" Nabik shouted. Cold air burst from his fingers and billowed through the crowd. Something crunched inside a dozen guns.

The air went quiet.

A soldier shook his weapon. Coconut shavings fell into his palm. Crumbs tumbled out of a dozen overturned gun barrels and bandoliers. The scent of roasted nuts, warm and homey, rose through the square. Infantrymen reached into their ammunition pouches and drew out chocolate cookies studded with candied almonds in the shape of bullets.

Nabik cursed and wiped a crust of powdered sugar from his palms. Had they seen him? Did they know?

"It's the wizard of the wood," gasped a fisherwoman. She caught a pouch as a frightened soldier dropped it. Then she pulled out a cookie and bit down. "She's here! She's come to aid us!"

"She can't cross the border," said a man armed with a steel umbrella. "Winter's bound her to the north. Maybe an apprentice?"

"Look lively, boys!" shouted a grizzled sergeant. "Grab anyone carrying a staff!"

"Enough!" Nabik bellowed. "Disperse! Go home! The last soul left on this street, I'll have thrown in jail!"

This time, his voice broke through. The fisherfolk grabbed their children and handfuls of cookies and scattered back down the hill. Soldiers escorted a group of shaken bankers out from the building to their autocars, then fell back into formation. Nabik climbed atop his horse, slouched forward in the saddle, and marched his men back to the barracks. Hoping his scraggly, half-grown beard would disguise his growing smile.

He whistled an old winter carol, stretching out his power to drink the city's relief. His wizard's heart, bright and strange, fluttered in his chest like a long-caged bird taking wing.

I'm sorry, Fydir. But I want my magic to be mine.

CHAPTER TWO

Powder with the Spark Gone Out

Drakne Zolkedna didn't remember how to walk.

At school, the grizzled old dancing master had made her practice for hours at the barre, neck straight, smile sweet, ankles burning. She'd been forced to lift furniture and sprint up hilltops carrying water jugs, all to strengthen her legs and back, and she'd spent hours on a mat, pushing her aching hips into a perfect split. With every practiced flick of her toes, she'd sharpened her magic like a knife. Now her flesh and blood felt heavy to wear, and whenever she coughed or drank the egg broth they gave her, she tasted metal. As her fever spiked and she shivered under the quilts, she held fast to one truth: she'd survived her brothers before. She could do it again.

The third time she collapsed while trying to leave the bed, the servants sent for Fydir. He dismissed them all as he entered, then sat down at her bedside and squeezed her hand. Fear surged through her body. She pushed her eyes open, and asked "Where's Nabik?"

"At his duties."

"When will he come back?" Her pulse pounded. Fydir held back his worst tendencies with their brother around.

"When he can, Drakne. He's a busy man." The words he'd

left unspoken were *too busy for you*. "You'd best not tell him any wild stories about where you've been. Understand? He'll bring everything you say right to me. And I won't have you making any more trouble for this family."

Drakne bit her lip. *That's a threat.* She changed tactics. "Have there been . . . any letters for me?"

"Letters? No."

Was he lying? She wasn't certain. What if one had come and he'd stolen it? Fydir would recognize a code if he saw one. *How much does he know?*

"May I have paper and a pen?" She pushed herself up to a sitting position. The effort left her panting for breath. "I want to write to my friends—"

"Absolutely not. And I'll tell the servants not to post anything you write. Anyone who lets you get into this much trouble is an unfit friend for a young lady."

You did this to me. You.

"May I at least have a candle?" she said. "The dark—it scares me."

He studied her. She held her breath.

"Have you learned your lesson?" he said. Drakne nodded. "Truly?"

"Yes. I promise. I'm sorry." Lies. All lies. But the trembling weakness in her voice was all too real.

"Good. Then we won't speak of this further. Let's put the matter behind us." He fished a waxy stub and some matches from his pocket and left it for her as he departed.

Three hours past nightfall, Drakne stumbled from the bed on wobbling legs and rested her weight on the small table by the window. She pushed the glass up in its frame—gasped at the cold—stuck the candle on the ledge, and struck a match. The wick blazed stubbornly in the night. Rummaging through the table's small drawer, she found a polished hand mirror and held it up to flash the signal—three long, seven short. Three long, seven short.

Great Winter, hear me, she prayed. She couldn't remember the last time she'd done that. *If Nabik can't help me, send me someone worse.*

The first thing she'd learned about the Rat King was that he did not give up easily. She'd ripped his first letter to shreds, burned the second, and flushed the third one down the lavatory. He'd switched his tactics. She'd been overjoyed when the school's new dancing teacher offered her private lessons—until the old woman revealed herself to be in the Rat King's pay. *He knows about your dancing magic. He thinks you can change the world.*

Drakne had learned enough about powerful men. Without even giving an answer, she'd run from the classroom, out into the night. Down the road she'd fled. Dark and cold had closed around her. She'd trudged down the road to town, toward the light of a factory. Perhaps the workers would help her find the train station.

Instead, when she peered through a window, she saw a woman and three children, a crew of maintenance workers, and a small stamp press. The largest part of the machine was the two exposed sockets on its side, each five feet tall, pulsing with purple light that tugged at her gaze like a magnet. The whole family was crying, all save the eldest boy, who helped his mother into a socket before climbing into one himself. Steel arms closed around them. Metal moved like liquid to cover their faces and limbs. The sockets tightened, the imprisoned bodies shrinking until they barely came up to Drakne's shoulder. When the children stopped sobbing, the foreman gave them a sack of flour and a small stack of banknotes.

Drakne turned away. The sorrow swelling inside her felt too big for her body to hold. She sank to the ground, shivering, arms wrapped around her knees. She missed her mothers.

Something scratched at her ankle. A little rat-shaped thing, made from twigs and rotting autumn leaves, a letter in its mouth.

This time, Drakne opened it.

Written in fine, delicate cursive, it read: *You can bring families like these back together.*

A warm hand curled under her cheek. "Hush. You're all right," murmured a soft, familiar voice. When acid clogged her throat and came from her lips in a wretched tide, calloused fingers turned her head to retch in a pan.

Nabik set the pan on a stool, frowning down at her beneath his harsh brows. "What happened to you?" he demanded.

Her stomach turned again. She gagged. Nabik passed her back the pan, swept her hair off her face. Bent double, she choked, sputtered, and spewed until her stomach was empty.

He sighed. "Was it something at school? Are there other girls ill like this? Have you been drinking?"

She shook her head. *Did he not notice—or care—that he hasn't heard from me in eight months?* Her hopes, small as they were, sank further. They hadn't been close in years. She'd written to him only once a month, and her letters had contained only a few curt lines. But once upon a time, Nabik's arms had been her one certainty as they huddled in cold, unfriendly places, waiting for their brother to return from work. Would he really go running to Fydir if she spoke the truth? She had to try. "Don't you know why I didn't come home all summer?"

"Saints preserve us," Nabik whispered. "Are you pregnant?"

Of all the useless—"Only with the urge to kick you."

"Good," he said. "The last thing I need is another Drakne to look after."

Drakne sat up. The sudden spike of anger made her feel almost human again. "You haven't *looked after me* in years." No, he wouldn't save her. But perhaps he might do something small. "Would you have a pen and paper on you, by chance?" Three days had passed since she'd first sent her signal, with no reply. It might take weeks for a response from her old dancing teacher, but it would at least be a start.

"Fydir said you weren't allowed to write letters."

She slumped back against her pillows. "You won't even wipe your ass without his say-so."

"Well, he doesn't even want me visiting you." Nabik plumped up her pillows, took a folded quilt from the chest at the foot of the bed, and laid it within her reach. "But he's off dealing with Kolznechian spies right now, so . . ."

"Foreign spies? In the city?"

"Three rat-soldiers hid in a crate that supposedly had been

sent south by Kolznechian ore traders. They bit off a soldier's finger before we got them in custody."

"I'm glad you caught them." Two rats had likely snuck by for every one they had found. Her brothers' ineptitude fueled her hunch: Fydir knew nothing about her role in the Rat King's scheme to weaken Szpratzia by sabotaging its factories. *If he did, he'd have plucked out my toenails to make me talk.*

She didn't intend to wait around for that.

Drakne rolled out of bed. Her left knee buckled. She stumbled, cursed, and recovered her balance. Nabik reached for her. She brushed his hand away.

"Where are you going?" Nabik demanded.

She pulled a coat from the wardrobe and belted it over her nightgown, shoved her feet into a pair of boots. "Anywhere but here!"

"Drakne! Stop!"

His *stop!* didn't scare her. For all his faults, he wasn't Fydir. Drakne pushed through the door and nearly tripped on the hallway carpet. She stumbled down the wide oak staircase, leaning on a balustrade. Housemaids and soldiers reached for her. "Are you well, miss?" "Miss Zolkedna, let me help you back to bed." She ignored them, focused on remembering how to walk. *One foot. The next. Weight balanced. Push forward.* Her weakened muscles screamed as she staggered through the hall into the foyer. But her rage kept her standing, burning in her chest like coals in a furnace.

What no one understood about soul-engines, not until they were trapped in one themselves, was how the magic *changed* you. For eight long months trapped in Fydir's gun, Drakne had possessed brass metalwork and lead shell casings for bones. Her hands had formed a gilded trigger. Cartridges had rested in the chambers of her heart. Compressed in that small space, each part of her had been twisted up tight like a powder packet waiting for a spark.

She was out. But in no way unwound.

As Drakne surged toward the door, it opened. A figure stepped into the entryway. She slammed into them.

"Blessed Winter!" gasped the girl now on the floor. "Am I a guest or a bowling pin?"

"I'm sorry," Drakne said. Her cheeks burned. She offered the girl a hand and pulled her to her feet. "Are you hurt?"

"I suppose I'll live. How are you? I have an awfully hard head, you know."

It was the first time anyone had asked how she felt in years. Her tangled anger and embarrassment began to ebb. "My pride is a bit bruised. I've had a—a difficult few days."

"Well, there's much worse ways to deal with difficulty than sprinting headlong through a hallway. I should applaud your thoughtfulness." The girl, perhaps two or three years Drakne's senior, wore a burgundy gown trimmed with a dark fur collar. Her brown hair, cut in a neat bob, matched the fuzz on her peachy cheeks. Garnet earrings hung in her long, round ears, red-framed half-moon glasses rested on her upturned nose, and as the corners of her lips pulled up in a smirk, her long incisors flashed against her lip. *Beastfolk.*

"Lady Ruba, of Znaditin," she introduced herself. "I came to have dinner with the governor."

"He's out," Drakne said curtly.

"Ah well." Ruba didn't sound overly upset to have missed him. "You must be Miss Zolkedna. You're ... taller than I thought." Ruba swept her gaze up the length of Drakne's body. "Though it's easy to be taller than a mouse."

"The beastfolk curse reveals your true nature, doesn't it?" Drakne said. Perhaps it was rude to ask, but she had always wondered. "Shouldn't a noblewoman turn into a wolf or a wildcat?"

"My true nature is more suited to a library than a battlefield. Have you ever thought what yours is?"

Drakne mulled it over. "Maybe one of those southern sea snakes with three tails and three ... other bits."

Ruba flicked open her fan, hiding her giggle with a plume of ostrich feathers. "The natural sciences are quite fascinating, yes! Do you enjoy zoology?"

"I enjoy making handsome strangers blush."

"Oh my." The light only brightened in her hazel eyes. She reached for Drakne's hand, hesitated, and then adjusted the ill-fitting coat's cuff, like that had been her intention all along. "Where were you off to in such a hurry?"

"I ..." Drakne bit her tongue.

The second thing she'd learned about the Rat King was that he knew what she wanted. In exchange for her services, he had promised to get her into the best ballet company in the Empire, to pay her well enough that she would live in luxury all her days. Where would she go without that? To work in the factories, to beg in the streets? She needed to contact the man, to confirm their bargain still held.

How, though? She had never met him in person, but his letters had come regularly since she accepted his bargain, brimming with bits of arcane theory and suggestions on how she might shape her magic. She had written of her progress and her questions on the back of the page, and he'd assured her, by his magic, he read every word she wrote. But she had no magic letters now, only the emergency signal. She missed his scribblings more than she might have thought.

"I'd love to hear more about your life in Kolznechia," she said. *Do you know how to reach the Rat King?* But what if Ruba told Fydir she had asked that? "Did you spend much time at court?"

"Frankly, I try to avoid it. A tedious place full of self-important blowhards, all led by an immortal melancholic bore."

Drakne laughed. If the Rat King had been boring, she wouldn't have spent the last few months spitting death from her throat.

Nabik leaned over the balcony from the second floor. "I'll take care of her, Drakne. You should be in bed."

"Ignore him," Drakne said.

"Of course," Ruba said. "Shall we have some hot drinks?"

An hour later, they lounged on a green-cushioned love seat in the salon, Ruba's head on Drakne's shoulder, mugs of molten milk chocolate in their fists. The scent tugged Drakne back to the life she'd lived long ago. Sitting by a fire, tucked warm between the mothers she barely remembered, while carolers sang and the scent of baking gingerbread filled the air.

"This was a good idea," she murmured. "I needed this."

"I'm full of good ideas," Ruba said. "We're Kolznechian. We know how to welcome someone in on a cold day."

Drakne smiled. Everyone in imperial society knew the archduke had elevated a Kolznechian soldier to his right hand; everyone always knew who her people were before they knew *her*. At school, her heritage had been a reason for other girls to shut her out. To Ruba, it was a reason to open a door.

Ruba plucked a walnut from the little bowl on the table and cracked it with the bifurcated silver tool beside the dish. "Do they still tell the legend of Winter and the nutcrackers in the south?"

"What?"

"When Winter created the mortal folk, in the shadow of the Great Mountain, the first tools she taught us to make were for opening nuts. So we could eat the bounty of her forests all through the coldest months. The nutcracker is a symbol of her motherly love."

"And a wonderful mother she is," Drakne said darkly. "Telling her children to be kind, then vanishing in a puff of snow while we torment and abuse each other." She believed in the goddess, of course. Magic had to come from somewhere, and no Szpratzian science could explain it. But she didn't believe that Winter truly cared, no more than she believed that Mama Zolka did. *If she cared, she'd be here with us. If she cared, she would have saved me from Fydir.* A piercing ache built in her chest. She changed the subject. "Ruba, why were you exiled?"

"Quarreled with the wrong noble. The Rat King took his side and cast me out. Can you believe that?"

"Of course. He's a rank bastard."

Ruba laughed. As she tipped back her head, Drakne glimpsed the cameo strung on a ribbon at her throat: a crowned rat. *Jewelry with the royal seal. A mark of the king's favor.* Perhaps Lady Ruba had received it in the distant past. But why still wear it?

She's hiding something.

Fydir's boot tapped in the salon entryway. Drakne jumped to her feet, nearly spilling her chocolate. Ruba stirred, yawning, and said, "Governor Zolkedan. Good afternoon."

He smiled at her and dropped into a bow. "My lady. Always an honor. I hope Drakne hasn't been bothering you."

"Your sister makes for delightful company. We've been discussing traditional Kolznechian folklore."

"I haven't heard the old stories for years," said her brother. "You must have heard them all, growing up in—Znaditin, was it?"

"Right you are. We're at the center of Kolznechian culture. I'm biased, but there's no Yuleheigh celebrations in the world like ours." Ruba flicked shut her fan, a garnet thing topped with black feathers, and tapped it thoughtfully on her chin. "I'd love to show you both. Charmers summon glowing beasts with fireworks, mummers dance on twenty-foot-tall stilts, and even the Great Mountain rumbles at our songs."

"It sounds magical," Fydir said. "Like the stories my mothers told."

"Magic, indeed." She gave him a smile. "Might you possess any magic of your own?"

Drakne froze. *No.* Fydir hated that question, even when their own folk asked it. It made him feel weak. If he had a gift, it was quieter, more subtle, than Nabik's or her own.

Fydir grinned, flashing his straight white teeth. "Perhaps I'll reveal my vast magical abilities on our wedding night."

Ruba gasped, then giggled. "That's no way to speak to a lady," she pronounced, but her smile only grew.

Of course he wants to marry her. Drakne's fists tightened. Under imperial law, all of a noblewoman's holdings would be transferred to her husband the moment they wed. At least that meant he had to stay on his charming side around Ruba. That, Drakne could use.

"How are things at the border?" Ruba said. "Is the Empire still planning to invade over a few rats?"

"The Empire wants new land and lumber. Souls for their soul-engines. An invasion is an easy way to get those, and they don't need much of an excuse." Fydir reached into the liquor cabinet and poured himself a thumb width of vodka. "The Rat King plays a dangerous game. Whoever he's hunting, he must think their head is worth risking war with the Empire."

"It's Prince Eugen Kutredan, I've heard. The last of the old royals. A wizard is hiding him near the border. The Rat King wants him found."

Drakne winced. Some foolish part of her had hoped the rats might be looking for her.

The third thing she'd learned about the Rat King was a hard one: you couldn't trust him to save you.

The first time she'd danced in a factory, she'd felt as free and lovely as the great swans of Dangichzuk. Two local musicians, hired with the Rat King's gold, played flute and violin as her toe shoes picked through sawdust. Bronze light flickered with each step she took. Between her teacher, the Rat King's letters, and her own experiments, she'd learned how to govern her power while she danced—to keep it in check so the Szpratzians would not suspect her when she performed, or to leverage all her strength until not even the archduke's machines could stop their victims from dancing along.

Soul-sockets popped open. Workers leapt from the great milling machines, joined hands, and spun in time. Laughing. Gasping in relief. Shouting their thanks. Triumph swelled within her, like nothing she'd ever known. Here she was, at the start of the grand career she'd been promised, performing for royalty by day, destroying their factories by night, made rich off the Rat King's largesse. She might even have done it for no reward—it felt good, right, to wield her power to help others.

But the second time, Fydir had discovered her. The musicians had hidden. The freed workers had fled. She'd faced him alone, with no company save the echoes of their every last terrible screaming argument.

And he'd broken her.

~

I can't wait for anyone else to rescue me.

"Ruba," Drakne said, "do you ever host balls?"

"Someone in this dreary city has to," Ruba said. "You both should come to my next one. Miss Zolkedna, I could show you my nutcracker collection."

"I'd love to," Drakne said, and meant it. *Careful. Don't let her charm you. Not until you know for certain how deep her alliance with Fydir runs.* "I think we'll be very fit friends. Don't you agree, Fydir?"

He stiffened. But he could not deny her this, not with Ruba watching. Slowly, he nodded.

White flickered at the window. Drakne turned in time to glimpse a falling, snowy feather, and saw herself reflected in the glass. Pale as fresh snow, bruise-like shadows hollowing her cheeks. Hair a dark river, eyes two new moons. A sickly and thin girl who looked like you could lift her up and tuck her away on a high shelf with one hand.

But if you tried, you'd find her heart weighed down by bullets, her guts stuffed with pistons and gears. A terror of the modern era, finding her own way.

CHAPTER THREE

Out of Joint

"A man nailed a wreath of dead rats to a baker's door." Nabik leaned across Fydir's desk, a stack of reports in hand. The office, lit by a single glass lantern, draped both brothers in shadow. "In Rot Hill, a Kolznechian neighborhood. We need to calm the city before someone gets killed."

Fydir reached up and grabbed a fistful of Nabik's hair. "When was the last time you cut this? Do you want the Empire thinking this family is no better than beasts?"

Nabik took a deep breath, closed his eyes, and counted to five. This time, going limp worked. Fydir released him. "I'll cut it. Listen—this snowfae girl, Talzne, the one who's helped stir up the strikes? An informant said she's planning a protest outside of Lady Ruba's ball tonight. If I arrest her and hold her a few days, things might calm down—but I don't want to punish her just for speaking out. Is there something else I could try?"

"You're too soft on these people. I already agreed to an open forum with the laborers and to hand out extra grain." Fydir pushed model tanks and soldiers across the map he'd bought from a ferret-eared merchant. *Kolznechia and the Greater Polar Lands.* Information decades out of date, if not purely fabricated, and yet he'd paid for it in gold. *Why does he need that?* Military governors had broad discretion with how they might use force within their holdings, but Fydir couldn't send troops north without Parliament declaring war. "Well? Go catch the snowfae. What do you need from me?"

Nabik sighed. "I just need to get into Lady Ruba's party. Might I come with you?"

"I wrote and declined her invitation." Fydir squinted at his model tanks like his knitted brow would make them fire. "No time to waste dancing. Ask Drakne if you can go with her. I'm sure she'll be happy to oblige. By the saints, I think she might be my new favorite sibling." Those last words tripped lightly off his tongue. Like a joke. To Nabik, they tasted bitter as vermouth and gin.

Since Drakne had recovered from her illness, she'd been the picture of courtesy—and Nabik loathed it. He loathed it when they ate breakfast in the cavernous dining room, Drakne rarely speaking save to say "Of course" after all Fydir's remarks. He loathed it during services in the cathedral, when Drakne smiled through the sermons and murmured piously along with every prayer. He loathed it in the evenings, when Fydir invited the local elite to dine, drink, and gamble, as Drakne praised their wit and wisdom and Nabik sat sullenly by the fire, waiting for the sister he remembered to resurface and start a table-flipping argument.

He wanted his old sister back. The little girl whose arm he'd tied to his when they slept in the children's shelter, the girl he'd taught to waltz on a snowy lane. The Drakne who argued loud enough to drown out Winter's call.

Because the voice on the north wind grew ever stronger. He'd wake at midnight, nose pressed to his forest-facing window, breath tracing fractal snowflakes on the glass. Icy patches spread beneath his boots if he stood still too long. Whispers blew into his ears whenever the gales sharpened. *Come to me, Nabik, child of Zolka. Serve me. Help me.*

It urged him to use his magic, to take reckless risks. Still, he dared not follow it north. He had to be a soldier, a brother. His family needed him here.

~

"You want me to take you to the party tonight?" Drakne laughed, not looking up from her bedroom mirror as she painted roses on her cheeks. Nabik stood in the doorway, his head ducked awkwardly beneath the low beam. "You hate parties. You hate people."

"But I like traditions." Kolznechians celebrated winter from the moment the first snowflakes fell, and the snow fell early indeed this far north. Since Drakne's incident with the archduke, Fydir had forbidden Nabik from so much as hanging a wreath. He missed the joy of it all. "Remember how Mama Zolka would bake gingerbread and let you lick the spoon?"

"I was four when she left," she said. "I barely remember those snowflake owls she used to send. All I know of her is what you've told me."

"She loves you," Nabik said. "It's not her fault—"

"Why do you have to make excuses for her?"

Nabik sighed. "Very well, I won't. Just—take me to the party."

"Say *please.*" Her teasing voice jabbed like a stick in the eye. "'Please, Drakne, take me to the party. I'm the only Zolkedan sibling with no invitation.'"

"I won't."

"You will."

He rolled his eyes. "Please, Drakne, take me to the party. I'm the only Zolkedan sibling with no invitation. Which is a good thing, because I've caught both you and Fydir wishing Lady Ruba will fall in love with you. Someone in this household needs to keep their head."

"Yes, you're quite good at keeping your head in these circumstances. That's why you've never been kissed."

He lowered his voice. "This is the Szpratzian Empire, and I fancy men. It's dangerous and you know it."

"That's never stopped me from kissing anyone I liked. It didn't stop our mothers from being happy together."

"Only because Mama Zolka could pass for a man in a suit. She had to wear one whenever she left the apartment, since that was what her documents said she was. She hated it." The wishes of her heart had always warred fiercely—to provide for her family, to be who she was. "We've all made sacrifices to survive in the Empire. Our family's well-being matters a great deal more to me than love."

"As your family, I beg you, go be happy. Or, if you'd rather make yourself miserable, leave me out of it."

What chance of happiness did he have? "You don't understand. At least you also like men. You could have a decent marriage—"

Drakne threw a hairbrush at him. "There's no happiness in giving up half your choices, Nabik. I fight for what I want. You could try that." She flicked open a tin of cheek powder. "Meet me downstairs in an hour."

~

Nabik dressed before his small room's mirror, adjusting his red wool dress jacket until his epaulets fell perfectly parallel with the line of his broad shoulders. The twisted, bell-shaped badge of the Eighth Regiment, cast in bronze, graced the brim of his black felt hat. He'd cropped his hair within an inch of his skull, which had left the face below harder and more stern. Aside from his lack of a mustache, he was the picture of a young Szpratzian officer. Polished as a porcelain eggshell. Maybe as empty.

I had a personality, once. As a boy, he'd greedily devoured fairy tales of Kolznechia's lost prince and the wizards who'd hidden him away. He'd befriended bakers and confectioners to steal scraps from their kitchens. He'd tumbled with a crew of traveling acrobats in a circus ring. And he'd dreamed of true love. Kisses. Promises. Forevers.

He'd let it all go. There was no room for it in the man his brother was building.

~

Traffic washed through the snow and slush of the main road, white and brown spraying up under wheels. Drakne swung back her skirts as vehicles passed. Nabik, lacking her dancer's grace, tripped on the ice as he dodged the filthy snow, and his fine hat tumbled into a drift. Drakne laughed.

"And Fydir thinks you've finally learned some manners," Nabik muttered.

"I don't need them around you." She laughed again. "You don't scare me."

Fydir scares you? That question felt too dangerous to say out loud.

Three inches of fresh powder had fallen since noon, but the hardy city folk embraced both darkness and snowdrifts alike. Factory workers slogged home in ancient boots. Farmers drove empty carts homeward through the throng. Marchers blocked a road, knocking barrels of salt fish into traffic, shouting about the mortgages on their fishing boats. A velvet-collared old man sneered down from the window of a black autocar, shaking his fist at traffic as brass hands swept snow from the windows.

Drakne led Nabik through an alley, past a trash heap, and across the edge of Rot Hill. Shoppers tucked frozen fish or plucked quails to their fur-swathed chests. Children darted about selling dried oranges, sparklers, and whirling toys on sticks. Carolers ringed the trees and sang ancient, lilting verses. Confectioners draped pines in chains of sugar candy as the two hurried siblings passed.

Nabik stretched out his power. A beggar on a corner wished for a warm coat, and his threadbare jacket turned to quilted down. A woman in an upstairs apartment wished her baby would stop crying, and the child settled into peaceful sleep. A girl wished for a wooden sword instead of her cornhusk doll, and one appeared in her hands, the hilt painted bright blue. The small acts of wizardry had become second nature since he'd turned bullets into cookies at the bank, and each one warmed his heart.

He sang along with the carolers. "Oh, here's where Winter sings and dances, here's where Winter meets her bride . . ."

"It's 'cold winds spark the fire inside,'" Drakne said. "Which makes no sense."

"That's the second verse, and the fire is a metaphor for the warmth we build together in times of cold." He hesitated. "It's been years since we spent winter together as a family."

"Since that last awful ball on Yuleheigh." She wrapped her arms close about her chest. "Why'd you swap my shoes that night?"

Guilt stabbed at him, like a dozen icicles. They hadn't spoken about it since it happened. "I'm sorry. I didn't know how dangerous dancing could be with the wrong shoes. Fydir said it would just make you uncomfortable, so you'd stop."

"It was Fydir's idea? Even then?" Anger rose in her voice, like a pot boiling over. "Why?"

"He wanted to protect you. Show Marinus your power was unreliable so he'd stop making you dance for him."

"Fydir took everything from me. You call that protection?"

Nabik flinched. It had all made sense at the time.

The week after Drakne had asked Fydir to get her out of dancing at their parties, Fydir had taken Nabik to see his patron. *Marinus has many gifted protégés. If he likes you, he might forget about our sister.* Only the day had been warm, and Nabik's magic wouldn't come. It didn't help that the archduke's loathsome wishes nearly made him vomit. With a frown, the nobleman dismissed him from the room. Nabik did not know what had passed between his brother and the old man next, but when it ended, Fydir raged at him for weeks.

Useless. Weak. Poor excuse for a man. I could set you out on the streets, you know? You'd be dead by morning.

I'm sorry, Nabik had told him, when he'd worked up the courage to go, sniffling, to Fydir's office. *I want to help.*

Well, then. There's one small thing you could do for me. And if it goes well, I just might be able to find you a place in my regiment. Don't worry. No one will get hurt.

He'd been not-quite-thirteen. He'd trusted his brother. Now, though, he wondered. Had Fydir known the risks? And why had he made Nabik do it when he could have done it himself? Sweat beaded on his temples. His stomach churned as a deep, dark fear surfaced from where he'd tried to push it away. *Did he mean to drive a wedge between us?*

"I'm sorry," Nabik said. "Truly. I should have looked out for you. Kept you safe."

Drakne drew a deep breath and straightened her back. "I don't need looking after. I need you to be someone I can depend on."

He nodded. "You can depend on me. And Fydir. I know you two have your quarrels, but perhaps I can . . . mediate, between you." She gave him another hard look. He reached for her with his magic. In her heart, she wished for nothing more than for him to take her side. But he couldn't pick one sibling over the other. He loved them both. "Drakne, please. I wish I could fix things between us all. I do."

A streetlight flickered. Sputtered. The wind picked up, whistling in their ears. It spiraled about them, tossing up great silver coils of snow. Passersby ran for cover, leaving the streets as empty as if time had stopped. Nabik shivered as flecks of ice pelted his cheeks. Drakne pressed in close to his side, a spot of warmth.

A shape swept through the billows: a great silver owl made of flurries, glowing like the full moon. With a flap, it perched atop his shoulders, its ghostly talons the lightest touch. *Drakne*, it called, and *Dance, dance, dance him awake!*

With gloved hands, Nabik fumbled for the owl. At his touch, the shape burst apart and blew away. His fist closed around something solid.

"What's that?" Drakne said.

In his hand lay a pine soldier doll with a holly-green coat and a prominent jaw. Limbs finely jointed, epaulets and medallions painted in intricate detail, carved chestnut curls poking out beneath his hat. A handle pressed out of his back. Nabik said, "It's a . . . a nutcracker?"

Drakne's eyes lit up. But if she knew what it meant, she didn't say.

～

Ruba's rented mansion hugged a hilltop, red brick lit by flickering electrics, snow-topped statues lining the wide front way: marble men and women, snowfae and leaping animals, each and every one of them draped in pine rope. Fume-spitting autocars nearly ran over Nabik and Drakne as they crossed the promenade. They ducked through the main doors, where the housekeeper exclaimed in dismay to see they'd come on foot.

"You poor dears. To think, Lady Ruba's future sister-in-law walking alone in the cold!" She clucked her tongue, helping Drakne strip off her dripping fur coat. Even that one gesture made her heart flip over. She was so starved for kindness.

Drakne's gown, a gift from Ruba, was creamy satin, soft as ancient vellum, shimmering beneath black lace and sequins patterned like roses blooming under gothic arches. The fabric glistened in the soft electric light. Porcelain pins sparkled in her smooth dark hair. Every eye in the hall turned to watch her, and flicker by flicker, she pulled back on her smile. *Stay calm. Collect yourself. Find a way out.*

"You look lovely," Nabik said. He held the nutcracker close, in the crook of his elbow. "I'm going to search the grounds for troublemakers."

"Give me the nutcracker first. It would make a fine gift for Lady Ruba."

He looked at her like she'd suggested a human sacrifice. "You're not giving this away. You saw the owl, same as I did. It's a message from Mama Zolka."

Drakne had seen the owl. But she hadn't seen her mother in years and wanted nothing to do with her now. "The owl said my name. It's for me."

"You would give it to some woman you've barely met?"

"I need friends. You certainly don't count."

"What do you mean?"

He didn't understand. *I wish I could fix things between us all.* Didn't he know some things couldn't be fixed? Would he make her rip off the bandages and show him the cuts on her soul? She reached out and snatched the nutcracker. "Have you seen Fydir's new gun?"

"Of course. He takes it everywhere."

Drakne turned and walked away. Nabik came up behind her, his boots clicking on the marble tile, and reached around, grabbing for the nutcracker. He got one hand on it before she twisted away. He tugged. So did she.

"It's a soul-engine," she hissed. "He put me inside it."

Pop! The little nutcracker's leg came off in Nabik's hand.

"No," Nabik said. "He wouldn't—"

"It's true," she said. "I can't stay in this city with him. And neither should you. Nabik—"

"Miss Zolkedna! You're here." Lady Ruba bound out through the ballroom doors, a flurry of chattering guests behind her. But Drakne was still looking at Nabik. She could see in his eyes that he believed her. But belief alone meant nothing.

As the noise and crowd drew closer, Nabik pressed the little nutcracker's leg into her palm. Then he took a step backward. His hand slipped out of hers.

"Later," he mouthed. Then he turned on his heel and made for the manor door.

Lady Ruba reached her just as she started to cry.

He put her in a soul-engine. Slick bile coated the back of Nabik's throat. *In his gun. He's been using her as a tool for his dirty work for months. How did I not notice?* He drank in Fydir's moods like water. If he'd paid half as much attention to Drakne . . . *what? I could have stopped it?* Who did you turn to, when the person hurting your family was part of it? How could he face his sister when the one thing he could give her was a *nutcracker*?

He didn't know what to do. But he still had his duty.

Winter air had swept through the manor grounds, turning statues into soft white puffs and coating trellises in glinting hoarfrost. In the snowdrift garden beneath the ballroom windows, where broken trellises and dead vines arched over shadowed pathways, Nabik strode through the gray afternoon. A hedge rustled. Green eyes flashed at the garden's dark edge. Nabik swore, reaching out with his magic—felt a bit of *something*—and then it flickered, and the glimmer disappeared.

Something rattled against the manor wall. Nabik looked up. A white-clad figure with a violet kerchief was climbing a windowside trellis, a banner slung over her shoulders. *Talzne. At last.* Nabik grabbed the trellis base and gave it a shake. The wood scraped along the wall, small icicles cracking off its frame. Talzne slipped, and Nabik braced to catch her—but the snowfae girl recovered her footing. She glared at him as she slid down.

Nabik took her banner, opened it, and read aloud. "'Noble pigs, your time has come.' You know making threats is against the law?"

Talzne frowned. The words vanished, ink melting and re-forming into a painting of three girls dancing in a winter wood. *Snowfae magic. Conjuring beauty.* Nabik was impressed by her quick thinking.

"You have no evidence I've done anything," she said.

"I don't need evidence. I have a warrant." He reached in his pocket for it. "I don't do this lightly, mind you, but—"

Talzne turned and ran.

Nabik swore, and followed.

Light as a heron and fast as a hare, the girl leapt over the garden wall and darted out into the city streets. Nabik's heart raced as he pursued, his arms pumping, boots slipping on the ice. Running was easy. He could pretend he was leaving the truth behind him. *I can't both fight for Fydir and keep Drakne safe.*

Talzne's white skirts grew closer. He lunged. His arms caught her about the waist. In a puff of powder, they slammed down into a snowbank. Talzne spat and swore. He grabbed her wrists and locked a pair of iron cuffs around them.

"Let me go!"

"This is only for a few days. Until the city calms down." Something flickered in the corner of his vision, a flash of bright red. He stood, dragging Talzne upright with him, and looked toward the border wall, half a mile away. An electric torch flickered on the ramparts, colored scarlet by a film. His heart sank. He knew that signal.

Malirmatvi was under attack.

CHAPTER FOUR

The Pinewood Prince

Nabik wouldn't help her. Drakne had told him the truth, and he'd fled. *What do I do now?* She wasn't certain if there was anything she *could* do. The Drakne who had plotted with the Rat King felt like a lost dream.

Ruba dabbed at her cheeks with a handkerchief. She wore a gown of warm vermilion, petticoats patterned with drooping floral blooms. A silver chain secured her glasses. An old-fashioned gilded net, studded with metal thorns, held her hair back in a bun. No taller than Drakne's shoulder, she hummed with energy, like a spark plug or a bomb.

"Are you all right?" she asked Drakne. "You look upset. Is there someone I need to knock a potted pine onto? I will. I've got at least five of them to spare."

Drakne hugged her. The mouse-girl's eyes widened, but she leaned in and patted Drakne's shoulder. The scent of mushrooms rose up from her skin.

"What was that for?" Ruba asked as she pulled away.

"It's just . . . I'm quite grateful. To know someone cares about me." Her schoolmates had treated her like a fool for being behind in lessons, though most of them had learned to read and write at the same age she'd been scrounging on the streets. For years, the closest she'd had to a friend was the Rat King and his letters.

"Dear, I just asked how you were doing. You need to raise your standards for what *caring* looks like. You can't spend all day cooped up with that dreary fool Nabik."

"I agree." A small smile crept across her face as she held out the nutcracker. "For you. The leg is broken, but—"

Ruba snatched it up and shoved the leg back in place. "Good as new. My most gracious thanks! I can already tell that this will be a *magical* evening. Now come along. Let's see if we can find you some more friends."

Arm in arm, Drakne and Ruba glided into the ballroom. Crackling gas lamps cast a warm glow on the dance floor. Garlands of holly berries draped the wood-paneled walls and heavy, gilded crown molding. Pines stood in the room's four corners, wrapped in silver ribbons, covered in glass ornaments and gleaming white candles. Guests in silk skirts and velvet coats shared plates of delicacies with servants in wool, for Winter demanded that all folk share her bounty alike.

A collection of nutcrackers stood in ranks behind the grand buffet, some as small as Drakne's hand and others longer than her thigh. Their wooden coats were painted in a rainbow of colors, reds, whites, and traditional Kolznechian green. Some were shaped like animals, owls with cracking beaks and hares with breaking paws, and one was shaped like a crescent moon. Ruba set Drakne's nutcracker down in the middle of the table.

"What do you think?" she said. "Who hosts a better party, me or the governor?"

Drakne shrugged. "My brother hasn't hosted anything since I ruined a ball by annoying the archduke."

"The archduke? The foul man deserves as much. His soul-engines are absolutely disgusting."

Drakne hesitated. She took a champagne glass from a tray, swirled the wheat-gold wine as her thoughts settled. "Fydir uses them. Does that bother you?"

"Of course. I've spoken with him about it. He says it's just to avoid insulting his patron. One day, the archduke will bow to him and he will never need soul-engines again."

And you believe him? Drakne nearly said. *You're too clever for that.* Then she remembered a day back before Fydir had hurt her, when she'd told him the archduke didn't own them. *Marinus is an odious man,* he had answered. *He'll be most surprised the day he bows at my feet.* She knew what the nobleman had done to her, to Princess Sofiya, to endless thousands of poor laborers. Fydir had been working for pennies in a stable when Marinus had recruited him. How had the nobleman exploited the young Kolznechian man who relied on him completely? What had made Fydir hate him so?

She didn't want to know, and she didn't think she cared. It would make no difference in what her brother had done to her. But she couldn't forget that Fydir had wants of his own, and wants were little levers that could push a man one way or another. If she dared to lean on them.

"Do you mean to marry him?" Drakne asked Ruba.

"Maybe," said Ruba. "Maybe not. I mean to better acquaint myself with him and your family before making that choice. But I do enjoy the company of tall men . . . and charming women."

She plucked a hazelnut from a bowl, popped it in the nutcracker's mouth, and pushed the handle down. *Crack!* "And I sympathize with Fydir's vengeful streak."

"You want revenge against the Rat King? For exiling you?"

"I have no shortage of enemies." Ruba tapped one short clawed finger to the tip of her nose. "So why not have some friends? Fydir is a self-made man. He knows what it's like to fight for something. To feel hardship. To feel passion. Best of all, he has command of a small army."

So it's vengeance that binds them together. Vengeance, far above any notion of love. Relief settled over Drakne. Ruba was playing with fire, but at least she knew it burned. *Vengeance, and power. The wish to see kings and princes crushed before them.*

Drakne could think of quite a few people she'd like to see crushed herself.

"Miss Zolkedna!" said a voice at her elbow. An old man, peering out from behind half-moon glasses. "Have you met my grandson, Ivan Ivanidan?"

The young man beside him wore a collar of genuine leopard fur, which he'd already ruined with a wine stain. Drakne smiled and nodded as he listed every animal he'd ever shot. Ruba started making up animals, and the fool insisted he'd shot those too.

"Never mind," Ruba said as Ivan extolled his prowess in hunting the six-winged vulture. "Let's try them." She pointed at two reedy young men in starched suits. "The one in blue is Hergor. University students. Nice fellows."

Hergor might have been as kind as Saint Cecilia, but Drakne saw nothing of it, as, in the presence of a girl, he could only stammer to his shoes. His friend had a great deal to say about his research in electric motors, in which Ruba was well-versed and of which Drakne knew nothing at all. She ducked away when the topic turned to wire shielding and hooked herself on the arm of a young officer, who proceeded to explain to her that traditional Kolznechian linguistics meant her name was pronounced "drake" instead of "drak-NEY."

"I know my own name, thank you," she said, and went to grab Ruba's elbow. "Isn't it time to start the dancing?"

"What's wrong?"

"They're acting like fools. Which means they all want to marry me."

"Well, of course. You're beautiful and intelligent. Is there some other future you desire?"

She'd never seriously considered marriage, not since the Rat King had offered her a future. But she had signaled the wizard-king night after night with no reply. It couldn't be all bad, could it? A husband might truly love and protect her. She could be a better mother than Zolka, easily, and her children would love her too. She'd never be able to tell anyone about her time in the gun, of her nightmares where her lips spat bullets into a crowded ballroom. But perhaps she could forget, and it would be like it had never happened at all.

She could escape. All she had to do was trade every piece of her future to one of these foolish, boring men. That life would never be enough for her. But it might be all she could get.

"You could always go to Kolznechia, if you wished," Ruba said. "The Rat King made it legal for women to hold property in their own names. And you could wed or bed whoever pleased you—man, woman, elsewise, or no one at all."

"The one skill I can make a living with is dance. Which might be a problem if I crossed the border, as I'm convinced right now I'd turn into a worm."

"Oh, the curse tends toward birds and mammals. It's about fifty-fifty if their feet fit into toe shoes. And that reminds me—I've never seen you perform." Ruba clapped her hands. All around the ballroom, guests fell silent. The very air seemed to hold its breath, waiting to come alive. "Orchestra! Give us a dance!"

The conductor raised his wand. Music swelled to fill the room. A flourish of trumpets, a scatter of notes on the violin like leaping footsteps. The rhythm, high and fast, was that of a triumphant march. Drakne's feet tapped in half-remembered patterns. Something clicked inside her, like a popped wire. A backfiring plug. Hot and white in her chest.

Dance, she told herself. *You're a dancer. Not a gun.*

"I'll lead," she said, and Ruba let her twirl them out onto the center of the floor. Their cream and red skirts meshed together like gears. Drakne firmly gripped Ruba's waist, spun her about with gestures light as air, dipped her until her rings brushed the marble floor.

The horns blared, notes steep and sharp. Cymbals crashed. Harps sparkled like moonlight off ice. The violin melody built into a cry. Weeping, mourning, full of glory. The magic of Winter inside Drakne flared to hot and burning life. She couldn't remember the last time she'd felt this strong.

She focused her power, keeping her magic under tight control. The little she used, she aimed at Ruba, helping her partner follow along. The girls matched each other, move for move, as bronze sparks flickered under Drakne's shoes. Her magic guided their every leap and spin as she held her hands high, arched her neck, thrilled in the burn of her muscles. Ruba jumped, and Drakne used her momentum to lift her off her feet, swing her around in a semicircle. Her spine ached, yet still she smiled. Ruba pressed in, close to her chest, their hearts racing as one, with only the satin of two bodices between them.

Drakne leaned down and pressed her lips to Ruba's cheek, to the dry skin just above her prickling fur. Ruba winked at her, then swept out to face the crowd. The girls curtsied as the guests applauded. Every eye in the ballroom fell on them. On Drakne. And as her heart beat hard, dark hair falling loose from her bun, she remembered the last time she'd done this.

A tall wooden building that reeked of smoke and fresh-cut lumber. Her stolen worker's uniform streaked with sawdust. A pounding on the door. A terrible, clenching fear that twisted her heart in its fists and didn't, wouldn't, couldn't let go—

The guests, wide-eyed and eager, pressed in around her. The boring young men. Children with caramel-streaked fingers. Footmen and maidservants. "Dance with us! Dance with us!" "Miss, are you well?" "Miss?" Her lungs grew tight and airless. Her stomach wrenched sideways. Fear seemed to clamp her in an iron vise.

"Enough!" Ruba shouted, in a voice that struck like thunder. The guests stepped backward. The mouse-girl pressed her hand to Drakne's back, ushered her back toward the buffet, and whispered, "Breathe. Just breathe. There you are. Keep going."

Keep going. But no number of calming breaths would change the fear now settling in her marrow.

What if Fydir ruined dancing for me?

"You need to eat." Ruba shoved a plate into her hand. Atop it sat a slice of chocolate cake the size of her head. "Do you not like chocolate?" Into Drakne's other hand, she shoved a bowl of popcorn. "These are caramel flavored, but we've got regular in the kitchen—"

"Thank you," Drakne said around a mouthful of chocolate. It was bitter, with buttercream frosting that melted on her tongue, but she couldn't bring herself to savor it. "I—I'm sorry. This isn't helping."

"Do you need water? A place to lie down?"

"It's the dancing," Drakne said. "It's—I'm scared—" She bit down a sigh, leaned back against the plaster facade ringing the fireplace. Atop the mantel, cavalry sabers lay in a nest of greenery. For a heartbeat, she dearly missed the simple life of a weapon.

"You don't have to be nervous," Ruba said. "Blessed Winter. When you dance, it's like a fire come to life." She spoke with the fervor of a bishop. "Your gift—it's true northern magic."

"You felt it?" Drakne said.

"Felt it? In all my time at the Rat King's court, I never felt any magic quite so strongly."

Crack! Across the buffet table, a child slammed down the handle on Zolka's nutcracker. A broken hazelnut tumbled from its jaws. Another child yanked the handle back, distorting its face into a monstrous, gaping thing. Drakne felt something like pity for the little machine. She knew how it felt to be used.

"Careful!" Drakne shouted as a third child picked it up and swung it like a bludgeon. She set down her plates and yanked the nutcracker away, held it in the crook of her elbow like an infant.

Ruba stared at it appraisingly. As if she'd just now noticed an old friend in the crowd.

"I think this one might be special," she said, almost softly. "Miss Zolkedna, I don't know what you're afraid of. And you don't need to tell me. But if you've always loved dancing, I think you owe yourself another try. Just . . . focus on the nutcracker. An audience of one. See if you can set the world aside, and dance with him."

Drakne braced herself. Ruba had the right of it. She needed to give dancing another try. And hadn't the snowflake owl told her to dance when it gave her and Nabik the nutcracker? "Right," she said. "Try to stop folk from laughing at me for dancing with a doll."

Ruba smiled and stepped backward, waving guests away to clear the floor. "I promise, Miss Zolkedna. If anyone laughs, I'll claw out their tongue."

This, Drakne could trust. Ruba would do as she wished, damn the consequences. Drakne only longed for the days when she might have done the same.

A violin melody spilled across the floor. As the sweet, plucking notes of harpsong joined in, Drakne slid onto her toes, tipped her head back, and spun. Holding the nutcracker close to her chest.

Music slipped into her gestures, into her pose. Light footsteps sped her across the polished floor. Her free hand flicked up, wrist curling in a perfect arc. She swung out her skirts in a spray of sequins. Arms spread wide, she leapt, and landed with her back arched, one leg lifted parallel to the floor. Every tap of her toes brought forth the ballroom's applause.

But when she closed her eyes, something clicked inside her,

like clockwork jamming, caught on something messy and organic. She inhaled and tasted metal. *No.*

The gun closed about her. Bullets rested on her tongue. And Drakne wanted nothing more than to fire them at the man who'd put her there.

"Is that a rat?" whispered a voice. "It's too tall," said another. One of the young men she'd spoken with? She couldn't remember all their names. Couldn't bring herself to imagine a life with them. "No, a *Kolznechian* rat—"

Drakne bit her lip and tuned out the crowd, spinning the nutcracker in an arc. Magic spun up her legs, through her chest, into the little wooden man. *It's only dancing magic. That's all I have, and it's not enough. It can't set anything to rights. Not my world, not my heart.*

The music crescendoed. Drakne spun, and broad hands, strong as tree trunks, circled her waist and lifted her aloft. A shock of surprise ran through her—but she improvised like a true performer. She arched her neck against his shoulder, craning her arms like a swan lifting in flight. *My empty arms.* She leapt away as he set her down, skirts fluttering about her— then their hands met, and she twisted into his chest as they closed the pas de deux.

A tall, broad chest of pinewood and holly-green paint.

Drakne swore.

"Where am I?" said the nutcracker, an archaic lilt to his voice—and then the windows shattered.

Amid a spray of glass, a dozen rat-soldiers leapt into the ballroom. Each four to five feet tall, they wore jackets of green livery atop their dark and spotted fur, clutched antique sabers and pistols in almost-human fists. Screaming guests grabbed their children and dancing partners. Servants dropped their laden trays and ran. Some fled out side doors; others ducked beneath tables or crouched behind the ribbon-wrapped pines. Ruba herself was nowhere to be seen.

"Prince Eugen!" A deep and wicked voice boomed throughout the ballroom. "It's been far, *far* too long."

The Rat King strode leisurely across the ballroom floor as guests sobbed in the corner and his long-toothed soldiers raised their weapons in salute.

Drakne didn't know what she'd expected. Certainly not a spindly, pale young man in evening dress, with glasses shaped like silver crescent moons, a choker of raw emeralds and silver wire at his throat. He tipped his slender top hat, revealing long skin-flap ears and slicked-back brown hair. In place of a cane, he carried a staff of black iron. Slimy mushrooms blossomed down its length. A wormlike tail flicked beneath his tailcoat.

"I would have done this sooner, but the wizards stole you away mere months after your ... *enwoodening*. Kept you hidden away for two hundred years." The Rat King lowered his brow, glaring over Drakne's shoulder at his target. "Thankfully, one of them had a daughter with a most interesting gift. Exactly the sort of magic that could help me find you."

Drakne stiffened. Was *this* what the Rat King had wanted with her all along?

"What's going on?" said the nutcracker—Prince Eugen. He stood as tall as Nabik, though less broad in the shoulder, garbed in an old-fashioned green coat and wide trousers. Tree ring lines flashed in his pinewood cheeks. His walnut curls lay stiff and unmoving. But the fear in his voice was all too human. "Two hundred—what?"

The Rat King advanced. From behind a ribbon-covered pine, an officer aimed his pistol. The wizard snapped his fingers, and the gun exploded into shards of peppermint. Screams rose as flying sugar cut skin.

"Miss Zolkedna." He grinned, like they were friends. His pink nose twitched. A diamond stud winked in his nostril. "Move aside, please."

"No," she said, and nearly clapped her hands over her mouth at her own foolish impulse. This man had devastated a whole kingdom. She should bow at his feet and plead for mercy. But he had offered her the world and abandoned her when she needed him most. She'd signaled him, hoped for him, hoped for so much from so many people who let her down. And now he had the nerve to ask her for something?

"Right," he said. "What can I do for you? I could give you a crown that would make all who gazed upon you fall in love, or a silver cloak like the ones that hide my spies from sight. Make the wish, and it's yours. But only if you step aside."

Make the wish. Her fists tightened. Her heart sped. Her eyes met the tyrant's, and all she could wish for was what the Rat King had. The power to walk into a room and leave the crowd cowering.

"Think quickly, now," he urged her.

"It's all right, miss," Eugen said, and stepped out from behind her. "Please. Don't risk yourself on my account."

I'll risk myself for whoever I please. Drakne stepped sideways, shielding him once more. She didn't know the boy. She didn't particularly want to die for him. But he was a danger to the Rat King. This prince could put the wizard off his throne. And she wanted the Rat King to sweat, for as long as she could make him. Let him feel a fraction of the fear she lived with every day under Fydir's roof. In that awful place where this creature had left her to rot.

The Rat King frowned and took a few steps toward her. Pinning her eyes with his, brown as weathered winter tree bark. The most human features in a visage with a hairy, ever-twitching nose and yellow incisors as long as her pinkie finger. Another step closer. Plague swirled in the air about him, a green miasma clinging like a cloak, humming with malevolence and the shadows of flies. With one clawed hand, he reached for her. "Miss Zolkedna. Truly—"

She spun and lunged for the fireplace. Drakne grabbed the ornamental sabers off Ruba's mantel, tossed one to Eugen, and lifted the other high.

"Thank you very much," said the prince, and he leapt at the Rat King, who swung his staff to block. The sword hit. Metal rang against metal. The Rat King knocked the blade aside. Air whistled as he swung at the prince's head. Eugen ducked, his wooden joints swift but jerky, and punched him in the stomach. The Rat King staggered backward, knocking into the buffet table. Punch bowls, candies, and nutcrackers spilled across the floor in a clatter of color.

With a shake of his head, the Rat King stood and stalked toward Drakne. She lowered the sword at his chest. She'd never used one before, but how hard could it be? *Point and stab. Like mending socks with a needle.*

A laugh formed on the Rat King's snouty lips. "I don't think so," he said. "You're no soldier. I know what you wish for." With a snap of his fingers, the blade transformed—into a pair of rose-pink dancing slippers.

Eugen lunged at the usurper from behind. The Rat King whirled, parrying with another metal clang. They circled each other, eyes locked, jaws set, neat fencing footwork transforming the duel into a dance. The prince feinted sideways; the Rat King lunged, and Eugen's sword left a neat cut through his waistcoat. The Rat King leapt at his enemy, sweeping his staff in a circle, and when Eugen stepped backward, his shoulders pressed against a candle-covered pine. The prince froze.

The Rat King laughed, lifting his staff high. "Farewell, Eugen. I don't know who I'll hate without you."

Drakne swung the slippers like a whip.

They struck the Rat King in the head with a satisfying *thwack!* Drakne pressed herself against his back and hooked the satin laces under his jaw, twisting, *twisting*, until she felt his throat spasm. Rage burned in her heart, in her stomach, in her arms and shoulders, filling her with raw, red might.

She had been wounded in a thousand terrible ways. For once, she wanted to make someone else bleed.

"Miss!" Eugen shouted as he grabbed the tree and shoved it over. Drakne saw it fall in the corner of her eye. She leapt away. In a great clatter of wood, it slammed into the Rat King. He pitched forward. Ornaments shattered. Tumbling candles lit branches aflame. The scent of sap filled the room as the rat-soldiers squealed, sprinting for their fallen king.

Drakne grabbed Eugen's arm and pointed at the ballroom door. "Run!"

CHAPTER FIVE

The Dutiful Deserter

As Talzne kicked and protested, Nabik dragged her to the nearest wall garrison, showed her to a maid's apartment, and locked her in. The moment the lock clicked, a scout ran up the stairs, bent double and panting.

"Sir!" he gasped. "It's rats. Two dozen rats beyond the wall!"

"Where's the senior officer?" Nabik said.

"You're the most senior man here, Captain Zolkedan!"

Nabik swore and followed him to the ramparts. *I can do this,* he told himself, squashing down his doubts. *I'm needed. It's my duty. I* must *do this.*

Snow and barbed wire covered the squat brick border wall, electric lanterns gleaming every twenty yards. Wind whipped down its length, and soldiers' teeth chattered even though they wore their heavy uniform coats. To the north, a cleared field marked the boundary between kingdoms, gleaming in the pale light of the full moon. Shadows seethed just behind Kolznechia's tree line—clawed shadows, fanged shadows, their green eyes flashing in the dark.

"Steady," Nabik commanded, squaring his shoulders. Most of these soldiers were no older than he, and even the blades of their bayonets rattled with their fear. Nabik had never fought a true battle, but he was certainly no stranger to violence. "Break some ice off the walkways if you can. Make sure your gun straps are fastened tight, and keep your ammunition close to hand. We have a strong position. Hold the wall, and not one rat will cross."

An invisible signal seemed to slink through the dark. As the spell passed him, Nabik somehow knew it for the Rat King's command. He reached for his own magic—no. His men would know it was him, the Kolznechian. This moment called for military discipline, not magic tricks. *Do as Fydir taught you.* But Fydir hadn't trained him to lead. Only to follow.

Ratfolk surged across the field in a clump of brown fur and green fabric. They shrieked and squealed, a high, harsh sound like ripping metal. Some soldiers clapped their hands over their ears. Some fired. The first gunshots cracked through the dusk. Bullets fell short and struck the field, throwing up earth and snow.

"Hold!" Nabik shouted. "Let them come to us! They can die in that field if they want to, but the gate is ours, the wall is ours, the city is ours—"

Then Nabik realized rats could climb.

They hit the wall in a wave and scurried up it, needle claws sinking into chinks in the mortar, and leapt onto the ramparts. Some brandished swords and some shot antique pistols, and one jumped atop a boy and drove its sharp incisors through his throat. Soldiers screamed. Blood spilled on the bricks. The smell of copper filled the air.

"Fire!" Nabik shouted. Concussive blasts struck his ears like rain. Two rats fell, tumbling backward off the wall. One collapsed, clawing at his shredded guts, and four more tripped over him. Shining bayonets stabbed down and through them. "Fire!" he screamed again, and then he couldn't hear his own voice, and his gun slammed into the meat of his shoulder as he pulled the trigger down.

But the rats were among them. Most of his bullets sailed off into the night. "Form ranks!" he called. "Stand together!" He looked to his left, his right—*where are they?* All was sound and flashes of fury in the flickering electric lights. A fur-covered figure leapt at him, and he struck out with the barrel of his gun, only for the rat to vanish into the fog of rifle smoke. A boy fell at his feet, clutching his tooth-torn guts. Nabik reached to help and slipped on the ice, cursing as his chin struck stone.

"Fall back!" another man yelled as he dragged Nabik to his feet and pulled him toward the stairs. "Retreat!"

"Get the other men out of here!" Nabik shouted, jabbing at the nearest rat with his bayonet. It screamed, skittering away as blood poured down its coat. "I'll cover you—"

A second signal-spell brushed the edge of his awareness. The rat he'd injured kept moving away, leaping back over the wall, and all its fellows moved as one to join it. In a river of brown, green, and bloodstains, they scrambled back across the moonlit field.

"Hold!" Nabik shouted as his soldiers took aim at the fleeing beastfolk. "Let them run."

They stared at him like he'd just commanded them to sing opera.

"Wait on the governor's orders," he continued, both wishing Fydir were there and wanting to retch at the thought of him. "This might be a trap." He wasn't certain about that. He just didn't want anyone else getting hurt, on either side.

Because it all felt the same to him. He couldn't stop his magic from soaking in pain: the fear of the dying rats and soldiers, the *no, no, no* of the friends who held their hands, the crushing shame of the boy who'd jumped down on the safe side of the wall and hidden as his friends screamed. Nabik had never been close to any other soldiers—Fydir forbade it, lest it distract him from his duties—but that did nothing to lessen the terrible weight.

Tears prickled in his eyes. He turned his head. They couldn't see their leader cry. He didn't need Fydir to teach him that much.

This is what it means to be a soldier, he realized. *How can I bear this?*

He wanted his mother.

His men carried the wounded to the infirmary. As Nabik helped them, he felt the doctors' wishes, then slipped extra bandages into cabinets and refilled empty bottles with painkillers. Where he dared, he closed a few wounds with a thought, strengthened a few fading pulses. A headache pounded at his temples as the power rushed out of him. *Any more, and they'll know there's a wizard here.*

Nabik went to the apartment where he'd locked Talzne. As he let himself into the small, dark chamber, the girl turned her back on him and gazed out a narrow window at the moon.

"Are you well?" he asked.

She didn't answer.

"Do you know anything about why the Rat King might attack

the south?" He thought it unlikely. But he'd take any scrap of information he could get.

She turned once more, to face him. Her eyebrows arched. "Even if I did, why would I tell you?"

"I know I have no right to ask this of you. I'm asking for the people of this city. They're in danger, Kolznechians and Szpratzians alike. My mother taught me that the snowfae call themselves Winter's daughters. Wouldn't our goddess want you to help bring peace?"

Her face fell. When she next spoke, her words were weighted with sorrow. "Winter hasn't appeared to the snowfae, to anyone, for hundreds of years. She's no more than a whisper now."

"What?" He didn't understand. "Is that ... because of the curse? The Rat King?"

"Her power has been fading for centuries. But the Rat King made everything worse." She shook her head. "You southerners think the curse only turns people to beastfolk. That's all you can see. But when that monster—when a *wizard*, blessed with Winter's power—took the throne by force, something terrible was unleashed. A blight. One that's been slowly turning Kolznechia's farms and fields to crystal."

"I've heard tales of the great crystal forest," Nabik said. "I never thought ... it must be quite hard to live there."

"I don't know what the Rat King wants. But he's no fool. He can't rule a dead kingdom. So maybe, if he's in Malirmatvi ... maybe there's an answer here."

The answer. Nabik swallowed. *Winter is calling me. She needs my help.* Would Talzne believe him if he told her that?

"Sir!" A soldier knocked on the door. "The scouts are back. There's been more attacks."

"I'll return soon," Nabik said. He ducked outside, locked the door, and went across the walkway to the officers' meeting room.

Over the next hour, scouts trickled in from the other garrisons. Nabik took their reports and marked every rat strike on a map. The Kolznechians had attacked three points on the wall since sundown, striking viciously and running back into the trees. *What is the Rat King doing? Making feints. Creating a diversion. Drawing our soldiers to the wall so he can do ... what?*

"Men of the Eighth Regiment!" Fydir swept through the doors, his tone as warm as melted ice cream. "What a victory we've won!"

Why does he sound so pleased by all this? The sight of his smirk felt like a slap in the face. *Drakne. He put Drakne in his gun.* "Sir, five men died."

"Only five? Excellent." He gave Nabik a hard look. "This is war. Folk die."

"We aren't at war with Kolznechia. There must be a way—"

Fydir frowned. "Men, wait here for my orders. I need a word with my brother." He opened the door and waved Nabik through it.

Nabik went.

They stood together, on the wooden walkway outside the second story of the officers' quarters, as Fydir shut the door on the other men with a click. A rattling tin overhang sheltered them from the drifting snowflakes, but Nabik still felt cold trickle down his neck.

He put Drakne in his gun.

"Everything is going as I planned it," Fydir said. His eyes were bright, like his soul was a sparking fuse. "First, Kolznechians stir up the factories. Then they attack our walls—"

"They're not one and the same," Nabik said. "Ordinary Kolznechians aren't the Rat King's soldiers. That's a prejudice, and a dangerous one. One that's turning folk against their neighbors—"

"Good. We can use that. By next week, Parliament will authorize the Eighth Regiment to enter Kolznechia."

"We're taking the regiment into Kolznechia? Next week?" Nabik's heart stuttered sideways, like a windup doll with rusted clockwork. "But that's . . . what about the labor forum? The factory inspections? Everything we planned?"

"We didn't come to Malirmatvi so you could play nursemaid to some hatmakers. We're here to get me an army. And once we cross that border, not even the archduke will be able to command me. Think of all the untouched riches in that land. All those souls for our engines." He smiled. "Don't you see, brother? This is our chance. In Kolznechia, the two of us can be as mighty as kings. Together."

Cross the border. Together. That was more than Nabik had ever dared dream of. To journey to the place where he could live freely as a wizard without leaving his family behind.

At the cost of countless innocent lives.

"No." Nabik stepped backward. His boots skidded on the ice of the walkway. "You can't do this."

"Of course I can. I have the best army in the modern world. The Rat King has only a rabble of untrained beastfolk and some antique guns—"

"You *shouldn't* do this."

"Merciful saints. Ever since Mama Zolka ran off to be a wizard, I've looked after you. Despite everything you are, everything you do, because we're brothers. What was it you said the other week? *I'm your man. That's all I've ever wanted.* So are you my man now? When I need you?"

Need. Need. The void in him tugged at Nabik. The hunger. The loneliness. The paranoia. This was why Nabik hadn't glimpsed this horrid plan in Fydir's wishes. He wished for *everything*. Nothing Nabik could summon him would ever be enough. *And he will make me bleed for my failure to please him.*

"You owe me this much," Fydir growled, and grabbed for him.

"No!" Nabik flung up his hands. Shards of ice flew from his fingertips. One sliced a red line across Fydir's cheek. His brother's eyes widened, his fingers clasped to his cheek. "I'm sorry, but I don't owe you this," Nabik said, more quietly. "I've stood by you too long, and it's hurt us all."

He turned his back and set off down the walkway.

"Come back here," Fydir bellowed, "or I'll have you arrested as a deserter!"

Nabik raced down the stairs. Fydir's horse stood in the courtyard, nervously pawing the ground. Nabik untied its reins from the hitching post, clambered atop the beast, and kicked it. Hoofbeats echoed as he bolted out into the night, the wind tugging at his scarf. *Drakne. Drakne.*

They both had to leave the city. Tonight.

~

As the moon rose high, Drakne led the pinewood prince through the ramshackle factories and warehouses of Rot Hill. The scent of salt and roasted meat hung heavy in the night air. One street over, a drummer played and a crowd clapped, but all sounds were muffled by the falling snow. A sense of danger hung in the air— was that gunpowder she smelled?—but happiness was right there beside it, and that alone made her quite proud to be Kolznechian.

"Where are you taking me?" Eugen said.

"To the border wall." Drakne pointed north. "You're not safe in the Empire. Archduke Marinus will take you apart bit by bit to learn how you work." With her next step, her foot tangled in the too-long men's coat she'd grabbed as she'd fled Ruba's manor. She wobbled forward. Her calf burned as she used all her dancer's training to keep from falling face-first in the snowy road.

"Will I be safe in Kolznechia?" Eugen asked. She didn't have the heart to tell him *most likely no.*

"Drakne!" a man shouted, his horse trotting swiftly down the lane. "Is that you?"

"Nabik?" She squinted. "Saints defend me, you look awful."

"Are you all right?" He leapt off the horse, looped the reins to a light post, and hugged her. Drakne froze. He dropped his arms and stepped back. "What's wrong?"

"I just . . . didn't expect that." Not after how they'd argued at Ruba's party. "What's going on? Rat-soldiers have crossed the border. They raided Ruba's manor. Is there fighting at the wall?"

Lamplight glimmered on the hollows of his cheeks, casting shadows that made him look much older than nineteen. "There is. The rats struck en masse. We fought them off, but—"

"Are you hurt?"

"I'm quite well." He spoke like something dead and heavy weighed on his chest.

"Nabik . . ." she whispered.

He turned to the nutcracker. "What . . . who are you?"

"I am Eugen Kutredan of House Teyodet, crown prince of Kolznechia." Eugen glanced awkwardly down at his jointed fingers. "My apologies. I must be quite the fearful sight."

"You're not even the worst thing I've seen all evening." Nabik gave him a thoughtful look. "You're who the Rat King's hunting. The snowflake owl . . . our mother sent you to us so my sister could wake you up." A smile crept across his face. "Drakne! This means she must be close. We need to get him to her. Now."

"What? Why?" She would see the wooden man safely out of town. No more. "We're her children, not her servants."

"What else can we do? This is clearly important."

"The last thirteen years of our lives were important." Rage welled within her, more than she expected, more than she knew what to do with. She didn't care about curses and lost princes. Zolka had left them, and now she was reaching out, not even with an apology, but with a chunk of painted wood. "Fine. You take him to the border and look for Mama Zolka. I'll go back to check on Ruba. The rats attacked her too."

"Then we should look for Ruba first. When we find Zolka, we're going north with her. To save Kolznechia."

"What?" She nearly choked on the word. Her voice seemed to twist itself into a frustrated knot. "What do you mean?"

"I spoke to a snowfae girl. Kolznechia is suffering. And it will only get worse." He took a deep breath. "Fydir means to mount an incursion across the border—"

"So we shouldn't go anywhere near him." Drakne shook her head. The news scarcely surprised her. She knew what Fydir was. "There's nothing for me in the north. We should go south. Back to the capital. Together. I'll work as a dancing teacher, audition for the companies, and you'd be free to do whatever you want. No Fydir. No Zolka. Just the two of us. *Please.* No one in this family has ever stood by me when I needed them. I need you now."

"Drakne, I'm a wizard. Like Mama Zolka. My place is in the north, with her. Nothing I can do here will set this right." True anguish filled his words. The sound of a man with his heart pulling him two ways. A wizard, yes, but a man still. He could choose to go north or south, wherever he wished. *I'm the one who can't just walk away. Not without money. Not without the help of someone I trust.*

"You can burn on the saints' coals in hell," she snapped. It felt good. Not as good as she'd expected, but good enough. "I'm done with you." She unwound the horse's reins from the street-light and swung herself up into the saddle.

"Miss Zolkedna!" Eugen said. "Where are you going?"

"Anywhere but here."

"Please," Nabik said. "Don't go. I can't let you get hurt."

Tears swam in her eyes. Beyond the road, festive poppers cracked in the night. Children laughed and shrieked. An old, weathered voice took up a song. *Here's where Winter sings and dances, where cold winds spark the fire inside.* Her heart twisted. Everywhere she looked, she saw what a family could be. What hers wasn't.

"You already have," she said, and galloped off in a spray of powder and pain.

CHAPTER SIX

The God of Cold Things

Torches, lanterns, and songs filled the night, and Drakne Zolkedna rode through it alone. A fragment of an old letter ran through her mind:

Dear Miss Zolkedna,

When you last wrote, you asked if I liked being king. I haven't asked myself that in—years? Decades? Does time exist for creatures thrust outside it? I digress. I do not enjoy king-ship. Neither do I despise it. The throne (if you will indulge my cliché) is my duty. I was the only one strong enough to claim it after the curse descended. The king was dead, his son turned to wood, the court transformed to beastfolk. I alone could step forward and guide my nation. And I have been very much alone since that day.

She'd thought over that particular letter so many times since she'd first read it. If even a king could be lonely, what hope was there for her?

Loose snowflakes tangled in her unbound hair as she rode. Pain churned in her stomach. She hoped Nabik hurt worse. *He wants to help the mother who abandoned us and a kingdom he's never seen. Not me. No matter how much I need him.*

An idea occurred to her. If Nabik crossed the border, he wouldn't need anything he'd left behind.

She urged her horse onward, ducking low against its hot neck in the snowy wind. Soon, the governor's manor rose before her. She tied the horse at the front gate and ran up the walk, her shoes sloshing through snow. She stepped through the door, then ran up the stairs, two at a time, leaving footprints of wet slush. Nabik's small bedroom was sparsely furnished, with only a desk, a bookshelf, and a narrow bed. Not many places to hide valuables. Drakne flipped the mattress over, found a rip in the seam, and pulled out a small leather pouch. Silver coins glimmered within.

She smiled. Yes. This would do.

Nearly tripping in her own slush tracks, she ran back down the hallway, pausing only to grab some of the brass candleholders from the wall and slide them inside her coat. She didn't bother with subtlety. The servants were gone. So were the guards. *All hiding, or fighting on the walls.* She would ride to Ruba's manor and make sure her friend was unhurt. Then she would go to the train station. Then—

Heavy boot steps pounded on the stairs. Fydir stepped into the hallway. "There you are," he said. He grabbed her by the collar of her coat as she tried to slip past him. The fabric fell open. Candleholders tumbled to the floor. Fydir's eyes widened. He stuck a hand in her coat pocket and pulled out the stolen purse. "Are you robbing your own house?"

"I'm leaving," Drakne shouted. "Just let me leave!"

"In a snowstorm? With the city full of rats?" He seized her by the wrist. "Blessed Winter, you should be grateful I'm not letting you get yourself killed!"

Rage burned in her chest. Dangerously hot and bright. "You don't care if I live or die."

"I care very much if you disobey me." His grip tightened. "You're my sister, Drakne. Until the day some foolish man takes you to wife, you're *mine*."

He hauled her to her bedroom door. She twisted and kicked, but he paid her no more heed than if she were a clawing kitten, and shoved her inside. She fell to her knees with a gasp of pain. The door locked behind her with a click that sounded like a bullet sliding into a chamber.

Blessed Winter. Will I ever escape him? Drakne yelled and pounded her fists against the wood. "Let me out! Let me out!"

No one heard her. Or if they did, no one cared.

Nabik led Eugen through Rot Hill like a fox inspecting an old den for snakes: nose-first, on his tiptoes, conscious of every flick and flicker of movement. His reflection shone, warped and ferocious, in wavered windows and patches of ice. The sleeves of his coat were marked and singed from powder burns, his black hair disheveled and his face red and puffy from sweat. His gray eyes were as haunted and wild as the beasts that had come screaming over the city walls.

It didn't help his nerves that he had to explain two hundred years of history to a nutcracker. The expansion of the Szpratzian Empire, the mass emigration out of Kolznechia, the invention of soul-engines and what it meant to be trapped inside one. How Zolka had been called away and trapped beyond the border. How Fydir planned to invade the north and raid Kolznechia for silver and souls. How the Rat King had cursed the forest kingdom and how even Winter herself could only call upon her mortal followers to make it right.

Eugen's carved eyebrows lifted higher with each word Nabik spoke. "Blessed Winter. The last thing I remember is that—that *Rat King* stabbed my father through the heart. I tried to save him. My limbs went stiff, and—and then I was dancing with your sister. Looking like this."

"I'm sorry," Nabik said. The death of King Kutreus was all but ancient history to him; to Eugen, it was mere hours past. "But there's no time to mourn. If the fairy tales are true, only restoring the rightful king will break the curse and set things right. You need to go north and take your father's throne."

"I'll do whatever's best for Kolznechia," Eugen said. "But are you quite sure you want me? I'm awful at trade negotiations."

What a strange creature he is. Eugen wore a painted coat of holly green, and his limbs and digits swiveled on carved joints. Wooden whorls marked his cheekbones, and his curls lay frozen under dark brown stain. His eyes jumped from sight to sight with a lively intelligence, unnatural in their carved sockets. A masterful sculpture, beauty, tragedy, and strangeness all caught in one figure. Curious, Nabik reached his power toward the prince—and felt a soul as bright as sunrise.

The yearning to do good burned in Eugen like a hearth fire. He wanted big things and small things, free schooling for Kolznechian children and the taste of lemon drops dissolving on soft human lips. He wanted out of duty, to do right by his country, and he wanted out of hope, his conviction the world could be much better than it was, but he wanted nothing out of anger or hate. For Nabik, it was like stepping into the forest and touching both the deepest roots and the treetops, the saplings and the greatest giants. A heart full of cheerful, thoughtful, welcoming wishes. A heart that felt like a home.

"I don't know much about being a king," he said. "But it seems to me you have the right character."

"That's not what my father thinks. Thought." Eugen shook his head. "He was this great warrior-king, and I . . . well, I've never done anything great. I was just born."

"My brother wanted me to be a soldier," Nabik said, "and I wouldn't call myself great at that either."

"It's difficult, isn't it? When you can't quite measure up. You either become the man they want, or become the embodiment of your own fear of failure."

Nabik winced. He felt that keenly. "I wish we had other choices."

"Well, *you* might," Eugen said. "What would you do if you could do anything?"

"I've always wanted to go north and learn wizardry. I have the gift, but . . ."

"You're a wizard? That's incredible."

"Didn't you have dozens of wizards at court? The stories say they built the Kolznechian kings a palace of crystal."

"That was long ago. The gift has grown rare over the centuries. But perhaps that's because people have grown crueler. They say Winter only gives wizardry to the most kindly, giving souls."

He gave Nabik a hesitant smile. His lips shone, polished

smooth as velvet. When Nabik realized he was staring at them, he blushed and looked away. "Thank you. I do want to learn magic. It's only that I've always put caring for my family first . . ."

"Ah," Eugen said. "I mean no offense, but considering what I just saw of you and your sister, you may wish to try something else?"

Perhaps. He didn't know how to explain his family to a stranger. "What would you be, if you could be anything?"

Eugen laughed. "Right now? I'd be human. Perhaps sitting on the throne will turn me back too. Or perhaps . . . if we go off fairy-tale logic, true love's kiss will restore my flesh."

True love. "That may prove a challenge. You're walking into a war. What sort of girl likes to hear *Let's take a romantic stroll and storm the palace?*"

"It doesn't have to be a girl."

"That changes nothing. I've never been kissed, but I've been on a battlefield. Hardly a romantic place." Nabik paused. Met those carved eyes and looked away, cheeks burning. They stood in the shadow of a pine covered in paper ornaments and hanging glass bottles. A dozen revelers about their age stood around the base, shouting and laughing, making toast after toast. Eugen had opened a door, and if Nabik could just bring himself to step through it, they would be just two young Kolznechian men out together too late on a winter evening. But nothing in his life had ever prepared him for a moment like this.

A ball of burning pitch streaked across the night sky and crashed into the silver-draped tree. Revelers shrieked and ran, dropping beer and plates of cookies as the paper ornaments ignited. Whipping wind lashed pine-scented flames toward the boys. Nabik swore and pulled Eugen farther down the avenue, away from the dangers of the heat and crackle.

"It's the prince," cackled a high voice. "And the soldier from the wall."

Nabik spun. *Rats?* They marched down the avenue, twenty, thirty of them, green uniforms spotted with blood. Fury glittered in their moonlit faces. Their wishes tasted hot and cutting. *Hungry.* They meant to loot Rot Hill of all it had.

"How did—"

"Your wall has a dozen little holes. Too small for humans."

Nabik cursed. "Right. Stand down. Leave this place, now, and we may yet have peace—"

"There is no peace. Not when the north starves and the south feasts."

"This is a poor neighborhood. Full of innocent Kolznechians. They're your kin. So am I."

"You're not one of us," said another rat. "Not while you wear the Empire's uniform."

Nabik winced. There was a grain of truth in that. He'd given up so much of who he was to be what Fydir wanted. *What do I want?* He knew. He'd always known.

"Brace yourself," he murmured, and sank tendrils of thought into Eugen's wishes. A note of longing, pure as a chiming bell, radiated from the prince. A need as strong as a second heartbeat to set his broken homeland right. Nabik wound the wishes about him like a scarf, focused on their goal—*open a route*—and flung the magic outward.

Ice exploded from the air, knocking the rats backward in a sparkling wave. Thunder clapped. They cringed, clutching their large skin-flap ears. "Wizard!" one shouted, and it came out edged in terror.

That's right. Nabik grinned and seized Eugen's hand. "Run!"

Scrambling down an ice-swept side alley, sliding over broken ground, the pair of them ducked into the ramshackle wooden maze of Rot Hill. The rats cursed and hissed at their heels. Dogs barked. Windows opened above them as children stared down at the chase and banged shut as their parents pulled them away.

Nabik and Eugen pushed northward. The shouts of their pursuers blended into the noise of a dozen other small battles. They turned one corner to find rat-soldiers surrounding a dressmaker's shop, placing torches to the wooden foundations. Nabik caught their wishes for plunder and summoned golden ribbons to bind the rats in shimmering cocoons. Snow flew up from Nabik's and Eugen's heels as they scrambled down the road—they passed a bakery with broken windows, and Nabik waved a hand to mend them with frosted white glass. A rat leapt from the doorway, claws out, and Nabik spun winter air about himself and the prince, knocking it away with a gust of wind. The power drained from him, like his soul was touched by seeping frostbite, as they stumbled out onto the main road.

"We're almost to the east gate," Nabik gasped, nearly tripping as his ankle twisted in a rut. "It's small, but it leads right to the border. Quickly—ah!" He leaned on Eugen's shoulder, panting heavily.

"Have you ever used this much magic in one go?" Eugen said. "Does it have a limit?"

"I don't know!"

"Right. Just do the best you can." He hooked an arm around Nabik, pulling him close. His wooden chest, though frost chilled, felt reassuringly solid. "I'll keep us moving forward."

Nabik clenched his fists, willing himself to keep going. Even with the prince holding him up, he staggered and wove. Shouts rang in his ears. Drawing closer. Closer. Shadows swept across the snow. A thrown torch ignited the hay on the wagon before them. Icy needles racked his lungs as he summoned a final burst of power. The flames cracked and snapped into a great pile of popcorn, the scent of hot butter filling the air.

Eugen dragged him forward. Past the cart, over a rubbish heap, down an alley. The small eastern gate of Malirmatvi rose before them—the iron doors chained shut.

"Surround them!" ordered a hissing voice. Rats poured out from the side streets, their eyes glinting green in the dark. Another rat patrol, grinning as they drew their weapons, came up from behind, cutting off all hope of retreat. Swords and guns pointed inward at Nabik and Eugen, the glinting moonlight turning them into a circle of sharp teeth.

"Lady Winter," Eugen whispered. "Guard us well."

Nabik had no prayers, not on the edge of collapse. He pressed his face against Eugen's shoulder, closed his eyes, reached with every thread of magic he could muster—and *called*.

A streak of white and wind—a weight crashed down just beyond the wall. The iron doors of the gate shivered and dulled, turning matte brown. *Chocolate*. It cracked and exploded outward in a thousand pieces.

The tallest woman he'd ever seen stood beyond it, cocoa dust on her fist. She was regal, strongly built. A worn fur coat covered her from her shoulders to her knees. Her cheeks were lined, hair white and weathered, and white feathers twisted down her nape. Behind her, the gray-flecked wings of a polar owl spread as wide as a house.

Zolka. His mother. At last, she'd come.

A silver wizard's staff glimmered like moonlight in her fist. She swept it across the sky in a glittering arc. Swords flew from the rat-soldiers' hands, shooting skyward and vanishing in the night. Blocks of ice locked around their feet, binding them in place.

"Hurry!" she called, voice clear and resonant. "Nabik, Eugen, to me!"

Nabik could barely set one foot before the other—but Eugen was already pulling him forward, to the point of no return. The line he'd dreamed of crossing, both in fantasies and nightmares. *I won't be able to come back for Drakne.* But she knew where she could find him. And for so long, he'd only lived to be what Fydir wanted. Now he wanted to be something new.

Together, he and Eugen crossed through the gate, tripping as they stumbled through the bullet-churned drifts beyond. A silver sleigh awaited them, magic brimming in place of a harnessed horse. A pistol cracked as they neared it. A ball stung his heels. Eugen leapt into the sleigh and pulled him up. Zolka waved her staff, and the sleigh charged off into the night.

"Thank you," Nabik gasped once he could speak, his exhausted head falling back against Eugen's solid chest.

"My sweet, gentle son." Zolka's hand cupped his cheek. "I'm afraid this will hurt."

And Winter sank her icy claws into his heart.

He seized, back arching, as his mother held him steady. *Nabik, child of Zolka,* called the voice of the wind and colder things. *Child of Winter. Your people crave your care.* And it was like all Kolznechia flew by beneath him, leagues and leagues of silver pines and deep, secret lakes, towns hidden against cliffsides and encircled by curling rivers, until the northern sky turned violet and the trees all turned to crystal. Gleaming gemstone pines ringed a city at the foot of a glacier. *Znaditin.* Where the pointed spires of the Crystal Palace, lacquered with sugar and butterscotch, brimmed with a magic that might choke him.

A throne towered above him. Tall, tall, as if he saw it from cringing on his belly. Beastly carvings covered every inch, wolves, bears, and lions, the gilt worn thin to show the chocolate beneath. Around it wrapped cords of crystal, as gnarled and twisted as the branches of a tree. Crystal roots threaded across the throne room floor. Rancid, rotting magic leaked from every inch of the sparkling stone, soaking into his flesh, waking and changing him.

Break its power, called Winter. *Save me. Save me!*

"I will," he gasped, and let the god of cold things claim him.

Drakne peered out her window and fumbled with her candle and mirror. *Three long, seven short. Three long, seven short.* Wind rattled through the manor's bones, seeping through cracks in the plaster. The scent of smoke came with it, as did the sounds of shouting and gunshots. She didn't know why she still bothered. Only that she had to push back against the part of herself that wanted to give up.

The window flew open. Drakne gasped, stumbling back. An airborne shadow sailed through—and smiled at her.

The Rat King's brown hair flew back off his shoulders, long and loose, his top hat gone missing in the night. His wormlike tail flicked behind him, pierced up and down with silver hoops. Long incisors flashed in his smile. "Miss Zolkedna." He bowed before her, took her hand, and pressed it to his lips. His claw-like nails were painted black. His padded fingers felt surprisingly smooth. "Drakne—may I call you that?"

"I'd rather hear my name than my mother's, yes."

"Drakne." This time, he said it like she'd given him a gift. "My apologies for my late arrival. Rest assured, you've never been far from my mind."

Drakne's heart sped. Should she be afraid? But she'd been scared ever since Fydir tossed her in his gun. The Rat King could do no worse to her. "Where is Lady Ruba?"

His eyes widened. "You care for her?"

"She's my friend. If you've hurt her—"

"She's fine. Keep your eyes open with her. Not everyone is what they seem." He hesitated. "Not even me."

He sounded oddly . . . vulnerable. Up close, with the everyday-ness of the wardrobe and vanity behind him, the powerful, immortal king looked . . . young. Nineteen or twenty. Like a thread of time had snagged the back of his coat and kept him there. At school, they'd taught her how to speak to a nobleman, how to curtsy, how to flatter. But she didn't see a king. Only a friend who'd betrayed her.

"What do you truly want from me?" she asked. "To dance open soul-engines? Or was that all a lie? Did you only write to me because I'm Zolka's daughter? Because you thought I could find Eugen for you?"

"It was both," he said. "I chose you because you care more about doing right than doing what society approves of. You were willing to burn Archduke Marinus alive for hurting women. I find that admirable."

"That was seven years ago. What if I've changed?"

"I'm sure you have. A good heart can harden. But a good mind stays sharp. You're cunning, Drakne. You can understand why I wanted to sabotage Szpratzian soul-engines, both as a king who doesn't want the empire on my border to grow stronger, and as a person with a sliver of a heart. Consider—am I truly the only monster, in the tale of me and Eugen Kutredan? He's the one whose family claimed the right to absolute power. He'll make a suffering kingdom bleed for his last name."

"You make a fair point," Drakne said. The Eugen she'd met didn't seem to care overmuch about power and conquest, but who knew what her mother might want with him? Perhaps she'd underestimated how much chaos her dancing would unleash. "You might have come sooner and asked me to wake Eugen for you, instead of just scuttling about in the shadows."

"Can you blame me for not trusting you?" He stepped closer, so close she could see his pulse beat staccato in his throat. A whiff of ink and paper hung beneath his mildewy scent. "Come now. Let's not mince words. I recruited you as a saboteur, one of my agents in the Szpratzian Empire. You vanished for eight months. Suddenly, a Szpratzian army is massing on my border. That hasn't happened in centuries."

"You think I had something to do with that?" Her voice rose with shock. "The Empire never invaded because Szpratzians are terrified of becoming beastfolk. Now they have my brother to lead them, and he isn't scared of anything."

"Your brother was very recently promoted. Is that why you turned on me? For him?"

"I didn't turn on you!"

"You tried to knock my brains out with a shoe. I pride myself on some intelligence; I can put the facts together." He shook his head. Moonlight lit the red mark on his throat where she'd strangled him. "No. Your whole family is in on it, aren't they? You made a deal with the Empire to overthrow me and install Prince Eugen as a puppet king."

As ideas went, it was diabolically simple. The Empire would likely have offered her family titles and mining rights in exchange for carrying out the coup. They would have become the richest family in Kolznechia. Empires would pay you well for betraying your own people. Fydir was happy to make that bargain; the thought of it churned her stomach. But what other conclusion could the Rat King draw? *He doesn't know about the gun. About any of it.*

The Rat King was angry, yes, but there was a curiosity behind it, one that almost reminded her of Ruba. He was lonely, and had clearly been betrayed before.

She could use that.

"Very well. You have it right. I have Prince Eugen." Drakne smiled. "In fact, I'm the only one who knows where he is."

The Rat King narrowed his eyes. "Tell me."

"No."

Cold swept through the room. A thicket of icicles sprouted from the air, each one longer than her arm, and pointed at her chest, her throat, her eye. Needle sharp and diamond bright, they sparkled. Drakne's heart jumped. She froze. Clenched her jaw. Said nothing. *He's playing with me,* she told herself. *He knows I can't help him if I'm dead.*

At last, the Rat King snapped his fingers. The icicles collapsed in a spray of water. He sighed. "Drakne. Dear. I need to kill him. It might be the only way to break the curse."

She stared at him. "It's *your* curse."

"You know wizards. We're quite powerful, and I might very well be the strongest of us all, but a curse of this magnitude . . . it was born of my magic, Winter's magic, and some magic I don't even understand. Every year, it changes and grows stronger. It's hungry. Vengeful." He sighed. "The Teyodet line has a dark history. They were cruel monarchs. Warmongers. They blasphemed against the goddess. My theory is that their extinction will strengthen Winter's power and placate the curse."

Winter. All Drakne could think of was Zolka. Cold, distant, demanding. "Killing him sounds quite important, then. So you should give me what I want."

"Very well. I can let our original deal stand. You'll have a position with the best dance troupe in the Empire, and—"

"No." That was what she'd wanted before. Before she'd realized Fydir wouldn't simply let her go live her own life. Before she'd realized that dancing only brought back what he'd done to her. She wanted what the Rat King had. The power to make sure no one would ever hurt her again.

The wish came to her like a flash of lightning. *Brilliant.*

The Rat King's hazel eyes widened. He could read the desire on her, even before she spoke it out loud.

Drakne smiled. "I want you to make me your queen."

"What?"

"You heard me. Sweep me off to your palace. Marry me. Crown me your queen. Then I'll tell you where to find Prince Eugen. And I'll get Fydir to halt his invasion. I'll make peace." She didn't know how she'd make good on those promises. But she'd work that out later. Once she'd escaped.

The Rat King stepped backward. His eyes darted about, as if he expected her to spring a trap. "An intriguing proposition. I shall . . . consider it. We'll talk soon." He pushed open the window. Snowflakes billowed into the room. He dropped into a low bow. His black cloak swirled around him. The scent of rot washed down Drakne's throat; she clutched her nose and gagged. A snap of leathery fabric, and the wizard-king was gone into the night.

Drakne went to close the window. As the latch clicked, she paused, gazing out to the north. Where hundreds of innocent families didn't know the horror Fydir planned to bring them. *I can't stop him.* He would most likely drag her along on his conquest. But she could find opportunities in the chaos. Especially if she kept her rage in check and didn't provoke him.

And when she was queen of Kolznechia, she would never live in fear of him again.

ACT TWO

Under Silver Pines

CHAPTER SEVEN

An Offering of Gravestones

Silvertree Forest, disputed Kolznechian-Szpratzian territory

Snowflakes caught like kisses on the loose hair that fell over Nabik's brow, flecks of white that nestled in the black.

Wooden hands held him in place as the sleigh jostled northward. White wings spread above him when the storm grew thick. Nabik tossed and turned, dreams racing through his head: red-furred ferrets chewing gashes in his tingling ears, soldiers bleeding hot chocolate as they died, a motorized soul-engine throne that held up Fydir's gold-crowned weight as he polished a gun with Drakne's face for a muzzle.

"I think his humors are out of balance," Eugen murmured. "We should bleed him."

Nabik stirred, buried under a weight of wool. *They've draped me in more blankets than a spinster's ottoman.* "Absolutely not, you fiend. Your medical knowledge is two centuries outdated. Humors aren't real."

"Oh, good. I never liked getting leeched. How are you feeling?"

Nabik opened his eyes. Eugen's face loomed above his. Too close. An animated visage with too-high eyebrows and jerking, painted pupils. Smiling like his birthright hadn't been stolen.

"I'm a bit disconcerted," he said. "Could you get your elbow out of my diaphragm?"

103

Eugen rolled off him. With the terrifying chatterbox out of the way, Nabik could finally breathe and look about in the noonday light. The magic-drawn sleigh pounded down a twisting, narrow road lumped with snowdrifts and flanked by white-draped birches. Wind whistled through branches, and the trees creaked as it blew. No other tracks save theirs marred the soft blanket of snow. Accustomed to the roar and reek of cities, he might have thought this clean and quiet place a gift, if he hadn't known a curse bound the land like iron fetters.

"Where's Zolka?" he grunted.

"Right here," hooted a soft voice. The owl dropped through the trees and perched on the back of the sleigh. "Thank Winter, you're awake." Blood stained her beak and talons. She folded herself back into human form, expertly balanced on the runners, and wiped her lips clean. "The Rat King's eagles are chasing us. I drove off two, but more are coming."

"We need to cover our path," Nabik said, shaking his head to throw off sleep. "How are they tracking us?"

"Most likely by the sound of your snoring," said Eugen.

"I don't snore!"

"You've never had to sit next to yourself sleeping off a magic hangover." Eugen jabbed a finger into his chest. "You snore like your nostrils hold a portal to hell."

Zolka waved her hand, summoning a staff of silver birch twined with ice-crystal feathers. She drove it into the brake shaft and pulled back, slowing them with a crunching metallic *scree*. "Start unpacking. We need to abandon the sleigh. It's too easy to spot from above. Even more obvious than a wooden boy."

"Wooden *man*," Eugen insisted. "I'm nearly twenty!"

Zolka, with every line etched on her face like a saga, gave him one look and killed the objection.

Nabik clambered out of the sleigh. With Eugen's help, he slid the blankets into canvas packs, along with their dried meat, heavy clothing, and fire kits. "I'll get that," Eugen said cheerfully as Nabik reached for one. Long wooden fingers clacked as they closed around the strap. "I don't tire easily in this body, and you're still recovering your strength."

"I assure you, I'm quite fit." Nabik entertained the idea that, along with his body, Eugen's mouth would never tire either. He shuddered, and not wholly from the cold.

"I insist!" Eugen slung the extra pack below his own. "I've moldered as a knickknack for two hundred years. I'd like to be useful."

"I've never heard of a useful prince. You know, Szpratzian princes buy themselves whole forests for pheasant hunts, then get drunk and accidentally hit the game wardens."

"That's awful. Royal blood is no excuse to be an ass. Or, in my case, royal sap."

"You're *cursed*. How can you joke about that?"

"My one other option is moaning. I might as well choose the cheery one. Dark times come over all of us. It's how we face them that determines who we are when the dawn comes."

When the dawn comes. Eugen made it sound so certain. Optimistic to the point of madness. "You're cursed *and* delusional."

"Oh, please. You're making me sound much more interesting than I actually am."

Interesting. Yes, Eugen was. But Nabik couldn't lose focus now. "Mother—Zolka—I dreamed about Drakne and Fydir. It was . . . terrible."

"I summoned a vision of Drakne in the ice," Zolka said. "She's at home with Fydir in Malirmatvi."

She's safe. Or at least, not trapped in a soul-engine. Nabik exhaled. *But how long will they stay in the south?* He knew Fydir. Knew what drove him. For years, he'd told himself his brother only dealt with the archduke, the soul-engines, the imperial military, to feed and house his family. Everything he did, even the cruelties, came out of love. He loved his family as much as they loved him. He only had a different way to show it.

But Nabik knew the wishes of his brother's heart. They tasted of fear and ambition, tangled in a strangling cord. If there was love, it was not the thing that drove him.

How do I tell her that her son is a monster?

"I know," Zolka said quietly. "I know what he's done, to you and to your sister. I know he plans to attack Kolznechia. And I'm sorry. For not being there. For leaving you three alone. For not helping Fydir be a better man. I'm more sorry than you can ever know."

"You wouldn't have gone north if you didn't feel it was necessary," Nabik said. "I understand. I'm not angry at you. But . . . Drakne is. She needs our help. And she won't come to us."

"She knows she has family across the border. Until Winter releases us from our bond, the best we can do is keep our doors open." She frowned. "And, if we get the chance, deal with Fydir."

"What do you mean, *deal* with Fydir?"

"To be honest? I'm not yet sure."

Neither was Nabik. In fairy tales, the heroes killed the monsters. But what did you do when the monster was your brother? He lowered his head. A loose lock of hair flopped down from his cap. He reached to brush it back—and froze. *I cut this just the other day.* This lock was twice as long as Fydir allowed—almost shaggy—and flecked with threads of white. Not the slender silver of age or stress. A thick, eggshell pearlescence of *potential*.

"It's quite cold. Take this, sweetheart." Zolka dug around in a pack of her own garments and offered him a coat of gray-flecked cream fur. The lacework ties and wide waist marked it as a woman's garment—though at least the woman offering it matched his own six feet of height. Nabik stared at it, confused. Fydir had taught him to work *maleness* into a shield. As a soldier, in the Empire, he'd been grateful for the protection. *Wasn't I? What about when Fydir laughed at me for wearing a too-slim, womanly watch chain, and I was so disgusted with myself that I threw it down a well?*

"Is there a way to . . . adjust this?" he said.

Zolka snapped her fingers. Wind twisted about the coat, turning the ties to sturdy leather and straightening the waist and shoulder for a square frame. He pulled it on over his torn and bloodied uniform.

"Thank you," Nabik said. "And . . . sorry. I should have been able to work that magic myself. I can't always find the right wishes. Will you . . . teach me?" Asking came hard. He was a man grown. He was supposed to be capable.

He didn't quite know what he was anymore.

"Of course!" Zolka beamed, and pulled him into her arms. Her grip was sure and steady, her embrace warm. Nabik froze, unused to hugs. His mother pulled back, still smiling. "It would be my dearest honor to teach you. But the most important lesson of magic is how it must be used. A wizard cares for the weak and vulnerable, holds the powerful to account, helps every town and village thrive. That's our purpose. Follow it, and all the other answers will come."

Nabik nodded. *Follow it.* Yes. He was good at that.

To the east, an eagle screeched. A shriek like human laughter answered. It was far away, but it was drawing nearer. Eugen shivered as he stood, wooden joints clattering, and slung the last of the packs on his back. "Which way now?" he said.

"We should follow the river," said Zolka. "Where the undergrowth is thickest. Take cover."

Down the bank they scrambled, beneath the overhangs once carved by swift-flowing water. Their boots cut the earth's frosty rime, and the scent of peat and clay bled up from the gashes. Bare branches laced above them like the domes of a cathedral, the cracked and green-flecked river ice its mosaic floor. Speaking only in low whispers, they made their way upstream. The thin sunlight cast everything in an eerie violet haze and glistened off the crystals that clung to the bulrushes and bedstraw blossoms. Nabik shivered to see that perhaps every fifth clump of greenery had turned to amethyst.

A shadow washed over them from above. The air pounded and thudded beneath the weight of wingbeats. Nabik glimpsed a flurry of brown feathers, human eyes narrowed above a great beak, the green sash of the Rat King's army—and a shot shattered the stillness. It was close, ear-stabbing. Nabik jumped back against the embankment wall. Tree branches cracked as a body plummeted downward. A broken wing beat frantically. An eagle shrieked curses in a garbled human tongue.

"They forget wizards have more tools than just our spells," Zolka said, grim and practiced, lowering her smoking rifle. The spice of gunpowder burned in Nabik's nose. "We'll follow the river three miles north. There's a village where we can shelter for a bit."

They pushed their way along the shadowed embankment at a trot, scrambling over smooth, loose stones and dodging the deceptively slippery patches of dark ice. Nabik followed, empty belly aching, calves burning as he sought purchase on unsteady ground. A hand rope had been staked to aid passage—but too low to the ground for anyone but a child to use it. Any *human* but a child.

The incessant prickling in his ears seemed to hum like swarming wasps. A shiver ran up his spine, full and consuming, as if his very bones were shaking loose to bend as the curse commanded.

"We're close," Zolka said. She pointed down into the frozen riverbed, where the twisted sticks and branches of a beaver lodge rose up to meet a hollowed-out tree with a door in the side, only three feet high.

"Is the whole town beaverfolk?" Nabik asked. "Do beast shapes run in families?"

"No, the shapes don't go with bloodlines. But beastfolk often build their own families, find kinship with those of similar shape and mind. Beaverfolk are drawn to rivers. A good number of them dwell here."

Eugen clambered up the bank and rapped on the door. "Hello? Is anyone home?"

No one answered the knock. The small glass portholes cut in the tree side remained dark.

"I'm sure they're just out for the evening." Nabik followed Eugen up the bank and clapped him on the shoulder. "Perhaps you should be glad to have missed them. They'd have chewed your leg off for a new postbox." He did not add *The beaverfolk probably fled into the river when they saw your rictus grin at the window.*

"Can you feel anyone nearby?" Zolka asked as she passed Nabik a lantern. The flame seemed wan against the purple sunset haze, casting harsh half-moon shadows on the trees.

Nabik reached out, feeling for nearby wishes. The wind shifted. On it came sorrow and the heavy smell of smoke.

He gulped. "Follow me."

Past head-high shingled rooftops and stone-lined firepits he led them, crossing prints made from tiny shoes and broad, sweeping tails. They entered the village proper, where some of the waist-high doors had cracked from heat; one blackened shell of a treehouse had burned out from the inside. A snow-dusted common square lay strewn with little stools and fishbones.

They found the beastfolk in the graveyard. Most were shaped like beavers, with some frogfolk and ferrety children among their number. Small they were, the tallest no more than four feet high, the shortest barely at his knee. Some stood up straight; others had backs bent beneath their hairy pelts. Their hands and feet were humanlike, or human enough for the purpose of moving about and doing labor. Some had black webbing between their fingers; most had tails, flat and wide. Some wore patched trousers, some wore long smocks, and some wore naught but looks of horror as they tossed palmfuls of soil on the graves.

"What happened here?" Zolka said. She knelt and took an old beaver-man by the hand. "What caused the fire? Mayhaps we can lay spells to stop the next one."

"It was poachers. From across the border."

Nabik winced. Guilt rushed through him like the ghosts of embers. *Beaver pelts. For hats. Atvidan and his damn factory.*

"Let me help," he said. With a nod, he summoned shovels to replace their single, bent-handled one. He waved off one of the gray-muzzled beavers, who was so old his spine looked next to snapping, and took his place filling in a hole. Eugen started digging beside him, and the mourners didn't question the presence of a wooden boy. Zolka drew two crying beaverfolk into her arms.

"Will you give your blessing to the grave?" the old man asked Nabik as he patted the earth smooth. "Send the spirits out on the winter wind?"

Nabik nodded and closed his eyes. He knew not what to say—wizards were not priests, for Winter asked her followers to share warmth, not to worship her. But in the old man's mourning lay a purpose he might serve. *Send them home.* He stretched out his hand and reached out with the fragile flutter inside him that breathed in wishes and pain. The earth shook and cracked open, rumbling under his shoes. Stone pierced up through the soil. Slabs of granite rose to mark each plot.

There, he thought, opening his eyes and wiping away tears as the little graveyard settled.

"Well done," Zolka said, low and solemn, yet proud.

"Thank you," said the old beaver. "It's quite the kindness."

I still can't make it right. No magic could. He could only make it mourned and settled. *It's not enough. I'm not enough.* He stumbled backward, a new wave of exhaustion sweeping through his chest. Eugen cursed and caught him. For half a heartbeat, the spinning in his head was such that Nabik let himself lean on, lean *into*, the strange boy beside him.

The back of his head fit perfectly against Eugen's shoulder. Fit *too* perfectly. His whole body fizzed with a hum of echoed incoherence, a wrongness in the bone. Eugen had caught him when he'd stumbled back in Malirmatvi, his sharp-carved nose digging into Nabik's ear. Now that same ear, prickling, potent, rested easily against Eugen's shoulder. Rested *wrong*.

Zolka's coat trailed loose on the snow. Two inches of hem too long.

He shouted—shrieked—yelped in shock, pulling away, stumbling over his hem, toppling forward into the snow. His hat tumbled free.

Dark hair streaked egg white fell in loose tangles about his cheeks and rough-stubbled jaw. His ears popped free in a click of cartilage. Reflected in shining ice, he saw their tips stretching high, pointed, curved, bristling at the edges with white fur. Saw a tall man—tall, but no longer towering—his canine teeth sparkling sharp at the point.

His magic had opened him to the curse, and it had collected its toll.

"Congratulations," said Zolka. "A white winter fox. A lovely and fitting aspect for a young wizard."

"Welcome home, child," said one of the beaver-women, smiling at him and his mother.

"Welcome to yourself," said her companion, dabbing at her reddened eyes. "Such a happy thing to see."

They see the curse as a blessing? He looked up to his mother. *Up.* "Why is a fox smaller than an owl?"

"All beastfolk change in their own ways. Some more, some less. The curse finds hidden aspects of ourselves and brings them to the surface. What it's saying is, perhaps you are not a man in the way you've come to expect, all tall and mighty. You're . . . your own self. The curse is showing you that." She smiled. "How do you feel?"

He didn't know. All considerations of *how he felt* and *who he was* had always come second to what Fydir wanted him to be. "Excuse me," he said, and stumbled off through the snow. He crossed the burned-out village square and slunk down to the river-bank, where the distance from the villagers meant he didn't feel so awkwardly exposed. Sitting on a log, he buried his face in his hands and shook as if weeping—but the tears would not come. It was as if the gears had jammed within him.

Eugen sat beside him and poked at Nabik's ear. Nabik slapped his hand away. Undaunted, the prince said, "Foxes are my absolute favorites. Tricksy cunning beasties. And they're adorable—not that I'm saying *you're* adorable, specifically. I mean, you're barely a tenth of the way transformed—"

A white winter fox. Part of him had always yearned to curl up in a quiet, peaceful den, surrounded by warm bodies. Part of him could snap, bite, and kill at Fydir's bidding. It fit. But he wished he could be something more. He wasn't sure what, precisely. But wizards were meant to care for those who needed them. All Nabik could offer these beaverfolk were graves.

"I don't think I can do this," he whispered. "Wizards are supposed to be wise. Leaders and protectors. But I've made so many mistakes. I've hurt people—"

"You're not the only one," Eugen said. When Nabik gave him a questioning look, he continued with "I mean, the kings in my family all made terrible mistakes. Started wars, made plagues and famines worse. When I turned eighteen..." Eugen took a deep breath. "My father told me a secret. One passed from each Teyodet king to his heir. When our ancestor, the first King Kutreus, fought to unify Kolznechia, Winter herself appeared to him. She denounced his violent ways and threatened to stop him. So he snuck into the caves beneath the Great Mountain. He found where Winter slept and cut out her heart with his sword."

"What?"

"It's true. There's a sacred relic, the Heart of Winter. The soul of the goddess dwells inside it. But it was separated from the rest of...her temple? Her body? I don't think mortal language has a word for what she was...connected to. But that's why she's become so weak. Why she needs wizards to do her bidding. Likely why she hasn't intervened to break the curse."

"That's terrible," Nabik whispered.

Eugen nodded. "To keep secret what they'd done, my ancestors hid the Heart of Winter inside our royal throne. When I have it back, I can restore the Heart to its proper place. I don't know if I'm capable of being a good ruler, or even if we have a chance to stop the Rat King at all. But I want to do whatever I can to set things right. That feels like a step in the right direction, doesn't it?"

Nabik took a deep, shaky breath. "Then I suppose it's my duty to put you in a place where you can do that. So we can help each other be what we're supposed to be." Their eyes met. Nabik gave Eugen an encouraging smile.

The wind shifted. An owl made of snow fluttered up to perch on Eugen's shoulder. "I'm summoning a funeral banquet," it said in Zolka's voice. "Come back soon. It's an insult if a wizard won't eat at your table." The snowflake owl blew apart. The smell of fish stew washed over them both, dampening the dry scent of ashes.

Eugen stood and offered Nabik his hand. "Well. Duty calls." His smile was back. A bit more stiff than before, but Nabik couldn't judge that. He took Eugen's hand and stood. The prince's fingers were quite long. And surprisingly warm.

The villagers held the banquet in the hollow beside a frozen waterfall, where icicles fanned down like a feathered aquamarine cloak. A river-carved outcrop of dark granite sheltered them from spy eagles and bats. A fire crackled in a pit, and Zolka had charmed the smoke to creep upriver. Besides the stew, the beaverfolk had brought a mash of ground river-tubers to share, and Zolka had summoned a silver-lidded tray she lifted to reveal steaming cinnamon rolls drenched in icing. Nabik bit into one. Spice, heat, and buttercream flooded down his throat. He squeezed his eyes shut, savoring. It didn't make everything better, but it was a start.

"The blight's grown worse," said a beaver-woman to Zolka. "The crystals build up in the fish and kill them. Our catch is nearly half of what it was ten years ago."

"I didn't realize it had reached this far south." Zolka waved her staff. Crates of grain and bags of flour appeared from the aether. Filleted fish and fresh red meat materialized atop banks of ice. "That should keep you a month or so."

But far too many villages wouldn't have a wizard looking out for them. "We need to go to Znaditin now," Nabik said. "We need to face the Rat King."

"You'll be no match for the Rat King until you've honed your magic," Zolka said. "We'll go to Stakte. It's a large town, lots of people, lots of needs to tend to. A good place to grow into your wizardry. The hard part will be getting there, though. The forest is dense, and there's no road. It'll take a full month overland on foot."

"Can't I just wish us there?" Eugen said.

"No, for the same reason you can't wish the Rat King overthrown. Wizardry has limits. It would take more power than my body and Nabik's can muster." She shook her head. "But there's other magics. Help the beavers put away their stores, and I'll show you."

Nabik lifted one bag of flour, Eugen lifted three, and along with the beaverfolk, they hauled the summoned stores to a hole inside a dead oak, where the cold would keep it fresh. The beaverfolk went back to their village, to the work of rebuilding, and Nabik tried to think what he might summon them to help as he and Eugen returned to the waterfall hollow. But he knew nothing of carpentry and construction, and he needed every drop of power he possessed for what lay ahead.

"We can speed our travel with the help of a powerful snowfae," Zolka said when they returned, warming her fingers over the fire. "Nabik, draw on my wanting and summon her here."

Nabik nodded. He stretched his hand—and his magic— toward his mother. Zolka's wishes rested at the surface of her, calm and orderly. *Queen Genna the Glacier-Born*. But he felt nothing else. As if all of Zolka's fears and longings lay beneath a glacier.

Nabik shivered. It had nothing to do with the wind stirring the snow flurries and everything to do with the cold inside his own heart. "What if this Genna is too far away to be summoned?"

"By the time a snowfae is that old and powerful, part of them is everywhere they've blessed with nature's beauty. You're not dragging her toward us. You're opening a door." Zolka looked sheepish. "I'd do it myself, but we've had a bit of a personal . . . falling out."

Nabik took a deep breath. Tried to concentrate. *What if I can't do this? Like how I couldn't do magic for Fydir and the archduke?* Magic twisted in his chest. Sticks of peppermint, sharp edged and cutting, erupted from the ground and stuck between them like a steel fence. Zolka broke one off and stuck it in her mouth.

"Good try," she said. "Keep going."

"I'm sorry. I . . . something's wrong," Nabik said, fumbling for words. In truth, he felt more like *he* was something wrong. "Your feelings—I can't reach them."

"I know. I'm doing my best to keep them contained. You aren't responsible for me in that way. I'm your mother, not the other way around."

"I'm a wizard. We're supposed to care for the people who need us."

"I love that you have such a loving heart." She softened her voice. "But even wizards have limits on how much we can care. Right now, you need to care for *yourself*."

Myself. That was the last thing he wanted to think about.

Who is that? Not a soldier. Not Fydir's instrument. A wizard. That was all he knew. *A wizard cares for the weak and vulnerable, holds the powerful to account, helps every town and village thrive.*

A wizard cares for others first.

On his next attempt to summon the snowfae, Nabik created a bridge of gingerbread across the river. On the next, rose vines cut clove-scented gashes through the biscuit, flowers blooming and shriveling under thin coats of rime. A rabbit made of packed snowballs skipped about his feet. A fountain of whiskey exploded from the earth. A herd of grazing reindeer bugled as they began to levitate, then raced off trumpeting through the sky.

"I'm sorry!" Nabik shouted as they vanished from sight.

"Try using Eugen's wishes," Zolka said. "Mine might be too heavy for you to work with."

"I'm sorry," Nabik mumbled.

"You don't need to apologize to me. You're just learning."

"You can do this," Eugen said, and put a hand on his shoulder. The weight was solid and reassuring.

Nabik steadied himself. Shook out his fingers. Reached out. Eugen's wishes hummed and skipped about him, like puppies and dragonflies, and somewhere in them Nabik found the queen of the snowfae. He *pulled*, and the world unraveled like a frayed thread. Snow billowed up into a burst of thunder. Clouds knit together as the sky went dark. Nabik clapped his hands to his ears and felt them crawl like caterpillars, fur and hair unspooling from his skin like noodles pushed through a press. Fistfuls of eggshell white bursting through his shrinking fingers as his nails went black and sharp.

"Well done!" Eugen laughed and clapped him across the

back, and it was real joy, not Fydir's backhanded, cutting compliments. Something in him leapt at the sound of it. Like he'd finally done something right. Like dawn might finally find him.

"I knew you could do it," Zolka said. Nabik barely recognized the emotion in her voice—*pride. She's proud of me.*

Genna the Glacier-Born arrived in a descending storm cloud. She was purple-eyed and mahogany-cheeked, her braids stacked high inside a crown of icicles. Lightning tumbled down her skirts like living lace, leaving rough block patterns in the snow. *Physics doesn't permit*—Nabik thought, but the effect was lovely, and loveliness permitted the snowfae a great deal.

"Zolka." Her deep, rich voice echoed off the ringing trees. Pines dropped their burdens of snow and needles. Gingerbread shook and chocolate cracked. "It's been a long time. Too long."

"Good day, Your Majesty," Zolka said, and curtsied. "Thank you for heeding our call. Allow me to present my son Nabik and Prince Eugen Kutredan Teyodet."

Genna rapped a fist atop Eugen's carved curls. "Fascinating spellwork. You don't get this kind of detail these days."

"We need to travel to Stakte," Zolka said. "So we might—"

The snowfae queen's lips flared, revealing teeth so serrated they were almost spiraled, like a crabeater seal's. "I know why you called me here. You need another favor. How many of those have I done you?" There was a note of familiarity in her voice—and in her heart, a wish to be held. Nabik didn't know which struck him more: that his mother had taken the queen of the snowfae as a lover, or that she had bungled it badly. "Why should I help you? You're still working to overthrow the Rat King. Snowfae don't interfere in politics."

"The snowfae are the daughters of Winter. She teaches us to care for each other in our most desperate times. Politics can be an instrument of service."

"Politics is the instrument of power," Genna said. "And mortals crave power so much they abandoned Winter's teachings and ripped out her heart." She shot a cutting look at Eugen. "We want nothing to do with their games. Not while they don't respect our goddess."

Nabik stepped forward. "Please," he said. "Winter's teachings—they still matter. Perhaps they matter now more than ever. We all have a part to play in making this right. I'm only one wizard, but I'm willing to do whatever I must. I promise."

His words felt thin, frail, insufficient. Genna studied him with eyes as dark as the night sky.

"Perhaps you haven't all forgotten your purpose," she said. "Very well. I'll take you to Stakte."

Oh. He hadn't expected that. But Eugen smiled, wide and satisfied, and Nabik realized the prince wasn't surprised at all. Maybe there was something to Eugen's optimism.

Maybe he was something worth believing in.

Nabik turned, to ask his mother what would come next, and quietly dissolved into vapor.

CHAPTER EIGHT

Of Maidens and Monsters

Drakne remembered the first time Fydir had fired his gun.

Trapped in the soul-engine, time had faded away as she waited for her purpose. A ballerina in the wings. A weapon in its holster. Then she'd awakened in a dingy warehouse. His hands pulled hers, now a gilded trigger. Her dancer's legs sprang up and down, absorbing the heavy backward shock of recoil. Fresh cartridge after cartridge dropped into the chamber of her heart.

Men she'd never seen dropped dead before her. Fydir shouted, swore, and raged. He was always angry when he killed, but never angry at the people he was killing.

The morning after the rats attacked Malirmatvi, Drakne met Fydir in the manor's salon. The gilded mirrors atop the piano cast her reflection back at her: a pale girl in a gown of white and eggshell, her hair pinned up tight, leaving nothing to grab. *I look like a corpse*, she thought, and then *I look like a bride*.

Fydir waited, hunched over, at the bench of the piano he couldn't play. A glass of whiskey, jagged chunks of ice poking over the lip, lay in his hand. He was chewing on the base of his pipe. Gunpowder streaked the velvet sleeves of his smoking jacket, and blond stubble lined his chin in unruly tracts.

"Are you planning to run away in that?" He gestured toward

her with the whiskey glass, not looking up from the maps on his knee. "Won't get far."

"I know." She took a deep breath. "I'm sorry about last night." The apology stung, and she wasn't truly sorry. But until she had her crown, she needed him on her side.

"Think nothing of it," Fydir said. "I barely remember it anyway. Had a few drinks after the fighting on the wall. What a disgusting mess it all was. We're marching on Kolznechia as soon as approval comes through Parliament. I'll see the Rat King punished."

"Is he the one you want to punish?" she said. "Or is it truly the archduke in your sights?"

Fydir quieted. Like waiting quicksand.

"He's never recognized your true value," she said quickly. *Flatter him. Secure his favor.* "You'd be well within your rights to tear him down."

"Did I ever tell you about the archduke's pet cat?" Fydir said. "He adored her. A purebred queen with long white fur and eyes like sapphires. One day, a roving orange tom snuck into his mansion and got her pregnant. The archduke was furious. He gave me the kittens. Two orange, one white. Told me to kill them."

"Did you?"

"I gave them to a friend."

He killed them, Drakne decided.

"Everything is disposable to that man. People, animals. That day, I saw my time would come, and he'd get rid of me too. He's cruel, petty, small-minded. I'm ten times the man—ten times the leader—he'll ever be. He's in our past, Drakne. From now on, we make our own future."

"Good," Drakne said. "Your service made him the richest man in the Empire. What wonderful things might you make for yourself?"

His brow furrowed. He sipped his whiskey, as if to buy himself a pause to think, but Drakne had already caught the flicker of uncertainty in his eyes. The praise warmed him. But he was a bit suspicious at getting it from her. "I tell you this much: I won't stop at securing a monopoly on Kolznechian lumber."

So this wasn't only about punishing the archduke. It was about money. And power.

Drakne brushed a hand over her bodice, where she'd tucked away the letter Ruba had sent her at daybreak. *I'm safe. Cleaning ashes from my ballroom.* Short and to the point, scrawled out in messy print. *Be careful, darling.*

"Where's Nabik?" Fydir asked.

"Gone," Drakne said. "He crossed the border last night."

Fydir's lips vanished into a thin white line. His eyes gleamed dangerously bright. "After all I've done for him, running away to—" He lifted his whiskey glass. Drakne knew that look of his. She dodged a full heartbeat before he flung it. Crystal shattered in the fireplace. She pulled her skirts away from the spreading amber stain.

"I know," she whispered. "I'm shocked too. But what else can we expect of a wild Kolznechian wizard?" *We.* She dared not emphasize it, but she needed him to understand.

Nabik was gone. Which meant Fydir had only one sibling in play, only one person who relied on him enough to be *usable.* He had to treat her with some care.

She had leverage, for now. Not like his. But a foothold.

"Well," he said. "I'm glad you're still here."

"So am I." Drakne smiled. Fydir had made her into his weapon. She would wield herself, until the whole world danced behind her.

Three days later, the Eighth Regiment assembled to march on the north. Massed men shivered at the border, uniform coats thin and tatter sleeved, worn boots shifting in the mud, as they prepared to cross and set their humanity behind them.

Drakne stood beside Fydir, the gate's iron teeth spiked above them. Snow rested in the brim of their rabbit-furred hats. A microphone hooked to a soul-engine amplifier crackled with static in his fist.

"My brothers-in-arms," he growled. "As children, we heard tales of the north's nightmares. But ours is the power of iron, lead, and souls. We fear no curse. Beyond that wall, we'll seize our fortunes!"

He nudged Drakne with his elbow. This idea, they'd come up with between the two of them. A dozen soldiers had deserted since the Rat King's attack. Fydir had ordered them caught and flogged, but Drakne knew it would take more than fear of punishment to keep them in-line when their flesh began to crawl. *Give them shame. Show them a girl can do it fearlessly.* Better cross and be a monster than flee and be less a man.

Great Winter, if you ever listened to your people, heed me now. You made me your dancer. Now crown me your queen.

Alone, head tipped back to taste the dusting snowflakes, Drakne crossed through the gate. Joy bubbled in her lungs like laughing gas as the bullet-blasted fields and shadowed, sulking forest unfolded before her.

Not a single brick lay between her and her destiny.

"Move out!" Fydir ran to her side, waving his soldiers forward. Some men murmured low fears or rubbed their pricking temples as they crossed. Even Fydir scratched at his ears. Drakne ignored the hairs stiffening on the back of her neck.

A heavy-treaded soul-engine autocarriage, made for harder terrain than city autocars, trundled across the snow. She shuddered to see a pair of churning pistols shaped from brass arms, but said nothing. *I have to be cautious,* she told herself as her stomach churned. She wouldn't make it anywhere if she fought with Fydir over a handful of souls.

Drakne climbed inside the carriage, closed the door, pushed the velvet curtains shut, and sat beside Ruba on the well-cushioned, front-facing bench. She swept snow off her skirts, careful to get none on the mouse-girl's green wool coat. A humming glass bulb in the ceiling lit and warmed the plush cabin. The strife outside seemed to vanish from sight.

"I'm glad you came along," Drakne told Ruba. "Though please— tell me you don't mean to marry Fydir on the road." *Please. Not yet.* First, she needed to become queen. She needed the protection of the crown before she dared tell Ruba the truth about her brother. Fydir would be furious if Drakne cost him a wife.

"Absolutely not," Ruba said. "If I marry, I want a grand wedding, at the Crystal Palace. A profoundly obnoxious spectacle." She gave Drakne a teasing look. "You did a nice bit of theater out there, you know? Myself, I've never understood why people fear becoming beastfolk. It's only a little crawling of the flesh."

"It's the lack of control," Drakne said. "It makes folks feel vulnerable."

She'd already decided how she'd remake herself.

On the other bench of the autocarriage sat a girl clad in homespun, her white hair twisted up under a kerchief, violet eyes lined with sleepless rings. Manacles bound her wrists, one end of the chain locked to the carriage roof. Talzne glared at her in bitter ire.

"Why am I here?" she demanded. "Nabik said he'd set me free."

"Fydir forbade it," said Drakne. "He doesn't want anyone giving the locals a warning of our advance."

"Of his *attack*." Talzne shivered. "And you're just going along with it? What sort of monster does that?"

Drakne flinched. A memory seized her. Fydir, holding her stiff gun-body, riding through the woods. His horse pulled up lame, and so he leapt off and ran. A group of cavalrymen charged down a dark roar. They cursed and reached for pistols at the sight of him. At the heart of their circle, an unarmed man gasped *Mercy!* Drakne opened her gun barrel lips and spoke them all red.

"I'm not the monster here." Drakne clenched her fists, forced herself to breathe evenly. When she'd steadied herself, she leaned across the carriage and unlocked Talzne's bindings. A boon, but also a reminder: Drakne held the power here. "What brings a snowfae girl to Malirmatvi?"

"Queen Genna sent me south to map the extent of the crystal blight."

"Then how did you meet with the union movement?"

Talzne frowned. "Why do you care?"

"It takes a great deal of courage to speak up for what you believe to be right." Drakne took a deep breath. "I could use some courage myself."

The snowfae girl studied her. Then, hesitantly, she said, "One day, I snuck across the border wall. Just for an adventure. And I met...Simon." Her voice wavered on his name. "He was kind, and funny, and loved with a heart bigger than the moon. But his father got too sick to work, and his family was hungry. So he sold himself into a soul-engine. For them."

"I'm so sorry," Drakne said. "So that's why you help the workers in Rot Hill?"

Talzne nodded. "I can't help him. So I help his people."

Tears prickled in Drakne's throat. She missed the days when she'd thought life was as simple as helping the people you cared for. She'd never imagined her own brother would break her. "It's quite admirable, what you've done. The Empire is so full of injustice. How they treat Kolznechians and common workers, how they use soul-engines—"

"You're making me ride in a soul-engine."

"It's my brother's soul-engine," Drakne said. "Do you think I want this? No! But I can't stop it. Not without power. That's why you're here. There's magic in my blood. I can dance folk out of soul-engines. I can free your love. But I need something in return."

"You can...truly?"

Ruba leaned in. "You should see her dance. It's wonderous. Magical."

"And..." Talzne hesitated. "What would you want in return?"

"I need you to help me marry the Rat King."

Beside her, Ruba erupted in a gale of nervous laughter.

Drakne sighed. "I know you and the king have a bad history." To the point where the Rat King had personally *warned* her about this girl. Not that she could trust him. "I wouldn't choose him over you. This is only a political match."

"Ugh. Court politics." Ruba snapped her fan open, the black ostrich plumes glistening atop the garnet fabric. "I wish I'd never gotten involved with them. Did I ever tell you of my feud with the Baron of Stakte?"

"Sounds like fun," Drakne said, imagining whatever the Kolznechian version of Archduke Marinus might look like, tumbling down a staircase after Ruba fan-whacked him in the back of his knees.

"It's a nasty matter, truly. I discovered he'd been kidnapping the wolf-children born on his lands. Taking them from their parents to serve as enforcers in his mines."

"Blessed Winter," Talzne swore. "What a bastard."

"He is. Which is why I suggested Fydir should strike Stakte first. We'll see how smug that bastard can look with a cannon shoved down his throat."

"Oh," Talzne said. "I . . . truly, he sounds awful. But is this the right way to stop him? Wherever this army goes, innocent Kolznechians will die."

"We aren't the one making the choices," Drakne said. "Not yet. When I'm queen, I'll ban the use of soul-engines in Kolznechia. I'll get the Rat King and Fydir to negotiate peace. And I'll give your Simon back to you."

Talzne hesitated. "Why . . . why can't you push Fydir to negotiate *now?*"

"He doesn't trust me now. I need to show him a side of myself that he will." Drakne leaned across the cabin and took Talzne's hands in hers. "Will you help me?"

The snowfae girl took a deep breath and nodded.

When they made camp that first night past the border, the three girls shared a well-guarded pavilion tent. Curled up beneath heavy quilts and furs, with Ruba pressed to her side, Drakne hid from the watching world in darkness. She reached beneath her hair and—teeth gritted—plucked a black feather from her nape. Blood glittered on the tip.

Just as she'd feared. She shook Ruba.

"What's that?" Ruba yawned, breath warm on Drakne's neck, and took the feather. Pulled on her glasses to take a closer look. "Swanfolk? Delightful. Fitting for a dancer who likes to honk and ruffle feathers when she's mad."

"I can't be a dancer here." Drakne crushed the feather in her fist. "And I certainly can't afford to be a *goose*."

"Swan, darling. They're closely related, but not the same. Swans are beautiful, and so are you."

Drakne hesitated. *Beautiful.* A word no one gave to tall girls with wide shoulders. A word no one offered to girls they valued not at all. *Swans are beautiful.* But power had a beauty all its own. "We're surrounded by predators. I can't afford to be prey."

"I'm prey. It hardly bothers me."

"Your beast . . . it suits you." And it did. Ruba could smile pleasantly from behind her polished facade, laugh and jest with the calculated ease of a monied girl, and most folk would convince themselves she held no depths. Just a common mouse. But Drakne loved to catch the glimpses of what lay beneath her surface. Her fiendish intelligence and her absolutely devilish drive. "But these feathers—I need more. Talzne?" Drakne rolled over and shook the shoulder of the girl on the small servant's cot. She'd offered to let her sleep in the main bed, but Talzne had taken a good look at her and Ruba and declined. "Do it. Just like I told you."

Talzne sat up straight. Her eyes glowed violet in the pale dark. Without a word, she wrapped her nail-bitten fingers through Drakne's hair. Magic soaked through her locks like warm lotion, like honey. Tugged her shrinking ears into wide, prickling points.

"Thank you," Drakne said. Talzne shrugged and went to lie back down.

"We have a deal," she said. "Not a friendship."

Guilt stabbed at Drakne. She'd never asked for anything in exchange for saving someone from a soul-engine. But she could live with the regret. She'd just add one more red-edged memory to her collection.

Drakne woke with flecks of gold threaded through her dark hair. By the third day, when they halted atop an icy bluff to establish a supply camp, it had gone as blond as Fydir's, curling just below her chin. Color and sinew flexed through her limbs, and a wild energy pulsed just beneath her heart. *At last.* Like a clay mold had shattered, revealing brutal bronzework below. The face of a queen and a destroyer. A woman declaring it was time for others to suffer, not her.

The crimson mantle tossed across her fur coat glimmered with Talzne's magic as she and Ruba crossed the camp. Men busy heating rations over cookfires and breaking ice off tank treads stopped to stare as she passed. Soldiers' ears, grown long and brown furred, twitched and quailed beneath her gaze.

Heat filled the officers' tent, a sauna of sweat and pounding heartbeats. Men clustered tight about the main table, gulping hot tea and sketching lines across scout maps. Fydir gave each his attention in turn—but when the girls entered, he lifted his hand and silenced them with a gesture.

"Lady Ruba." He kissed the mouse-girl's hand, dwarfing it in his own. "And—Drakne." Fydir grinned at his sister. His hair and beard had grown unruly from its military cut. His teeth stretched sharper, glinting in his smile. "Good morning. How lovely you both look today."

Drakne's eyes flashed golden as she sat beside him. She cracked her knuckles, which were thick with burgeoning tendon and bone. A feral smile spread across her frozen mask. Beauty mattered most in the beholder's eye, and Fydir would love nothing more than a sister who looked just as much a part of him as his right hand. *A hand so close it could choke you.*

Her long nail ran along the crinkled skin of a map, charting the overgrown road to Stakte. "What do the scouts say?"

"An old fort guards the road into town." Fydir ran his pen along the map, circling landmarks for her. "When he sees we're approaching, the Baron of Stakte will mount his defenses. That hotheaded bear will likely wager all his men to defeat me in one gambit. Old beasts don't dare look weak before young bucks."

"Promise me you won't destroy the whole town," Ruba said. "Please?"

"Such a tender heart." His lips brushed the top of her head.

"I'll have mercy. I mean to rule the town, not destroy it. Once it's mine, we shall construct a factory. Employ the local beastfolk assembling artillery and war vehicles." Fydir smiled. "It's good practice for them to learn to work the imperial way."

Drakne fought the urge to flinch. "How many soldiers will you take to attack the fort?"

"Two hundred." He grinned. "And you."

Me. He needs me. Just like back when she'd used her dance to serve the archduke. *He needs me alive, well, and helping him. He needs me unharmed.* So she would be his twin. And trust them all to forget that the lioness caught more prey than the lion.

They traveled onward, Fydir's soul-engines cutting a roadway through the forest, and visions of swan-maids cooking on spits invaded her nightmares. Amber pooled in her dark eyes, the irises leaking into the white. Her ears grew level with the top of her head, curved edges dissolving into fuzz. Her stomach grumbled whenever soldiers carried raw meat to their cookfires. With her wheat-yellow hair and the gold of her gaze, it seemed as if she were remaking herself into a living crown.

Nightly, she, Ruba, and Talzne tore out her feathers and buried them in the snow. Daily, the three of them sat in the autocarriage, growing quieter with each mile they traveled toward battle. Beast-folk dragging carts and hoisting bundled firewood scurried back into the bracken as the Eighth Regiment marched past. By the second week, the roadsides were empty of all save footprints and jutting shards of crystal, some the size of a man grown.

The morning they approached Stakte, Drakne rose early, her guts churning. She sorted through her trunks, staving off her fears with thoughts of fabric. *What does one wear to a battle?*

Ruba rolled off the bed and draped a fur-lined wool coat over Drakne's shoulders, a mottled white and brown to blend in with the snow. "You stay warm out there," she murmured, leaning in close to Drakne's ear. The fur on the edge of her cheek prickled as it brushed Drakne's neck. "I'll be in the command tent. Giving officers the lay of the land." She hesitated. "Be careful. This venture would be much more boring without you."

"Saints forbid that you'd be bored for a moment." Drakne reached up and gave Ruba's long ear a playful tug. Ruba tripped and purposefully sprawled backward in Drakne's lap.

"I'm glad you two are having fun," said Talzne. "Didn't we speak about how the baron kidnaps wolf-children to raise as soldiers? Do they deserve to die at Fydir's hands?"

"He won't send the youngest to the battlefield. They'd be useless." Ruba shrugged. "Anyway, the day won't be less bloody if I'm somber about it."

"And you, Drakne?" Talzne turned to her. "You don't have to help him. You could claim sickness, or faint—you could claim to have your courses, and—"

"I need him to trust me. I need to be useful." Drakne closed her eyes. "You don't need to agree with me. But you will respect me." She took a deep breath, drawing the cold into her lungs. Her head throbbed. The back of her neck ached where a black feather unfurled ingrown. "Stay in the tent while we fight. Consider that an order from your future queen."

Throwing the coat over her shoulders, she strode out to greet the dawn.

A gentle snowfall had begun, sunlight slipping through the clouds to dart off dancing flakes, which dissolved against her cheeks and red cravat. Soft layers of white crusted the gaps that tanks and artillery carts had cut in the soil, transforming machines of war into odd-shaped huts and boulders. If not for the clamor of shouts and echoing gunfire, she could have imagined winter had the power to paint the world pure.

The soldiers moved like dreamers lost in sleep. Long-nailed fingers ran through shaggy hair, tugging at ears grown long or feeling for those vanished in feather whorls. *Try monthly bleeding and you won't be surprised when your own flesh betrays you.*

The fortress sat on the bluff where the road forked and led down into the town of Stakte. Beyond boulders and a wooden palisade, antique cannons fired at the Eighth Regiment. All shells fell short of their modern guns. The tanks blasted fire like pounding drums, chewing stone to pebbles and ripping holes in wood and beastflesh. Screams rose whenever shots and splinters hit live targets. Drakne tried to tell herself they were only the howls of the wind.

Fydir grinned when he saw her. Her brother towered above his officers. Many beastfolk shrank in stature as the curse claimed them; he loomed large as a king. "They sent two platoons against us." He swept an arm at a mass of too-still flesh in green uniforms. Bitter bile rose at the back of Drakne's throat. "Didn't stand a chance against our guns. Shall we dance, sister dear?" He offered his hand. His red sleeves were pushed up to the elbow. Thick golden hair prickled down his wrists.

"I'm ready," she said. "Just give me a gun."

"I don't need you to fight in the flesh, little lioness." He caught her hand in his and laced their fingers together. The joints in both were growing thick and broad, fingernails darkening to sharp points. "But your soul can sing the song of victory with mine."

He nodded. An orderly opened his gun case. The wide-open soul-socket pulsed a sickly purple, a brass clamp hungry to bind and fold her into metal.

Drakne's breath caught. A million sparks, like snapped and sputtering wires, fizzed down her spine. Something shattered. Something screamed inside her. Her pulse raced; her head spun until it felt like it was lolling sideways. She could feel his fists close around her, his weight and strength dragging her to her destruction, her heels drumming fruitlessly in the dirt.

But Fydir hadn't grabbed her. Not yet. He wanted to see how she reacted.

If she would *volunteer*.

He was testing her loyalty.

So she would test his usefulness.

"When Stakte is ours," Drakne said, willing her voice not to tremble, "we should reach out and parley with the Rat King. You'll hold the kingdom's best mines; you can negotiate near anything. Offer him my hand in marriage in exchange for peace. Then we'll rule Kolznechia together." *Me as the queen, and you as my lovely lion-pelt rug.*

"A marriage to the Rat King?" Fydir mused. "Good idea. You've been quite full of those lately."

"It's almost as though I have a military genius in my family."

Fydir laughed. "You have my word, Drakne. Now." He hoisted up the gun.

Drakne made herself breathe, though the air felt like she was sucking it through a straw. *It must be done.* No one would come to help her, lift aside the obstacles in her path, carry her to safety like a princess in a tower. *I hate him,* she thought. All the rebellion she could allow herself in the moment. *I hate him, I hate him, I hate him.* She wanted to hate him like he hated her, and more, because the hate would hold her together.

Even if her own hate tasted like drinking poison.

It's fine. I'm fine. Keeping him happy would secure her path to the crown. At least in this moment, she was choosing him as much as he was choosing her. And the weapon understood her well.

The gun case lay open in the snow. Fydir offered his hand to help her step inside, like a footman guiding a lady into a carriage. The brass pins of the socket reached up to embrace her. Her arms stretched down the barrel, fingers unfurling around the muzzle. Her knees bent and locked across his back, secure in jointed brass. Her head came to rest on his shoulder, her eyes high and focused on the fortress beyond.

Once more, her heart was full of bullets and her head burned with borrowed rage.

CHAPTER NINE

Lord and Lady Lion

Stakte, the Kingdom of Kolznechia

The wind shifted about Nabik. Like a released breath, the storm let go. Flesh and pine and Zolka's flailing feathers, the three of them dropped down into a world that reeked of soot.

"Well," Eugen murmured from the bottom of the pile, his elbow jammed deep in Nabik's gut. "At least we've made it somewhere. And she didn't swap around any of our limbs."

"Could a snowfae do that?" Nabik said.

"Perhaps. If she thought you'd be more beautiful with my limbs on your body. Though I quite like all your limbs where they are." It came out so earnest and matter-of-fact that Nabik's guts seemed to tie themselves in an elaborate bow. He couldn't breathe, and wasn't sure if that was from the wooden elbow digging into him or something else.

"Zolka!" yelped a fearful, pleading voice. A needle-nosed ferret-woman hurtled down the tree-lined avenue where the snowfae had dropped them. "Thank Winter, you're here!" She flung her arms about Zolka, hugging the wizard close to her chest like a shield.

Zolka hugged her back. "All will be well, Nivni. I'll see to it. I swear."

Nabik stumbled to his feet, coughing. Soot already seemed

to coat his lungs, painting the eggshell-white streaks in his hair back to black. His empathy rolled outward—and hit anguish. Exhaustion. For the first time since he'd crossed the border, the forest's slow curse and his own roiling wretchedness concerned him naught. Something in Stakte had broken terribly deep.

Genna had carried them across the forest with her magic, as Zolka had asked her. But the snowfae hadn't told them how long the journey would take.

What has Fydir done with that time?

"What's going on?" Nabik asked the ferret-woman.

She shuddered. "Szpratzian invaders have captured the town."

A wave of dizziness swept through him as he looked around and *saw*. Bullet tracks and claw cuts marked the shabby wooden buildings and the tree trunks that ringed them. The streets lay empty, reeking with fear. Sobs filled the air along with the pressing din of drills and stamping metals.

From every wall and tree trunk, soot-streaked posters flapped liked the feathers of pinioned geese, each bearing a sneering, cold face. Wild-maned and cold-eyed, lips peeled back over curling fangs, black ink lines thick and hurried, as if the artist behind it had longed for nothing more than to finish and flee his subject's gaze.

Fydir, Baron of Stakte, will spare your life and household in exchange for your hard labor.

Nabik shivered as they walked through the town. Stakte sat atop an ancient silver mine, so old that awls and drills made of mammoth bone had scraped the first few layers of earth away.

Over thousands of years, the folk of the north had chipped away at the base of the cliffside. Pines and oaks had grown up in the crumbling gully beneath it, fueled by mad magic, laced together like a dancer's skirts until the miners' neighborhoods and the forest were one. Some were green and growing, and some were shining violet crystal, and all were covered in laundry lines and glistening wizard-light fungus. The tallest point of Stakte, on the east hill, was where the baron's manor stood beside its fellows, ringed by walls of crumbling stone, lording its half-ruined glory over the town. And between the hill and the cliffside, at the town's heart, sat a clear-cut circle where clapboard factory walls enclosed great machines that belched smoke skyward.

Nabik seized on the party's frantic wish to not be seen as they passed it, and wove a low fog about them to nudge away eyes. They slunk around gashes and ruts in the earth, ducking the gaze of soldiers in Eighth Regiment colors. Beastfolk in worn clothes lined up outside the factory door.

"What are they doing?" Zolka whispered. "Why are they writing down their names?"

"For the waiting list," Nivni said. "After they killed the old baron and took his manor, the invaders made us build them a factory. You can sign up to be put in their machines, and while you're in there, they'll give your family a month of grain. They also hire for hand work—I've got a shift later assembling tread axles—but they only pay coppers."

"And people volunteer?"

"The new baron said we had to. Or he'd *volunteer* us."

Zolka swore. Nabik had forgotten she'd left the Empire when Marinus's inventions had only just been prototypes. The soul trade had hooked itself quickly into every aspect of Szpratzian life until it felt like a pillar of the world. And now Fydir was wielding it as a weapon, as a threat. Something shaped to crush lesser beasts with fear.

Is this enough to finally make him happy?

"But they don't let folk out," Nivni said. "I've tried to free them and I can't. I've always been good at tinkering, but never used this southern equipment till now. I'm not even sure what we're building." She shivered. "And we're all scared it's weapons."

Eugen's voice rose. "What will Fydir do with more weapons?"

A pair of soldiers shot them suspicious looks. Nabik narrowed his eyes and drove more will into his spell. *All you see is common-blooded beastfolk and a gangly living pine.* Not even a lie.

"Whatever he's doing," Nabik said, "we'll put an end to it. I swear."

Down toward the base of the cliff they went, where the trees grew fast around small wooden cottages. The greatest trunks had been hollowed out into apartments, candles glowing in hand-carved windows, their squirrelfolk residents leaping from branch to branch. Ramps of snow and packed stone made smooth paths over jagged gashes cut in the earth. The high cliff blocked out the wind.

"The meeting house is right through here," Zolka said, pushing on a flat stretch of stone. Beneath her touch, it transformed into a wooden door. "Good to see my protective spells still work. Not even the Rat King himself could break in here."

Nabik stepped through the door into an egg-shaped, oblong cavern. A strange smile perked the corners of his lips. It felt as if he'd slid back in time to the neighborhood he'd grown up in. Fires leapt in three open hearths, casting dancing shadows across stone walls laced with flickers of silver. Listless, lowered-brow miners set down their cups and flocked to Zolka, who greeted them with hugs and a booming laugh. A fiddler with a goose's neck played a warm, familiar tune. Under his breath, Nabik hummed along. *Colder than the heart of blizzards, brighter than the moon and stars, clearer than a spire of crystal, Winter shows us who we are.*

"Hearth's welcome," said an old man, dark-cheeked and stooped under reindeer horns, the traditional greeting of the traders who ran routes across the Great Pole, and Nabik murmured "Night's warding" as Zolka had once taught him to. Two children tussled over a wooden doll in the corner. Nabik shaped its twin from a swirl of snowflakes and handed it over. "Thank you," said the boy, and their weary mother shot him a grateful nod. Nabik's skin prickled all over as his limbs and digits warmed. As Fydir's soldier, life had rubbed against him like a too-tight shoe. Now everything *fit.*

Zolka smiled at the sight of the children playing. "I miss when you all were that small."

"What was Fydir like, back then?" Nabik asked hesitantly. *How did he become what he is?*

"He was wild. Full of life. He led neighborhood children into trouble, charmed candy from shopkeepers, trained street dogs to leap and bark at a word. We always wondered if he had some small magic of his own, or just your mama's charm."

Warmth crept back into her voice. "When you were born, he ran out on the street and bellowed *I've got a little brother* for half the city to hear. He put all his toys in your cradle, even before you could grasp them, and asked me every week when you'd be big enough to play. When Drakne came, he went to work for the farrier so he could buy her a real porcelain doll. We set it up on a shelf so she wouldn't break it, but he took it down for her and she flung it at the wall. He cut himself cleaning up the shards."

Nabik thought of the little white line on Fydir's right hand. "So he does care for us."

"He did," Zolka said, as gently as if her words held a cracked egg. "But he's not caring for you now, and he hasn't cared in a long while."

A sob rose in Nabik's throat. He bit it down.

"All's well," Zolka said. "You can cry. You *should* cry, if you want to. It's a sad thing."

"I don't want to," Nabik said. "I don't want to feel any of this."

"But you *do*."

But he shouldn't. All his sorrow, all his hurt—what he felt was so much bigger than him. *Especially now.* Even with heavy socks on, his too-small feet were slipping about in his boots, and he'd nearly tripped on his coat hem twice on their walk to the meeting house. It was like the curse was taunting him, revealing to the world what he tried so desperately to hide. A weak man. A small man. *Vulnerable.* No. Perhaps his true strength lay in magic, rather than in any might of arms, but he was still strong. He had to be.

"Nivni!" he said, and turned to wave at the ferret-woman. She and several of her fellows stood by the hearth, warming their hands. "Have you seen Drakne in town?"

"The lion-lady? She never leaves Fydir's side. The pair of them are absolute terrors."

"What?" No. Drakne loathed their brother. Why would she be helping him? Nivni had to be mistaken. He'd need to find Drakne soon, and bring her to stand by them. "Never mind. Have you been planning anything to deal with the factory? Fydir and the Empire think they can loot Kolznechia for silver and souls. We need to show them that we won't be exploited for their gain."

"Oh, we want to tear it down," said Nivni. "Break open the soul-engines. Smash and burn the rest. We've been planning as much, me and the rest of the tread crew. Four in five of us would start flinging dirt in the gears at the first chance we got—but Fydir has an army."

"An army that doesn't know this ground. Who's terrified of the beastfolk curse and how it's changing them." Nabik smiled. His sharpening teeth sliced his lip. This felt right. *A wizard cares for the weak and vulnerable, holds the powerful to account, helps every town and village thrive.* "You have wizards on your side, Nivni. If you rally the workers, I'll find a way to hold off the soldiers."

"Well, then," Nivni said, and smiled back with needle teeth. "I'll hold you to it. Quite a useful boy you have here, Zolka."

"I'm proud of him," Zolka said. "But wizards alone can't do this all. We need each other, and we need our prince." She looked back over her shoulder and reached out an encouraging hand. "Eugen?"

Nabik started, realizing he hadn't heard Eugen's chatter since he entered. The pinewood prince lingered in the doorway, buried in shadows. Slowly, hesitantly, Eugen stepped into the light.

Beastfolk turned toward him. Some leapt or gasped; most were too tired to voice shock at the sight. Eugen's fearful eyes darted over the crowd and found Nabik. He smiled. How unlike a prince, to freeze up when speaking to a crowd.

"You can do it," Nabik mouthed. "You never shut up around me."

"I," Eugen said, and the one word trembled as he spoke, "am Prince Eugen Kutredan of House Teyodet, rightful heir to the throne of Kolznechia. I've come back to overthrow the Rat King, to break the curse on you and the curse on me. I swear by my ancestors and Winter herself."

"It can't be," groused an old grouse, and "It is!" whispered a hopeful girl with cat ears. "He'll drive out the invaders!" swore a boy with a toy sword, "and I'll help, I will, I will!"

Beastfolk clustered around Eugen, prodding at his wooden boots and thighs, pleading for royal blessings and beseeching aid. The prince stood stiff as a rail as he answered them. Perhaps the townsfolk saw that as the product of his woodenness. Nabik knew better—he could feel it.

He's scared. He wishes so deeply to not let them down. It's strangling him. Nabik wanted nothing more than to take Eugen's hand and lead him out of the crowd, help him get some air. *No. We need him to show Kolznechia a perfect prince. He isn't just some common boy I can fancy.*

But I wish he was.

Nabik's lips tingled, like he'd been bee stung without realizing. He pressed one pointed fingernail to them, unable to let go.

~

The Rat King's eagles wheeled in the sky above Stakte's crumbled northern watchtower, the site of their planned parley. Drakne and Fydir climbed the broken and eroded road up the hilltop, flanked by soldiers in Eighth Regiment red. The new Baron of Stakte had draped himself in a gold-embroidered jacket, hasty stitches marking where it had been lengthened—twice—to fit the growing bulk of his shoulders. His mane, grown wild from his hair and beard, spilled out over the fine fabric. Drakne wore an ankle-length coat of soft blond pelts fastened by brass buttons in the shape of gears. Her ears twitched in the wind, fangs distorting her lower jaw as she spoke urgently in her brother's ear.

"He's not as fearsome as you might expect," Drakne said. "Beyond his flash and power, there's a loneliness. He likes to talk. If you spark his interest, he won't do you harm—"

"I've dealt with kings and nobles since you were squalling in a cradle. I know what I'm about." Fydir glanced back at his soldiers. "Stay there," he ordered. "I don't want the Rat King to think he scares me."

Side by side, Drakne and Fydir stepped into the shadows of the crumbled keep. The Rat King leaned against the frame of an ancient window. Thin sunlight lit his long brown hair and diamond diadem; he wore a somber black suit and black-rimmed spectacles, like he'd come to a ball at a graveyard. Charmed mushrooms and sickly yellow flowers bloomed at his feet.

"A beauty and a beast," he said. "The magnificent Drakne."
He took her gloved hand, kissed her stolen amethyst ring. A delicious shiver spiraled down her spine. *Careful. Don't let his charm trip you.* All she needed of him was royal power. She'd wed a sack of potatoes for an edge over Fydir.

"Rat King," her brother said with a stiff nod.

The Rat King reached out and pressed Fydir's heavy, fur-flecked knuckles to his lips. "How kind of you to pay me homage."

"Unhand me," Fydir growled, shaking loose.

"Gladly. At the wrists or the elbows?" He met Drakne's eyes and winked. She giggled.

Fydir took a step closer, pressing the Rat King back against the wall, crushing the small yellow petals under his feet. "For all your cunning tricks, you're still a rat," he breathed, hot and meaty, onto the Rat King's neck.

"And you're a big, strong lion, right until I turn your bones to jelly and watch you melt." The Rat King vanished in a puff of black smoke and reappeared, laughing, behind Fydir. The lion-lord cursed and spun to face him. "Where's Prince Eugen?"

Fydir raised an eyebrow. Drakne held her breath. She hadn't told Fydir about her conversation with the Rat King in Malirmatvi. She could only hope that he was smart enough to play along.

"Yes, Prince Eugen," Fydir said. "I imagine you're quite invested in finding him."

"I am. A great deal."

"But you're in no position to make demands. I'll speak directly: The Empire doesn't truly care you burned some houses in Rot Hill. Kolznechia has wood, metals, and souls for our engines.

The Empire wants your resources, and what it wants, it gets. I can continue to take your territory by force, or we can make a deal. The choice is yours."

"How generous." The Rat King snapped his fingers. Screams rose from outside the keep—howls of mortal terror, echoing off the stone. *Our guards.* Drakne tightened her fists and told herself not to look afraid. Footsteps echoed behind her. A man ran into the crumbled keep and collapsed at her feet, gagging. His tongue lolled out, bloated, blobby. Mushrooms clogged his throat like hair in a drain.

"Stop this," Drakne said. "Are you here to negotiate, or play games?"

The Rat King sighed and waved his hand. The choking soldier stood and spat out a mouthful of mushrooms. "Get out," said the king, and the man ran from the keep. Outside, screams faded into whimpering sobs. "They'll live. Now. What are the terms of your deal?"

"I want lands and a title," Fydir said. "Good lands, not poisoned by the crystal blight. I want you to pass laws so I can buy materials for my factories at a discount. And to seal it all, I want you to marry my sister."

The Rat King betrayed no surprise at hearing the third condition. He looked to Drakne with narrowed eyes. "Why are you so interested in a broken soul?"

She folded her arms. He had sounded more curious than suspicious. "Why do you call yourself broken?"

"The curse affects me too. Don't they put that detail in the children's stories?"

"I never had the patience to sit for story time."

"A queen needs a good deal of patience. The work is mostly attending long dinners and teas. And you have to be nice to everyone, even insufferable bastards. I thought I'd have a grand time with the job. Now look at me."

"You're a king," Fydir said.

"I'm a prisoner of my own success. For two hundred years, I've sat on that ugly old throne. But it's as if I live the same few months, over and over. I'm bound to never grow a day past when I seized power, in body, mind, or spirit."

Drakne gave him a studious look. He wasn't like the young men she'd met in the Empire's cities; nor was he like the gray-beards who leered at her on the street, though he'd been born back when their fathers' fathers drew breath. He was a creature from outside time, as much a creation of magic as a master of it. She didn't quite understand that, but she didn't think he quite understood himself. It made her a good deal less afraid of him. "That would explain why you're so scrawny."

"Jest if you will. But if you share my throne, you'll share my curse. You'll never age, grow, or change. You'll always be as you are, the moment you speak your wedding vows."

"That hardly sounds like a curse. To be handsome, strong, and cunning forever?" Fydir grinned.

The Rat King lowered his head. Diamonds glittered on his brow, as heavy as the earth they came from. A tired sadness filled his voice. "Neither of you understand what you ask for. Enough playing about. I will send my agents into Stakte. They will rip Eugen from wherever your mother and brother have hidden him and chop him up for kindling. When he's dead, I'll send you fleeing from my kingdom. And that will be a *mercy*."

The Rat King clapped his hands. Lightning flashed. Thunder cracked. The very stones of the old keep rumbled. Drakne threw her hands over her eyes as Fydir flinched backward. When she looked up, blinking away spots, the Rat King was gone.

Her heart pounded. *No.* She hadn't come this far to fail. There had to be some way to win his hand. *Agents. He's sending spies after us. To find Eugen.* That was how the Rat King worked. His soldiers couldn't best theirs. He had his magic, but he was only one wizard—if he thought Nabik and Zolka stood with them, he'd hesitate to draw them into a fight. *His spies are his best choice.*

If she could capture them, the Rat King would have no choice but her.

~

"We need to go to the wolves," Nabik told Eugen as they slurped porridge at the meeting house's long central table. Zolka had been called away to help deliver a baby. She'd instructed Nabik to make himself useful and practice wizardry. She might have only meant for him to summon bags of flour or repair some of the town's broken rooftops, but he itched to do more. To prove himself.

"Why the wolves?" Eugen said, fumbling with a small spoon in his wooden fingers. He'd refused to drink the porridge from the bowl, said it wasn't mannerly. The spoon dropped, splashing spots of white down his painted chest.

"Apparently, they were the old baron's elite guards," Nabik said. He'd spent all the last evening meeting with the locals, drawing maps of the factory grounds and where his brother's troops were quartered, all while Eugen had attempted to darn Nivni's socks and somehow sewn the tops shut. "Since the battle, the survivors have holed up in their den, trying to decide if they'll serve Fydir or not. I want to show them who's fighting for the town."

"You," Eugen said. "Our new wizard."

Nabik elbowed him in the side, and cursed as his nerves struck wood. "*You.* Our royal savior."

Eugen laughed, cleaning porridge off his chest with a rag. "How very royal I am right now. No. You and Zolka will do the real work of saving Kolznechia." He said this with no bitterness, as only a statement of fact. "I know I'm mostly a figurehead."

"You gave a fine speech last night."

"You liked it? Honestly, I felt like an utter disaster. If I still had human fingernails, I'd have bitten them bloody. All those people, looking at me? Like I'm . . . I don't know. All I could think was how I might disappoint them."

"How would you disappoint them?"

"By . . . being a coward, I suppose."

"Your country is starving and under siege. Who would judge you for being frightened? I don't."

"My father would." Eugen shuddered. "For my tenth birthday, he took me on a hunting trip. He cornered a stag, gave me his gun, and told me to shoot it. I couldn't. I didn't want it to suffer. So he made me stand outside our tent, in the snow, until sunrise." He looked down at his wooden boots. "If these came off, you'd see I'm missing a toe."

Nabik, who loved nothing more than family, said, "I'm glad your father's dead."

"Me too." Eugen sighed. "He beat me a few more times after that. Nothing so bad. He realized he shouldn't kill his only heir. But I never forgot that he *could*. That was the hard part."

"Did you at least have friends at court? People to look after you?"

"I had...a handful of friends. I won't deny, being a prince comes with great advantages. But my father made it fashionable to hate me, and his court was eager to join in. The folk who didn't bully me or shun me wanted to use me as a pawn. It's quite rare for someone to like me as *just Eugen*."

"*Just Eugen* is incredible," Nabik said, the corners of his lips twitching upward.

"No, I'm not. I'm absolutely average at everything, from tax policy to gardening. If I wasn't born to be king, I don't know what I'd do."

"Stop that. You're miraculous. Do you have any idea how hard it is to make me smile?" They were both smiling now. Nabik had never felt anything like this. Eugen treated him like some marvelous new star, a whole world he'd just spotted in his telescope. And Nabik couldn't help wanting the prince to discover him. Softly, he said, "This isn't your father's kingdom anymore. It's quite normal to worry that people won't like you. But anyone who doesn't is missing out on a true friend."

"Well," Eugen said. "I suppose we'll learn if the wolves agree."

Following directions from Nivni, Nabik led the two of them on a winding switchback path up the cliff. Miners scrambled downward past them, rushing to their shafts as their family members bustled toward the factory. The crisp scent of crunching snow and the sounds of chatter and laughter drew Nabik out of his own roiling thoughts, leaving his head blissfully clear. Bright sun sparkled off the red-and-green mineral-rich icicles that hung off the cliffside, and at last he had a purpose that belonged in daylight.

"Do you even think most Kolznechians want the curse broken?" Eugen said. "So many of them find meaning and purpose, even identity, in their beasts. And what if I take the crown, everyone cheers, all the beastfolk turn human, and no one can fit inside their houses? It's winter. They'd have nowhere to go. If it wasn't for the crystal blight, I might just run away and let it all be!"

His voice peaked, anxious, fearful—and making a very good point. "There *is* a crystal blight," Nabik said. "It must be dealt with. And it's wrong that the curse changes your life and body without your consent. It makes the kingdom poorer too. Outsiders are too afraid of the curse to come trade with us. And beastfolk are treated so cruelly in the south. Kolznechians in the Empire won't even visit their families because they don't want their children sprouting fur and feathers."

"Good and bad on both sides, then." Eugen huffed through his wooden teeth. "So no matter what happens, thousands will hate me for it. Excellent."

"That's what it means to be a leader." Nabik shook his head. "It must be hard to bear. But Kolznechia's choices are either you, the Rat King, or the Szpratzian invaders. I know who I'd vote for."

"I'd sooner vote for a rock."

"Unjustified pessimism is *my* bad habit. I won't let you steal it." With that, Nabik scooped up a snowball and flung it in Eugen's face. The other boy jumped, powder dripping down the painted green of his chest.

"You can't just strike a prince!"

"I didn't. The snowball did."

Eugen grinned and swept his long arm along the cliffside wall, knocking a wave of powder down across Nabik's chest and arms. "Right. This means war!"

Nabik darted behind a rocky outcropping to scrape up ammunition. Eugen's snowball struck him on the leg. He yelped and returned fire, his missile bursting against Eugen's shoulder in a cloud of white. Crystals caught in his wooden joints. "It seems you're going to lose this war to one common man, Your Highness!"

"Absolutely not!" Eugen straightened his shoulders, a snowball in each hand, three more tucked in the crook of one elbow. "Even to suggest that is treason, Nabik Zolkedan, and it's punishable with a handful of snow down your collar."

Eugen charged. Drenched in powder, his heart pumping, Nabik fled. He darted around a bend in the cliffside trail. In the shadow of a boulder, he knelt, balling more icy missiles—

"Ambush!" called a voice from atop the boulder. Eugen kicked a month's worth of snowfall down on his head.

Whump! The world flashed off and on again in a wink of cold. Eugen laughed as Nabik shook off the snow. White dripped through his hair, which fell loose about his shoulders, and thoroughly soaked his underclothes. He'd never felt so warm.

"What are you children playing at?" A wolf-woman in a thick coat leapt down from the lip of a cavern. Beneath a scarred brow, her eyes narrowed. "This is our den."

"My apologies," Nabik said, straightening and knocking

snow from his clothes. Of all things, he dared not come off as *childish* here, even if he was now acutely aware of how his chin only came up to Eugen's shoulder. "My name is Nabik Zolkedan, and this is Eugen Kutredan, of House Teyodet." Quickly, he explained who they were and why they'd come. "Are you the pack leader?"

"I'm Dreba. Svalge leads the pack. You can come speak with him, but be quick about it. He's expecting an important guest."

The wolves' den lay far back in the cliff, set with wide shafts for hearths, its furnishings newer and sturdier than those of the meeting house below. Veins of silver flickered in the walls, and lanterns hanging from purple crystals filled the room with sharp-edged light. Dreba even offered them use of a coat hook by the entry, though Nabik kept his on.

This is what they got from enforcing the old baron's order, he realized. *The highest place on the scrap heap.*

"Dreba," said the spindly russet-furred wolf-man on a cushioned chair near a fire. Other wolf-folk napped on benches or drank in silence, but all eyes and long ears flickered to him when he spoke. *Svalge. The pack leader.* "What's this? A fox and . . . a southern kitchen appliance?"

Nabik cleared his throat. "Sir, we need your help." Sparingly, keeping details vague, he laid out what he could of the budding plan to sabotage the factory. "With your strength, we could force Fydir's soldiers out of the factory. Perhaps push them out of town entirely. The people of Stakte would be forever grateful."

"Grateful?" Svalge said, and gulped from a great mug of beer.

"What am I supposed to do with that? Under the old baron, I ruled this town. If you want my help, pay me what I'm worth. Don't insult me by offering a bowl of potato stew from the meeting house pot."

"It's good stew," Eugen said.

"Shut up, puppet. Don't make me crush that wooden jaw."

Nabik flinched and put a protective hand on Eugen's arm. "Winter teaches us to use our gifts to help each other."

"No one's seen Winter in centuries, boy. She's abandoned us. But gold can't run away." A clamor rose at the tunnel's mouth: hisses, growls, and one pained lupine shriek. Svalge grinned. "Ah. Another party, come to bid for my work."

Drakne strode into the cavern. *She's safe. She's alive.* His heart leapt, though his guts churned with guilt. There was still hope to make this right.

His sister was scandalously dressed, wearing trousers and a vest beneath her long coat, and her high-held chin said she'd eat anyone who dared mention it. "Hello," she said to Nabik, light darting off her fangs. "Little brother. I've missed you so."

"I'm eighteen months older than—" but she ruffled his hair as she passed, showing off her new inch—or two inches—of height on him.

"Svalge. I'm here to make a deal." Drakne leapt atop a table. Sunlight curled through a sky vent, painting her golden. She opened a sack and poured out coins, and they were more golden still.

Svalge grabbed two coins, rubbed them together. "What sort of job do you need us for? Your brother's got a whole army to serve him."

"I don't need soldiers. I need hunters who understand the local ground and can help me catch spies."

Nabik wouldn't have marked her for a lioness. They were silent, deadly hunters, and Drakne lived for the sound of her own voice and the heat of a spotlight. And he couldn't see her and Fydir as the same beast, as if she were his mirror.

"What are you doing?" he said, lowering his voice. "You're not anything like him."

"How do you know? Because we were close, back before your voice cracked? I'm allowed to change."

"Because you want to, yes. Not because Fydir is making you. I know what he does—"

"You know nothing about it," she growled. Claws flashed along her fingertips. "You know nothing about me."

Did she think she could scare him? "Listen. Zolka and I can help you. We can get you away from Fydir. He's doing horrible things—"

"I know," she said. "I'm not a fool. I have my own plan."

"What sort of plan?"

"If I tell you, you'll try to stop me."

"If it's that dangerous, then I should. You're my sister. You should have at least one brother who looks out for you." What if this plan of hers angered Fydir? If she was alone with him, what would he do? *I didn't even get the worst of him, and I*—Nabik tried to imagine Fydir's wrath, and his stomach flipped with panic, just from the thought.

"Miss Zolkedna," Eugen said, "if you and your brother could—"

She swiped at the nutcracker, claws shining. He jumped backward and clattered into Nabik. Both of them stumbled, gasping and cursing, up against the cavern wall.

Drakne laughed, and Svalge did, too, clapping like he'd just watched a performance at the royal ballet. "I like this girl. The fox and the wooden boy have nothing for me. Get them out of here."

Dreba took Nabik by the shoulder. Another wolf grabbed Eugen's wrists, and together, they were firmly dragged to the cave lip. "For what it's worth," Dreba said in a low voice, "some of us do care about the folk in this town. But our pack comes before that, and our pack follows Svalge."

"Thank you," Nabik said, albeit grudgingly. "You can always come to us if you change your mind." He glanced back over his shoulder, into the cave, where Drakne helped herself to Svalge's beer. The wolves flocked eagerly around her. She gave Nabik a wink and wiped foam from her lips.

It was all very *Drakne* of her. After all he'd been through, he couldn't help but smile, ever so slightly, to see his sister's face. They were family, still, in their very bones and marrow, no matter what.

But he couldn't escape the reeking, repugnant truth: The two of them were now at war.

CHAPTER TEN

Fairy-Tale Logic

The wolves toasted their bargains with beer and games of dice. Drakne joined in eagerly. She lost three of her brass buttons to Dreba and didn't mind. Far too long had passed since she'd last played at anything. The wolves laughed as they shared tales of chasing children and ferretfolk through the town, and Drakne told herself it was likely all exaggerated. It warmed her chest to be welcomed in the den, and she needed all the friends she could get.

As the sun set and waxing moonlight spilled into the valley, Drakne strode, hooded and shadowed, through the streets that wound about the great pines. Light and laughter poured through the windows carved in lichen-draped tree trunks, but all mirth died as beastfolk glimpsed her and her lupine entourage. Eastward they went, toward the baron's manor. Her eyes flashed green as she wove through packs of bedraggled workers and beggars with crushed limbs, her pointed ears twitching to catch every sound, every whisper. Waiting. Hunting.

She looked every inch a queen fit for a monstrous king. Beneath her long coat, she wore trousers of red wool and a finely tailored vest of golden beige like a wash of desert sand. At her throat, a cameo on a choker secured a crimson neckerchief. A neutral brown lipstick and soft pink blush evened out a face grown forward to fit her new canines. *Beauty,* Talzne had promised her, and it might not be the beauty of dance, but it would serve her.

A hot, spicy scent wafted under her nose. *Fresh gingerbread.* Memories woke within her, so old they came only as formless wanting. *Warm hands. Yuleheigh evenings.* Hugged so tightly by her mothers she couldn't feel where one stopped and the other began.

A boar-man sold gingerbread from a cart by the factory's side. Drakne's thick, clawed fingers struggled with the ties of her purse before finally pulling out a fistful of coins. The boar-man scowled as he took her money.

"My family used to bake this for Yuleheigh evenings when I was small," she said. "I never thought I'd taste it again, not until—"

"Off with you, lion-lass. No one will buy my wares if they see me selling to invaders."

Ugliness cut through her reverie. The first flicker of warmth she'd felt in weeks evaporated. "I'm not an invader," she huffed. "I'm as Kolznechian as any of you. I belong here."

"When are you and your brother letting folk out of his great machine, eh? When's my sister coming home?"

Heat rose in her cheeks. A painful prickle of shame beneath fine golden fuzz. She dropped the gingerbread and crushed it with her boot.

A trio of fox-girls with matching green hair bands laughed beneath a pine tree draped in silvery wizard-light lichen. "Have you seen anyone unusual about town?" Drakne asked them, and they leapt into the hole at the tree roots, tails flashing. A tern-maiden ran across the street, holding an infant tight to her chest. From behind an upper-story lichen curtain, a low voice cried "Killer!" Someone threw a pail of night soil down at her feet.

They envy me, she told herself, though part of her knew she'd earned their fear, knew she'd put it there deliberately. All so she could take one more step toward that throne. *They want to be me.* She didn't know quite who she was any longer. But she did know these normal, happy townsfolk were lashed on Fydir's lead. *Normal* meant you had nothing but a handful of peasants to rely on.

"Are you lost, dear girl?" A cat-man with thick gray fur at his temples laid a hand on her wrist. His soft finger pads were flecked with fur. Orange smoke coiled where his skin met hers.

Drakne started and hissed. She was no one's *dear* anything, and—

And . . .

And she couldn't remember why she was so angry. Wasn't she just running errands? Picking up candlesticks and fresh-milled flour so she and Nabik could make dinner before Fydir returned from his day's work in the mines?

"Feeling better, are we?" said the old cat with a kindly smile. A golden pendant winked on the chain around his neck, marked with the seal of a mushroom and a wizard's staff. The Rat King's seal.

"Yes, much. Thank you, sir." Drakne curtsied, then turned and trotted back to the baker. "Sorry. I dropped my gingerbread— could I buy more? For my family back home?"

"Get out. Before we chain you up and trade you to your

brother to get our folk freed," grumbled the boar-faced baker. The crowd pressed in, frowning and tight, as the gray cat vanished into the twilight.

"What's going on?" A nervous snatch of laughter flew from her lips. "What did you say about my brother? Rokte? Idni? Why's everyone looking at me funny?"

She'd never seen the townsfolk so upset. And she'd lived in Stakte for years, ever since Zolka had brought her family north with her. These faces were as familiar as their little cottage beneath the pines, a cramped yet cozy space Nabik jokingly threatened to bring the tallest possible husband into. Why was Idni scowling at her when Drakne had helped birth her baby last spring? Why was Rokte lifting their rolling pin like a weapon, when Drakne was the only soul in Stakte who laughed at their bad jokes?

"Miss Zolkedna." Svalge pushed through the crowd, reaching for her arm. She gasped and jumped backward. "Come with me. Quickly."

"I'm not going anywhere with you!" The wolves terrorized Stakte. Why would she trust them?

"Your soldiers beat my da senseless!" Idni shouted at her. "You and Fydir had best run back south, or we'll chase you there!"

"I don't . . . understand." Fydir could grump and glower, but his violence began and ended at swatting away flies that disturbed his nap time. "You're my people. This is my home." Stakte, where the townsfolk pitched in to pay their rent that summer Mama Minka was recovering from the flu and couldn't work. Stakte, where she'd shared her first kiss with a ferret-boy beneath a sparkling oak.

161

"She's gone mad."

"Stakte will never be yours!"

Tears welled in her eyes. Great, ugly, uncontrollable things. "Why are you saying that?" The baker slapped Rokte on the back. An old woman bent double, cackling down at her knees. Their laughter rose. Jeering. Taunting. A dozen slaps on every side. "Tell me why you're so cross with me. I deserve that much. I need—"

A crown. A crown, a crown, a crown.

All her warmth rushed out like air from a punctured tire. A brief, lovely flush of memory, from a life she'd never lived, trickled down into Stakte's gutters. Drakne clawed at her ears, rubbed her eyes until she had to blink away dark patches. The cries and mockery rose around her. And she, too, was laughing, gasping, fleeing. Her thin-soled boots slipped in the ice and slush as she sprinted for the safety of the baron's manor and her brother's troops.

One of the Rat King's spies. With magic. How dare that bastard play with my head like that? But this was war. She'd chosen to come here. *How dare I be softer, kinder, joyful in a life where I'd never been hurt? How dare the world hate me when so much of me is made of other folk's sins?*

"Drakne!" Dreba ran up to her. The wolf-woman's eyes widened with concern. "What happened? Are you well?"

Drakne wiped tears and snot on her coat sleeves, tightening her fists. *I'm fine.* She couldn't escape her scars. But she could transcend them. What she'd faced at Fydir's hands had made her stronger. Every time Nabik and Zolka had failed her was fuel for her fire. With the fury of a thousand hellhounds, she would suss out the Rat King's agents and rip out every laughing peasant's tongue.

She was alone, like a crown was: It took only one to make you a queen.

~

Drakne marched into the high hall with an army of wolves at her back, grinning like she'd drunk herself silly on moonlight instead of Svalge's beer. *I'm a lioness, whereas Nabik is only a fox.* A creeping, skulking thing that stole its prey from better hunters. Too foolish to realize he could make of himself what he chose.

Fydir flung a dripping vertebra at her foot and chortled as she jumped.

In better times, the lords of Stakte had built a long hall, framed and molded in gilt, with murals of cherubs and snowfae dancing on its walls. But beastly hands couldn't fit gold sheets or guide paintbrushes, and the last few barons had possessed no interest in art or beauty. They'd let the hall fall into decay. Years of dried fat and blood spatter coated the mock-marble columns, and the cherubs' faded faces had been ripped through with claws.

Fydir ate his way through a cow as a butcher carved it directly into his silver bowl. Blood ran into corner trenches where mice-folk mopped it away, shying from the gruesome feast. Clotted amber liquor swirled in the blown crystal wineglasses they'd brought from Malirmatvi. Ruba sat beside the lion-lord, carving a plump turnip with a knife and fork. Red specks from Fydir's feasting dotted her garnet skirts. Drakne assumed she'd chosen that color to match the mess.

"Sister, dear." Fydir didn't rise to greet her.

She'd passed a sleepless night as the curse claimed him in full. His howls, curses, and even whimpers had echoed through the manor. The magic had shattered and rebuilt his legs, shortening the thighs and lengthening the ankles, drawing fur down his skin and twining a tufted tail from his spine. Drakne hoped she wouldn't have to ask Talzne to do the same for her. The pain would be excruciating. And with lion's legs, she wouldn't be able to dance.

The regimental tailors hadn't quite finessed the shaping of Fydir's trousers around his tail—the pants he'd worn to parley with the Rat King had fallen apart practically the moment they'd left—and the long smocks beastfolk of all genders wore, he'd dismissed as dresses. Draped in a gold-trimmed coat stolen from the old baron's wardrobe, shoulders bulging with muscle and laden with his thick, full mane, Fydir radiated lethal power—as long as he didn't stand up and expose his privates.

"I present Captain Svalge of the town guard," Drakne said. "I've hired him to help me find the Rat King's spies."

"Welcome, Svalge," Ruba said. "Best of luck with the hunt. You appear to be a man of great intellect. It should be no trouble at all for you to find the Rat King's best agents."

Drakne arched an eyebrow at her friend. That sarcasm had come out a bit too sharp. "Do you know any of the Rat King's spies?"

"Why would I want to?" Ruba said. "I'm perfectly capable of attracting trouble on my own."

Drakne laughed. Though she noted the answer was not quite a no. "Perhaps you can tell me more about this trouble you attract. Later tonight."

Ruba unfurled her fan and winked at Drakne over the top of the black ostrich plumes. Garnets glittered in the gold-wire frames of her glasses.

"I was just telling Lady Ruba about my factory." Fydir placed a hand on Ruba's shoulder. He met Drakne's eyes and flexed his grip. The message was clear: *You might flirt with her, sister, but in every way that matters, she'll be mine.* "We're weeks ahead of schedule. Tanks, cannons, and more—they'll all be ready by Yuleheigh." He drained a bowl of red wine and motioned for a servant to refill it. Ruba held up her fan in warning—*He's had enough*—and the servant blanched and stepped back.

"My lady," Fydir said. "I need it. For the . . . discomfort in my legs."

You need it for what's in your head. Drakne knew that, even if Fydir pretended differently. For the drinking, at least, she could not blame him.

"Excuse me, my lord," she said. Her jaw prickled fiercely, aching to expand into a beak. "I need my rest."

Fydir waved her off. Drakne ducked out of the hall and climbed the stairs to her bedroom. The Eighth Regiment had haphazardly repaired a chamber in the broken tower for her and her companions, nailing in new floor slats over rotted ones, slapping tar across the roof. But wind still whistled through the chipping masonry, the gaps between the window and the frame. Even with the hearth blazing, the room felt like the doorstep of winter.

Talzne stared out the window, at where factory smoke met the clouds. A low gray blanket hung over Stakte like a quilt of cold. The snowfae girl was yet too young to fly on the breeze like her elders, but every inch of her clearly yearned for the freedom of the sky. Guilt squirmed in Drakne's guts. *Why am I doing this to her? I know what it's like to be a captive.* Only she knew it all too well. She would do whatever it took to never know it again.

Drakne sat atop the window ledge. "My face. Now, please."

Talzne sighed. "My magic is strong, but it can't hold off the curse forever. Your swan nature is fighting to reassert itself."

"We just need to keep it going a while longer. Then we'll go back south and free your Simon." *Remember what you're getting out of this.*

Talzne set her hands firmly on each side of Drakne's jaw. Heat poured into her cheeks, burning and liquid, like molten honey. Her nerves and tendons twitched, thickening, as her bones slid forward. Fur prickled down the sides of her face. Pain like little lightning bolts shot through her gums. Her fangs grew even longer, sliding up from her lips and curling down into a wicked smile.

"You're still doing this?" Ruba said, ducking through the door. "Is that why you came back drunk, to numb the pain? Why are you hurting yourself? To appease Fydir?"

"I have my reasons," Drakne said. It was a struggle to speak through her shifting lips. A globule of spit slid down her chin. "I like me better as a lion." She felt safe. And strong. Not as safe and strong as she wanted to be, but closer.

"You do? Because you're not happy." Ruba lowered her voice. "I don't think I've ever seen you happy."

Drakne flinched.

"Listen," Ruba said. "I'm not here to pry. You don't have to confide in me. But sometimes we cut ourselves just so we can see our own blood. Talk to me. I can't make it right, but I can help you pull it out of the shadows. *Please.* I carry quite a few regrets. I don't want that for you."

"I don't mind if I'm wounded," Drakne said. She caught a little glimmer of anger in the corner of Talzne's eye. The snow-fae didn't mind either. Likely wished for it. This was a war on many fronts, and wounds were what you got when you fought them all.

"You should mind," Ruba said. "You don't have to be here, and you don't have to be doing this. All you need to do is dance. Use your magic, open yourself to the beastfolk curse, and you'll have wings to fly by morning. You could go anywhere."

I could leave. Fly a thousand miles through that soft gray winter sky. Fly, eat bugs and minnows, get shot and wind up on a hunter's trophy wall. *No.* The sky could not protect her, and no wind would blow the clouds from her head.

Some people seemed to live in whole gardens of joy, where their desires sprouted like fresh flowers. Drakne had never been planted anywhere she could grow toward the light. When the cat-spy had attacked her memory, she'd seen how happy, how loved, a girl named Drakne Zolkedna might have been in a life that showed her mercy. But that Drakne had died the moment Zolka chose to leave her family. All she'd had left was dancing, and Fydir had spoiled that for her. Now she might have a crown. That would need to be enough.

It will be enough, she told herself. *At least Ruba will stand beside me.*

"You won't get rid of me that easily." Drakne pulled on a sad smile.

"Good." Ruba smiled back at her. "I want you to stay with me. Truly. I've been lonely longer than you even know. But I want *you* to want that. The road ahead of us is hard, and we are far beyond the warmth of Winter's arms."

"We can make our own warmth." Her smile kept growing. Foolishly. Ridiculously. It felt like a coal had kindled in the space between them. One small, good, bright thing in this frozen, bloody world. "All we have to do is light a fire."

"You two are the absolute worst," said Talzne. "Just go on and kiss."

Hesitantly, Drakne looked to Ruba. The mouse-girl nodded. Drakne took her by the hand, stood, and tugged her toward the door. There was a storage room beneath the stairs where they might find privacy—

"By the way," Ruba said, "have you seen Nabik in Stakte?"

"Pardon?"

"Nabik. Rumor has it he's been spotted around town. With Prince Eugen."

Drakne hesitated. She could only think of a handful of reasons for Ruba to ask that question, and all of them put Nabik in danger. "No. I haven't seen him."

Their eyes met. Ruba's eyes shone with wanting, but not for her. A desire that would pierce right through Drakne on its way to its target.

Drakne dropped Ruba's hand. "I should wash up." She stumbled out of the bedroom, shut the heavy wooden door, and learned back against it. Breathing hard. Trying to think. *If I can't trust her*—Drakne bit her lip and tried to feel rage. Rage would keep her standing. Instead, she found a sorrow that howled inside her like a hungry abyss.

If I can't trust Ruba, who in the world can I trust?

~

The next morning, after a sleepless night spent counting Ruba's breaths, Drakne sat atop the manor wall, sketching the Rat King's twitchy-nosed, beaming face in a notebook. She tried to fill in the rest of his body, but her pen slipped and it looked like he wore a waistcoat of inkblots. *There's something about that smile of his.*

Fydir paced the snow-dusted courtyard, leaving leonine prints on bare gray stone. His ruby-red coat bore fresh blood spattered against gold embroidery. Sweat lifted his mane into a frizzled haze.

"You incompetents!" The oak branch he carried whistled down, cutting another stripe down the back of a kneeling soldier. "Letting those local troublemakers steal fuel from my factory?" Another *smack*. A factory worker rolled over, weeping, blood streaming through spreading dark fur. "I gave you all work! This is how you repay me?"

"Is this really necessary?" Drakne said, leaping down from the wall. "So what if a few peasants dipped their hands in the coal barrels? They can't work if they freeze to death in the night. And who will be loyal to you if you beat them?"

Fydir rounded on her, eyes glittering like pools of molten gold. His whites had gone two days ago. "I don't tell you how to pirouette. You don't tell me how to rule."

Careful, she told herself, biting her tongue. Fury rattled about inside her, a bomb with nowhere to explode. *You can't push him too hard. Not here. Not now.*

She had prey to hunt.

~

Clad in pale trousers and a black riding jacket embroidered with gold floss, Drakne stalked through the manor gate, stomach growling. The first flakes of a fresh snowfall gathered in her bristling bangs. Hammers rang from scaffolds where soldiers and townsfolk were repairing the chinks in the manor wall.

"The soldiers told me Lady Ruba likes to take an afternoon walk around the manor district," Dreba said. The wolves trailed behind her as she walked down the snowy lane. "She goes through the ruins and ducks into an old house. I've been watching her, just like you asked—she left ten minutes ago."

"Good," Drakne said. "Then we can catch her tail." Did she want Ruba to be a spy? On one hand, taking such a valuable informant from the Rat King would weaken his position. But if the little mouse had only befriended her on the king's orders . . .

Her heart twisted. *Everything I am, everything I care about, is only leverage great men use to make me a pawn in their games.* She mattered naught at all in the grand order of things.

Time to make herself matter.

Thrill at her own power surged through her veins as she stalked toward the ruined manors across the hill. Some remained occupied by the late baron's allies, some had been seized by officers of the Eighth Regiment for their own uses, but many lay crumbled and abandoned. The perfect place for spies to hide away.

"There!" said Svalge. A small figure, shrouded in a cloak, ducked out from within a kitchen tower. Drakne glimpsed clawed feet and a flash of brown fur before Dreba tugged her back behind a tree.

"Is she heading back toward the baron's manor?" Drakne said.

Svalge shook his head. "She took the path toward town."

"Maybe she's looking for Prince Eugen. Or that cat with memory magic who bespelled me." Drakne smiled. "Quickly. Maybe we can catch two at once."

The pack trotted after their prey. Ice and bracken crunched beneath their feet as they tromped through overgrown hedgerows, past abandoned wooden scaffolds and carriage houses with their whitewash weathered and cracked. The curling path led to the low wall that rounded the hilltop manors. They leapt over the tumbled-down stones and followed small, clawed footprints down the way.

Fydir's factory, its fresh-cut wooden walls yellow and bright, rose before them. Plumes of smoke billowed up through the holes in its yet-unfinished roof. Drakne looked for Ruba. The cloaked figure had vanished amid the workers arriving for the afternoon shift and the folk lined up to sell their souls for grain.

"Spread out," said Dreba. "Get a better vantage. If you see Lady Ruba, grab her."

The pack split. Dreba climbed the switchback stairs leading to the factory roof, and Drakne followed. Wood creaked and swayed beneath them, wind whistling through rickety slats.

Smoke washed through her lungs. She peered down into the factory, where the great soul-engines howled and screamed as they spat fabricated metal onto conveyor belts. Workers with busy hands ran up and down the line, sorting pieces, inspecting joints, but of the eight mice she spotted, only one had Ruba's brown hair, and hers was streaked with gray.

Drakne's fists tightened. Her pulse hammered hard. She crossed the rooftop walkway and looked out toward the mines. Haggard beastfolk dragged handcarts of ore up the pine-covered slope. Peddlers and bakers gathered where the cleared square met the shadows, hawking wares. Beggars pled. A white-bearded goat-man played the flute. Fabric flapped on the breeze—

There! The girl in the cloak! The wolves who'd remained on the ground saw her as well. They surged forward, clawed feet flinging up snow, Svalge in the lead. He grabbed the girl, pinned her by the throat to a pine. She shouted and squealed. Her hood fell backward. Tall, tufted ears flicked flat in fear.

Squirrelfolk, Drakne realized. *It's not Ruba.*

But Svalge didn't let go.

Drakne swore. She turned, waving Dreba to follow her, and darted down the stairs two at a time. Her boots pounded on the wood, and when they hit the snow, she took off running. Her lungs jolted up into her throat as she pounced; she grabbed Svalge by the shoulder and hauled him backward. The squirrel-maid fell to the snow.

"What are you doing?" Drakne demanded.

"If you want to catch spies, you need the common folk too scared to guard them. Trust me. It works. If you burned down some of the treehouses, they'd hand over the Rat King's spies themselves."

"Or they might try to burn out my brother and me as revenge."

Svalge laughed. "Are you scared?"

Drakne bit her lip. Could this be truly what was needed? The people of Kolznechia had no love for the Rat King. They surely wouldn't act to safeguard his spies. *Unless Fydir and I are so brutal that the Rat King looks like a saint.*

On the edge of her lion's hearing, she heard a gasp.

A streak of movement. A flash of snow. Out of the corner of her eye. Drakne turned to see a short girl in a red dress darting into the shadows behind a cart of scrap iron.

Ruba? She wasn't sure. She wasn't sure of anything, not anymore.

"Stop her!" Drakne ordered. She and the wolves lunged together. Workers screamed, darting from their path, tripping on ice. Drakne's claws scored scarlet lines down someone's shoulder as she forced her way forward—then she was through the crowds. Her hands reaching, her jaws wide open, Svalge and Dreba at her back, flanking the target. Saliva filmed on Drakne's tongue. The air tasted of sap and mushrooms.

A boar-woman, stout and powerfully muscled, swept the girl in the red dress behind her and threw up her hands to shout "No!" The Rat King's gold medallion sparkled at her throat.

Drakne froze. *Another spy.*

Svalge flung out an arm and knocked Drakne away. She tumbled back across the snow as magic washed throughout the open air. A column of wind and sparking electricity wove a crude barrier between her and her target. It hummed like a thousand bees and shimmered like a tower of mirrors.

"She's getting away!" Drakne shouted, rolling back onto her toes. She coughed from Svalge's blow, blinked to try to see through the light of the sparkling storm. The girl in the red dress vanished down a back alley. Drakne hadn't even clearly glimpsed her face. "Svalge! Move!"

But he couldn't. The sudden, solid thunderstorm had caught him like a fishing net. Distorted through the waves of wind and magic, he moved in blurs, faster even than a lion's eye could track. The squirrel-maid, who must have been caught in the spell as she scrambled to get away, huddled at the edge of the storm. Then she moved closer to him. Snatches of shouting, speaking, laughing rose from within.

"Svalge! Out! Now!" Drakne shouted. For a heartbeat, his wolfish amber eyes met hers. All the anger in them had drained away. Only sorrow remained in his gaze—and something *knowing* in them said he sorrowed for her most of all.

The air screamed. Like the very universe was a twisted, rusty spring pushing *back*. In a billow of snow and ice chunks, the column collapsed. The scattered townsfolk pressed in close to see what had happened, for once not fearing the lion in their midst.

The boar-woman's magic had crafted an entirely new nightmare.

Out of the falling snow, a girl stumbled forward. Not the same one the spell had caught—a rabbit-girl of five or six. *Where did she come from?* Svalge stood hand in hand with the redheaded squirrel. A thick beard covered his chin and jaw; gray streaked his temples. She had grown wider and heavier in the chest and hips, and held another squirming child in her arms.

"What," Drakne said, "in the name of all the saints, is this?" They looked like kin, the adults and the children. *Children that didn't exist a heartbeat ago.*

Dreba ran toward her pack leader, eyes wide with shock. He reached out and embraced her. Shaking. Weeping.

"It's so good to see you," he gasped. "My wife, our children, and I—we've waited ten years to break free."

Drakne froze. The watching crowd cowered, murmuring in shock. Her thoughts spun like gears as she calculated. If she'd made a misstep, a decade of her life would have dissolved.

She might even now be a content, smiling member of that little time-bound family. All her vigor and venom stripped away.

Though at least then someone would care about me.

"Drakne!"

A warm hand found her shoulder and guided her to sit atop a cast-off crate. She realized she was shaking. Someone pressed a mug of hot chocolate in her hands.

Drakne looked up into a long, gold-beaked face. A white-haired woman smiled down sadly at her.

She was surprised she could still recognize her mother's face.

"All's well." Zolka spread out her wings to shelter them from the crowd. "Drink. Breathe. The boar-woman ran off. I'll keep an eye out for her making more trouble."

Drakne shivered. For years, she'd told herself she didn't care about the mother who'd abandoned her. But the shock of what she'd just seen echoed through her. Now all she wanted was to bury her face in Zolka's arms. *But can I trust her? Can I let her see me weak?*

Instead of reaching out, she asked, "How did the boar-woman do that?"

"Some magics are for wintertime," said Zolka. "When cold winds blow, the people need their wizards to care for them, the snowfae to spread beauty, to fill the long, dark nights with strength and joy. But some magics—like yours—belong to summer. When the sun blazes and the days run long, hearts come into conflict and the great powers fight for control."

Drakne flinched and looked about her. Svalge, Dreba, the squirrel, and her children were encircled by the protection of the wolf pack. She stood outside it. "That's what my dancing is? The magic of a monster?"

"No. Your magic is a catalyst for change. It simply takes wisdom to use that gift for good."

"Wisdom," Drakne snorted. "Like yours?" Was Zolka about to start shouting orders at her? "The wise wizard who abandoned her children and ran off to another country? You could have brought us with you. You never should have left us behind."

Zolka lowered her head. Her wings drooped, too, the long primary feathers brushing the snow. "Your mama and I—we talked about it. Bringing the whole family north together. But you all would have become beastfolk, and the Empire would never have welcomed you back. We didn't want to make that choice for you."

Oh. Drakne sipped her chocolate, considering. Letting the warmth and sugar feed some life back into her. Was it her mother she was mad at, or Winter herself, who'd bound Zolka to break the curses on this frozen land? But she *wanted* to be mad at her mother. It was easier to be mad at someone you could reach.

"I wish you had," she said quietly. "Better a beast than . . . than whatever I am now."

"I know what Fydir did to you," Zolka said, even more quietly. "I wish I had been there to stop him."

"You should have," Drakne agreed. Her heart lurched sideways. There was so much she wanted to say. Wanted to scream.

"You can scream if you'd like," Zolka said. "Or you can strike a real blow against him. Come with Nabik and me. We could use your help."

My mother wants me? It was something she'd never expected to hear. But the joy that leapt inside her was snuffed out by her rising tide of rage. *Too late. She came for me too late.* Drakne had found her path. There was no place on it for her mother. Not for any of the people who had failed her, again, and again, and again.

She snarled. "No. You and Nabik need to stay out of my way. This town is mine."

Zolka flinched and stepped back from her. Hurt flashed in her eyes.

I sound like Fydir. Drakne smiled a wicked grin. *Good.*

CHAPTER ELEVEN

Of Fires and Foxes

Nabik trod dutifully along in a handmade hamster wheel, turning posters into marzipan.

A small electric generator powered a smelter and a cable lift that ran deep into the mines. The townsfolk without more pressing duties took shifts walking the cliffside wheel that powered it. Staring out over his shoulder as he paced, rickety wood and iron shifting around him, he stretched his power through the pines of the low town to the factory. It climbed up walls and signposts, changing Fydir's printed visage to honey and almond meal.

"Not bad," Zolka said, trudging up the cliffside, leaning on her staff of silver birch and ice-crystal feathers. "When you have more practice, you'll be able to summon up a staff. It'll help focus your magic."

"Would a staff make me strong enough to overcome the factory guards?" The tight red knot of smoky misery at the heart of town pulsed like an abscess on his heart.

"Perhaps you don't need to overcome them by force."

"Not that I even could." He looked up to her. By now, his eyes barely came level with her chin. "Why did the curse make *you* tall?"

"It didn't. I did that to myself. For quite a few years after I came north, I let the curse shape me small. More how women look in the south. Then I realized—the women of the south don't decide who I am, and I quite missed being the tallest in the room." She gave him an encouraging pat. "You'll have that same mastery, too, one day."

"One day." He brushed shining white hair back behind his ears. Both hair and ears were growing unnaturally long. "What sort of wizard can't even reach a high shelf?"

"That's not what makes a wizard. Remember?"

Nabik shook his head. "I want to do more than turn a treadwheel."

"Very well, then. Come with me."

Zolka led him down the cliffside and up into the town, to a tangle of squirrelfolk homes nestled within great oaks. At her bidding, Nabik knocked on the frames of tiny windows and on round porthole doors. The squirrelfolk answered eagerly, offering up their wishes. He summoned needles and thread spools, glue pots and fur boots, and in one case—Nabik grinned—a red-handled nutcracker.

They went next to the roped-off entrances of an abandoned mine shaft, where Stakte's ferrets and star-nosed molefolk dwelt in tunnels. He summoned hammers, chisels, and sturdy wooden scaffolding to shore up their ceilings. To the northern well they went next, where folk of all beast shapes gathered. Nabik felt lighter than a cloud as he passed out jars of oil, bottles of medicine, and fistfuls of fruitcakes, drinking in Stakte's smiles.

They want me here. They truly want me.

Maybe he could suffice for them all.

"We can take the factory from within if we act quickly enough," Nabik said the next morning, as the conspirators in the sabotage plot gathered in the meeting house. "I'll sneak onto the grounds and disable the guards' weapons. Then I'll give the signal, and you can jump on them, tie them up, and smash the factory equipment." He took a deep sip of the hot cider he'd summoned for the breakfast table, letting the warmth bolster his courage.

"Won't the guards notice you?" Nivni said.

"I served with the Eighth Regiment. The guards won't look too closely if I show them what they expect to see."

"You're sure?" Nivni asked. He nodded. "Well, best of luck. I'll see you in there."

"I'm coming too," said Eugen. He sat on a bench, peeling potatoes while Nivni made mash. He'd already passed her a two-foot-high pile. "Someone's got to watch his back."

Absolutely not, Nabik nearly said. He couldn't lead his prince into danger. Too much depended on him.

A group of children rushed across the cave toward Nabik. They tugged at his homespun robe, pulling him down to sit among them, wishes jabbing at him like swarming honeybees. Lemon drops and cupcakes spilled from his hands, a tide of meringue and chocolate. A girl delightedly bit the legs off a gingerbread man, and Nabik charmed it to scream.

"Off," Eugen said, pointing a long finger at the ox-boy who'd clambered onto Nabik's lap, half crushing him. "You're too big for that, Rudin."

The children darted backward and dropped into hasty, clumsy bows. "Your Majesty. Your Princeliness." They grabbed their toys and scrambled for the door with eyes low and tails twitching. The cavern of the meeting house felt colder in their wake.

"You'd make an excellent schoolteacher," Nabik told Eugen. "You terrify them."

"Is that the only qualification for the job?" Eugen asked. "The ability to strike fear in the hearts of children?"

"That, and nice handwriting."

"Well, then. I suppose it's a little like being a king."

Nabik laughed and climbed back up on the bench beside him, absentmindedly resting his hand on Eugen's knee. The prince's wishes washed over him. Wishes for luck, for success, for many things, but not for a throne.

It struck Nabik he'd never felt Eugen wish to be *king* much at all.

"Come sabotage the factory with me," Nabik said. "You'll feel better once you've made yourself useful."

"Thank you." Eugen smiled. "I look forward to proving myself as your partner in crime."

"You couldn't even steal tea from a grandmother," Nivni said. "You don't have the spine for it."

"Nivni!" Nabik said as Eugen's face fell.

"What? Crime's a skill. It takes time to master. Now, my first crime ended when the baron sent wolves after me just 'cause me and my friends chucked dung at his carriage. They beat me half to death before Zolka jumped in."

"She saved you?"

"And lectured me senseless in the doing. Said I couldn't waste my potential. I had to step up and lead. Find ways to make some use of making trouble." Nivni laughed. "I needed to hear that, I did. You wizards always know the right thing to say."

~

As the sun rose high, Nabik and Eugen crept uphill from the meeting house. The tangled roads of Stakte bustled with life, workers and cart drovers winding their way around blooming crystal sproutlings and pines draped in silvery lichen. Soldiers patrolled in groups of four and five, and local beastfolk scattered where their shadows fell. The two boys approached the factory, where the rising sunlight bounced off the raw wooden walls. Green flashed behind Nabik's eyes as he led Eugen across the no-man's-land between the pines and work yards.

"You're wanted on deck," said the guard at the door, looking at their summoned Eighth Regiment uniforms and naught else, certainly not the faces hidden under low hats. Nabik had made an extra packet of cigarettes appear in the man's pocket, and he was far too pleased about that to inspect anyone closely.

Light and heat billowed over them as they entered, like they'd stuck their necks inside a burning bell. Hammer strikes and half-yelped shouts echoed up and down the maze of wooden walkways. Sheets of molded metal, newly pressed, rolled down conveyor belts and under the eyes of huddled hawkfolk inspectors. Chained vats of molten slag swung across the ceiling on heavy chains. Fumes roiled, and Nabik fought the urge to gag—and then he saw what lay at the factory's heart.

An enormous stamp press drank raw metal through its three

wide throats, its eighteen arms slamming down in a ceaseless rhythm. It arched against the unfinished roof, bent as if an old man beneath a heavy load—but the souls inside it ranged from twenty to eighty, brass visages peering out with wide eyes and wrinkled brows and stretches of bared fang. *Almost thirty of them,* Nabik counted, an icy focus stealing over him. *Drowned in living metal.*

"Blessed Winter," Eugen whispered. "What a disgusting thing!"

Nabik nodded and waved Eugen to follow him up the ramp. "Hurry. They'll keep their extra weapons in the supervisor's office." He'd already turned the door guard's bullets into popcorn. He had to get the rest before the man noticed what he'd done.

The workers on the ramp should have been given masks and goggles to shield themselves from flying scrap metal. Without proper equipment, they made do by wrapping their faces in heavy scarves. As Nabik and Eugen pushed past them, their fur bristled, and one badger-woman yelped, but no eyes looked further than their uniforms. The supervisor's office was a small room built atop the upper platform. The door was locked, but with a wish from Eugen, it popped open.

Nabik slammed the door shut behind them, nearly knocked over a freestanding coatrack, and yanked open a cabinet full of papers. "Check below the desk," he told Eugen, who stood staring out the tiny window onto the floor. "The guns could be anywhere."

"How could you stand working beside a man who used these awful machines?"

"What could I do? He's my brother." The words came out too

terse. Nabik caught himself. It wasn't Eugen he was mad at. It was Fydir. It was himself. "I told Fydir I didn't care for them. But I could have done more. Should have done more." *I should have saved people. I should have fixed things.* "I . . . I don't know why I couldn't find the words."

His eyes skittered across the papers, desperately seeking— something. *Schematics.* Marked with the logo of Archduke Marinus's manufacturers.

Nabik understood the basic mechanics of soul-engine presses and autocars. But this new tank design packed souls more tightly than in any soul-engine he'd ever seen. *What does Fydir need that much power for?* He flipped through the pages. An article torn from the *Journal of Industrial Mechanics*, urging factory owners to rotate the souls in their engines weekly, lest they become attuned to the mechanism—

"I think this is it." Eugen pulled a coat off a crate and forced open its wooden lid. A dozen long rifles shone inside. Nabik waved his hand. The weapons turned into flaky marzipan, the scent of sugar and almonds filling up the room. "Let's go tell Nivni."

"One minute," Nabik said, heart thrumming like a caged hummingbird's wings. "I need to—to look this over." A second schematic lay beneath the first: a long-barreled, slender rifle, fitted with brass filigree. *Fydir's gun. His pride and joy.* Nabik had never even so much as been allowed to breathe near it. If he had, he might have recognized the soul it carried.

Drakne. His stomach flipped over. His blood pounded hot in his ears. Fydir had grown so vicious with that new gun in his fist. Hunting down and shooting the archduke's enemies, where before he'd arranged accidents or crafted subtle poison. *He wanted her to feel that. All of that.* Of course Drakne hadn't wanted Nabik to help her, back in the wolves' den. He'd failed her when she'd needed him most. *Why didn't I do more? When she stopped answering my letters, I could have traveled to her school, or at least written to the headmistress.* But any mention of Drakne could put Fydir on edge. He hadn't wanted to upset things.

Because Fydir terrified him.

Wood cracked. Splinters flew. A monster, with a pelt of blinding gold, broke through the door. Nabik froze.

Fydir, Baron of Stakte, stood seven feet tall and four broad at the shoulder. His medal-studded red uniform jacket shone in the flickering electric light. He grinned with a jaw so thick it could break stone, his beard and mane as wild as summertime bacchanalia.

"Little brother," he sneered. "So this is what you are on the inside. A skulking fox-child. A scavenger of garbage heaps. Too cowardly to do a real man's duty. And yet you thought you could run from me?"

Each word hit like a blow, meant to make him feel as small as he looked. But now was no time to cower. Nabik lifted the schematic. "Why did you do this to our sister?"

"Don't make this about Drakne. You're the one who walked away from us. You're the one trespassing in my factory. You're the one *hurting our family.*" Unsheathed claws glittered on his fingertips.

"I—I hurt our family?" Shame pulled on him like a siren's call.

"You abandoned us. Your regiment. Your sister—"

"No," Nabik said. Threads of steel crept into his voice. He knew beyond a doubt that Fydir had no right to say anything

185

about Drakne. "You failed us. You failed Drakne. I remember. All the screaming, breaking plates, mocking her behind her back. And don't tell me your rage is at the archduke and the Empire, that you're only trying to help our family advance. How does it help our family if we all live in fear of you?"

Fydir snorted. Low and dismissive. Nabik flinched. "You're afraid of me? What, because I expected you to do your duty? I treated you better than any man in the Empire would." He stepped forward. His claws glistened. He wished a thousand punishments on his runaway brother.

Nabik scrambled backward. His back hit the wall. He had nowhere to go, and no way to block out the rage that radiated off Fydir like the sun.

"Ungrateful, deviant boy. It seems I need to teach you a stronger lesson. Just like Drakne."

Images of guns and soul-sockets flooded his head. His heart raced. "Don't!" he gasped. "Fydir, please—"

"Excuse me, but I hope this hurts like hell." Eugen grabbed the coatrack and swung, hard. Wood cracked. The shaft splintered on Fydir's skull.

The lion dropped like a stone.

Spurred into motion, Nabik seized Eugen's frantic desire— *Protect us!* Coils of rope appeared out of the air, binding Fydir's wrists and ankles. For good measure, Nabik summoned a gag in his mouth. He didn't need the lion biting, and he didn't want to hear one more word from his brother.

Fydir, still staggering from the blow, hissed and spat as Nabik helped him stand. A purple lump bloomed on his forehead. *He'll need Zolka. Her healing magic.* "Come with us," Nabik said, pulling his brother along as he stumbled on his bound feet. All he could think of was getting Fydir care—until they led him out of the supervisor's office, and the workers on the floor erupted in cheers.

"Stakte is ours!" Nivni said, and turned her wrench against the heavy bulk of the stamp press. A single *whack*, and the metal dented. Three vole-women began knocking over barrels; salt and screws spilled across the earthen floor. A wide-shouldered pig-man barred the front doors. A pair of soldiers ran in from the back—with a snap of his fingers, Nabik sent them crumpling into sleep.

"This is glorious!" Eugen said eagerly as the clamor rose all around him. The nutcracker prince slammed his shoulder into an industrial drill rig, knocking the heavy machine on its side. Dust flew. The machine's oaken frame cracked and splintered. Fydir squirmed, growling through his gag, glaring at Nabik with eyes of simmering gold.

Nabik smiled, trying to look as proud as if he'd caught the lion himself.

He couldn't let anyone know he'd been scared.

"This is it!" Nivni said. "The factory is in ruins. The lion-lord is ours. Those Szpratzian bastards will never wring another penny from our people!"

The meeting house erupted in cheers. Exhausted workers banged beer mugs on tabletops. Children laughed and spun one another in dizzy dances. Nivni pounded a drum, and a goose with a violin struck up a jaunty chord. Even Nabik found himself smiling.

It was hardly a complete victory. The soldiers had withdrawn from the factory and the lower town once they'd heard of their leader's capture, but a thousand men still occupied the manor district. After treating Fydir's head wound, putting him in an enchanted sleep, and locking him up in a supply cabinet, Nabik and Zolka had spent hours trying and failing to open the soul-engines. *There's magic tied up in these machines,* Zolka had said, and Nabik had thought of Archduke Marinus and his dark interest in Kolznechians with gifts. *Only the owner can open the sockets. It will take a power more forceful than ours to break through.* Still, they'd done a great thing and shown the Szpratzian Empire what Kolznechians were made of.

Nabik climbed atop a bench and clapped Eugen on the shoulder. "And here's to the man who struck the lion down! When the rest of Kolznechia hears what we've done, they'll rise for their rightful king! From the border to Stakte, to Znaditin and the Crystal Palace!"

All eyes turned to Eugen. He dropped into a courtly bow. "Speech!" shouted a ferret-girl, and "Speech!" called a reindeer-man.

Eugen straightened up. His wooden joints went rigid as he braced himself. "Thank you. I will most certainly remember the lessons I've learned here once I sit on my father's throne. I . . ." A strange, dry, clacking noise came from inside his throat. "I . . . I . . ."

"You can do this," Nabik whispered.

"I'm about to learn if nutcrackers can vomit. Say something. Please."

Nabik raised his voice once more. "Tonight, we celebrate Winter's blessings with the folk and friends we fight for. Tomorrow, we keep on defending our homes and the work of our hands. May Winter cheer us all."

He stretched his arms wide and called power from the air. Over the empty wooden tables it flew, looping through minds and growling stomachs, flowing out and solidifying atop plates and trenchers. Roast hare and rich stew, cracked marrow bones, and peppered, pickled cabbage. Apples carved in coiling strips and almonds topping hearty cakes. Kegs of beer and wine casks. Noodles and potatoes drenched in butter and fried with vinegar. Whole turkeys leaking stuffing of bread, celery, and dripping gravy.

This is who I am. A wizard, meant to serve the people who need me most. Everything he'd ever been seemed to hum inside him, brass and iron breaking into liquid slurry for reforging. Soft and molten. Ready to be something new and bright.

Snowflakes danced around him, a flurry, an embrace. He pulled magic like thread through his body, reshaping himself. Surrendering to the beastfolk curse—no, to the chorus of the people who'd found life and meaning inside it. Nabik stepped forward, small and fine featured, his long white hair falling down his back, tufted tail swishing out beneath his frost-blue robes. Different, yet true, yet free, as if he'd been drowning all his life and only now found air.

A staff of peppermint, twined with mistletoe, appeared in his hands. The crowd applauded. "Well done," Zolka said, and patted the seat at her right hand. "Here. Wizards take a place of honor."

Nabik grinned and dropped into the chair. *I have a place here. A place that matters.*

Older women in faded skirts and trousers drew a knot around Zolka, asking if she'd come around that night to grant their wishes. "You could slip in through my chimney shaft," said one. "My children sleep like the dead; they'll never hear you." Younger men and women flanked Nabik, filling his plate before he could even ask for seconds, complimenting his spellwork, his bravery, his beastfolk form. One boy even brushed a finger down the furred length of his ear and suggested he might pierce it with a line of golden hoops.

"Where am I to get gold?" Nabik asked. "When the invaders are gone, we'll need to have a serious conversation about compensating your wizards."

They laughed, the sound full and riotous. His cheeks flushed crimson. Of everything he thought the beastfolk curse might bring out in him, he hadn't expected to develop a sense of humor. But the laugh he cared for most was absent.

Where's Eugen?

Musicians struck up a melody on a bass fiddle and a pair of pipes. Children pounded along on drums. Zolka clapped her hands high, and her companions spun around her in a circle. Folk pushed the tables and benches against the cavern walls with a great scraping of sound. Nabik waved his staff and summoned little lights to dance along the ceiling. One shone on the nutcracker, who was sitting alone on a bench in a shadowy corner.

"Join us," Nabik said, drunk and giddy, dropping down beside him. "Come on. You're a prince. You must have had a thousand tutors teaching you to dance."

"The minuet, perhaps. Not these swift folk dances." Wistful yearning filled his voice. "I wouldn't know where to start."

"I'll teach you."

"Thank you, but . . . would it even be appropriate for me to join in?" He stared down at his wooden hands. "I don't know the etiquette. What if I do something wrong? Every festival I've ever gone to, I had some royal role to play."

"Play *just Eugen* tonight. Dance with me."

Like his words had cast a wild spell of wanting, Eugen stood and curled his broad hand around Nabik's delicate, dark-clawed one. A scrawny mole-child caught his other and led them both into the ring. The steps Zolka had taught Nabik as a child returned with fluid ease. *Hand up, wrist cocked, chin high, skip left.* The music swept him into the tide of his people, and he pulled the prince with him into the joyous clap and leap of sound.

His world dissolved into melody and rhythm, clapped hands and low knees and feet pounding the floor like they could wake the world itself from slumber. Dust and glittering motes of light swirled through the hall. Zolka smiled through the darkness. A dozen dancers shouted his name. A warmth wrapped about him, one no snowstorm or even a lion's claws could pierce.

When Eugen squeezed his shoulder and whispered "Outside," Nabik nodded and eagerly followed behind him.

Up the hill and under snow-laden tree branches they clambered, arm in arm, swaying, clumsy, until they dropped into a nobleman's ruined garden. Statues of dancers worn blank-faced by the years twirled beside a long-since-frozen fountain. Slender pines poked up from where broken stone tiles left exposed earth, their needles scattered on the snow. Lichen had devoured one bench and left the other suspiciously cracked. Nabik conjured a circle of warmth at their feet, marked in silver sparks that occasionally broke from his spell and drifted heavenward. Eugen snatched up a bundle of loose pine branches and wove them into a garland, which he draped across Nabik's shoulders, pulling him in closer.

Together, they watched a silver-tailed meteor streak across the stars.

"You summoned a whole feast," Eugen said, stroking Nabik's hair, running his wooden fingers along one pointed, white-furred ear. "Even though it exposes you to the curse?"

Nabik smiled. *I could tuck my head under his chin now*, he thought, and did so. The feel of hard wood on his skin was a strange one, but that was Eugen, and Nabik wanted the texture of him everywhere.

"I don't mind," Nabik said. "In truth, I'm beginning to like this form." There was a beauty to it, a queer masculine beauty that a more artful soul could write poems of. It felt right. It felt interesting. And in a petty fashion, he liked that Fydir *didn't* like it. But he wouldn't mention his brother here. Or his nagging sense of shame that he hadn't been able to save himself from the lion-lord. "Quite fitting for a wizard, isn't it?"

"Quite so." Eugen took his hand. Their fingers curled together. "Can you tell what I wish right now?"

"Let me try," Nabik said. He'd grown attuned to the prince's presence since he'd first read his wishes in Malirmatvi, the fabulous gold-and-sapphire edges of his wanting—but now he found something new rising to Eugen's surface like the silver sparks drifting skyward.

Something joyful and terrifying all at once.

"You want me to *kiss* you?" Nabik shook his head. The garden spun around him. The tips of his ears blushed, hot as newborn suns. Sweat trickled from places he didn't know could sweat. "I would, but . . . I've never kissed anyone. I don't know how."

"Then I'll teach you." Cradling Nabik's head gently as a porcelain eggshell, Eugen leaned in and met Nabik's nervous mouth with his own.

Nabik froze. Shivered. Pushed forward. The wooden lips were cold, like licking an icicle. But sculptured, textured, new—and wanted. His lips ran past the carved divot under Eugen's nose, the rough bump of carved mustache stubble. His tongue slid past polished, too-smooth teeth; he drank in the taste of snow and stain. A moan fluttered free of his throat, where it felt like it had been trapped since they first met.

A boy kissing a boy. A strange creature kissing a stranger one. A prince kissing a common soldier, and those wooden hands held him so gently it *hurt*. Nabik whimpered, and Eugen laughed in his ear. "So you *do* like me?" the prince whispered. "I was scared."

"Of course," Nabik breathed. He had so little experience with feelings of any sort. Certainly not like these, leaping flames he yearned to embrace and let devour him. A wanting in his mind, body, and heart stronger than a steam engine. It had been building since he'd first seen Eugen, but only now did he know its name. *Love.* Or something like it. A first step on a journey more delightful than a dream. "I've never felt so much. I didn't know I could."

Eugen hugged him close. Nabik brushed his lips down that wooden neck, overwhelmed by the light blooming inside him, his kisses shifting to tiny licks.

"Wait a moment," said the prince. "Wait. Can you feel my heart beat?"

"What's that matter?" He couldn't kiss a beating heart. Nabik wondered if he should move his lips up or downward. That long, proud nose deserved a whole bouquet of kisses, but *downward* led somewhere beautiful and strange.

Then he remembered. What Eugen had told him back in Malirmatvi. *If we go off fairy-tale logic, true love's kiss will restore my flesh.*

Cool disappointment slapped him like a winter wave.

All this magic. Everything I am. Everything I feel.

Am I truly still not enough to save him?

CHAPTER TWELVE

Starlight in Exile

In Fydir's absence, dinner in the baron's manor was colder than the winter wind. The feast table in the gore-streaked great hall was piled high: baked ham covered in pineapple, mashed potatoes swimming in gravy, peanut cookies, and free-flowing wine. The full moon shone through the narrow windows, casting a strange, hard light around everyone who'd come to dine. Fydir's officers spoke in low tones among themselves; Drakne watched, ears twitching, straining to eavesdrop on the men. Every few breaths, Ruba glanced nervously at Drakne over her vegetable platter.

Does she know I suspect her of spying? No. Ruba was smart. She would have fled. She would have known better than to trust that Drakne would spare an enemy. *The advantage is mine.* But she didn't feel like a victor. She felt as if she were suffocating.

What will be left of me if I drive her away?

"Shall we have a song?" Ruba said.

Drakne nodded. Anything to drown out the roaring in her head. She took up the verse of an old carol. "Oh, cast my soul in steel and satin, put the trigger in my hand. She who died was merely asking; I will claim what I demand."

Ruba took up the next line. "Crown my head in gold and mushrooms, all the bounty of the land—"

The hall doors banged open.

"My lady." Svalge's voice had only grown gruffer with the ten years the boar had drained from him. A heavy sack hung over his shoulders. He crossed the hall and bowed before the feast table. "I came to tell you I'm leaving Stakte."

Drakne sat up. "I don't understand." Shock trickled through her veins like cool water. "I hired you because you're the most vicious man in town. I have plenty of work for vicious men."

"I've been vicious a very long time," Svalge said. "The old baron dragged me from my mother's breast. Raised me to rend and terrorize. I had the anger for it. But time's drained that away, and all I've got left is regrets. My children deserve a peaceful father. We're going to buy some land and start a beet farm in the winter wood."

"Beets?" she said. "I'm going to be queen. I can pay you the weight of a beet harvest in rubies."

"You can't eat rubies," Ruba pointed out. "That's why most of Znaditin lives off lichen or buys costly imported food. The crystal blight has starved the city for decades. Now if you could farm some beets, ship them north, you'd have a market. They'd be delicious with some fresh lettuce and bean sprouts—"

"Just because you look like a mouse doesn't mean you need to eat like one," Drakne said.

"Real mice are omnivores. They eat anything. Even their own young. I, on the other hand, am a vegetarian."

Drakne shrugged. "More meat for me." Perhaps she should be glad the factory workers took Fydir hostage. She didn't want him to get ideas from that *eating your young* concept. And it wasn't like Nabik or Zolka would let him get hurt. They'd watch over him. Likely better than they'd ever watched over her.

"Thank you for your generosity," Svalge said, "but I'd like to build myself a life I can be proud of." He tipped his cap and turned. "I hope your family finds the peace that mine has."

"Very well." Drakne looked down the hall, to where Dreba stood sentry at the door. The wolf-woman stiffened, looking as uncomfortable as if her whole spine were one great itch. "Dreba? You'll take command of my wolves. For my first order—"

"We're going with him," Dreba said. "Me, and all the pack."

Drakne's fists tightened. "I thought wolves were loyal."

"We are. To our pack leader." Dreba shook her head. "Best of luck. Visit if you'd like; we'll keep a place for you at our hearth fire." She put her hand on Svalge's shoulder. Together, tails twitching, they and the remaining wolves left the hall.

Fools, Drakne thought as the door slammed shut behind them. *Running off into danger. A beet farm is no shield from this world's violence.* But they could do as they pleased. She was a lion. She needed nothing from lesser beasts. Certainly not friendship.

The wolves would regret the day they abandoned her.

"What do you think of the townsfolk's demands?" she asked Ruba. Perhaps the mouse-girl's reaction would reveal something of her loyalties. "In exchange for giving back Fydir, they want us to withdraw from Stakte completely. They say we can keep most of the baron's gold if we go—"

"With all due respect, Miss Zolkedna," said an officer sprouting the snout of a donkey, "we'll negotiate with the rabble to free the baron."

"He's *my* brother," Drakne growled.

"And if he were here, he would want us to protect you. No. If we can't free him by tomorrow, I'll take fifty soldiers and escort you home to Malirmatvi."

She could have thrown her plate in frustration. To the men of the Empire, she was just another girl, another pawn. Fydir didn't see women as his equals, but she was his sister, and she shone in his eyes so long as she reflected his own light. If he wasn't here, she'd have to find another champion. By any means necessary.

"Please excuse me, gentlemen," Drakne said as she rose. "I need my rest."

She had to make the Rat King hers. Tonight.

Clad in a coat as pale blue as icicles, she slipped from the manor and followed the path Dreba had shown her days before. The ruins atop the hill were riddled with hiding places. Somewhere amid them was where Ruba slipped off to every day.

Drakne poked about crumbled carriage houses, high halls with roofs of tumbled timber, courtyards claimed by bird nests, lichen, and creeping violet crystals. Lion's prints stretched out behind her as she strode through the maze of snowdrifts and tumbled-down gray stone. Into a broken keep she climbed, dodging rotted floorboards, and found a descending stair. Her eyes flashed green as she followed it into the earth.

The blaze of candles blinded her like sudden sun. Warm, still air washed up around her, carrying the scent of dusty pages and fresh ink. *Magic.* A library lay beneath the ruin, bookshelves stacked high with leather-bound volumes, enclosed in cozy comfort by some unseen enchantment. *Wizardry. This is the Rat*

King's hand. She could almost taste him in the air, bog water and sweet molasses.

She prowled through the rows of shelves. Before a small, round window stood a desk with the four carved feet of a dragon. Beneath it, sticks, blankets, and loops of dark hair had been heaped up into a rat's nest. Books lay open on its surface, scrawled with arcane sigils, astronomical charts, and phases of the moon. A music box topped with a dark-haired ballerina waited silently. Above, sickly, pale mushrooms bloomed from green wallpaper.

Beautiful, Drakne thought. She picked up the music box and wound the knob. Nenye's "Lullaby for Saint Valchassia" tinkled as the porcelain girl spun. Broader in the shoulders than most young dancers—

It's me, Drakne thought. But this figure smiled, joyful and proud, and Drakne held it to her chest as if she could hug herself. *I wish it could still be me.*

"What are you doing?" said a soft voice. Drakne whirled. Ruba stood behind her, face unreadable.

"Looking for answers," she said brusquely. Barely holding in her screaming fury. "You told me the Rat King exiled you. So why is your little hideout filled with his magic?"

She expected the other girl might deny it, try to flee or fight. But her hazel eyes held neither fear nor anger. Only sorrow, a boundless sorrow, so deep it threatened to drown them both.

"It's a long story," Ruba said. "I'm not sure where you'd even want me to start."

"Start with why you *lied* to me."

"You broke the Rat King's trust long before I came to Malirmatvi.

Can you really blame him for wanting answers from the girl who betrayed him?"

"I didn't betray him! I was—" Drakne hesitated.

"Yes?"

"It doesn't matter." She wouldn't tell Ruba what Fydir had done to her, not now. She had already made herself so foolishly vulnerable to this girl.

"It matters a great deal." Ruba folded her arms across her chest. She glared at Drakne from behind her black-framed glasses. "The fate of Kolznechia hangs in the balance. Where is Prince Eugen? Where did Nabik and Zolka hide him from me?"

Blessed Winter, it's always about them. Drakne growled and threw the music box. The little dancer cartwheeled through the air. Ruba yelped and ducked as the porcelain shattered. Then Drakne was atop her, knocking her to the ground with her knee. She pinned the mouse-girl to the floorboards, pulled a ball of twine out of her coat, and bound her prisoner's hands. She tried not to look at where the rope cut Ruba's skin.

I don't need her, she told herself. *I need my crown. I need my power. I need—*

A spasm of pain shot through Drakne's legs. She bent double, curled against her prisoner's back, biting her tongue and cursing at the taste of her own blood. Her bones trembled. Burning. Stretching like flesh should never stretch without snapping. Her limbs lengthened. Her toes twitched, melting together. Webbing bloomed between them, loose, blobby skin, and Drakne *howled.*

"You can't run from what you are forever, swan-girl," Ruba said. "I know. The curse knows—"

"I'm not some bird. I'm a lioness." *I'm a weapon.* Drakne

pulled out a handkerchief. "You can come quietly, or you can come gagged."

~

"Where's Ruba?" Talzne asked when Drakne returned to her bedroom.

Drakne gave her a warning growl. *No questions.* She had panted and cursed all her way up the tower, limping along on limbs as wobbly as rotting wheat. "I need you to change my legs. Now."

"Your legs?" Talzne hesitated. "Drakne, your own nature is fighting against you. Whatever I do to you won't hold, not for more than a week or so."

"Why do you care?" She sounded like Ruba. Worrying. Concerned. Blessed Winter, had all that been a lie? The one true friendship she'd ever had? *It doesn't matter. What matters is I can make her pay for it.* "I only need a few weeks. Once I marry the Rat King, none of this will matter." She would share the curse laid upon him by Winter. She would be a lioness forever frozen in body, spirit, and mind, and never need friendship or feelings to make her strong.

Talzne sighed and knelt to rummage through a trunk. She dug out leather belts and a wooden hairbrush. Drakne lay back on the bed; Talzne strapped her feet to the metal frame and wrapped her hands around the other girl's scaled, birdish thighs. "You said you wanted to be a lion because it would make Fydir trust you," said Talzne. "But he's not here. You're not trying to trick him. You're trying to *be* him."

Drakne flinched. It was true, but the shame of it still stung her. Fydir was a monster, a killer who trafficked in souls. Was that what she'd have to become, to escape him? Did she have another choice? "Shut up. You want to see your boy Simon again? Fix my legs, or he'll rot in some damn engine forever."

Fear flickered in Talzne's eyes. "Right. Very well. But this is going to hurt."

"I expect it will." Drakne locked her teeth on the hairbrush handle and waited.

Pins and needles, heat like springtime and then hottest summer, rolled down her legs. Energy burst from her skin like fireworks, painting trails of yellow fur where it licked her. Her dancer's feet prickled. Drakne grimaced as the first joint popped. Then the next. The next. Bones shifted under her skin. Claws erupted from her feet as her toenails broke free in a spray of blood.

The hairbrush shattered in her teeth. Drakne gasped and choked as the splinters cut her tongue. *I will not scream. I will not scream—*

Her femurs twisted out of joint and locked, forward facing, back into her pelvis. The bed frame shattered as she ripped her legs free. Her spine swelled as a black tide rolled down it and burst out of her. For a heartbeat, the world was dizzy darkness.

The next thing she felt was the soaked layers of her petticoat, freezing all about her.

She threw water over me, Drakne thought, before realizing what soaked her legs was her own sweat. Buckets of it, and the reek of something fouler. But it had worked. Golden fur sheathed her legs, shaggy against her haunches, fine against the long bones of her foot where tendons stood in sharp relief. Claws like grappling hooks fanned out from thick, crushing feet. Her tail twitched beneath her skirts, jerking like a limb severed as new nerves sought to map themselves across her brain. She stood and nearly toppled over, the shift in her hips forcing her to lean her weight forward.

I will never dance again. But she'd grow used to it. She could grow used to anything.

~

The baron's manor had no dungeon, so Drakne had chained her prisoner in the abandoned chapel, which had been built in a bygone day when Szpratzian traders still braved the north. Wall panels framed in gilt vines held murals of saints sweeping the holy up into pink-brushed clouds and gleefully tormenting the sinners. The pews had been carted out eons ago, leaving the black-and-white tiled marble floor broken and bare.

The altar was carved in the image of Saint Clovis lofting his tormenting bell, a hundred tiny lions cavorting up and down his robe. She'd tied Ruba to it. Above her head, a cracked stained glass window showed Saint Valchassia spreading owl's wings.

"Where is the Rat King?" Drakne said.

Ruba laughed. Her glasses, cracked from when Drakne had knocked her down, nearly fell off her nose. "You don't know how to find him yet? I thought you were the witty one in your family. Don't rage about. *Think.*"

Think. Frustration boiled inside her. What was she supposed to think about? Her enemies? Her fears? Herself? This strange new girl she had to be, and hated? Rage came easier. *Rage.* Like she truly had become Fydir. He raged at her because she disobeyed him. She raged against him because he'd broken her very soul. *Only I can't rage against him. Not now. Not yet. He'll destroy me.* Her rage had only one place it could go.

Drakne grabbed her prisoner by the neck. Ruba froze under her fist. "Talk. Where is he?"

"Where," Ruba gasped, "is Prince Eugen?"

"Blessed Winter. You and the Rat King are both obsessed with him." She tightened her grip. Ruba's pulse fluttered against her palm like a trapped bird. "I don't have the prince. Nabik does. He's had him ever since they crossed the border. You think we're working together? Why? Because we're family? My family doesn't care for me. I only have you. Only I *never* had you."

Drakne reached back over her shoulder and unslung the case she'd stolen from Fydir's office. The clasps parted smoothly at her touch, revealing the brass-and-iron finishings of her brother's gun. The soul-socket pulsed purple beneath her fingers, calling to her. Sucking at her mind like the aching hollow left by a lost tooth. She ignored it, holding the weapon in one hand and seizing Ruba by her short brown bob cut. A moonbeam shone down on the altar. A bell tower began to chime midnight's golden peal. "Tell me where the Rat King is."

"You wouldn't."

Drakne pushed Ruba closer to the socket. Energy pulsed through the mouse-girl's face and chest. She stiffened. A film of brass built upon her lips, her chin. The fuzz of her cheeks took on a metal shine.

"Try me," Drakne hissed. Loathing bubbled in her belly—for her family, for her friend, and for herself most of all. *How can I be doing this? What choice do I have? What else can I do?* Her own body wished to melt into something feathery, flighty, something Fydir would mock and despise. Her brother's soldiers would ship her back south without her say. "Maybe you'll want to talk once I've taken you for target practice."

Ruba *howled*. Her incisors lengthened, sticking through her lips. Her cheekbones arched, her pale features stretching out behind a sharp chin. The ropes binding her snapped free, morphing in her fist to a staff of black iron laced with mushrooms. Her black gown drew itself up into an elegant dark suit, a waistcoat fastened by buttons of silver skulls.

Drakne swore. The gun fell from her hands. She tried to scramble backward but stumbled on her new feet and fell. Her head struck the floor and rang like a bell. Her skin crawled, imagining his magic already inside her, creeping into her tissue and melting it from her bones.

"My darling Drakne," the Rat King purred, digging his staff into the tender meat below her chin. "It's not every day the mouse catches the lion."

One of the mushrooms on his staff popped open. Blue fluid oozed down on her neck.

At the cool touch, she realized he'd been playing with her all along.

Drakne's heart twisted. She wanted to scream. But she couldn't let this bastard win.

She arched her back, flung her legs upward, and kicked the

staff from his fists. It clattered onto the floor. He swore, summoning green fire to his fists—but Drakne was already standing. Wrapping a clawed hand around the lethal vein in his skinny thigh. Pulling him close.

"You don't scare me," she said.

"I'm not trying to scare you. I'm trying to keep myself out of that damned soul trap!"

Reasonable. She didn't let go. A growl filled her words. "I wouldn't have needed to threaten you if you'd been honest."

"And I wouldn't have needed to deceive you if you hadn't betrayed me to fight for the Empire!"

"I'm not fighting for the Empire. I'm fighting for me, which no one else does. I won't apologize for that."

"Was what I offered you not enough? A place on the stage? The career of your dreams?"

"I want more." Dancing couldn't keep her safe. Only power could.

"You want to be my *wife*?"

Drakne laughed. It jerked and coiled out of her, like some awful sickness extracted from her lungs, and he was laughing, too, sheepishly, like a child with their hand caught in the cookie jar. *Wife.* An absurd little word. Like she was already chasing squalling brats about a kitchen while he read the morning paper and bemoaned his unfair boss.

"I don't want to be a wife," she said, releasing his leg. "I want to be a queen."

"Understandable. Weddings always felt to me like a woman's devil bargain. You bind your fate to a stranger and pray he's not a monster."

A thread of curiosity tugged at her. "What's your true name? Are you a man, or a woman, or something else completely?"

"My name is Ruba Otyeda"—the suffix on the patronymic was gender-neutral: *child of Otye*—"and whether I'm a man, woman, or *elsewise* wanes and waxes like the moon. I appear as I choose, and you may address me as I appear. It matters little to me. The world outside my court hears *Rat King* and thinks *man*, and I let them live in error so I might walk among them and spy."

"You make quite the spy. You convinced me we were friends."

"I *do* consider you a friend. I've known you by letter for years. I like you a great deal. How could I not? A passionate, angry soul, who wears her heart on her sleeve and dances like the dawn sun? Anyone who doesn't want to be near you is a fool." He reached for her, then paused. It was Drakne who closed the distance between them and took his cool, soft hand.

"That's why I hesitate to wed you," he continued. "I told my spies to show you what you'd lose. The happiness you might have in a simple life. The softening of pain that comes with change and time, the growth the curse denies me. I won't keep you from this marriage, not if you truly wish for it. I only want you to know what it's like to dwell in shadows before you choose to join me there."

Where the chapel roof was broken, a meteor blazed silver across the night. Drakne looked up at the moon, which was flanked by the shimmering stars that Szpratzian folktales called Saint Gicha's Veil. Kolznechian folktales said the stars were Winter's sisters, goddesses of suffering and death, and though Winter had banished them from her world, the love they bore each other kept them bound together in the sky.

If even dark goddesses didn't walk the night alone, perhaps Drakne didn't have to either. In another life, with another heart, she might have loved Ruba, all his shadow and drama. But she held so much brokenness inside her, it felt they'd only ever be strangers joining hands to fumble down a moonless road. Paltry. Damaged.

And shockingly necessary. Ruba was all she had left.

She shifted from foot to foot, thinking, and hissed as pain shot through her calves.

"I can numb the ache," Ruba said. "If you'll allow me."

"Absolutely not. What if you give me pig's legs?"

"Then you would have a funny story to tell."

She laughed. "If you must."

His clawed fingers gently brushed the side of her neck. There came a scent like forest earth overturned, a rustle of growing things. Green light simmered in the dirt that poked up from beneath the broken marble, sinking deep into her remade flesh. The ache she carried faded and died.

"Do you know," Ruba said, "that I'd forgotten I could heal?"

There was such agony in his voice. Drakne hesitated, then asked, "Why did you become the Rat King? You don't have to tell me anything private, but . . . how did you feel, once you seized the throne?" *Tell me it was worth it. Please.*

"I felt . . . satisfied." A small smile crept across his face. "Especially once I saw Prince Eugen clapped in pinewood. You see . . ."

He told her a story. A tale about a broken friendship and a sacred relic, about theft, betrayal, bloodshed, heartbreak. A wound on his soul that would not heal. With every word he spoke, her bile rose, fuel for her fury. *Blessed Winter. All we've been taught about the Rat King's rise is wrong.*

"It still feels like yesterday," Ruba said. "The moment won't fade. Won't release me. I'm caught in it, while all of time moves forward."

"But there are worse fates," Drakne said, thinking of the soul-engine. "If that's the price of the throne, I can accept that. It's my fate to choose." No other acceptable fate was open to her. "Now, shall we go find Eugen? He's likely still with my brother. And I could track Nabik's scent anywhere."

Ruba leaned down and brushed his lips to hers. A brief, gentle touch, one that tingled with delicious electricity. "Let's go hunting."

Hand in hand, the betrotheds set after their prey.

CHAPTER THIRTEEN

Colder than the Heart of Blizzards

I *failed him.*

Nabik pulled back from Eugen, just an inch. The ruined garden's snowdrifts shone in the moonlight. The silent statues stood as ice-crusted witnesses to his failings. *True love's kiss. To make him human*—and the thought of those same lips, but soft and yielding, might have made him collapse if he hadn't already been leaning on the nutcracker prince.

"I don't understand," Eugen said, his voice trembling. "That should have worked. I've never felt so deeply about anyone."

Nabik shook his head. "It's my fault. It must be."

"Bravo," purred a low voice, deep with threat. "Even I couldn't fill Eugen's last moments with anguish like *that*." The Rat King stepped through the garden gate, clapping theatrically. Drakne, claws out, stalked behind him. Nabik and Eugen both leapt to their feet. The fox-wizard stretched out his hand, summoned his peppermint-and-mistletoe staff, and hoisted it like a weapon.

He hadn't even sensed his sister coming. Had the Rat King's magic shielded her, or had he let himself get so wrapped up in Eugen, he'd spared no thought for their safety? *Some wizard I am.* He felt for Drakne's wishes, reaching for answers—*Why is she standing next to the Rat King, of all folk?*—and hit a wall of rage. Loss. Fire.

She's in pain. But she's too immutably stubborn to wish she wasn't burning.

"I don't know what you're doing, Drakne," he said. "But it won't make you happy."

She paid him no heed. "Listen. The Rat King told me something you need to know. About Eugen."

"What?" Nabik scoffed. "Why would I trust him?"

"You won't." The Rat King laughed. His eyes flicked from Eugen to Nabik. Glee jumped in his gaze like popping corn. "But you'll trust his shame. You'll feel him wish he'd done everything differently. History has forgotten this tale, but I haven't. The two of us were close once. Back when we were just Eugen and Ruba, two young outcasts in the royal court, struggling to survive a cruel king. We were all each other had. Which is why Eugen trusted me with his greatest secret: that his ancestors had stolen the Heart of Winter."

"I did trust you, Ruba," Eugen said. "And then you stabbed my father."

"No," said the Rat King—*Ruba? The same name as that noblewoman from Malirmatvi?* "That's not how this started. You told me the secret. And you told me what your father said it would do to you. That the stolen Heart froze Kolznechia's kings. Hardened them against any growth and change. You were terrified. You asked me to help you steal it, to restore it to its proper place. We plotted how it might be done together. I even asked my brother—who was only a common stablehand!—to prepare a cart for us so we might carry it back to the Great Mountain." Ruba lifted his black iron staff like a hammer. "And you betrayed us to the king."

"I had to tell him!" Eugen gasped. "He knew I was plotting something. He threatened to beat me black-and-blue—"

"But he didn't," Ruba said. "He didn't need to. You crumbled like a house of cards. You told him everything." His voice went flat, heavy with centuries of echoed pain. "And because I was a wizard, and you were his heir—because we were both too *useful* for him to punish us—he had my brother hanged." His knuckles tightened on the staff. "You are the curse on this kingdom, Eugen. You are the blood of the men who maimed a goddess. You are the man who lacked the courage to save her."

"No," Nabik whispered. "Eugen would never. He's—" The brightest star in his sky. His hope that dawn could come.

"I'm so sorry," Eugen whispered. "I failed you. I betrayed you. I have no right to call myself anyone's king."

No. The cold seeped through Nabik's skin. He glared at the prince. "You hid that from me. My mother and I are risking everything to put you on the throne, and you didn't even tell us why the Rat King hated you to start with!"

"I didn't know what to say!" Eugen answered. "Ruba killed my father and turned me into wood. Then I woke up centuries later, hundreds of miles from my home, and I saw you—" Something clacked in his throat. "You said you needed me to save the kingdom, and I wanted to be everything you and Zolka saw in me. And no one left alive but me and Ruba knew what happened. I thought it would stay in the past." The prince shuddered. "And now... now I've hurt you too."

~

Tears welled in Nabik's eyes. He didn't even seem to notice them blooming. Drakne took a single hesitant step toward her brother, her footfalls hushed by the snow.

"I'm sorry," she said.

He didn't hear her.

"Nabik!" she said, and he jumped. "Listen to us. You and Zolka are making a mistake. What you're doing won't help Kolznechia."

"What else can we do?" he said. "It doesn't matter what Eugen has done. Not in the grand scheme of things. The curse will only end when he takes the throne."

"Are you sure of that?" she said, and saw in his eyes that he wasn't sure of anything.

"This curse is ancient," Ruba said. "It grew and changed when I took power, yes, making beastfolk and spreading the crystal blight, but it's hung over the Teyodets for generations. Enthroning Eugen puts us back where this all began."

"So you're going to... what? Kill him?"

"It could work. Curses love the taste of blood."

"Why don't you just put the Heart of Winter back where it belongs? Maybe that's a better course of action than *murder*."

"Don't you think I've tried? It fights me. Every time I've tried to free the Heart, I see my brother swinging in a noose, over and over, until I forget my purpose, until I want to claw out my own eyes. It wants a tyrant king; wants the people to suffer until we turn away from each other in the coldest times. It wants all memory of Winter's kindness washed away."

"Nabik, listen," Drakne said. "The true problem is so much deeper than we've been taught." How much of the conflict in her own family had bloomed from the seeds planted when her Kolznechian ancestors fled home? This simply *couldn't* be a matter of one wizard, one prince. All this pain grew from roots sunk deep in Kolznechia's heart.

"And Eugen's the problem? After all we know about Fydir and the Rat King, how could you take their side?"

"Why would I take yours?" Why did he need to act like he was always right, especially when she'd just shown him how much he was wrong about? "Saints above. It's like you want to save Kolznechia from *me*."

"No. I'm trying to save you from yourself."

She didn't need him to save her. She needed him to stand beside her. To be her brother, the boy who'd first taught her to dance, the hand she'd held at her mother's grave. But he held back his love from her, like a cruel man tossing bullets in a beggar's bowl. He loved Mama Zolka. He loved this wooden boy. He had served Fydir loyally for so many years.

He had nothing to give her.

Tears brimmed in Nabik's eyes. Not just from his own pain, but also from his sister's. She wanted him to listen. She wanted him to love her. And yes, he wanted that, too, but the future of

Kolznechia and all its people balanced on the fulcrum of this moment, and what he felt and what she felt didn't matter.

He wiped his face on his sleeve and imagined his heart was frozen, five feet deep under ice. His kingdom needed a wizard to fight for it. He could not fail. Not now.

Nabik lowered his staff at Ruba. "Whatever pain you carry, wizards are meant to serve. To care for the weak and vulnerable, to hold the powerful to account. Not to rule. You've betrayed your nature, your people, and Winter herself. This will only end with you torn off your throne."

Ruba spun his staff. A dozen minor longings flitted off his skin. Nabik grabbed one and hurled a rope of black hair at the enemy wizard, snared his hands in ebon locks, and dragged him forward.

"You wish to duel?" Ruba sank a thorned thought into him— dragging up his idle wish for *heat*—and dissolved the hair bonds in a flicker of fire. "I'll show you how a wizard dies."

A roast ham and a dozen meat pies leapt out of the aether and struck Nabik in the chest. He flew backward and hit the garden wall. Pain jolted through his chest. The scent of rosemary and crackling washed over him.

"Don't hurt him!" Eugen shouted.

Drakne snarled, springing through the night like a golden dart. "You're *ours*," she said, and shoved the pinewood prince sideways. He grabbed at her shoulder. They slammed down onto a broken bench in a puff of snowflakes and spores, wrestling in the dim glow of wizard-light. Wood clattered. Claws flashed. Eugen's back arched, straining, as he threw Drakne off him and ran for the Rat King.

"We were friends once!" he shouted. "Stop this!"

Ruba struck the ground with his staff. Dark ice appeared beneath Eugen's feet. The prince slipped and crashed down in a bed of pine needles. Ruba stalked toward him. Nabik snarled. Buttercups and bluebells bloomed up from the snow, grabbed Ruba's limbs, and pulled him to his knees.

"You think you're clever?" Ruba laughed. "A million little tricks and you've never learned to strike at the heart."

"Eugen!" Nabik ran toward the prince as Eugen struggled to stand. "Are you—"

Hot buttered popcorn forced its way out of Nabik's throat in a bursting flood. He doubled over, gasping. *That bastard of a rat.* Nabik stretched out his staff, steering through Ruba's desires like a boatman through a channel. Pushing down past the surface for deeper wishes to fuel sharper spells.

A leather-bound volume of fairy tales, large as Ruba was tall, pounced upon the wizard-king with teeth of hardened parchment. He howled. Playing cards with razor-sharp edges flew at Nabik, screaming like a cloud of bats. He dodged, gasping as they tore through his robe and cut red lines down his side.

I need more. Nabik searched. Pushing through the layers of pain Ruba wove around his heart. Memories rose from him like smoke, laced with wanting. Slogging through snowdrifts in a pine forest, scraping lichen off a boulder with a jawbone. A laughing older boy who told stories as they worked, his face forgotten save a red veil of pain.

His brother. This tender place was twin to all Nabik's own. The wish to have a family once more.

Nabik hesitated. It felt wrong, to turn that wish against him.

216

"I know what you want, little fox." Ruba smiled. The garden pines trembled and cracked. Roots stretched up from the earth. Needles fell to the ground in a puff of snow. The wooden trunks folded in on themselves, carving themselves into joints, painting themselves red and green, with grinning faces and empty eyes. An army of man-size nutcrackers stepped up to ring Nabik, sabers drawn, jaws open. "But he's too cowardly to give you happily ever after."

"Don't listen to him!" Eugen swung a branch, knocking a head off a nutcracker. It dissolved into a scatter of snowflakes. "I'll fight for Kolznechia—I promise—I'll do my best!" His voice cracked. He sounded nothing like a fairy-tale savior. Only someone painfully, shamefully human.

Nabik ducked beneath a saber strike at his head. Skirted a stab at his chest, all his scrapes and bruises burning. *This is how Ruba sees him. Not me.* The Rat King, who'd broken a kingdom to soothe his own pain. So brokenness, Nabik gave him: in the shape of the crystal-lined crevasse that burst open beneath his feet and sent him tumbling ten feet down. Bone cracked. Ruba howled. The nutcrackers vanished into puffs of white.

Nabik grinned, a flash of victory and white fangs.

"No!" Drakne shouted from behind him. "If you hurt him, I'll—"

He whirled around and felt his heart go as cold as a blizzard. Drakne, her eyes wild, held the head of a broken stone dancer aloft. Eugen lay pinned beneath her leonine foot.

"I'll crush him to splinters," she growled.

~

Drakne held death in her fists, and felt nothing but the wind, cold as a tomb. Was this strength? Her heart raced. Her chest seized. Was this power, or panic? *What am I going to do?*

"Please," Eugen whispered. "Not in front of him."

Nabik only stared at her, slack-jawed. "You wouldn't. You *couldn't*." She could have cried, or cheered. At last, he wasn't simply looking past her. And all she'd had to do was threaten someone he loved more.

"You don't know what I can do." She could bring the bludgeon down. Crush him. For Ruba. For Kolznechia. To stab a thousand icicles through Nabik's soul. But *why* could she do it? How could such terrible things come naturally to a girl who just last year had dreamed of justice? *There is no justice. Only rage.*

"Enough, Drakne!" A white owl swooped down from the night sky and landed in a spray of pine needles. Zolka straightened, her wings folding neatly into a cloak of feathers. Horror blossomed in her eyes.

Mother. Something wet and heavy, sob shaped, stuck sideways in Drakne's throat. *Help me. Help me, please.*

"Stop her!" Nabik shouted. Zolka waved her hand, and the stone Drakne held imploded into a puff of feathers. Through her palms they tumbled, down onto the grime-streaked white of her coat. All the mess of her, made terrifyingly real.

"Take your foot off the nutcracker, daughter," Zolka said. "Come with us. We can help you."

"Crush his throat." Ruba clawed his way out of the crevasse. He stood, his suit streaked in earth, and spat out blood. "Kill him, dearest, and let's be away. We have a wedding to plan."

"Wedding?" Nabik swore. "Drakne, you can't—"

"You have no right to stop me." Beneath the pad of her paw, Eugen lay, as still as death. She pressed her weight down. The wood of the prince's neck shuddered and strained. The boy let out a faint moan.

Zolka held out her hand. "Sweetheart, I know you're angry. And that's allowed. But you can't just—"

"You can't just abandon me!" Judgment. Always judgment. Telling her what she *should* do. Never once reaching out to where she was—at the bottom of the pit they'd tossed her down.

"Please," Zolka said. "I'm sorry. I love you."

Those words felt like poison in her ears. A fishhook. A trap. If Zolka loved her, she would have saved her from Fydir. *I hate her. I hate her.* Could Zolka read her wishes like Nabik did? *I wish for you to know I hate you, Mother, you and every choice you've ever made.* Silent tears poured down her mother's cheeks. *Good.* "Your *sorry* doesn't matter. Not anymore."

Drakne kicked Eugen away. The prince coughed, rolling through the snow. She didn't even glance at him; she knew her true target. Drakne shifted her weight back on her haunches and sprang at her mother.

White flashed. A tail flicked. Nabik lunged between them as her claws came down.

Blood sprayed across the snow.

And Zolka screamed.

She flung herself over her son. A wave of force surged out from her chest and knocked Ruba and Drakne backward, sending them tumbling head over heels through the snow. Drakne grabbed the base of the ice-slick fountain, pulled herself up—and slipped again, pounded by a downdraft, as a massive white owl rose into the night. Her wings were as wide as a house, their every beat like a crescendo of drums. Her talons clutched Nabik and Eugen close to her breast.

"He got away." Ruba cursed. "Well. We'll get him after the wedding. We'll have forever to hunt him down."

Down to the cliffside they hurried. From what the wolves had told her, Drakne knew the meeting house was concealed near the base. Zolka's magic shielded it from Ruba, but the people of Stakte were happy tonight, celebrating Fydir's capture. Joy would make them foolish. It was a weakness Drakne lacked.

Two drunks with a lantern stumbled out of a gap in the rocks. Drakne marched forward and knocked both men sprawling in the snow. She ran her clumsy, clawed fingers over the boulders until they grasped the ice-cold handle of the enchanted door, and wrenched it open with such force a hinge splintered.

Screams echoed through the egg-shaped hall as Drakne stalked into the meeting house. Factory workers leapt up from the cooling remains of a feast. Musicians dropped their instruments. Squalling children ducked beneath a table to hide. The air reeked of roast meat and sugar cookies. She waved the scent away from her nose.

Ruba entered behind her, clomping along on iron-toothed snow boots. "Bow for your king," he said. At the sight of his staff, the whole room dropped to their knees. Drakne followed a muffled banging sound to a back closet. She threw open the door. Fydir's eyes met hers above a thick cloth gag, wild with relief.

A slice of her claws, and she freed him. His thick arms wrapped her into a rough hug. "Knew you'd come for me," he grunted. "Whose blood is that, eh?"

Drakne gazed down at her chest. At the crimson splatters and the white feathers. "Nabik's."

He chuckled. "Blessed Winter. I love you."

No, you don't. You only love yourself.

But maybe there was nothing left of her besides what she'd become to survive him.

CHAPTER FOURTEEN

Bride of Kings

Three days after she ripped open her brother's face, Drakne Zolkedna set off to the Crystal Palace for her wedding.

Her autocarriage lacked the fortitude for a journey into the mountains, but Fydir had made his factory assemble him a new vehicle. Her fine new sleigh, fitted with the souls of six micefolk scurrying in brass down the treads, breathed cigarette trails of black smoke as it raced northward up the snowy road, the Eighth Regiment following at a march.

Fydir sat beside her. Perhaps it was only natural for a brother to attend his sister's wedding, but his presence made her nervous all the same. "Are you sure you don't want to stay in Stakte?" she asked him. "What if there's more unrest? What about your factory and your war machines?"

He'd gone up to the factory after she'd freed him. She didn't know what he'd done there, but the next morning, the workers had returned to their stations without question. Without even so much as a noise. Days later, the folk of Stakte still only spoke in whispers around her.

"Stakte is mine. Forever." Fydir grinned. "Who could take it from me? Nabik and his rabble? I'll never understand why Winter gave *him* the gift of wizardry. All that power and he's completely useless."

Once, when she was a small child, Drakne had asked Fydir if he possessed a gift of his own. His face had grown red, and he'd bellowed her out of the room, not even bothering to answer her question. *He has so much power. His army. His might.* And yet it bothered him, that they had magic. One small scrap of something that was their own.

"It's a bit shocking that Lady Ruba turned out to be the Rat King, though," Fydir said. "Not sure how I feel about that."

"Are you sure you don't mind me marrying someone you were . . . attached to?"

He shrugged. "I'll have no trouble securing a wife with my sister on the throne. No woman of taste could refuse me."

No woman of taste. Was that an insult aimed at Ruba? Drakne considered, and let it slide. Why would she fight with him now?

The light shifted to an eternal twilight haze as the sleigh bore them onward. Oaks changed to pines, which changed to slender, bowed hollies made of polished crystal with sparkling ruby seeds. Snowfae and beastfolk watched from the roadside, slipping through the rainbows cast by prismatic leaves, scraping lichen and low mushrooms from the rock. Villages of pink and purple hide tents fell behind them.

Soon, one-room homes of gingerbread and white buttercream mortar stuck up through the gemstone trees. *The lower city. Ruba grew up here.* Narrow snowpack trails split off the main road, winding into smoky groves and shadowed caverns. Beastfolk struggled along under heavy packs; carriages laden with velvet-wrapped packages jingled past them. The air smelled of snow and sugar; somewhere a singer sang and somewhere an infant wept. Hollow, fearful eyes watched their sleigh. Watched the bound souls work the gears.

"It's not every day they get to see a queen." Fydir grinned. He waved to the crowds. Beastfolk turned away from him, their tails whipping back into their burrows. His face fell. His fist tightened on the handle of his gun case. "Little cowards. They'll make good engine fuel, eh?"

Drakne stiffened. She felt the phantom tug of the soul-socket pulling her in. Trapping her. Her heart raced. Her palms went damp with sweat. *Soon. I'll be safe soon.* Nothing else mattered.

They turned a bend in the icy road. The Great Mountain rose to pierce the sky, a sharp, steep lone peak that cut out of the earth like a knife, its sides covered in snow. *The womb of Winter, they call it.* A waterfall poured off its back into a calm blue lake. On its shore stood the Crystal Palace, whose six clear glassy towers lifted gold-leafed conical spires high above its great halls. The sleigh and the soldiers sped toward it

The crowds grew dense as they drew nearer. Servants and tradesmen leapt from the sleigh's path; carts laden with rugs and statuary pulled off the narrow road to make way. Drivers stared and cursed. The gates, barred in gold worked into thin harp springs, rolled back with an E-major chord to admit them.

Small wonder Ruba captured it with just a few spells, she thought, dismounting in a courtyard lined in ice sculptures and poisonous poinsettias. *All glitter. No fortifications. You could bring down a dynasty with a slingshot and some rocks.*

Ruba, clad in a garnet robe and his male form, met them on

the sparkling sapphire entry steps, flanked by two dozen rat guards in livery. He caught Drakne's gloved hand and helped her from the carriage. "Darling Drakne. Lord Fydir. A pleasure to welcome you both to my humble palace."

"It's made of *sugar*," she whispered as they entered the keep, grudgingly enchanted. Dyed candy crystals and sheets of molded butterscotch covered the walls, shaping patterns of singing birds, waving wheat, and blooming wildflowers. Mosaics of golden sesame brittle covered the high-arched ceiling.

"The curse turned the forest to stone," Ruba said. "But this palace has been sugar since it was built. The Teyodets made their wizards conjure their palace out of children's dreams."

Drakne tried to remember what she'd dreamed of as a child. The center stage of the royal ballet. All the lights on her. A fuzzy fantasy of crowds tossing roses at her feet. *All the dreams that matter are right here.* "When do we marry?" *When am I crowned?*

"At sunrise tomorrow." He squeezed her hand. "Vows, coronation ceremony—it will be a dreadfully long day. And a dreadfully long night, if you'd like it to be."

He spoke like molten caramel. Drakne tried to summon some delicious shivers. She was about to marry a king who'd set her on a throne and ensure neither hunger nor Fydir nor Winter herself could touch her. She was about to marry Ruba, who was grand and wicked and the truest friend she had.

But all she had inside was aching. It went deeper than the bruises of their fight in the garden. Like she'd walked a dozen miles and wanted to drop dead in the streets. Like ice had swallowed her up the moment she put her claws through Nabik's face.

I struck my brother. I could have killed him. Part of her trembled in confusion to remember her own rage. Fydir stood beside her now, and he'd hurt her far worse than Nabik could. Where was her anger for him? *I have no reason to fight him. Not on the very precipice of victory.* But this victory tasted like ashes.

All you are, when you swear your vows, shall remain part of you forever.

"Here, come see. My inventions." Ruba led them into a smaller, interior courtyard paved with glass tiles cut like snowflakes. The scents of a thousand spices bloomed wild in the air. Traders called greetings in a dozen tongues—*human* traders, each cloaked in something like a shimmering blue film, touting crates of fabric, boxes of jewelry, slabs of marble. "The Hall of Portals."

Archways lined the courtyard walls, each filled with a single great blue bubble—and each bubble held a window to another land. Pink sand beaches under bright blue skies, a green plain stretched out before a white obelisk, a city built inside a shining silver leviathan. "It clings to every person who passes through," Drakne said. "It's . . . the air of their homeland, sealing them away from the curse?"

"Precisely!" Ruba said. "I get all the benefits of international trade, none of the worry I might cause a diplomatic incident giving an Anyiri artificer whiskers. I've hired dance troupes from fifty nations to perform at the wedding feast. You'll love it, Drakne."

I don't think I could watch anyone dance without hating myself. She didn't want to think of what she'd given up. Quickly, she changed the subject. "What does Kolznechia trade to the outside world?" If she was going to be a successful queen, she needed to know how he kept the books.

"At present? Mostly crystal." Ruba laughed. "How do you think I've fed Znaditin all these years? Alas, the price of the exchange has grown steep. We have too much crystal, and our need for food is dire indeed."

"Kolznechia could be rich, if we sold lumber to the south," said Fydir. "And if we opened factories near the border. With soulengines, we wouldn't need to waste a penny training the labor."

"No soul-engines," Ruba said. "They disgust me."

Drakne felt a flicker of guilt. She remembered shoving Ruba toward the socket of Fydir's gun. *I scared the Rat King. Me.* And the memory clung to her like mold spots. "It's the way of the future," said Fydir. "We can't outcompete the Empire if we don't modernize."

"But why must you compete with them? You have your land and title. I've confirmed Stakte and its silver mines as yours. I'm marrying your sister. What more could you want?" Ruba shook his head. "You're a hard man to read. I can never quite tell what would make you happy."

"*Happy* is a word you only hear in fairy tales. Me, I want my new home to prosper. Drakne, don't you want that too?"

She flinched. The promise she'd made Talzne and Ruba on their northward journey came back to her. *When I'm queen, I'll ban the use of soul-engines in Kolznechia.* But her power felt thin as sprinkled sugar under his gaze.

She would stand up to Fydir. Tomorrow. Today, she would compromise and change the subject. Drakne cleared her throat.

"Fydir. Ruba. Our first priority should be securing the throne. Both against Prince Eugen and any further Szpratzian aggression." There. Something they could all agree on.

Ruba nodded. "We can talk economics once the pinewood prince is dead. I want to mount his wooden head on the grand staircase newel post. The left side, I think. I don't even care if it wrecks the symmetry of the hall."

Lord Maznun, the old cat who wove memories, and Lady Eba, the boar who spun time—who was apparently his wife—joined them for a welcome feast. In a hall lined with mirrors, each framed with little gilded songbirds, they dined on fresh mango and tender veal. Every brush of Maznun's fingers sent another silver-clad beastfolk lord spinning in a dizzy oblivion of false memory. Drakne and Fydir both declined his drugging touch, though they drained their wine bowls dry.

"With a gift like yours, you must have had a wizard in your family," Fydir said to Lady Eba as she aged a glass of wine with a tap of her hoof-hand.

"My father," said Eba. "He allied with Ruba and earned a title for his trust. Zolka killed him in a wizard's duel ten years back."

Should I apologize? Or subtly gloat about my family's strength? Court games reminded Drakne of her days at school. If she offended Eba, would the boar-woman stuff a rotten onion under her mattress? She took the middle ground. "If only Zolka had stayed with us in the south. Then neither of us would have felt such a loss."

"Loss is inevitable." Eba shrugged. "Tragedy has long shrouded Kolznechia. The Szpratzian invasion is only the latest incarnation of our doom."

"Doom?" Fydir laughed. "Come now, I've brought you a queen. I've turned my army to your side. Mark my words—one day, you'll think my invasion was a blessing."

Maznun shook his head, his neck and shoulders drooping under the weight of his own gray fur. "I can conjure a hundred different memories. Yet even I can't turn a war into a blessing. Violence leaves scars across the mind. It matters not if they were carved by righteous causes. They still bleed."

Palace servants swarmed about them, garbed in crisp green uniforms. A flutist played in an alcove, the gilded songbirds on the mirrors opening their little throats in harmony. Golden platters glittered in the candlelight, meat laden, juicy and hot. Drakne drank wine bowl after wine bowl until a belch pounded out of her throat. "You're disgusting," Ruba said admiringly, clinking his bowl to hers. Red slopped onto their wrists.

Drakne downed her dregs, drowning in the taste of cherries. "At least I can still walk. Fydir will need to be carried back to his room."

"Now, now," Fydir said. "Respect to your elders."

He'd spoken teasingly, but Drakne's breath still hitched in fear. "Oh. I'm sorry."

Ruba gave her an odd look. Drakne dodged their gaze. To say more felt harder than feeding a family by scraping lichen off rocks. She couldn't reveal why she feared Fydir without uncovering her scars, and she wanted them to stay buried. To pretend they were nothing but shadows.

How could she find it easier to claw Nabik open than to tell her own betrothed the truth?

The next morning, as darkness still cloaked the land, a small army of black-gowned maids garbed Drakne in silk as yellow as butter, embroidered with peonies and bluebells. Her cheeks they painted white; her eyes they lined in black. For jewelry, they draped her in gemstones and crowned her with a fan of diamonds. Her neck ached by the time she reached the small tent off the courtyard where she'd wait for the processional.

"Your brother's come to see you, my lady," said a maid. "To wish you luck on your wedding day."

The lion-lord swept in past the tent curtain, clad in his best dress uniform: the red velvet with gold-trimmed epaulets and medallions, crisp black trousers cut at his furry knees. "Congratulations, Drakne." He pulled her into a hug. Drakne pressed her face into his shoulder, willing herself to feel *something*. "Blessed Winter, I'm so proud of you."

Those words should have meant something to her. She and Fydir shared so much: flashing tempers, a hunger for attention, wild joys and melancholies. Now he offered her the love he'd ripped away all those years ago. A love that felt like safety. For a cost.

"What can I do for you?" she asked cautiously.

Fydir gestured to the maids. They ducked out of the tent. When he and Drakne were alone, he forged ahead smoothly. "I must have my soul-engines. The war machines I'm building in Stakte require them. It's critical for my plan."

"What plan?"

"With my regiment in the north, Malirmatvi is undefended. We can secure the city—all its factories, all its gold—for Kolznechia. For us."

Her stomach crawled. *War. More of it.* The pavilion tent seemed to close tight around her. The gems on her head and neck seemed to push her down.

"You're not usually this quiet." Fydir leaned in. The tent candles turned the edges of his mane to gold. "Drakne, I've supported you with this whole marriage plot. You *owe* me."

"We'll speak after the wedding," she said.

"That's not an answer."

"We'll work out ... a compromise." Drakne hated how weak that word felt on her tongue. She just needed him gone. "I promise. You'll be happy. Now, go. I need a minute alone to finish preparing."

Smiling like a child with a Yuleheigh gift, Fydir ducked out of the tent. At Drakne's command, two soldiers ushered in Talzne. The snowfae girl's fingers trembled as she tightened her spell. Shaping graceful arms into crushing claws and nimble feet to break and trample. Pain shot through Drakne's limbs. She bit her lip, willing herself not to sweat through her makeup.

All you are, when you swear your vows, shall remain part of you forever.

"Thank you," Drakne said. "When the ceremony is done, I'll put plans in motion for our journey south. To free your boy Simon from the soul-engines."

Talzne shook her head. Heavy, bruise-like rings lay beneath her eyes. Her skin looked thin as paper. "What if Fydir doesn't let you?"

"He'll have no choice," said Drakne, and she tried to say it strong. Like Fydir hadn't written fear of himself into her bones. "I'll be queen. What can he do to stop me?"

"All he has to do is say no." The snowfae girl sighed. "I've stood by you, Drakne, while you and your brother did terrible things. I thought you could help me. But you can't even help yourself. I know how he scares you. If you can't face him now, you never will."

Drakne flinched. She couldn't find anything more to say to that.

"Really? Now you go quiet? Blessed Winter, I've wasted my time on you." Talzne turned on her heel and walked from the tent.

"My lady?" A maid stepped inside and placed a bouquet of poinsettias in Drakne's arms. "It's time."

Drakne buried her blank visage behind the flowers as she stepped into the grand main courtyard.

A hundred thousand white rose petals covered the frozen earth. Music swelled from the strings of a twenty-beast orchestra, a slow and lumbering dirge better fit for the funeral of an unliked cousin than the wedding of a king. Nobles in silver gowns and glittering tuxedos rose from their benches, turning as one. Whispers swept their polished ranks, gossip swelling as scarlet reptilian eyes, mole eyes ringed in rhinestones, pale feline eyes fell on her, sharp and targeted as bullet fire. Prettily they all shimmered, but they reminded her of nothing but her cruelest schoolmates.

Do I really want to spend the rest of my life dealing with them?

At the top of the aisle, Fydir hooked an arm through hers. As one, they started down.

The orchestra pushed up the tempo. Horns and drums and

creeping cellos all played a military march. A sweat sheen built on Drakne's chest and armpits, prickling like feathers about to break free. Beneath a great crystal pine, Ruba waited for them atop a raised dais. In female visage, she wore a cloth-of-gold suit with tight trousers, her jacket as ruffled as a full skirt.

As they reached the wedding arch, Ruba gave her a hesitant nod. Her glasses almost slipped off her nose. "Drakne," she said. "Do you still want this?"

Want. A small and awful word. So close to *hope*, and hope required a *future*. Raw hunger could only sustain her for so long. The fuel she'd made of her own combustion was fast sputtering. She wanted Ruba, the smooth dark hair, the menacing power, the winks behind her glasses, the too-long skittering fingers. Wanted the embrace of someone who knew and understood pain. Someone who could hold hers.

"If you do this," Ruba said, "there's no going back. This is who you are, and who you shall be forever."

She would never dance again, and never want to. She would always be the lion she'd become for Fydir, the lion who'd struck Nabik with her claws. How could she be a good queen if she couldn't defy one man? How could anyone love her if she carried such cruelty in her flesh?

If I do this, I will always be afraid. And afraid on a throne was better than afraid in Fydir's power. But she didn't want to be afraid forever.

Drakne hesitated.

"Enough," Fydir said, and turned to face the crowd. "Let me tell you a fairy tale, people of Kolznechia, and let you know it to be true."

Thunder rumbled in his voice. Lending it a strange new dimension. A certainty. *Enchantment*. As one, the gathered beast-folk stilled. Twitched their ears toward him, to listen. Human guests, clad in foreign finery and blue films of magic, murmured nervously to one another. Some ducked out toward the Hall of Portals. Eba and Maznun linked arms and slipped out the back. *What's going on?*

"Once upon a time," Fydir said, "a poor boy in a great city sought his fortune. He was strong and handsome, golden-haired, but his greatest gift was the magic in his blood. A power that let him command any beast of the field or forest to do his bidding. The nobles in the city made him tend their horses and the crown prince made him bid mice drown themselves for sport, but it wasn't until he caught a great duke's eye that he learned to make birds his spies and dogs his soldiers. Holding his pagan magic a careful secret, the boy grew to high manhood at the Empire's heart—and returned to his homeland to rule."

Do you have a gift? Drakne had asked Fydir once, and always wondered. Now she knew. He lacked Nabik's wizardry, envied it—but small as his own power was, the right hands could make it monstrous. *Beast-speaker. Charmer of animals and wild things.* A useful gift, for a spy. And in a country draped in fur and feathers, his words held more power than Winter herself.

"No longer will you decry me as an invader," Fydir said. "To-gether, we will modernize this backward land and build an in-dustrial empire to rival Szpratzia's. I am your king, you are my subjects, and I command you to love and fear me with the ado-ration due legends!"

"What's going on?" Ruba said as the crowd cheered. "What are you doing?"

Fydir grabbed her arm. "You will marry me and become my queen. Your throne is now mine." As shock flared in her eyes, he added, "Smile. This is our wedding day."

And Ruba smiled a ghoulish grin.

Together, they spoke the binding words and dusted each other with grains of coarse sugar. Ruba drank from the wedding chalice, then held it up to Fydir. She smiled so widely that the wine dripped through her open lips. "Winter bless the king!" cried the crowd as Fydir took his sip, and "Winter bless you, my lady!" The new-made queen placed a crown of golden sunbursts on Fydir's brow. He lifted his arms, and the crowd cheered as a dozen white doves streaked across the sky.

Drakne stepped down from the wedding arch and tore off her headdress. Diamonds tumbled to the stone. Black feathers pricked up from her hair like crocuses poking through snow. Talzne's glamour, wearing off at last. She shook her head. It felt like casting off slumber. *I'm not a lion. I was never truly a lion.*

Good.

Because she could still change. Not be the girl she'd been that terrible night in Stakte.

Maybe there was hope for her yet.

Under Sugared Spires

CHAPTER FIFTEEN

Useless Love

Znaditin, capital of Kolznechia

The Great Mountain stood tall above the city of Znaditin, with a glacier saddling its back and a deep, sapphire-blue lake at its foot. The glimmering Crystal Palace rose from its shores. Gemstone pines ran from the castle gates to the glacier's base, past the city's borders and down the southern road, where the huts and tents of lichen foragers wove about the shining trees. The hulking brass shapes of a dozen soul-engines, their pipes belching smoke, trundled past them. The sky was cloudless, and the air was still. All the city held its breath.

The snowfae made their home atop the mountain's glacier, where the emerald aurora swirled each night and the cutting wind drove off outsiders. The walls of their fortress were made of rough-hewn gingerbread, mortared by frozen buttercream. A palisade of sharpened peppermint sticks and hewn crystal poked up beneath it. Peanut-brittle buildings shingled in gumdrop shavings lined the grounds. The scent of rising blizzards blotted out all but the faintest trace of sugar from the air.

Nabik lay abed and dreamed that sweetness was his own flesh rotting. He woke up tucked into a cot, inside a softly lit room with chocolate walls, his face swathed in bandages.

"All's well," Zolka said, her hand on his brow. "Don't worry, child. All's well."

Nabik laughed ruefully. Pain shot through his jaw. He clutched at his cheek. All was broken. Hopelessly so.

He didn't know what to do next.

"Where am I?" he murmured.

Zolka explained. Her long, labored flight through the darkness, up the northern road, over the sleeping city. "The snowfae don't trouble with the business of kings, but they'll keep us safe, for now. Blessed Winter, do we need it."

"What?" *We're not supposed to need protection. We're supposed to be protectors.* "What happened?"

Zolka took a deep breath. "A snowfae girl just arrived from the Crystal Palace. She has ... hard news. Do you remember how skilled Fydir was with dogs and horses?"

What? Why did she ask? "After you left, he found work in the city stables. He could soothe horses quicker than anyone. The archduke saw him. Recruited him ..."

There was a terrible darkness in her face. The sort that hinted at terrible truths. "The archduke recruited him to spy. Because he has a gift. He can make animals obey him."

No. Nabik froze. It made sense, it did. Why else would a poor Kolznechian be offered so important a role? *Oh, Fydir.* His heart ached for his brother. Whatever Fydir was now, he'd been only a boy when the archduke had found him. And the nobleman had used him most cruelly.

Zolka spoke of a wedding, of vows extracted by vicious magic, of noble guests fleeing and common servants ensnared. The Rat

King's banners had been torn down and Fydir's had been hung up in their place; three footmen had slipped on icy ramparts and fallen to their deaths in the rush to replace them. The Rat King's soldiers had barricaded themselves in their barracks; war machines had torn through the walls and Fydir had forced them all to kneel with one word. Even now, soul-engines trundled through the narrow city streets, crushing what they did not care to steer around, playing wax-cylinder recordings of Fydir's voice. Binding the beastfolk to love him with their hearts and serve him with their hands.

"I see." Nabik had never felt so terribly small as he did then. Was this what Fydir had wanted all along? Had he only been biding his time until his soldiers were far enough transformed that they wouldn't turn on him? How could someone Nabik had once loved with all his heart hold so little love inside him? "What about the people of Stakte?"

"I cast a scrying spell. The factory's up and working. But Nivni and the workers are alive and, as near as I could tell, unharmed."

"He must have forced them back to their stations." Nabik tightened his fists. Nivni and her crew had fought so hard to free Stakte. And now they, too, were but pieces in Fydir's great war machine. He wanted to run back to Stakte and burn the factory to ashes. He wanted to charge into the Crystal Palace and toss Fydir off his cursed and stolen throne. More than anything, he wanted to disappear.

"Careful," Zolka said as he sat up on the cot. His head spun from the sudden shift in position. "You're still quite hurt. You're lucky you didn't lose an eye."

Drakne. She struck me. And part of him felt he deserved it. How long had her feet taken to heal, that night he'd swapped her dancing shoes and left her blistered? The bond between them never had. He'd failed, utterly and completely. Both as a wizard and as a brother.

The gauzy curtain that sectioned off his small sickroom slid aside. Eugen stepped into the chocolate nook, wooden footsteps echoing strangely on the sugar floor. "You're awake!" He grinned, then hesitated. "Blessed Winter, Nabik, I'm so sorry. About everything in Stakte. Everything I kept from you."

"Did you tell Zolka about it?"

"He did," she said. "We've been sitting here together. Looking after you."

They truly care for me. Warmth flickered to life in the pit of his stomach. Perhaps he shouldn't have needed their care. Perhaps he should have done everything with Drakne differently so she wouldn't have—*No. Don't be silly. It's not your fault she struck you.* Part of him wished it was. Because if he had brought it on himself, he could ensure it never happened again. *Eugen and Zolka care for me. Even when I fall flat on my face. But what's the use of their love if Fydir crushes Kolznechia beneath his boot?*

Nabik took a deep breath. "Eugen, what passed between you and Ruba is your affair." He understood why Eugen had betrayed the plan to steal the Heart of Winter. He understood why Ruba hated him. Even the sweetest souls had their fears and flaws. He could accept that.

What frightened him was that wizards were meant to have answers. Eugen was meant to be the answer. The leader Kolznechia needed. But it had been Nabik and Zolka leading him forward. Eugen had gone along, desperate to please them. *Is he truly ready to be king? Will putting him on the throne make anything right?*

"And?" Eugen asked. Waiting on him.

"Forgive me," Nabik said. "I don't quite know what to do."

"How do you feel?"

"It doesn't matter."

"It does," said Zolka. "For your own sake. We wizards have our heads full of other folk's wishes. Even the greatest of us can lose track of who we are, and Fydir spent years trying to mold you into what he wished."

"So long as I can be a great wizard, I don't care. *Myself* is a small sacrifice for a whole kingdom—"

"If there's sacrifices to be made, I'll make them. You are my son, my student, my responsibility. My children have suffered enough for this country." Zolka shook her head. "You don't have to talk to me or Eugen. But you need to talk to someone."

"I will," he lied. "Later."

"Very well. Get some rest. I'll deal with—"

"Actually," Eugen said, "Queen Genna wants me to bring him to the audience hall."

Zolka sighed. "At least let me take off his bandages."

With slow, steady hands, she unpeeled the bandages from his face. A mirror appeared in her hand. She lifted it to show him: three red lines running from the middle of his cheek to his chin. As he turned his head, they prickled and tugged. He shivered at the sight. Soldiers had scars, yes, but he was enjoying the new shape of himself. He didn't wish to see it marred.

"The snowfae might be able to pretty that up if you asked

them," Eugen said. "But I'd wait a while. They don't presently think of you in the best regard. The snowfae who brought word of Fydir—her name is Talzne, and she knows you from Malirmatvi."

Nabik swore, buried his face in his hands, and swore again from the pain. The past snapped at his heels like a hungry dog, hounding him even to the icy edge of the north. He swung his legs off the bed. "I'll speak with the snowfae. They have a right to hold me to account."

Zolka nodded. "I'll be right there if you need me. Take heart, Nabik. I love you dearly."

Why?

With a wave of his hand, Nabik summoned a fresh robe of eggshell cream, fur-trimmed, with mistletoe embroidered along the hems. His long hair pinned itself at the back of his neck with a holly comb. With a flick of his finger, he banished the smell of travel and sickness. He felt like a wizard again, or at least he looked like one, and that was enough. He would face his consequences.

A pair of elk antlers framed the doors of the towering main hall, twelve feet from tip to tip. Nabik held himself straight as he entered, Zolka and Eugen following close behind him. The hall was strewn with stools and benches; fire danced in a grand brass brazier at its heart. Dozens of snowfae milled about. Some were cleaning fresh-caught fish and pounding mushrooms into powder. Some were playing at a game of ring toss and passing around a pipe. Each looked different from her sister, in height, age, or color, their hair like ice or snow. But all of them, when their eyes found Eugen, frowned and whispered. *Heart thief. God reaper.*

Queen Genna sat on a wooden throne, its backpiece set with caribou teeth, mammoth ivory, and whale jawbones. Her gaze fell on Nabik as he bowed before her, and behind her violet eyes lay her cool wish for justice. He wondered if she might find him more beautiful as a puddle of snowmelt.

"Nabik Zolkedan," she said. "Our sister Talzne has told us quite the story about you."

The crowd shifted. Nabik looked back over his shoulder and saw Talzne. Her face was weathered, tired, a bit smug. She was now several inches taller than him.

"I'm sorry," Nabik told her. "I shouldn't have detained you. You were only trying to help folk."

Talzne's smile widened. She looked as if she wanted to rub things in a bit. But her queen continued. "Talzne knew what she risked, dabbling in mortal politics. We keep ourselves separate for good reason. You cannot be trusted." She gave Eugen a hard look. "It was the Teyodet kings who stole the Heart of Winter and plunged the goddess into unending slumber."

"That was centuries before he was born," Nabik said. "It wasn't his fault."

"Some fault is mine," Eugen said. "I had a chance to free her, and failed. I could have stopped all this from coming to pass."

"Go on." Genna tapped long purple-painted fingernails on her chin. "I will hear your account of it, boy."

Eugen nodded. "It all started when my father told me the Heart of Winter was hidden inside the Teyodet throne—"

Shocked whispers spread through the room. Genna leaned forward. "In the throne? That's where they put it? The nerve."

"I told the secret to a friend of mine. A young court wizard, born to a poor family of lichen farmers—Ruba Otyeda."

"Otyeda?" Nabik noted the neutral patronymic. "Are they even a *he*, then?"

Eugen shrugged. "It changes with whatever form they take."

So it was the same Ruba from Malirmatvi. Nabik thought it over. *How would it feel, if I could change like that?*

"Ruba and I," Eugen continued, "had a plan to take back the Heart and restore it to its rightful place beneath the Great Mountain. But my father grew suspicious of us. When he interrogated me, I betrayed us. Ruba's brother was hanged for it."

Nabik felt Eugen wish with all his heart he had been braver. "You had good reason to fear him," the fox-wizard whispered.

"I remember Kutreus," Genna said. "A monster of a man. But you shouldered the fate of Winter of your own free will, Prince Eugen. You shouldn't have begun what you were not prepared to finish." She frowned. "I am interested to hear that the Rat King acted out of vengeance. That makes a great deal more clear."

"Such as?"

"Long ago, before her heart was stolen, Winter told me a story. A rival goddess had blamed her for the death of her child and put a curse upon her world. An evil that fed off violence and hurt, taking the natural order of life and twisting it. Only the power of Winter—only the care we showed each other in the coldest times—could hold it back. I thought it was merely a parable." She looked to Eugen. "Did Ruba ever go beneath the Great Mountain?"

Eugen nodded. "They went looking for the place Winter slept. What they found was an old temple, full of silver pillars and beacons of ceaseless rainbow light, all overgrown by roots of violet crystal. Ruba broke some away and brought them back to the palace for study. I remember . . . the roots spoke to me. In my mind. They told me I should kill my father for what he'd done to me. They said they would *help*. I was horrified."

"And so it goes," said Genna. "And when Ruba's brother died, I imagine the roots made them the same offer."

"Ruba stabbed my father with one." Eugen shivered. "In front of the whole court. I remember running forward, grabbing them, trying to wrench them both apart. The root sank into the throne. Into the Heart. My fingers turned to wood. Fur bloomed on Ruba's face. They looked at me with fear in their eyes, and—and then I was in Malirmatvi. Dancing with Drakne Zolkedna."

Genna nodded. "This curse has grown beneath Kolznechia since the dawn of our world. When the Heart was stolen—when mortals built kingdoms and empires and industries—it fed off our pain. It began to grow. It found a vessel in Ruba for its ultimate goal: to pierce the Heart. To not just weaken Winter, but to take control of her, to use her and all her power to destroy the world she loves. I have journeyed beneath the Great Mountain. Her temple lies in ruins. Putting the Heart back will not save her. We must free her from the crystalline corruption that has filled her. Only then can she break the curse that binds us all."

Break the curse. Nabik's heart sped. This was what they needed. "So I'll go get the Heart. Right now. I'll—"

He turned. Pain shot through his face. With a sickening gasp, he bent double, clutching his cheek.

Feathers rustled behind him. Zolka put a hand on his shoulder. "You won't be getting the Heart today. Back to bed."

Nabik shook her off. "It has to be now. I have to—"

"Genna and I will work out a plan. Go get some fresh air. Walk around a bit."

Low and shaky, Nabik bowed to the snowfae queen. Then he slipped back outside, sliding through the ranks of snowfae, stepping out into the sparkling, noon-lit day. The cool wind numbed his cheek, but not the fire blazing inside him. *Drakne. Winter. Curses.*

All my mistakes. Everything I can't get right.

Tail twitching beneath his robes, snow crunching under his feet, he crossed the small fortress and peered out over the peppermint palisade. Sunlight winked off the crystal-and-gumdrop rooftops of Znaditin. Roasting meat and sugar scent rose from the city. New banners hung from the walls of the Crystal Palace, green with the image of a roaring gold lion. The glimmering marvel of a castle seemed so small he could cradle it in his hands. *Is Drakne there now? Blessed Winter, keep her safe.*

"How's your face?" Eugen said softly, leaning on the rail beside him.

"It's fine." It hurt, but everything hurt.

"No. It's not." Eugen reached for Nabik's shoulder. Nabik turned away and paced circles before the palisade. "Nabik. Please. At least—tell me where we stand. We kissed!"

"I don't know where we stand," Nabik said. "Whatever that kiss did, it still wasn't enough to make you human." *Winter. She can break the curse. If we free her.*

"I didn't kiss you to break a spell. It would have been nice, certainly, but I kissed you because I wanted to kiss you." Eugen hesitated, then reached out. Nabik let himself lean into Eugen's palm. The prince swept a loose lock of Nabik's hair back into his comb. "You know what I want. You always do. But what do you want from me, Nabik Zolkedan? Say it. It's yours."

Nabik's heart twisted. He didn't know what to say. How to face this. *Love. Beautiful, useless love.* Everything he felt was useless. Kolznechia needed his help, not his heart. Eugen and Zolka could try to comfort him, open him up, rifle through his feelings like thieves in a lockbox. All they could do was distract him. He had work to do. His kingdom needed its wizard.

"Could you fetch me a blanket?" he said. "I'm a bit cold."

"Right away." Eugen turned and set off back through the snow.

Once more, Nabik fixed his eyes on the Crystal Palace.

He had to find the Heart of Winter. Now.

CHAPTER SIXTEEN

The Dance of Owl and Swan

The pain struck the moment she changed her wedding gown for a dress of sensible black wool.

Drakne sent the palace maids to find Talzne. They returned with nothing but a pillow for her to scream in. She curled up with it in a corner of the stable as her lion's legs contorted, joints snapping and popping backward. Her hair fell out in great downy waves as feathers spread like a cap down her head and back. Her tail retreated, wormlike, into her spine and flourished out again as a knot of feathers. Curses, blasphemies, and pleas for mercy rose from her lips as the snowfae spell shredded itself.

At last, all was still, and a sweat-streaked Drakne was left to face the world she'd created.

Fydir's speech at the wedding hadn't bound her. She bore him no love, and certainly not the respect he'd demanded. She wasn't fully a swan, not yet. Until the transformation advanced further, Fydir couldn't control her. But the day would come when he could bid her smile, and she would gladly kneel to kiss his ring.

I should leave. Now. Talzne was gone. Eba and Maznun had fled. But Drakne didn't know what to do. She felt as if she were sleepwalking.

The throne room at the keep's heart had been built large enough to host whole orchestras. Mirrors covered the walls, their brass frames worked in the shape of a musical score. The floors of frozen white fudge were marbled through with brown veins dark as forest roots. The ceiling rose in two hexagonal domes, painted with the ruddy faces of ancient Teyodet kings hunting foxes through a lively green wood. At the back of the room, a fluttering velvet curtain concealed a stage.

And the throne itself rose atop a dais. The gold—no, chocolate covered in gilt foil—was molded in the shapes of roaring lions and howling wolves, mice and hares and pigeons crushed under their claws. Great roots of amethyst crystal pierced through its back and coiled about its feet. Rage and malice seemed to leak from the shining surface, and the air felt slightly colder whenever she drew near. Fydir sat atop it with a satisfied smirk, the only chair in the room large enough to fit his broad frame.

If you share my throne, you'll share my curse. You'll never age, grow, or change. You'll always be as you are, the moment you speak your wedding vows. Fydir had forced the marriage and seized the throne, and the curse that held Ruba would claim him too. But she bore him no sympathy—that, she would save for his subjects. What might her brother do with *forever*?

Fydir leaned down from his throne, addressing the handful of nobles who hadn't escaped him. "Kolznechia has slumbered, mild and pleasing, while Szpratzia built its empire." He drained his wineglass, then tossed it away. Servants rushed to clean up the shards. A girl gasped as she cut her hand. "Now we rise to craft our own. I'll need guns and bullets. My soldiers will need uniforms and fresh socks. The time has come for you to open up your pockets and provide for the growth of our great nation. Ruba, tell them what you told me."

"The curse affects every inch of land under Kolznechian control," Ruba said. She sat at the foot of the dais that held Fydir's throne, on a step stool upholstered in gold-flecked reindeer skin. Fydir had ordered her not to use her magic without his permission, and her voice trembled now, vulnerable and unsure. "When Fydir conquers Malirmatvi, all its people will become beastfolk. They will be transformed into his loyal subjects."

Horror pumped through Drakne's veins, as burning hot as engine oil. *He'll be able to control them.* Fydir could *do* it. Make war on the south. Bind every soul he conquered to his will. Rule forever and ever, or at least until the crystal blight devoured every last green thing in their land. He would bend the world before him. With his carelessness, with his cruelty, he would *kill* it.

"Drakne," said Fydir, looking to her. "I barely recognized you." He laughed. "A goose girl. How fitting. I should have known you weren't a true lioness the moment you hesitated at the ceremony. Only a prey animal lets fear get between her and what she wants."

I don't want to be you. "You . . . you're going south?"

"Not until after Yuleheigh."

"Yuleheigh?" The winter solstice festival was only a few days away.

"Smile, Drakne. We haven't celebrated Yuleheigh together since that incident with your shoes."

Why was he thinking of that? Today, of all days. Perhaps because it was a moment he'd seized power over her. But he'd always had power over her. A man, a soldier, a spymaster to the archduke could do as he liked to a girl only armed with dancing magic. *It's only dancing magic.* He'd said as much, that day she'd gone to his office to beg for help. Then he'd made Nabik swap her shoes and sent her, bleeding, off to boarding school.

Why did you hurt me? Why are you still hurting me? She wished she could bring herself to ask those questions. She wished she had the courage to scream in his face. As a girl, she'd been brave enough to dance the archduke toward the fire. But Fydir had ground that courage out of her.

A messenger ducked into the hall—a slender stoat-man clad in green livery, trembling as he spoke. "Your Majesty. Beg pardon. An enemy wizard has been spotted on the palace grounds. A white winter fox."

"Nabik," Fydir growled. He stood and climbed down from the throne. Courtiers and servants scrambled back from his path. Voices hushed. Laughter died. "I'll be back soon. Need to finish what Drakne started and rip his face off. Ruba, go to your quarters. Now. And you're not to leave without my permission."

Ruba stared at him. Stood—and staggered forward, as if he'd struck her. Her stool tumbled away across the fudge marble floor. The sweep of her golden coattails shimmered in the mirrors. Candlelight shone on her glasses, in her sudden tears. She turned, her eyes finding Drakne—

Who turned and stumbled out the hall's back door, cursing under her breath—at her brother's cruelty, at her own cowardice. Into a service tunnel she fled, through a hall chipped in ice and sugar, the passage twirling and twisting down past permafrost and into mountain bedrock. She stepped out onto a wooden platform. Beneath her, a frothing river crashed through a blue-lit cavern. Pulleys and levers from shafts above lowered castle laundry down. Servants sloshed stained sheets through the icy cascade.

"Hurry up!" an old laundress called to her fellows. "If we're caught slacking, the king'll have us all put in engines!"

Drakne stood still as a statue, letting the cold seep into her, soak through her bones, buy her a moment of calm. *What do I do next?*

An icicle snapped behind her. She whirled.

A short fox-boy in a robe embroidered with mistletoe stepped out from a crack in a violet seam of sugar, holding up his hands.

"Please," Nabik said. "I'm here to talk. Just—don't hurt me."

And Drakne felt his fear—of *her*—keener than a dagger in her spine.

His sister stood shivering in the icy tunnel, river spray caught in the fuzz of the feathers down her head and neck, her lips now turning blue. She looked like nothing so much as an icicle. One that sparked a primal terror in his blood.

"I'm sorry," she said. "Nabik, I'm so sorry."

Pain shot through his jaw. Her eyes found the scar, and for all the world she wished to make it go away. But no magic would erase what had passed between them. It hurt. He hated how much it hurt. He wished it could be any other way.

"Ah, well, I was getting too pretty." He pulled on a thin smile. "I'll count it as payback for what happened with your shoes."

"The shoes." She paused. "Fydir...he told you that swapping them would show the archduke my power wasn't reliable? Would stop him?" When he nodded, she said, "But if he truly wanted to stop the archduke, he could have. He could have killed him at any moment. It's so obvious, now that I know about his magic. A mouse could have poisoned his tea. A horse could have thrown him on a hunt. Fydir could have sold some of his gold tea trays and brought us all north to Zolka. We could have been together all this time. If he'd only wanted it."

"He's never wished to do anything good for his family," Nabik said. "At least, not since his first few years in the archduke's service. Listen. I must get into the throne room. The Heart of Winter is hidden there—if I can find it—"

"Everyone in that room knows who you are and what you look like. You won't stand a chance." Drakne considered. "But Ruba is still queen; she might have some authority here. She can't retrieve it herself, but maybe she can get you close."

Could he trust her? "Remember, I'm a wizard. I'll know if you wish to do me harm."

Drakne lowered her head. Ashamed, he realized. "I know," she said. "Follow me."

~

The royal quarters lay in the upper levels of the keep, a great fortress with walls buttressed by hardened chocolate and pocked with tooth-shaped windows looking out on the mountain and the sky. The door to the queen's chamber was set with prancing stags stamped in gold foil. Two guards stood before it, clad in matching green livery and frowns. "No one gets in to see Her

Majesty without the king's permission," said the one on the right.

Nabik pulled a flask of brandy from the air. "I don't suppose you take bribes?"

Neither guard reached for it. Drakne shrugged and knocked on the door. "Ruba! It's me. Let me in."

Soft footsteps. The creak of a hinge. "Let her through," Ruba murmured, and the still-frowning guards stepped aside. Drakne and Nabik slipped inside and closed the door tight behind them.

Ringed by glimmering silver curtains and bas-relief murals carved into white fudge plaster, Ruba sprawled backward on a bed big enough for an elephant, the golden tails of her coat fanning out beneath her. Her fingers twitched. Her breath came heavy. As if the fuel to her fire had all been drained away.

"How are you?" asked Drakne.

"Awful," Ruba said, and glared at Nabik. "What is Eugen's lover doing here?"

"Eugen isn't the trouble right now," Nabik said. "That's Fydir."

"You're all trouble," Ruba said. "Your brother made me *marry* him. Why didn't you warn me about what he was capable of?"

"I didn't know about his magic," Drakne said.

"But you know his nature."

"I was ... frightened." She shivered. Nabik took one step closer to her. Gave her an encouraging nod. It was a show of support, and it didn't feel like quite enough, but it was what she had. "He ... he put me in a soul-engine."

"*What?*"

"He put me in his gun. To punish me." Her voice grew stronger. "Because I was doing what you recruited me to do."

"*What?*" Nabik said. "You were working for her?"

"Yes, for years, not that you ever cared enough to notice. Ruba told me I could dance souls out of engines. She theorized I could wake up Eugen too. We had a deal—"

"How long did he keep you there?" Ruba demanded.

"Eight months."

Ruba swore. She turned to Nabik. "And you let this happen?"

"I didn't know," he said. "Fydir always shouted and yelled when I mentioned Drakne. I was scared to break the peace."

Drakne winced. For years, she'd thought Nabik safe in Fydir's favor. But who would feel safe next to the man who'd so easily discarded his own sister?

"Drakne." Ruba's voice went soft. She took Drakne's hands, her claws cupping fingers backed in feathers. "Blessed Winter. I'm sorry. I never should have chosen you for—"

"No. I'm glad you did. I was happy to do it." As she spoke, she remembered the truth of those words. Ruba had given her a sense of purpose when she'd needed one most. "How it ended wasn't anyone's fault but Fydir's."

Ruba pulled her closer. Drakne felt her racing heart, how, in this small body, her head fit neatly beneath Drakne's own. Ruba smelled of moss and growing things, and if there was a hint of rot, well, rot spread through every healthy forest. Drakne wanted nothing more than to kiss her pale forehead. *Merciful saints, if only Nabik wasn't here.*

A fist banged on the door. They leapt apart.

"The king is on his way," a guard grunted. "Make yourself presentable, Your Majesty."

Drakne turned back to Ruba. "We need to leave. Hurry."

Tears bubbled in Ruba's hazel eyes. She lifted up her glasses and wiped them furiously with a gloved hand. "This is unfairly devious of you, Drakne. Making me feel things. I'd let you carry me to the end of the world in a satchel. Annoyingly, I can't even cross the threshold."

"You can't walk." A sudden spark lit in Drakne's mind. "Can you dance?"

Humming a bawdy song she'd learned at school, Drakne swept her foot in an arch and rolled onto her toes. Bronze light shimmered in her path. Following the roll and leap of the tune, she shifted her weight from foot to foot, hopping, skipping, clapping in time. "Fourteen saints in gold and garnet, marched to heaven's gate—"

"I can't believe you know this song," Nabik said. "I wish *I* didn't know this song."

"With a graying snake named Ivan atop a silver plate." She skipped in a wide, dramatic loop, holding out a hand to the spellbound queen. Ruba took it, and the two of them leapt gracefully toward the door.

Nabik sighed and hummed along. Drakne twirled Ruba under her arm, golden tailcoat and black skirts spinning together. Their hands clasped. At a distance, they whirled, each step faster than the next. Bronze light swirled about them like stage curtains blown back in a wind. As Nabik flung open the doors, Drakne pulled Ruba close to her chest. The mouse-girl's head tucked neatly beneath hers. Drakne held her breath, hoped, then dipped Ruba down low.

And slid her partner backward over the threshold.

Something twanged, like a violin string snapping. Ruba stumbled into the hall, shaking her head as if to knock off cobwebs. "Drakne? It worked. You look . . . impressive."

Prickles ran up Drakne's spine like sewing needles, re-stitching her. Her lips and nose sank into a long, stiff scarlet bill. Bones clicked and clattered in her neck as it stretched, new vertebrae dropping out of old. Scales wrapped her legs. Webbing sprouted between her toes. Magic laced up her arms, unhooking and refiguring her bones, stretching them thinner and lighter. Feathers bloomed down their length. Her wings unfurled in a cascading sweep as she flourished out her arms in a performer's curtsy.

Lovely, she thought. *I truly am.*

Then she realized. And gulped, down the whole length of her long throat. The beastfolk curse had crawled in through her magic and remade her. A swan-maiden. Vulnerable to Fydir's commands.

And a lion's growl rumbled out from one floor below.

We must get to the Heart, Nabik thought. But as the sound of Fydir's footsteps drew near, all he could think of was Drakne. How he'd failed her. He had to see her safe now.

Nabik followed Drakne and Ruba out through the doors of the royal apartment. Both green-clad guards shot him uncertain looks. He held out his hand and summoned a staff of peppermint and mistletoe. "You don't like brandy," he said. "How about gold?"

"Hmm," one said thoughtfully, and Nabik caught the edge of a wish. With a flick of his hand, he turned the guards' boots into solid gold.

"Run!" he shouted, and he, Drakne, and Ruba charged down

the hall, into a maze of walls dyed butter yellow and black as empty hearts. They shouldered past foragers laden with moss and root vegetables and butchers touting smoked fish and sausage. Down the servants' stairs. Across the main floor of the keep. Drakne bowled through a pack of mincing nobles and Ruba ducked around a pair of maids staggering under the weights of hatboxes.

A roar sounded at their heels. The spun-sugar floor trembled underfoot. Servants gasped, dropping tools and packages to sink into bows. "Your Majesty!" gasped an elk-woman draped in diamond broaches.

Fydir. Nabik knew without turning around. The gravity of his soul, the well of endless hunger—his wishes lashed at Nabik's soul like cutting blades, each one eager to rip into him. *Be a soldier for me. Be a man.* But Fydir was a monster, as well as his brother, and Nabik knew who he was: the wizard who would cut him down to size.

Nabik swept his staff out behind them and summoned a wall of chocolate studded with almonds and filled with jagged crystal shards. Fydir broke through and *howled* as quartz and diamonds stabbed at his face.

"You really can be a nasty little bastard," Ruba said approvingly. "If you weren't in love with my nemesis, I think we'd be friends."

Drakne had already darted down a spiral stairwell. With a flick of his staff, Nabik flattened the stairs into a chute. He and Ruba leapt after her, and the three of them spilled down the seamless sugar river, whirling about until they fell in a jumbled heap onto the courtyard stone. Nabik stood, head spinning. He looked about the courtyard, which was still decorated for a wedding. Drakne and Ruba, recovered and running, were already halfway to the gate.

"Go!" he shouted. "I can hold him!"

Drakne spun, reaching for him. "Nabik—"

"Hello, little brother."

Fydir's kick landed between his shoulder blades. Nabik fell forward, skidded across the courtyard on a sheet of ice, and slammed into Drakne's knees.

His brother stalked forward, blood trickling from the gashes down his face like poinsettia petals. He towered over them, muscles rolling in his shoulders as he cracked his fists. Nabik scrambled for a spell. Terror whipped his thoughts into slurry. His soul and spirit screamed in discord, until he could summon no more than a scatter of snowflakes from his sleeves.

Drakne. Nabik stumbled to his feet. He met Fydir's eyes and said loudly, "*Stop.*"

"Stop? Stop what?" Rage seeped out from the lion's voice like poison gas. "Stop trying to look after my wife and family?"

"Stop trying to control us."

"Are you really that scared of me? What sort of wizard are you?"

"The sort who wants his brother to care!" The words came out half a yelp. The cry of a wounded child. He didn't care. He needed Fydir to hear him. "Since I was thirteen, you made me your lackey. You isolated me, terrified me, and made me bend my life around your rages. I never wanted to be your soldier. But you were all I had. I wanted you to love me, and you wanted me to play the part. So I gave up myself for you."

Fydir scoffed. "You make it sound like I tortured you. You

were my right hand. I trusted you. But I won't make that mistake again." The gold of his mane gleamed like sunfire. "Your magic is *mine* to command."

The words cut like scalpels into Nabik's neck, through fur, flesh, and tissue. The world flashed and then went dark, his vision flickering in and out as the world came back *duller*. Chains of iron and worked brass squeezed tight against his soul as every fleck and flurry he'd reclaimed of himself bent back to serve Fydir's will. His peppermint staff shattered and dissolved into mist.

Nabik screamed.

~

It was a terrible sound, the cry of a fox with its neck in a toothed trap. Drakne couldn't help but wish herself possessed of a rifle and the means to end it.

Fydir continued, commanding. "Now, Nabik. Punish your sister for trying to steal my queen."

Ruba doesn't belong to you! Drakne meant to scream. *None of us do!* But then a thousand knife-sharp crystal pine needles flew at her, and her breath caught in her throat as she leapt aside.

"Get away from me!" Nabik gasped. Streams of burning brandy shot from his palms, melting the frost fractals on the courtyard stones. *What do you think I'm trying to do?* Drakne wanted to scream as she dodged, burning alcohol scorching her hem and tail feathers. But now she saw it, the watering misery in his eyes as Fydir's commands took hold. As miserable as she felt every time Fydir growled at her. The despair born of realizing you would always, always be used by him.

A horror Nabik had come to face, when he could have fled and vanished deep into the winter wood.

He'd come for her. Everyone she'd ever cared for had disappointed her, and she'd disappointed them. Still. Nabik had come back.

"Isn't this fun?" Fydir said, grinning like a ghoul. "We're together again. Like family."

"You're no family of mine," she spat, rolling onto her webbed toes and prancing toward him. *Step. Step. Step.* She hummed under her breath. Bronze flowed from her feet, winking filaments of magic that knocked him backward as she drew him into the dance. The web of power trembled around her, looking for music beyond her wobbly hum, a place to anchor and grow—

"Release me," he growled. Thunder crackled as his power sank deep inside her. *Like fire meeting fire.* The fears that lived inside her like tiny nesting mice sliced lines across her courage. Who was she, to challenge a king? Who was she, to challenge her brother? The last time she'd danced anywhere near him, he'd cut her passion out of her.

Cold snapped through the courtyard. Clouds wove across the sky, turning it gray as a dove's underbelly. Snow showered downward. Hailstones pounded the harp-string gates. A howling tide of wind spiraled about Fydir, icy claws catching him in their grasp. Out of the dark dropped an owl. Zolka stood up tall in her human shape and lowered a staff of silver birch and ice-crystal feathers between them.

"You," Zolka told Fydir, with the force of an iceberg calving, "need to *stop*." She turned to Drakne and Nabik, already rolling back her sleeves for battle. "And you need to run."

"No," Nabik said. "We won't leave you!" But Drakne already had hold of his wrist and was dragging him backward. Fydir stood between them and the gate, but the palace was full of disused rooms and hiding places. *If we can last until nightfall . . .* Drakne's head spun. The spark of an idea hummed deep within her breastbone.

"Inside!" she called. Clawed feet clattered on stone as Ruba followed the two of them back into the keep.

The stairs to the royal apartment remained a solid sugar slide—Nabik flicked his fingers at it and cursed when his bound magic refused to flow. "Through the library," Ruba said, and waved them through an archway of candy canes.

The three of them trampled across the red wool carpet, snow and gravel clinging to their heels. Bookshelves rose five stories high, made accessible by long ramps that spiraled up about the room. Light poured through tall sugar windows dyed with scenes of snowfae dancing. Charms painted on gingerbread floated aloft, flying to distant shelves and carrying back requested volumes.

But at the library's heart stood a soul-engine cannon, its barrel twenty feet long and equipped with three sockets on each side. Soldiers stood on guard about it, clad both in red and green. Nobles watched attentively as a sergeant shoved a squirming mouse-boy inside. The child howled and screamed as the brass swallowed him.

"Let him go!" Drakne shouted, and all eyes turned to them.

Ruba grabbed her arm and pulled her up a staircase, along a narrow walkway, knocking a beaverfolk librarian back against the peppermint rail as she went. Nabik broke off a sharp stick of the candy and hoisted it like a halberd, protecting their rear.

A pair of soldiers turned away from the pack of engine guards and ran for them. Troops in green livery poured through the entry arch, shouting "Catch them!" and knocking clerks and students to the floor.

"How dare they bring those machines into my castle?" Ruba said, panting and sweating.

"You're the one who let Fydir bring them across the border," Nabik said, throwing his makeshift weapon at a soldier. The man stumbled back into his fellows.

"I didn't *let* him." She sighed. "I might have done more to stop him."

"Don't let them escape!" Fydir's voice echoed up the corridor outside.

Drakne's heart sank. Her mother had barely bought them a few minutes.

"Up!" she shouted, extending her neck and *hissing* at the librarians in their way. Beastfolk trembled. Books dropped from their hands. Drakne flung open a side door and waved Nabik and Ruba inside.

Up they ran, up spiraling sugar stairs, the crystal walls about them etched with curlicues. Afternoon sunlight danced, refracted, shattered through each frosted inch. Drakne felt like she was running through a rainbow—a flight of air and fancy that would take her nowhere much at all.

The stairs ran out. Her stomach dropped. She set her jaw. *He won't take me. He won't rule me. Never again.* "The fire door," she gasped. "Onto the roof!"

Ruba jumped onto Drakne's shoulders and pushed a sheet of shaved pistachios sideways. Winter wind rushed inside. She leapt through the gap. Drakne caught her hand and scrambled up, pulling Nabik along behind her.

"What now?" Nabik demanded as Drakne slammed the foil-wrapped panel back in place. They stood atop a turret; the conical spire was steep, and the frost-swept gilding left it treacherously slick. Shivering and shaking, they balanced on wobbling knees. The wind whipped snow about them with a keening, piercing howl, pouring off the side of the Great Mountain. The sky shone clear, blue, and merciless above.

"We wait and hope," Drakne said. With her swan's eyes, she could see down to the courtyard. There was no sign of Zolka. "If we can hold out until nightfall—"

The roof exploded into chunks of pistachio and gold foil. Fydir leapt through the hole and perched easily on the balls of his clawed feet.

"Get back!" Ruba shouted, hoisting a buttery brick.

"Drop it," Fydir ordered. The missile fell from her hands. It clattered down the roof and vanished as it tumbled out into space.

"What did you do to our mother?" Drakne demanded.

"Zolka knew the consequences of defying me." Fydir shrugged. "I'll deal with her later."

She's alive. Her clenched fists relaxed.

"That's a nice scar you gave Nabik," Fydir continued, slinging his rifle off the strap on his back. The soul-socket pulsed purple, like a bleeding gum where a tooth had been ripped out. "Time to finish what you started. In the socket. Now."

Thunder crackled in his voice. Swan's legs and sweet fog pulled her feet forward. "No!" shouted Ruba. Nabik cursed, calling her name.

Nabik.

He and Zolka had come back for her. Her, alone. The un-loved sister a mighty king would write out of history. Who'd sought out cruelty to make herself strong. With neither crown nor magic to compel them, they'd come back for her. Because she was someone they *could* come for. Someone they could love, even if Fydir didn't. She was a dancer and a fighter, a bad student and a worse bride, and she was done letting this man grind her down.

The soul-socket on the gun blazed red-hot. Metal warping. Screaming. Calling to the familiar taste of her soul, but not suck-ing her down. *It's like it's part of me,* she realized.

And what was truly *her* blazed like holy sunrise.

She wrenched the gun away and fired high above Fydir's shoulder. Shocks pounded through her sternum, cushioned by the bulk of her wing muscle. Fydir jumped backward and clung to the gold of the dome. Foil tore beneath his claws.

Fear glittered in his golden eyes. His mouth opened and flut-tered shut. Wordless.

Drakne grinned and pivoted, tossing the gun and its strap over her shoulder, then reached out. "Grab on!"

Ruba grabbed her hand. Nabik froze. Staring.

Please. Please, trust me.

Nabik wrapped his arms around her waist, met her eyes, and nodded.

Drakne took a deep breath and leapt skyward off the dome.

The others screamed, clawing at her, gasping and shouting as they plummeted. Open air claimed them. Winter air and grav-ity spun them around. Gold-topped spires and snow-capped mountains flashed by. The white of the waterfall, the aquamarine of its shores. Wind howled. Winter glistened.

Drakne braced herself and flung her arms outward. Black wings, wider than a field of horses, stretched out across the blue. Cold winds rose beneath her, caught her, lifted her up. Pain and crunching weight pressed downward through her chest as she pushed, *hard*—

And swept them soaring into open sky.

CHAPTER SEVENTEEN

A Nation of Small Curses

Drakne Zolkedna shot across Znaditin, her wings a current of night against the endless blue. The muscles in her chest held taut, firm as an iron rod, though they burned with agony as the weight of her two passengers dragged her down. A dip of her shoulders, and she spun. The white-capped Great Mountain and the sugar city pivoted about her, and wind howled in her ears as she danced with the sky.

"How do I land?" she shouted.

"There!" Nabik yelled, pointing to the lake. Drakne aimed herself like a dart. The smooth depth of the waters shattered as she crashed down.

Cold flooded her. Kicking madly, craning back her neck, she broke the surface in a tide of bubbles. Ruba scrambled up onto her shoulders. Drakne folded her wings to her side, feathers shedding water, webbed toes opening wide. Nabik paddled along like a soaked cat, dragged down by the wet weight of his robe.

"We have to get back to the snowfae," he said as they clambered up a steep side bank and onto a narrow trail. His teeth chattered as he shook water off his fur. "Quickly. I can't cast a warming spell, or summon fire, or anything."

Drakne's fingers trembled, and not from the cold. Her feathers pinned heat to her chest—heat, and the flush of victory. The soul-engine gun hung from her shoulder, all the power and protection she needed. Whatever came next, she wouldn't dance the part Fydir gave her. She didn't need to deal with the snowfae, especially if Talzne would be there, reminding her of all she had to be ashamed of.

"I'm not keen on the snowfae," Ruba said. "I've always respected their autonomy, but they hold little love for kings. They won't involve themselves in a political squabble of mortals."

"It's not just political. It's the very Heart of Winter at stake. Perhaps we can get them to see they *must* support us. Besides, Eugen is there."

"Ah, good idea. We can fling him off a cliff and see if that breaks the curse."

"He isn't the only one to blame, and you know it. You carried those crystal roots into the throne room—"

"Enough," said Drakne. "Ruba, where might Eba and Maznun have run off to? Do they have a house in the city?" When Ruba nodded, Drakne said, "Good. We'll walk to the snowfae fortress. Nabik, you'll go in and get Eugen. See if you can convince them to help us, but don't take too long. Then we'll seek out Ruba's agents and see what they can do about Fydir."

To the eastern gate of the fortress they hiked, past cliffs lined in lichen, pines sparkling with jeweled leaves, and small cottages carved from peanut brittle. As the sun sank, the world was blanketed in soft gray and sunset-cast violet sparkles. Silence rose around them, broken only by distant elk trumpets and the singing of wind through crystal pines. Bent branches and hoofprints marked the lakeside trail, stretches of flat-packed snow broken by drifts that soaked Drakne's petticoats whenever she stumbled into one. She was shivering by the time they reached the peppermint palisade, from a cold that only grew as six snowfae slipped outside the gate to surround her.

Talzne stood at their head, her violet eyes burning with righteous rage.

Drakne swore. Right. From this vantage, the snowfae would have seen her in the sky.

"Oh, dear Talzne—" she started. Talzne waved her hand. A white lace scarf appeared and gagged her.

"You manipulated me every step of the way here." With each word she spoke, the scarf twisted tighter. "You and Fydir will be the death of Kolznechia. Nothing good can come of you."

Drakne reached for her gun. Lace scarves appeared and bound her hands, her ankles. She tripped forward and tumbled face-first into the snow. A ragged *honk!* rose from her throat at the bruising push of pain.

"We need to speak to Queen Genna," Nabik said. "We need to work together now. Kolznechia is in danger—"

"We know!" Talzne snapped, and her voice was cold with fear. Tears bloomed in the other girl's eyes. Distant shouts rose through the sunset afternoon.

"What's going on here? What's wrong?"

"Fydir's soldiers came to the south gate. Genna went to face them. He brought *war machines* to our doorstep."

A cannon boomed. Drakne gasped, her heart jolting sideways. Talzne pivoted.

"Eugen!" Nabik said, and sprinted toward the sound. Talzne and the other snowfae ran after.

Ruba untied the scarf from Drakne's ankles. "The snowfae can't be bound by his magic. They're not beastfolk. He'll want to beat them down."

The wind picked up, roaring with a lion's rage. Drakne swallowed hard, fighting not to shiver. A flurry of snowflakes fell on her brow. "I need to go after my brother."

"I know," Ruba said. "Let's find him."

The snowfae had left the gate wide open. As the snowfall picked up tempo, the two girls ducked through and ran toward the shouting and booming. A snowfae woman saw them and waved her arm. Thick white cloaks, fur-lined, fell onto their shoulders and covered them in camouflage. "Thank you!" Drakne shouted. She wiped snow from her brow and squinted hard into the billows. Where had the storm come from? It had been calm just moments ago.

A white-winged owl shot through the driving sleet. *Mother.* Her heart twisted. *I'm sorry.* Fydir had bound her to serve his commands and bring his wrath upon the snowfae. Gunpowder flashed. Gingerbread and peppermint cracked. Drakne threw up her hands as sugar shards flew. Zolka swept northward, and for a moment, the storm died, and she could *see.*

A war machine had flattened the south gate.

Four times as tall as any man, it rose, treads chewing at the ice, three tiers of guns fanning out like the ruffles of a layered petticoat. Plated in armor a handspan thick, the five turrets down its back swiveling like owl heads, it crawled across the earth like a metal crocodile. Beastfolk mouths ringed the gun barrels, fangs, beaks, and whiskers caught in brass. Clockwork mice and the wiry arms of ferrets turned the great gear wheels of the treads. And yet, still more soul-sockets lay open and exposed above the top ring. Pulsing and hungry.

A fifty-person soul-engine. Ten sockets unfilled. Drakne froze midstep and did not realize what she'd done until Ruba squeezed her hand. Her throat felt clogged and airless, as if bullets had flooded back down it. Her fingers shook, as if at any second they'd fold back into triggers. *Don't let them see you. Don't let them see you, or they'll stuff you in.*

"Give the king his coronation gift!" boomed a soldier. "His Majesty offers all folk of Kolznechia the chance to serve him!"

Soldiers ringed a group of tiny snowfae girls, herding them forward. Sockets pulsed with purple light. The children's eyes widened as they were drawn in. Metal prongs closed across their backs. Mouths of milk teeth froze wide open as bronze washed down their throats. Small cries rang out and stilled. Businesslike soldiers went row by row, making note of the filled sockets on a chart.

"Can you shoot them?" Ruba said.

Drakne squinted at the soldiers. At the children mixed among them. The wind blew fiercely. "I . . . I don't think I can risk it."

"Found him!" Paws scurried along the snow. Nabik ran up, hauling Eugen by the wrist. The prince gave her and Ruba wary looks but said nothing. "We need to go. Now."

The four of them fled, stumbling, following a group of snowfae to the south gate. Drakne held the soul-engine gun close, feeling her connection to the metal spark once more. *Fydir isn't here,* she told herself, fighting the urge to freeze. She held the gun now.

"Here!" Talzne stood by a section of palisade where the mountain slope dipped. She waved her hand, and a cluster of peppermint stakes turned into bursting bubbles. "Out into the city!" Snowfae stumbled past her. Her eyes met Drakne's with the force of a slap. "*You*. Are you going to stop this?"

"I'm not going to die," Drakne said. "And I'm not going back in their damned machines."

"Come with us," said Nabik. "We know someplace safe."

Talzne looked to Drakne. Then back up the slope, where the soul-engines hungered.

"We run," she said. "And if you fail me now, I'll turn your heart to lace and eat it."

The wind scoured the mountain slopes as Nabik and the rest crept down from the glacier and into the shivering city.

The crystal trees were the beauty and curse of Znaditin, a lovely backdrop for a palace and a terrible obstacle to all forms of civilian infrastructure. Roads, buildings, sewers—all had to be built around trees that would shatter and slice if one tried to remove them, and the stone roots ran both deep and wide. Some crystal trees had been half broken with hammers, but the city, for the most part, merely coiled around them, fitting itself in where it might.

They crept through curling, snow-dusted avenues in the darkening evening, a hush hanging over them like a held breath. Beneath the snow scent, the air reeked of soul-engine smoke and echoed with the discord of grinding gears. The scant few folk who braved the streets hurried along with their heads lowered, speaking only in whispers. Soldiers patrolled, in Kolznechian and Szpratzian uniforms alike. Nabik led them around the occupying army, his fox ears flicking at the slightest sound.

It's nearly Yuleheigh, he thought as they slunk through the streets. *If ever there was a time to show each other warmth, it's now.*

Her head lowered, bundled tight in her cloak, Ruba came up to Eugen's side.

"Ruba," Eugen whispered when he saw her. "I cared about you and your brother. I didn't betray you out of spite. I'm sorry. I was so scared of my father. That's all the answer I have, and I know it's not good enough."

"You could have defied him," she said. "You could have *tried.*"

"I know. I'm not mad at you. Not for . . . killing him. It had to be done. You have my forgiveness, my pardon—if it means anything to you. But what must I do to make amends? So we can stand together and save our home?" Eugen sounded so plaintive. Exhausted. Nabik rested a supportive hand on his side.

"What will you be saving, if you take your father's throne?" said Ruba. "The kingdom? Or just his dreams for you?"

"I'm not interested in the dreams of a dead man."

Ruba's eyes flickered to Nabik. "So this time, it's a living one."

"What?"

"I know your wishes. You've never once wished to be king. You spent most of your life wishing to change your name and run off to a small fishing village. But here you are, fighting for your father's throne. Because Nabik Zolkedan wants to put you on it."

Eugen flinched. Nabik spoke up. "First and foremost, we're here to break the curse. The snowfae think its corruption has infected the Heart of Winter—"

"Yes, it has," Ruba said. "It likes to invade and transform things. That's what it does."

"—but if we can get the corruption out of Winter, then she can bind the curse's power. That's what Queen Genna thinks." Nabik glanced back over his shoulder, at the snowfae fortress on the glacier, smoke still rising from its walls. He hoped everyone had gotten out. But how many were caught in soul-engines, or simply dead? How many more people had he failed?

Ruba sighed. "How do you plan to excise the corruption? With a chisel? The Heart is threaded through with crystals smaller than your eye can see. You couldn't remove the stone without destroying it."

"What if we . . . get Winter out of the stone?"

"Right now, we don't even have the magic to make chickens cluck. How do you propose we *do* this? The curse is stronger than any wizard. When I shoved that crystal root into King Kutreus—when it grew and pierced the Heart of Winter—all the magic in the throne room went wild. Eugen—the magic seized on my anger at you and tried to take you. I almost let it. It was all I could do to turn you into *this* instead of letting it destroy you completely."

Eugen stared. "I thought . . . you wanted me dead."

"I wanted you punished." Ruba spat. "I thought the curse lingered because I didn't let it finish you off. End the cruelty of the Teyodet kings forever. But I was a bad king too. Two hundred years I sat on that throne, and yet it all feels like a few awful weeks now that I'm off it." She shivered and pushed her glasses up her nose. "Fydir will be the worst king of all. But he is what he is because his ancestors fled Kolznechia, because Winter called his mother north, because of *me*. The punishment doesn't end. It circles back around and gets worse. Forever and ever."

"We don't have to feed it," Eugen said. Then, quietly, "I miss you."

Even more quietly, Ruba said, "I miss you too."

Briefly, they ducked beneath the awning of the Znaditin's public library to catch their breath. The building had been constructed leaning near sideways between two twisted crystal pines.

Drakne wiped frost off the placard by the door. *In Memory of Rosken Otyedan.* "Quite the tribute," she said. Ruba only stared.

"I forgot I built this," she said. "I thought it would . . . settle my mourning. Stop it, somehow."

Drakne squeezed her hand. "It never stops. My mama— Mama Minka—she died twelve years ago. I'm still angry about it. Zolka—if she'd stayed—she could have saved her."

"Maybe," Ruba said. "Maybe not. Not even Winter herself can save everyone."

"From what I've heard you and Nabik say, she can't even save herself. I've always thought Winter was like Mama Zolka. So powerful and capable. So that when she hurt me—when she abandoned me—it was all on purpose. But if it wasn't her choice . . ."

"You can be powerful and still be a victim," Ruba said. "There's always someone stronger. Or, at least, there's always someone crueler."

"What's the point of power, then? If you can still lose people? If folk can still hurt you?"

"I don't know. If you want wisdom, you'll have to ask a better wizard than me." She looked out at the street, where the bright electric beam of a soul-engine shone out between two nearby gingerbread houses. "We should keep moving."

Through a back alley they wound, where three interlaced crystal trees meant the taller members of the party had to crawl on their hands and knees. Nabik came to her side as she fought to pull her wings through. "How are you feeling?" he said.

"Can't you tell?"

"I can tell what you want, which is dinner. The rest . . . it's like a coal after a bonfire."

Drakne sighed. "Ashamed, mostly. And my arms hurt from all that flying."

Nabik nodded. Up ahead, Eugen laughed at one of Talzne's jokes. Her brother smiled. "Drakne . . . ah . . . what are you supposed to do when you're in love?"

"Do you think I know?"

"You did all that kissing at school. I read your discipline file."

"That was kissing. Not love. There's a difference."

"Oh." The tips of his ears turned purple. "I suppose I've never thought of it that way. But I do love him. It's not just kissing. Is it silly of me, that I'm so sure?"

She patted the top of his head. "Extremely silly. Keep it up."

Lady Eba's manor stood in the heart of a grove of crystal trees, the worn walls overgrown with glimmering wizard-light fungus. The whipped-cream tower tops shifted gently in a breeze laden with the salt scent of taffy. A wizened beaver-woman in livery waved them through the gate. "In the greenhouse," she said. "My lady is expecting you." They followed a walkway, its stones made of hardened fruitcake studded with raisins and limes. Carved gingerbread arches, icing and ice painting them with abstract lace, guided them through the manor's windswept gardens to a great glass greenhouse.

As Drakne entered, humid honey-scented heat rolled over her. Beneath shining electric lights and panels of glittering glass, palm trees and potted pines grew side by side. Crimson flowers bloomed within whorls of thick black thorns. One fanged plant snapped flies from the air.

And they were entirely alone.

"Where are they?" Ruba said. "Eba and Maznun are cautious, yes—they're *spies*—but they know me."

"We do." Maznun entered behind them, silent on padded paws. A long velvet smoking jacket fell to his furry knees. "And we know you'd never travel with Eugen Teyodet of your own free will."

Cat-quick, he lunged. His paw caught Ruba's cheek. She collapsed to her knees, her wide eyes staring desperately at something Drakne couldn't see.

"Rosken?" she whispered, tears brimming in her eyes. "No. No!"

"How dare you?" Drakne hissed, wings spread, neck arched. She reached for the cat.

Talzne grabbed at her arm. "Don't hurt him!"

Maznun caught both their arms at once—

And then she wasn't in the greenhouse, but in an auto-carriage, rumbling northward. She was in Talzne's memory, her hands bound, surrounded by enemy soldiers and staring at a dark-eyed girl who bore her no pity. Terror drenched her, terror and betrayal as heavy as crushing stone. Drakne Zolkedna

279

danced open soul-engines. She had promised to save the boy Talzne loved. This girl should care for justice. Not hold her hostage so she could chase a crown.

No, Drakne told herself as her heart twisted. This wasn't her pain.

She'd just caused it.

For nothing.

She'd promised Talzne—promised herself—that she was going along with Fydir only to stop him. But she'd never have power over him like he held over her. She didn't want to be as much like him as she'd need to be to do that. Still. She'd been *enough* like him. She'd been angry. She'd been cruel. Whatever chance she'd had of friendship with Talzne, she'd burned to ashes.

Drakne blinked away her tears and made herself focus on the greenhouse. Talzne was staring down at her hands.

"The dancing," the snowfae girl whispered. "The *pain*. Blessed Winter. I had no idea."

"I'm sorry," Drakne said. The words were heavy as lead on her tongue, and saying them made nothing feel better. But it had to be said. "Truly, Talzne. I am."

The snowfae girl just shook her head.

Nabik stared at Maznun. "What did you do?"

"I distracted the Rat King to search her memory. To see if Fydir sent her here to kill us. And when the two girls made a fuss, I showed them both a memory that causes the other pain."

"I still don't understand," Talzne whispered. "Maznun showed me that Yuleheigh when Fydir had Nabik swap your shoes. The archduke used you so horribly. And Fydir was so cruel . . ."

"He's always been cruel," Drakne said.

"You helped him win his patron's approval. Why push you away? It makes no sense. Don't you see?"

See what? Drakne bit her tongue, holding in the urge to snap. "No. I don't see. What is it? Please."

The pain in Talzne's eyes grew sharp. Focused. "He was in his office. You asked him for help. He said your magic was weak, so you made him dance. He dropped his cigar. He was *terrified*."

What? It was utter nonsense. Like some made-up words in a children's book spoken when a witch cast a spell. Fydir, afraid of her?

But then she thought further.

"I . . . I can *make* him dance," Drakne said. "He can't stop me."

Every face in the greenhouse turned to her. Every eye was wide with hope. Her throat tightened. *Blessed Winter, do I really have to face him once more?*

"Are you really so eager to throw your life away, Miss Zolkedna?" Eba, clad in solemn black, entered through a back door. Servants paraded in past her, laden with dishes, and began to set a great table. Chattering guests in Yuleheigh finery followed behind them. "Come now. Before you run off to get killed, have some food."

CHAPTER EIGHTEEN

The Feast of Endless Yule

The five of them stared slack-jawed at the waiting feast. Beast-folk in velvet robes and silver capes gathered about the long table, one heaped with puddings and plums, roasts and radishes, cakes and croquettes. A trio of enchanted instruments—a horn, a drum, and a violin of white wood—hovered in midair, playing in the corner. Lady Eba, in a flowing scarlet gown and a garland of holly, stood at the head of the table. Maznun pulled a cracker, and scraps of thin colored paper popped into the air.

"Enjoy yourselves," Eba said. "It's nearly Yuleheigh."

A group of children ran past Nabik to drape a popcorn chain around a potted pine. *Nearly Yuleheigh.* The days had grown shorter and shorter. The winter solstice was nearly upon him. But the darkness felt natural to his mood.

"Sorry we've shown up uninvited," Ruba said, looking altogether unrepentant. "We need your help, old friend."

"Of course. But we can discuss politics later." Lady Eba waved her cloven hand. "Eat! Drink! Make merry!"

"Fydir is taking control of Znaditin *now*," Nabik said. "If Drakne can stop him, then we need to act. There's no time—"

"This is my house," Eba said, "and I say we shall have time enough."

A servant lifted a tray to offer Nabik sugar-dusted plums. He took one, bit in, and gagged as dark, sweet juices flowed down his throat and chin. The scent of meat and pastries set his stomach grumbling. His feet ached from walking; his head swam with fears.

Everything was wrong. He missed Zolka. *Why would she sacrifice herself for a useless lump like me?* He needed her here, to tell him what to do, because he was trying so hard, trying with every part of him, and failing. He'd been trying since Mama Minka died, since he and his siblings were first put out on the street. He'd tried to keep the peace, to protect Drakne, to care for Fydir, to be a good brother. He'd tried to help the poor in Malirmatvi, to free the people of Stakte from Fydir, and despite all his trying, he'd done nothing more helpful than dig a few graves. *If there's sacrifices to be made, I'll make them,* Zolka had said. She'd also said *talk to someone*. But what could he say? That he wished Fydir had caught him? How could he admit weakness when they needed a wizard to lead them?

He reached for another plum. The instruments played a jaunty tune. Talzne filled herself a large bowl of popcorn. Ruba and Drakne went to sit beside Eba and Maznun, who served them chocolates off the length of a ski. Nabik packed down the brandy-infused plums until his fox feet scrabbled for purchase on the greenhouse's slick peppermint tiles.

A strong wooden arm swept Nabik up onto Eugen's lap. "Now this," the prince said, and the warm electric lights shone off the whorls in his carved cheeks as he smiled, "is exactly the sort of living I've been meaning to do."

He leaned forward. Nabik held his breath. Their lips trembled, a mere inch apart when, just outside the manor, a cannon boomed and—

~

The five of them stared slack-jawed at the waiting feast. Beastfolk in velvet robes and silver capes gathered about the long table, one heaped with puddings and plums, roasts and radishes, cakes and croquettes. A trio of enchanted instruments—a horn, a drum, and a violin of white wood—hovered in midair, playing in the corner. Lady Eba, in a flowing scarlet gown and a garland of holly, stood at the head of the table. Threads of lightning shone outside the greenhouse walls, a gauzy, sparkling curtain that wrapped around the manor like a cloak.

Some sort of protection spell? Perhaps. Something was wrong. *I was about to kiss Eugen—and the brandy—*Surely he hadn't passed out from drinking so little? *Though I'm littler now than the last time I drank.*

Winter bless him, he'd wanted that kiss. He couldn't remember the last time he'd wanted something so thoroughly.

"Sorry we've shown up uninvited," Ruba said, looking mildly confused. "We need your help, old friend."

"Of course. But we can discuss politics later." Lady Eba waved her cloven hand. "Eat! Drink! Make merry!"

Hadn't she said that before? "Something's wrong," Nabik murmured.

"You heard my wife," Maznun said, placing his hand on Nabik's wrist. Orange smoke puffed out from under his fingertips. "Nothing is so wrong that we can't celebrate. It's nearly Yuleheigh."

"Fydir . . . " Nabik said, and the rest of the thought slipped away like a silvery fish. This was a party. What did he have to do but celebrate? He grabbed fistfuls of peppermints, stuffed them in the pockets of his robe, and took Eugen by the hand. His heartbeat sped, but he wasn't afraid. He knew who Eugen was. He trusted him.

"Come with me," he whispered, and Eugen went.

As the cloak of lightning glimmered against the night sky, Nabik and Eugen snuck into the manor and found an abandoned salon. Beneath portraits of boar-lords and Ruba's winking male visage, atop a gilded chaise imported from some distant land, Nabik discovered that, while Eugen's trousers were carved onto his body, his lips and hands were free to move in a dozen decadent, distracting, delightful ways.

This is what my body is made for, he thought. *Not war. Not violence. Only this.* The more time he spent in this form, the more Eugen looked at him with wanting, the more he *wanted* to be wanted. He wanted to be very different indeed than what he'd been told to be.

Quivering, they held each other until the first cannon boomed.

The five of them stared slack-jawed at the waiting feast. Then Nabik grinned and rushed into the revels. The world and all its terrors melted away. All he knew was fresh plums, sugar and brandy. Teeth and tongue, wooden lips and soft ones. Up his ears, down his belly, every part of him that the curse had made new.

Every part of him that time and practice made less afraid.

He crushed green and yellow cupcakes against Eugen's carved chest, smearing sugar and icing across it as they came together. In a hayloft, in the stables, at the very heart of the greenhouse in the fourteenth—fifteenth?—cycle. The guests cheered as Nabik climbed on the table to kiss Eugen from above, leaving marks with purple lip paint they'd stolen from the baroness's boudoir.

He'd never done anything like this, never *lived* like this, and strange and wild energy now burst from every bare inch of his skin. He'd always bragged of being older than Drakne, even if only by a handful of months. He'd always felt aged before his time. Now, the world had flipped over. He felt young again, and eager. Alive.

"You're getting better at this," Ruba said, lying sprawled across a table, cheeks stuffed to bursting with candied hazelnuts. "Only took you two whole days to finally claim him in public."

"Kiss the Rat King or get out of my way." Drakne shoved Nabik by the shoulder, moving with the tottering gait of a drunk, and climbed atop Ruba. The runaway queen ran her lips down Drakne's neck. The swan-girl preened as chocolate splotches bloomed where dark feathers met pale skin. "At least you still have working lips."

"Oh, Drakne," Ruba said. "I can think of several positively wicked uses for that beak."

"You two are the worst," Talzne said, and stuck a meat-laden fork in her mouth.

Nabik cleared his throat. A terrible realization was cutting through the haze. *Two days?* How might it have been that long? He'd lost track of something. Something vital. He looked to the head of the table, where Maznun sat. *They want us to forget.*

Nabik turned on his heel and darted outside the greenhouse. His heart hammered in his mouth as he scrambled down the fruitcake walk and peered out through the manor gate.

The world outside seemed to speed past, double, triple time. Soul-engine tanks rolled through the streets. Soldiers hung green-and-gold lion banners off the houses across the avenue. Carts and caravans, laden with fleeing beastfolk, rattled down the road. Soldiers waved their guns, and the beastfolk ran in fear.

"No!" Nabik said, and reached for them. His fingers hit the sparkling barrier and bounced off it. He caught hints of wishes for safety, for justice, and knew with the pain of a branding iron that he could do nothing to make them come true. A gray fog filled his heart where his magic should be, turning the world dark and fuzzy about the edges.

Nabik rushed back into the greenhouse. He pushed his way through the guests and approached the head of the table. A footman was whispering in Eba's long ear. The boar-woman nodded and waved him off. She stood and waved a hand at the enchanted instruments. They sped up the tempo and volume of their song, turning it into a lively jig. Her guests clapped along, rising to step with the meter on clopping hooves.

"What's going on?" Nabik demanded. "Why have you trapped us here?"

"Nothing to worry about, fox-child. We're all safe here."

"What did the footman say?"

"Go feast and be merry—"

"What did he *say*?"

Eba sighed. "Fydir has issued an order for everyone in the city to come to the palace. The crystal blight is spreading rapidly.

He says the kingdom can no longer bear the expense of feeding those who aren't properly employed, and they must serve in the soul-engines to earn their keep. He plans to march south with his machines tomorrow."

Nabik stared in shock. "What . . . what are we going to do?"

"Stay quiet. When Fydir leaves the city, we'll be able to sneak out of here. Flee across the Great Pole. Start new lives in distant lands."

"Absolutely not," Nabik said. "Kolznechia needs us."

"Us? Or my husband and me? You don't seem to have magic at the present. You're volunteering us for battle. Do as you please, fox-boy, but we're not going to die for you."

"I'm not asking anyone to die," said Nabik. "There must be a way to stop him. With Drakne's magic, perhaps—"

"Enough," she said, and placed her hand on Maznun's shoulder. "Push any further, and we may just need to make you forget your own name."

Nabik backed off, all the way down the length of the table. His shoulders slumped. His heart sank. He didn't know what to do. Not without his magic. *But I must do something. It's my duty.* Duty too heavy for shoulders that couldn't even hold his sister's needs. The buzz of alcohol had faded. The truth had crept back in. He had no power. Only failings and a blinding need to hide.

"What's wrong?" Eugen put a hand on his shoulder as he walked past. "Why look so dour? We're at an everlasting party."

"Remember Fydir?" Nabik said.

Eugen's face fell. "Oh. Now I do. I wish I didn't."

"Eba and Maznun are hiding us from him, the cowards." Nabik

drew a shaking breath. His tongue felt heavy. "I suppose I understand why they're doing it. I'm scared of him too."

"I still fear my father," Eugen said. "And he's two hundred years dead."

"It's a hard thing. We're supposed to be men, to fear nothing. And for years, Fydir never even used worse than words against me. Not like your father—"

"It's never *just words* when you're hurting someone who loves you. No two scars look alike. That doesn't make yours less real than mine."

"A wizard shouldn't be—"

Eugen tipped up his chin and kissed him. *Oh.* Nabik pressed his lips against those cool, polished ones, relaxing with a sigh. Smooth, firm hands cradled his jaw and the back of his head. Wooden joints caught in his hair. Eugen broke away, muttering apologies as the pair of them untangled themselves. Then, with a smile, he tucked a liqueur-filled chocolate into Nabik's cheek. *Sugar and cream brandy. Blessed Winter.*

"It's not who you *should* be that I care for. It's who you are." Eugen cupped Nabik's chin in his hands. "It doesn't matter to me if you're not a great wizard. I want you to be happy."

Happy. Such a small word. Such a silly thing. So far out of reach. He couldn't remember the last time he'd felt happy. *Fydir taught me that my feelings mattered not at all. He said he was teaching me to be a good soldier, a good brother. But all he taught me was that I had to play a part to please him. I had to play a part to survive.*

"I'm *scared*, Eugen. I'm scared I'll be cast out in the cold if folk have no use for me. It feels as if I must shape and polish every inch of me into some sort of tool. A soldier, a wizard . . . I need to be something *for* people. I need to slot into their lives as neatly as a soul into a soul-engine. Or who could love me?"

"I could," Eugen said. "Your mother loves you, and even Drakne does, deep down. You don't have to be anything but . . . you."

"Me. I'm not sure I know who that is."

"Then I'll help you find out."

Nabik smiled. "I would . . . I would like that a great deal." The words were simple honesty, and yet to speak them felt like a weight lifting off his shoulders. "What about you? What do you want to be? The king of Kolznechia? Truly?"

"I'd do anything to help Kolznechia. To make right what my family and I made wrong." Eugen took a deep breath. "But if there's another way to break the curse, one where I don't have to sit on that cursed throne—I'll take it. *King* is only what I've been told I must be. There is nothing in it that could make me happy."

Nabik winced. Eugen was right; all the light inside him would dim the moment he put the crown on his head. Nabik could tell it was already wavering like a candle flame. *This might ruin him. I might ruin him.* "I want you to be happy," he whispered. "King or not. We'll free Winter. We'll break the curse. We'll find a way forward."

"Thank you," Eugen said. A smile crept across his face. "Come on. Let's convince Eba to break the time spell."

"How? We don't have magic. We're just two fools who kissed at her party." Nabik considered. "Unless . . ."

"Yes?"

"I have an idea." Nabik explained. Then he took Eugen's hand

and led him across the greenhouse, to where the enchanted instruments hovered in the air. "Let's make music together."

Eugen's voice was deep, rich, and resonant. Folk songs, bawdy songs, and ballads leapt from his throat. Nabik joined in, and the instruments played along. Their voices blended in an even harmony. At last, they settled on a tavern song, a children's chant: "Xachi and the Squirrel-Fur Slipper." "Fool Xachi had one fur shoe, no idea what to do, sought to buy a matching mate, traded in a golden key, never could escape his fate, slippers he had three. Fool Xachi had three fur shoes, no idea what to do, sought to buy a matching mate, traded in a hen alive, never could escape his fate, slippers he had five—"

"Stop that," Eba ordered when they reached thirteen, swiping her cloven hand at the air. "It's not funny."

"Trust me," Eugen said, "by the time we reach one hundred eighty-one, it gets *very* funny."

Oh, Nabik thought. *I want to sing with him every day for as long as I live.*

The cannon boomed. Time spun backward. Hand in hand, Nabik and Eugen ran back to the instruments and took up the song where they'd started. Two hundred and one. Three hundred thirty-five. Four hundred eighty-seven.

"Should only take another hour or so to finish," Eugen assured Lady Eba when they hit five hundred. The guests were glaring at him and Nabik. They might have lost themselves in the revels, in the lure of Maznun's magic, but this sort of music stuck itself in your mind. The cat reached for the pinewood prince. Eugen knocked his hand away. The orange smoke coiled across his wooden skin and dissipated.

"Oh my," Eugen said. "It seems that trick of yours only works on flesh."

Nabik kept singing. His throat ached, but he drew strength from Eugen, whose wooden treble resonated until the cannon boomed. Whenever the feast restarted, the burn eased, and he took Eugen by the hand and rushed onstage again. The horn blew. The enchanted bow danced across the violin's strings. The guests laughed and danced along. Lady Eba's frown only deepened.

This is what it means to be a wizard, Nabik realized. No, better—what it meant to be *him*. To be a note in the music of this joyous, starving land.

"You're persistent," Eba grunted. "I'll give you that much."

Persistent. It didn't feel like enough. It was all he had. She was listening to him. He couldn't give up now. "You can't run from Fydir. He'll come for us all in the end. The curse feeds off pain and suffering; it'll use his violence to devour the world. We need to stop him now." Nabik took a deep breath. "I don't have the magic to defeat him. But I have a plan. And I have hope. Please. If you'll just listen."

Eba stared at him. At last, she sighed. "Very well. What's your plan?"

"Drakne!" Nabik called. "We need you!"

CHAPTER NINETEEN

Where Winter Sings and Dances

Drakne, or some significant part of her, would have preferred to stay in Eba's manor and eat chocolate. Nevertheless, she followed her brother out into the hazy purple day.

Six fresh inches of snow had fallen on the avenue outside Eba's manor. They picked through the drifts on wooden shoes, leather slippers, beastfolk paws. Tread tracks from soul-engines marred the powder. Every one of their small party held their breath.

"It's the morn of Yuleheigh?" Talzne said. "Already?"

Drakne grinned. Not even a tyrant could take her people's defiant cheer.

Candles glowed on the branches of every crystal pine along the roadway; a cluster of hare-maidens in bright green gowns walked about, lighting each one with long tapers. Children darted around underfoot, tying red ribbons and green-and-silver glass orbs to every branch. Mummers wearing masks of lacquered holly twirled atop tall stilts, emerald pennants hanging from their arms. Passersby exchanged tokens and trinkets, clasping arms, murmuring well-wishes. Smoke flavored with meat and crackling sauce rose from cooking pits. Fireworks leapt skyward and burst with whistles and pops, showers of sparks glittering in the crystals of the trees.

"Don't they know about Fydir?" Nabik said. "And his edicts?"

"That's why we're doing it, boy," said a woman with the long ears of a bat. "He's told us all to come to his palace. Sent those brass-mouthed machines around, the ones that play his voice. We're bound to go to him. But we don't have to go fast."

"What if you did?" Nabik said. "The city folk outnumber his soldiers ten to one. If you all charged into the courtyard, you'd overwhelm him."

"We'd be a thorn in his side. But he'd force us all into the engines soon enough."

"My sister can dance people out of engines." Nabik nodded to her. "Drakne. You'll help them, won't you?"

Drakne hesitated and curled her hand around the strap of her soul-engine gun. It felt like a great deal to promise. She hadn't danced anyone out of an engine since Fydir had caught her. What if she'd lost the knack?

Soldiers clad in the green of the Rat King's uniform ushered a small group of whimpering children down the avenue. Ruba lifted her chin and stepped out before them. "Stop," she said. "By order of your king—queen—"

They pushed right past her. One laughing soldier shoved her down into a snowbank. Drakne rushed to her side and helped her stand.

"It's like they don't even remember me." Ruba brushed snow off her long golden jacket, its ruffled tails now noticeably worse for wear. "Every hour Fydir sits a-throne, his grip on them grows stronger."

"We need to stop him now," Talzne said. "We need to bring the folk of the city together."

"We need to *dance* them together," Nabik said, and once more looked to Drakne.

She gulped. *Dancing.* After everything she'd been through, the last thing she wanted was to try to free souls. It was too much like what she'd done on the day Fydir had broken her. It would only ever remind her of her pain. That she had to live with this weight on her forever.

But perhaps she could make sure these folk were spared it.

And perhaps she could ruin Fydir's Yuleheigh.

The folk of Znaditin flooded into the streets that wound about the crystal trees, making their way toward the palace. In the crowd, lanterns bobbed in hairy fists, and ribbons waved in the hands of children set atop their parents' shoulders. Lichen farmers wearing crystal crowns and crystal shoes passed out mats of spiced mushroom for free. An old song drifted skyward. *Here's where Winter sings and dances, cold wind sparks the fire inside.* Drakne thought about Winter, a goddess torn apart so a cruel man could become a king, and about her mothers, pulled from her by death and magic.

She began to dance. Slightly. Nothing grand. A step to the left. A clap of her hands. A shift of her hips. Nearby, a drummer noticed and took up the beat. Bronze threads of magic flickered in her footsteps. The boys beside her fell into step. A woman with a babe on her hip swayed along. Someone clapped. Someone cheered.

Drakne closed her eyes, letting her body take over. She drove the threads of magic in her steps outward, through the city streets, into houses and hovels, spinning a web. *Come out and dance.* Doors opened. Eager hands pushed tent flaps aside. The crowd doubled, tripled in size. Fiddles and flutes took up the song. The very city seemed to pound with the sound of their footsteps.

More. More. Her power sank into the soil like the roots of the deepest trees, burned in every heart it touched like an ember. Wherever a thread of Yuleheigh music sounded, wherever Fydir's soul-engines spoke his orders, folk heeded Drakne's call and came. *The king wants his people at his palace. Let's give him what he wants.*

With a crowd of ten thousand behind her, they pushed open the palace gates.

In the courtyard of the Crystal Palace stood three dozen soul-engine war machines. Terrible bronze shadows, of the same make and model of the one that had attacked the snowfae fortress. Ice clung to their treads. A hundred cannons shimmered in the dusk. Beastfolk trapped in metal seemed to watch the dancers with hungry eyes.

In the shadow of their bulk, three wolf-guards in royal livery urged a crying knot of children toward a soul-engine. A golden-haired boy, big for his age, twisted and thrashed in the hands of the wolf that held him. One little mouse-girl had her thumb in her mouth as they pushed her toward the socket.

They looked up to see Drakne and every soul of the city marching their way.

The soldiers turned and fled.

"Quickly!" Nabik said as Eugen went to gather up the children. "Drakne! Dance open the engines!"

Drakne looked about the courtyard. The nearby crystal pines reflected the pink and purple light of sunset. The tallest tree, a flawless diamond pine, had been decorated for Yuleheigh, hung with gilded ornaments and wrapped with strings of popcorn, candles gleaming on each branch. She tried to focus on that, and not the horrors all around her. Hundreds upon hundreds of souls, crushed by Fydir's will.

"Look what I brought along," Eugen said. He opened a case, and a trio of instruments leapt out—a horn, a drum, a violin carved of white wood. They floated through the air and, merrily, began to play.

"Dance!" Ruba urged her. "Remember my ball in Malirmatvi? When you made even a mouse graceful? I'd never seen anything as lovely as you."

She'd been lovely, in that moment of hope. She'd believed she might have a life of stage and travel, worn toe shoes and blisters, spotlights and applause. Fydir had dimmed that light inside her. "I don't even have a dancing costume—"

Talzne waved a hand. Drakne's skirts shivered, lifting and fluffing themselves up into a black lace tutu. Seed pearl and garnet beading bloomed down her shoulders and bust. Black leather toe shoes laced up her ankles.

"What?" Talzne said, when Drakne gave her a questioning look. "I'm still angry. I'm helping you do what must be done."

Nabik nodded to the floating instruments. The warp and warble of a traditional carol rose from the enchanted violin. Notes flurried skyward, ringed and muffled by the fresh-fallen snow. Eugen sang, rich and fervent. "Here's where Winter sings and dances, here's where gates stand open wide." The gathered beast-folk turned to watch her. Drakne's throat went dry. She slid the gun off her shoulder. Then she rose onto her toes, swan's neck arched, wings spread about her like a cloak of midnight.

How pointless, whispered a voice that sounded a good deal like Fydir. Dancing was nothing but footsteps and hand flicks. Only what she'd loved, when she'd had the light inside her to love anything.

"Show me," Ruba said. "All the strange beauty Winter has wrought in you."

Drakne took a deep breath. She met the mouse-girl's piercing eyes, recalled steps Nabik had taught her as a child, and let herself start. A skip on her left, a hop on the right, two claps, *spin.*

Eugen waved the children forward, urging them to mirror her. Ruba wheeled a reel, hand in hand with two bent-backed fishermen. Nabik leapt into the dance, twirling in a circle of reindeerfolk as hoofed feet stomped along. Bronze light spun from Drakne's skirt and footsteps. Sweeping over the snow. Sliding up the trees. Joining with the candles' glow as her magic wove the tired and scared city folk together into a body of laughter and song.

The dance shifted, and she and Nabik faced each other: him small and frost white, herself tall, black feathered, magic swirling about her as she stood poised on the edge of flight. They pressed together, chest to chest, heart to beating heart.

"I'm sorry," he whispered. "I tried so hard to be the man Fydir wanted me to be. Even when it wasn't who I was at all. I tried to give you what I thought I should give. Even when it wasn't what you needed. I'm not a great soldier, or a great wizard. I'm just your brother. And the one thing I can do is dance beside you."

"That's more than enough," Drakne said. "I missed this. I needed this." Music. Laughter. Friendship. Herself. "I understand, Nabik. Fydir made a weapon of me too. But I'm so glad we're here. Together." Her family was more than just Fydir, and she was more than her pain, and dancing had always meant more to her than the cold refuge of a crown. *I'm going to be happy again,* she realized, and a honk of snotty, ragged laughter flew up her long throat.

Soul-sockets trembled, shook, and popped open. Brass pins flew across the snow. Metal retreated from the bodies it bound, dropping folk to the earth. They gasped, stunned, reaching for one another as their feet carried them up and into the dance. Snowfae girls and toad-men, fur-faced children and gray-muzzled elders, all joined hands and spun as the violet light of the sockets dimmed away.

The sound of heavy footsteps, a terrible, too-orderly pound, rose beyond the castle's harp-string gates. *Fydir's soldiers.* Drakne swallowed. They'd been sent out to bring the folk of the city to the palace. But the people had gotten ahead of them, and they'd had naught else to do but race back to enforce the king's command. They rumbled toward the gate with the force of a rockslide. The city folk had barred it with some old furniture, but it would not last long.

Though it only needed to last long *enough.*

"Here it comes!" Nabik said.

Lightning crackled through the dusk, bright rushing rivers of silver. Thunder pealed. Bolt after bolt struck the ground around the army. Eba's magic seized the men, a shimmering, nearly reflective barrier threaded with light. They shouted silently, rushed forward, slammed their fists against the spell. And then—

The men of Fydir's army began to *shrink*. Their thick beardy whiskers faded into uneven fuzz and scruff. Uniforms slipped off scrawny shoulders. Weapons tumbled to the ground. The air itself seemed to squeeze and twist as time raced backward.

Within the spell, a thousand children began to play.

Shouts rose from within the keep. Horns blew. Alarms whistled. Guards rushed out, fell into rank on the sapphire stairs, and lowered their rifles. Drakne froze.

Cold snapped through the courtyard. A flight of snowfae soared overhead, clad in armor as white as the moon, carried on the wind in a frosted tide. Silver arrows and golden spears flew at the guards, who shouted, stumbled, and took aim. "Fire!" one called. Bullets streaked across the sky in a percussive rattle—and turned into spools of ribbon that fell harmlessly to the ground.

Genna dropped from the whirl and perched atop a soul-engine. A spear shone in her fist. "This abomination of Winter's gifts ends now!" Guards turned to flee at the sight of her. Talzne waved a hand and bound the men in taffeta. Genna floated to the ground, shimmering with fury, and pulled two newly freed snowfae girls into her arms.

"Thank you, Drakne," she said, meeting the swan-girl's eyes. The lace of her skirt was stained with soot and blood, but her eyes were resolute. "Now, you must act quickly. Your mother needs you."

~

Nabik's blood ran cold at the words. "What has he done to her?"

There was no need to clarify which *he* was meant. Only her eldest son could do Zolka harm.

"My scouts attempted to break into the throne room and free the Heart of Winter. Fydir is in there, holding her hostage. He said he'd kill her if we got too close." Genna shuddered. "If he would shed her blood—Winter could not withstand such cruelty. She and Zolka both would be lost to us. He must be pacified. And the only folk who might succeed are those who know him best."

Blessed Winter, don't let me fail my mother again.

"Let's go," Drakne said, snatching back up her gun. "Talzne, can you lead the city folk into the keep? If we block the halls, he won't be able to run."

Talzne looked to her queen. Genna nodded. "Go, with my blessing. No neutrality can serve us now. We will dispatch his guards while you confront him. *Hurry.*"

Eugen and Ruba sketched out a map of the keep in the snow—the attics, the doorways, the service stairs. Nabik committed its twists and turns to memory. "There's two entrances to the throne room," he noted. "One goes directly onto the stage. For when the kings would have musicians play."

He looked up and met Drakne's eyes. Her beak quirked up in a monstrous grin. Changed and spell touched as they were, it was like they'd slipped back to the days of their childhood, dancing in a snowy alley. Holding each other tight against the cold.

"Into the palace!" Talzne shouted, her voice raw and triumphant. "Fill the halls and galleries! Pack the corridors and side stairs! Make it so he can't escape." The shout rippled through the crowd. With a great shuffle and stomp of feet, the folk of Znaditin surged forward, flooding up the great sapphire stairs.

"Winter bless the king!" they shouted, and it was a threat. "Winter bless the king!"

"Good luck," Talzne told them, and ducked into the throng.

"How do we get to the throne room?" Eugen said. "Drakne can't fly carrying all of us. I'm not precisely aerodynamic."

A low voice coughed from behind them. A harrumph. A bellow. A family of reindeerfolk approached their conversation on all fours, clad in scrappy garments and saddlebags dripping with lichen, little human about them save their eyes and unusually dexterous hooves. Hooves that *hovered*. Every deer in the herd floated several inches off the ground.

"I knew I'd find you somewhere," said the lead stag, lowering his head to face Nabik. "I remember you, little fox—you and your magic lessons back in the silver forest. Me and my children can hardly keep our hooves on the ground since you cursed us. One idle wish that it might be fun to fly like the birds do—"

"Right," Nabik said, swallowing and sweating. "I remember. Good Mr. Reindeer—if I could have your name—"

"Rutri," he bellowed. His long snout glowed red with a massive wart.

"Rutri, I blessed you and your kin so you might, er, save Kolznechia. We need your help. Can you get us onto the keep roof?"

"I'm the fastest flier in Kolznechia." Rutri puffed out his low barrel chest. "I daresay I could span the globe in an evening— twice, if an old lover were chasing me."

Nabik sincerely doubted that. But this was what they had. It would have to suffice.

CHAPTER TWENTY

Pas de Deux

Drakne shot across the evening sky, wings outstretched. Three reindeer charged behind her, running on a road of air and fog. On them rode a cursed prince and the wizard who'd cursed him, and a white fox urging his mount to overtake his sister. She rolled her eyes and aimed her path high through the night until, kicking out with her black leather toe shoes, she perched on the ice-slick roof of the keep.

The reindeer drifted down beside her. Eugen was first to leap down off their backs. "Bit silly of my ancestors, really," he said, bringing his fists down on the scalloped almond-shaving shingles. Nuts cracked. A hole opened into the dark. "Pretty, yes, especially with sugar crumbled on the edges, but a palace of foodstuffs? Not practical."

Nabik dismounted, scrambled across the roof, and peered down into the darkness. "What will we do with Fydir once we've got him?"

Drakne reached up on her shoulder and patted the soul-engine gun. "I'm going to kill him."

"*What?*" said Nabik. "Please. Don't. There must be another way to stop this, for your sake, if not his. You don't deserve to live with that on your shoulders."

"Doesn't the curse feed on violence and cruelty?" Eugen said.

"The curse will have a good deal less to feed on when he's dead," Ruba said. "Shoot him if you want, Drakne. You know your own conscience. I know mine." She reached into the waistband of her gold-trimmed trousers and pulled out a carving knife, one Drakne had last seen at Lady Eba's table. "I don't want to think what that bastard would have done to me if you hadn't gotten me away."

"Everyone in Kolznechia deserves justice for what Fydir has done to us," Eugen said. "Whatever we bring to him must serve the purpose of setting this right."

True justice. Drakne didn't even know what that would look like. If it even existed. "Well. We can work that out when our mother's free." It was easy enough to say. She was the only one of them with a gun.

Nabik tied a rope around Rutri's chest. "When we're all down, pull off and fly to safety. If we fail, take your family and flee across the Great Pole." He grabbed the rope and dropped through the roof. Eugen followed close behind, with Ruba leaping down after.

Drakne took a deep breath, fluffed out her tutu skirt, took up the rope, and plummeted into the darkness of the castle hall.

The abandoned attic was stocked with frozen fudge blocks and dusty carpenter's tools, boxes of theater costumes and mirrors in cracked frames. Wind howled through the cracked roof as Eugen pried up the trapdoor leading downstairs. Drakne shivered. The black lace and beading trembled down her tutu.

"You're almost ready." Ruba slid on her tiptoes and pulled a charcoal from her sleeve. With a few quick swipes, she painted dark, dramatic lines around Drakne's eyes. "Best of luck, my vicious darling."

Drakne leaned in to her ear. "Promise me this won't end with you backstabbing us all and declaring yourself king once more."

"Wouldn't that be awfully funny, though?"

"What would be even funnier is me dancing your ass into the lake." Drakne pinched Ruba's cheek. The mouse-girl smiled.

"You can do this," she said. "I would never bet against you."

"That makes one of us," Drakne said. "Thank you."

Eugen waved Ruba to his side. Nabik gave Drakne a searching look with his amber fox eyes. "Be careful," he murmured, and led the three of them away before she could point out, *We've snuck into the fortress of a man who wants to conquer the world; it's the least careful thing we've ever done.*

She drew herself a map of the castle in her head, trying to remember what Eugen and Ruba had told her, to still the fearful race of her heart. The last time she'd done something this risky, this defiant—

A factory, soul-engine arms slicing the air like saw blades. Toe shoes in sawdust. Arms arched to the steam-stack ceiling. Her breathing sped. Her skin crawled. Her heart fluttered at the base of her very long throat and threatened to smother her. *Before I was broken.*

Before she'd realized that he'd done it all to make her too scared to fight back.

Drakne clenched her fists, then crept down into the lush hall below.

~

Shouts and pounding footsteps rumbled through the keep's shadowed hallways as Nabik, Eugen, and Ruba approached the throne room door. The air hummed with the same pressure as just before a lightning strike. The guards had rushed to the courtyard, to face down the snowfae, or hurried downstairs, to block the advancing crowd. The heart of Fydir's power was as lonely as an unmarked grave.

"It can't be possible," Fydir growled as Nabik opened the door just a crack. A faint hint of panic rose under the golden king's bluster. "That's nearly my whole army down in the courtyard. I spent years planning how I might bring my forces north. Now they're nothing but a lot of squalling children."

"You should be grateful for it," Zolka said. "They're still alive."

"I didn't ask for your opinion. You're here to serve me, nothing more."

Something broke in her voice. "Oh, my little lion cub. All you need is for someone to help you off that throne. I could feel the curse sinking its grip into you from the mountaintops. Step down. Be happy. I'm here. I love you. I'm sorry I couldn't be there when you needed me. It's not—"

"Enough!" Fydir yelled. "No more, or I'll—"

"Hurry!" Nabik said. Eugen pushed open the gilded door. Hinges creaked. Candlelight spilled out from inside, a gold that left them blinking. Hand in hand, he and Nabik entered, Ruba following just behind.

The throne room lay deathly still. Green velvet curtains covered the shuttered windows, falling down all the way to the creamy butterscotch-fudge marble floor. The mirrors framed in musical scores reflected freshly painted ceiling murals of Fydir, royally garbed, hunting boar and reindeer through the woods. Sugar crystals dangled from a chandelier that shone with the light of a hundred candles. An emerald curtain hung behind the throne, sectioning off the disused stage.

Fydir sat atop the beastly throne, its gilded chocolate sculpted into howling predators and screaming prey. Roots of violet crystal spread out under his feet and unfurled from the back of the chair like shining wings. Zolka knelt before him, thinly clad in worn trousers and a shirt of faded olive, her white-blond hair falling loose down her shoulders. Chains bound her, wrist and ankle, pinning her to the floor.

"No," Zolka gasped as she saw them. "Nabik, *run*."

"It's all right," he said, and hoped she would trust him. He dared not mention the plan out loud.

Eugen tossed their enchanted instruments aloft. Violin and drum took up a jaunty, leaping tune with a strong beat. Nabik's clawed feet tapped a rhythm on the marbled fudge. Ruba skipped along. Eugen hummed under his breath.

"You think to drown me out with music?" Fydir chuckled. Nabik could tell he still wished for control, still felt the howl of emptiness within him, and that more and more he believed fulfillment would never come. He wore a fine robe, regal emerald trimmed in white fox fur, yet scraps of food still clung to his beard and the fur of his chest. The crystal roots that pierced the throne shimmered and pulsed. As they grew brighter, the room grew colder. "Little fool. I can shout louder than any violin."

"I've noticed," Ruba said, and cracked her furry knuckles. "It's time someone shut you up."

Nabik stepped forward, his frost-dusted paws sliding carefully across the floor. Pacing with the music as Eugen's wooden feet tapped the meter. "Time to step down and surrender. Your army is gone. Even the snowfae stand against you. It's not too late to come peacefully. Give us wizards back our magic. Let us bind your tongue and break your spells."

"Why? So you can keep me as a house pet?" Fydir rose and descended from the dais, stalking toward his brother. Claws flashed from his fingertips. "I'd skin you alive before I'd bow to you."

"Don't!" Zolka shouted. Fydir didn't even look at her. Nabik swallowed, fur prickling down his spine. He could already feel those claws tearing into his flesh. But he also saw the brother who'd once cared for him, and for his sake, Nabik couldn't give up without trying.

"We won't hurt you," he said. "That's what you do to us. We're not you."

"So what will you do, little fox?" Fydir laughed and rolled on the balls of his feet. He was toweringly tall, and he knew it. "You think you can talk me off my throne?"

"That throne destroyed my family," Eugen said. Fydir wheeled to face him, his tail and his coattails spinning out behind him. The nutcracker stood between him and the dais. "It destroyed Ruba's. Don't let it destroy yours. They deserve better."

Warmth stirred in Nabik's belly. Eugen *cared*. Even with all his faults and failings, he imagined a bright future and worked to make it so. All his wishes shone like sunshine. And next to him, Nabik felt—something else.

A wish as ancient as the world. A wish for community, for family. A wish strangled by crystal roots and centuries of rage.

Winter. Or the last scraps of her.

Genna had said the curse was ancient, rooted in a darkness beyond their understanding. But Nabik thought he saw the meat of it. Some great apparatus that trapped folk inside it and used them to fuel terrors? It was just another soul-engine.

Fydir barreled toward Eugen, swinging a clawed fist at his head. Eugen feinted backward, limber as no nutcracker should be, hooked his ankle around Fydir's, and pulled his leg from underneath him. The lion crashed backward to the floor. Howling, he tried to rise—and Ruba drove her foot into his stomach as she spun to stand beside Eugen, the two of them as graceful as dancers in a minuet.

Nabik strode back and forth before the foot of the dais, a third body keeping Fydir penned. Every step he took fell in tandem with the sparkling, leaping notes of the violin. Something like pity tugged on his heart, a reflex of empathy for any caged beast. *Fydir built this cage for himself,* he thought, but that made it no easier to watch.

"Stop, Fydir!" he barked. "Surrender, undo your commands on us, and we'll grant you clemency."

Fydir coughed, reaching for Ruba. His fist closed on open air as the mouse darted sideways. Her knife sliced at his back, ripping through his emerald velvet coat. "You think I'll give up everything that makes me strong—"

"You have a family. *We* can be your strength." Heart pounding, Nabik took one step closer to his brother. "Say the words. Come *home.*"

For a moment, doubt wavered in those deep gold eyes. Nabik drew a deep breath, steadying himself. He had power here, even with no magic at his fingertips. He could choose to forgive or condemn.

Scythe claws shot toward his side. Nabik lunged backward—too slow. Pain lanced up his leg. He gasped. No, not today. His brother would not change today.

"I'm done with you," Nabik said. "You will have nothing more of me. I'm done."

"Nabik!" Zolka gasped, pulling on the weight of her chains. Eugen ran toward the fox-wizard. Fydir seized the opening and jumped to his feet.

"Stop this wretched music!" he screamed. He swung his fist at Nabik—and spun in an arc of his own momentum, pirouetting on one clawed foot. Graceful and quicksilver fluid, Nabik leapt backward without missing a note, injured leg burning as he sailed into Eugen's waiting arms.

The music grew, thickened, singing from the enchanted white wood of the violin. The drum beat with militant certainty. The horn blew as loud as a dozen trumpets. On the stage, the green curtain fluttered.

"You will *obey* me!" Fydir howled. "Stop those instruments. That's an order. You are *mine*."

Nabik shook his head, which was still cradled against Eugen's chest. The prince knotted a torn strip of his shirt about Nabik's wound as he hopped from foot to foot on the beat. Fydir's command broke like a wave on a rock, washing away.

"How does it feel?" Eugen asked, cupping Nabik's cheek.

"Much better with you here."

"Aren't those two adorable?" Ruba said. She advanced on the

king, grinning wildly, knife shining in her hand. "Unfortunately, Fydir, our own love story is a crueler tale. Surrender, sweet husband, and submit to our justice."

She lunged. Her knife flew in a graceful arc and sliced him from hip to shoulder. Blood flew. Something broke in Fydir's eyes. He pivoted, scrambling at the curtain, feeling for any escape—

And bounced backward as some invisible force sent him tripping to his knees at the base of the stage.

"What are you doing to me?" he howled as the curtain fell.

Behind the fluttering green stood a ballerina, a soul-engine gun strapped tight across her shoulders. She spun en pointe as the hovering horn played a royal salute.

Drakne grinned. "Brother dearest. Now you're dancing with me."

Fydir roared.

The gilded walls and vaulted ceilings trembled with the force of it. The shudder of an empire collapsing. The echo of a captured will.

"How *dare* you?" he growled, swiping at Drakne. All his clawing fell short of her waist. She spun him sideways, twirling him about her like they were two ballerinas in the opening steps of a pas de deux. A toe tap, a flash of bronze, and he leapt backward across the room and crashed down in a graceless heap on the fudge marble floor.

"Careful," Ruba said, positioning herself between Fydir and the door. "Don't play with your food. We won't get the jump on him twice."

"Oh, I won't let him get away. I've been waiting years to dance with my family on Yuleheigh." Drakne's smile widened, a horror on a face with a swan's bill. "How kind of my dear eldest brother to oblige."

"You still see me as your brother?" Fydir grumbled, thunder rolling impotently off his tongue. "I see geese and foxes, rats and owls. Vermin of the wood and farm. We aren't *family*. This I command: When you look on me, you should only see a lion."

And that order, Drakne let slip through her enchantment.

Ghostly fire crackled through Fydir's chest and neck. Muscle swarmed across his shoulders, ripping through his shirt and royal robes. He dropped to all fours, face melting like hot wax behind a thick snout and crushing jaw. Drool dripped from lips not shaped for spoken words. His humanity boiled off like mist on a lake as his mane thickened and his tail lashed the air.

Nabik laughed, the sound wild and barking, his hair sweeping out behind him on an unseen breeze. A staff of peppermint and mistletoe appeared in his hand. The violin played a jig of triumph as he waved his hands and a dozen jingling silver bells joined the song. "Well done, Drakne. You've silenced him!"

"He silenced himself," she said, panting, blistered, still poised on her toes. "He ordered me to see him as a lion. Well, now everyone will."

Ruba's staff appeared in her hands. With a flick of her wrist, the chains binding Zolka broke apart into red, rusty dust. Zolka stood, staggering, and ran to Nabik. Her hand shimmered as she held it to his wounded leg. Ruba went to Drakne's side, shifting into male shape as he did, tattered golden suit transforming into one as lavender as sunset. Drakne pulled him into her arms. They spun about each other, the Rat King laughing in dizzy delight.

Then Ruba gasped a curse. "*Look!*"

Drakne released him, turned—and froze. Despite the conjured music, her careful pose, the arch of her neck, Fydir still advanced on her.

A lion couldn't easily be made to dance.

She ducked under the swipe of his paw as Ruba scrambled away. Claws snagged the flight feathers of her wings and pulled them loose in a bloody, mangled mess. Gasping, she swept her feet balancé, and flickers of bronze tangled in his legs as she scurried backward.

"Help me!" Drakne called.

"You! Brute! Over here!" Eugen shouted, flinging a candlestick. It bounced off his shoulder, and Fydir snapped his teeth at him, but his golden gaze stayed locked on Drakne.

"Fydir!" Zolka said, grabbing for his neck. He shook his head and sent her sprawling, still stalking toward his sister.

He'll devour me, she realized. *He knows I'll never bow to him, so he'll destroy me.*

Fydir lunged—and slipped, as Nabik summoned ice beneath his feet. His claws caught her side as she leapt away. Red bloomed down her hip as she stumbled back behind the cursed throne. The fire of her anger drowned out the pain. "Come and get me, you bastard!" She pulled off her blood-soaked toe shoe and flung it, striking the lion in the nose. Fydir charged toward her, and Drakne pulled her gun up against the meat of her shoulder. She peered down the barrel, bracing herself to shoot.

A paw swiped at her, so close she glimpsed the tiny white scar on its pad. She pulled the trigger. A gunshot boomed through the narrow hall. *Wide. It went wide.* Staggering from the recoil, her head spinning as her heartbeat spiked, she slammed shoulder-first into a mirror. Glass shattered. Pain shot up her arm. She fell to her knees amid the glistening, bloody shards.

Fydir loomed above her, larger than the sun.

"Hey!" Eugen shouted. "Here!"

Fydir turned, eyes frantic. Drakne caught her breath. Eugen stood on the dais, a jointed wooden fist curled around the back of the throne. "Step away from her," he said, "or I'll destroy it. I will."

Fydir snorted, with a note of feline skepticism, and turned back to his sister. His jaws widened, pink and salivating. Drakne fought to think—

There came a crack. A rip. Eugen tore free the throne's backing, spun, and drove his foot through the seat. Gilt foil popped. Crystal shattered. The scent of dusty chocolate filled the air, heavier than history.

A small metal ornament flew out from the broken backing and skidded across the floor to land near Drakne's hand. A disc scarcely eight inches across, made from metal more silver than silver, shaped like a six-pointed snowflake. Unearthly light shimmered at its center. Drakne picked it up, wincing as cold stung at her fingers.

"I've always hated that ugly old throne," Eugen said. "I have one kingly act in me, and I plan to make it count. By the birthright of my blood, I declare the Kolznechian monarchy abolished."

That was all he could muster before Fydir lunged at him. Like a comet of feckless gold, he sailed across the throne room, claws out, snarling—

Eugen shoved the throne into his chest. Fydir struck them both in an explosion of crystal and chocolate. The nutcracker flew back into the wall. Mirrors broke. Wood splintered.

And then, all was terribly still.

"Eugen!" Nabik rushed across the room as Fydir lay stunned atop the ruined throne. He scrambled through splinters and knelt beside the fallen boy. Eugen's spine and the handle in his back had *shattered*. "What have you done?"

"The right thing. I hope." He laughed. It turned into a choking noise. With a trembling hand, he brushed the loose hair off Nabik's cheek. "I suppose you'll have to see if it was right or not without me."

"No," Nabik said. Fumbling for magic, for wishes, for answers. "Eugen, don't move. We'll get a doctor, a something—"

"Don't fuss," Eugen said, voice already fading. "Kiss me. Until I dissolve into starlight."

Nabik bent and pressed his lips to those cold wooden ones. Kissing him over and over, he drank in Eugen's shaking breaths as the prince held his cheek. Every stolen second was like springtime.

"I love you," Nabik whispered. "I only wish—we'd had more time." How much of it had he wasted, crushed by the weight of all he wasn't, when he might simply have been happy?

"I would have been king for you," Eugen whispered. "Thank you for still loving me when I said no."

The prince stilled. A void tugged at Nabik's soul. He wanted to vanish so deeply inside himself that he might never resurface.

"I'm sorry," Drakne said softly, putting a hand on his shoulder. Her other hand held tight to the Heart of Winter.

"I don't know how to fix this," he whispered.

"I know. I'm still here. I love you."

Tears slid down his cheeks. Her wishes washed over him. *I want a fresh start with Zolka,* he caught, and *I want us to be better than what we've been* and *I want us to be happy. Both of us.* And somewhere, in there deep: *I want to break the curse.*

"You ... can," Nabik realized. He would have seen it sooner if he hadn't convinced himself he had to do it all. He wasn't the person who could save Kolznechia. He never would be. Because he wasn't Drakne. "I can't do it. But you can."

"What?"

The throne room shuddered. And Fydir howled in pain.

The broken throne would not die easily. Crystal roots had reached up from the debris. They writhed and twisted, spreading like a spiderweb across the fudge marble floor. They had already coiled around Fydir's legs; now they closed about his chest and forelimbs. Where they touched, purple crystals bloomed on his skin.

"Run!" Drakne said. But the curse raced forward like an avalanche. Crystal roots wrapped around Zolka, caught Ruba around the chest, and lashed about Nabik's thighs. He yelped and fell. Drakne scrambled backward, trailing blood. Her back hit the cold glass of a windowpane. With the crackling, grinding sound of stone on stone, crystal roots reared up before her, like vipers ready to strike. Then—they hesitated.

They seem to *recognize* her.

I know you, it said. *I know your sorrow. Your rage. Don't worry. This can still end how you wanted it. I will make you a queen, an empress, a goddess. Worlds will bow before your power. Just like you wanted. All I need is the Heart.*

Her breath caught. She hadn't thought of this. That, with her magic and the curse's might, she could do everything Fydir had dreamed of.

"The Heart of Winter!" Nabik called. "Drakne! Dance with her! You can dance Winter out of the curse's claws!"

What? This wasn't a soul trapped in brass, a prince turned to pinewood. This was a goddess, caught up in a curse as old as time. *A goddess of warmth, community, and care. A goddess who did nothing for me when I needed her most.*

Someone I could tear down and usurp.

Someone as wounded as I am.

"You can do it!" Nabik gasped, and the crystals coiled around his neck.

"Nabik!" she shouted.

Give me the Heart, the roots said. *I will give you justice.*

Justice. She looked to Fydir, toppled and bound, moaning as shards of purple devoured his skin. Trapped in the curse he had so willingly fed. A thousand raw feelings coursed through her heart.

The one she least expected was pity.

She already had *her* justice. She had dancing back. She was loved. And that knowledge burned inside her like a blazing

317

hearth, a warmth that would not, could not, go out. She needed justice for her family, for her country, for a world gone frozen and cold. *Winter is the time we come together. To do the work of setting wrongs to right.*

Drakne held up the Heart. The cold scorched her fingertips. The cuts down her arms stung. Crimson blood dripped onto the torn black satin of her tutu. Her foot wobbled. The crystals reached for her.

No. She braced herself, blinking away tears. Rising on her toes, she poured all her grief, all her rage, into the pool of bronze light gathering at her feet. *Dance with me, Winter.* The light grew. It twirled up her chest, wheeled around the Heart, reaching for something—something—that seemed to slip from its grasp.

What even is she? Drakne's compulsion could trap mortal souls. Winter was something different. A thousand flickers of lightning. *Whatever you are, it matters not. Dance with me.*

Blood welled at her feet. The curse called her name. Balanced on her right leg, kicking with her left, Drakne spun her fouettés. The room whipped round and round about her. Her back burned. Her calf cramped. Pain pulsed where her toe shoe rubbed her right foot, all her weight pressed down on one point, growing sharper and sharper with each turn. Yet Drakne did not falter or fall.

The Heart glowed bright as the moon. Snow spiraled out from the metal. It flew about the throne room and gathered itself into the shape of a tall, thin woman, her features ageless, her nose crooked, her brown hair coiled in ringlets. Her fingertips brushed Drakne's, and all her wounds vanished to nothing.

Thank you, Winter said.

And Drakne said, "Fix this."

The goddess nodded. Wind howled. Windows broke. Curtains billowed inward. Drakne ducked away from the shower of glass as every violet crystal in the room turned to dust. Nabik, Ruba, and Zolka stumbled to their feet, gasping. Fydir rose, too—but talons of ice seized the massive lion, pinning him in the center of a maelstrom. He fought and snarled, muscles bulging, but Winter held him fast.

The curse is bound, she called. *Now bind the king!*

A peppermint staff appeared in Nabik's hand. He lowered it. Shards of hard candy, a sharp and jagged rainbow, lashed Fydir's cheeks and flanks. The lion howled, clawing at his face. Yule-heigh garlands leapt from the aether and snarled him in knots of pine. One tore, and he swiped at the fox. Drakne twisted her wrist, driving all her will into the flourish. Fydir's blow fell short.

Zolka raised her hands. Snowflakes streaked white across the gilt and splendor, her torrent of icicles joining the stream of candy pushing Fydir down in his frozen bonds. Ruba, grinning wickedly, summoned biting flies from his staff to join the flood of torments.

"Hate to miss the grand finale, darling," he said with a wink.

You won't finish this without me. Drakne glided forward en couru, neck arched, chin high. Cradling the gun that once held her captive. The soul-socket pulsed with violet light. A glow that was reflected in Fydir's golden eyes as they flickered wide with fear.

A bullet to the head. Forever in a soul-socket. She could do what she pleased to him.

Drakne snapped her feet back into first position and bowed. Bronze threads vanished. The music died.

"Just keep him from hurting folk," she said. "I'm done with him."

The torrent collapsed inward. The frozen bonds of Winter shattered. A fist-size crystal orb rolled out from the ice and chocolate debris. Zolka caught it and lifted the snow globe to the light.

Inside, a tiny blizzard blew through a frost-scarred wasteland. A thumbnail-size lion wandered alone through the trees.

"I'm sorry," she said, like the closing of a book, and slipped the ball into her pocket.

~

Nabik doubled over, panting, clutching his chest where the magic had rushed out of him. Sorrow, sweet and piercing like a swan's song, threatened to bleed him dry.

"Are you hurt?" said a familiar voice. A shaky hand rested on his shoulder. A *human* hand.

And the hand was connected to a human boy in an old-fashioned green coat, his cheeks as pale as pinewood, his eyes dark as the northern sea. His smile—and his wishes—as welcoming as a wide-open door.

"Eugen?" Nabik whispered.

The boy nodded. "Winter said that I . . . I should have another chance."

And what a chance it was. *The curse is broken. Winter is free. Drakne did it. And all I did was help along the way.* That was enough for him, he decided. He slid into Eugen's arms and cradled his head against that newly beating heart, stilling to let himself be held. Drakne wrapped her wings around her brother, Zolka embraced all three of them from behind, and even Ruba didn't step away from the family's warmth as the wind flooded through the broken windows and, far below, the city burst out in song.

Entr'acte

After the tearful hugging wound to its inevitable awkward end, Drakne and Ruba went to the window. Songs and laughter rose up from the courtyard. Lanterns bobbed and green lion banners went up in flames. In the city streets and in the forest beyond, crystal treetops shivered, fresh pine needles trembling in the wind as the glistening monoliths turned back to green. Drakne grinned at the sight. The Rat King looked somber.

"Where did Winter go?" he said, hazel eyes darting nervously about behind his glasses. "You don't suppose she'll make trouble for me?"

"I think she's a forgiving goddess," Drakne said. "But perhaps you shouldn't make more trouble for her."

Ruba nodded. "Then I should depart. My shadow has lingered over Kolznechia far too long. The people should move forward without the Rat King in the way."

"You're . . . leaving?" Her heart sank. "Will I ever see you again?"

"If you wish to." He kissed her hand, brushing her feathery skin with his thin lips. "Put a candle in your window. Three long flashes, seven short."

"And you'll come quicker this time?"

"Of course. If I dally, you'll knock my brains out with a shoe."

Ruba hopped onto the windowsill and waved his staff. On his shoulders, a sable traveler's cloak appeared, snapping about him as he spun to face the night. Then he was gone.

Drakne told herself not to spend too long staring at the place he'd disappeared. There was work to be done. Nabik's and Eugen's eager glances betrayed that they'd soon rush off to a castle bedroom, and she'd rather clean up a castle than chance hearing the noises of what would come next.

"Agreed," Zolka said in response to Drakne's unspoken wish. "Will you come with me? I should check on things in the courtyard."

Drakne nodded. Zolka stepped up to the window beside her. Both women spread their wings and leapt.

Swan and owl, black and white, they flew beneath the sweeping stars.

They set down in the chaos of the courtyard. The air smelled of ozone, the lingering touch of lightning from Eba's time magic. The children who'd once been Fydir's soldiers wandered about the yard, their oversize uniforms dragging in the drifts. The children freed from the soul-engines mixed with them happily; they all ran about shouting, crying, or waving popcorn garlands. Many soul-engines had tipped over in the snow, immobilized with all their sockets empty. Snowfae stood guard around them. They watched the crowd with wary eyes.

"Zolka!" Genna appeared in a thunderclap and ran to the wizard's side. "Are you—"

"I'm sorry," Zolka said. "I'm so—"

"No. It's not your fault." The snowfae queen took Zolka's hand. "And your children?"

"Alive. Fydir is bound." Pain shot through her voice.

"I'm sorry." Genna pulled Zolka into a hug. She squeezed the other woman close, then let go. She raised her voice, and magic carried her words on the wind. "The lion-lord has fallen! Kolznechia is free!"

The snowfae and the city folk managed a chorus of ragged cheers at that, then returned to the matter at hand: organizing. Only a scant handful of the children had family to look after them, and the rest had to be sorted into shelters for the evening. Zolka summoned them baskets of cinnamon buns, quilts stitched like snowflakes, and piles of pens and paper to make records of the foundlings.

Lady Eba's servants had carried down the leftovers from her endless Yuleheigh feast. Some foragers had dug wild turnips and onions out of a hardy crevasse between two boulders; children heaped up dung and twisted paper to stoke a cookfire. Drakne dropped roots in a pot as a reindeer-woman stirred. Eba herself walked up to join them, limping and exhausted. Maznun stood beside her, holding her hand. Her brow hung heavy and her chest trembled with each breath, but satisfaction glimmered around the edges of her smile.

"You know, I've never liked children," she was telling her husband. "This does nothing to change my mind."

Drakne offered her soup. "It might interest you to hear that Eugen destroyed the throne and declared the monarchy abolished."

"Hmm." Eba thought it over, sipping her soup. "Who rules now?"

"Ruba left. He said Kolznechia should make its own way. Which means those of us who can compel folk's choices shouldn't interfere." She took a deep breath. "My purpose is in the south. Yours could be too. The Empire won't give up on Kolznechia's souls and lumber. But you could defend this land without firing one shot."

"I'm a bit old for heroism."

"But you're never too old to make trouble." Drakne stood and squeezed Eba's shoulder. "Be sure you make the right kind."

Drakne drained her soup bowl, the broth rich and salty, and walked off, humming a tune. *Let her think over what I've said.* Zolka stood by an abandoned soul-engine, sweeping her staff through intricate patterns while the metal crumbled itself down for scrap. A little girl, no more than three, grabbed at the wizard's leg.

"Owl!" she gasped. "Big owl! Big owl!"

Zolka chuckled, sweeping the child into her arms. "Aren't you a mess!" She snapped her fingers. The girl's ragged dress transformed into a fluffy petal-pink petticoat, her tangled hair twisting into ribbon-tied pigtail plaits. "That's what you wish to wear? Well, it's a bit fancy, but if it keeps you warm—"

Drakne's stomach sank as Zolka bounced the child on her hip. The same sickly feeling she'd get at school when the other girls didn't hold a seat open for her at dinner. "She's sweet," Drakne said, and winced. "Did you . . . expect to get that back? For me to be the same daughter I was when you left? I can't. I'm not. I don't want to be."

Hurt hovered in the air between them. "Sweetheart," Zolka

said. "I . . . I'm sorry things are so awkward between us. Fydir, at least, I knew before I left, and Nabik and I have such similar souls, but with you . . . truth be told, I'm not quite sure *how* to be your mother. Not yet. Not when you're already the sort of person I always wished I could be. You're brave, determined, and you don't give a damn what anyone thinks of you. I'm so deeply proud that you're my daughter."

Proud? Of me? "I went along with Fydir's war plan. I nearly killed you."

"And I don't need magic to tell that you wish to grow beyond that." Zolka shook her head. "Some folk won't forgive you. But you're my daughter. My joy. I know that we'll need time to make things right—but whatever you want or need from me, it's yours."

She'd spent so long trying to escape her family. She'd never even known what she might ask of it. But seeing the little girl tucked under Zolka's wing gave her direction. "Can I have . . . a home with you? Just to know I have somewhere safe to go? Where I'll always have food and clothing, and . . . where you'll take care of me, if I need it?"

"Absolutely." Zolka hugged her close, tucking her beneath her other wing, white and warming. "You will *always* have a safe home with me."

The realization trickled through her like sunshine seeping through the clouds. Never again would she fear the streets. Never again would she need to gamble desperately to escape a man's control. With a wish and a wing, she could dance right back into a place of safety. Whatever she risked, whatever she chose, the cruel winds wouldn't cut her to the bone.

At long last, Drakne Zolkedna was safe.

"Please don't ever tell anyone how soft I just got." Drakne laughed. "I have an image to uphold."

~

For weeks, havoc ruled the halls of the Crystal Palace.

Three rulers had claimed the throne. Fydir was trapped in a snow globe. Ruba had vanished on the wind. Eugen had scribbled a declaration abolishing the aristocracy and reincorporating Kolznechia as a constitutional democracy, signed it with his father's signet, and hidden from crowds and influence-seekers in the castle library.

Zolka and Nabik had summoned representatives from every village and town in the country, moderated quarrels as the people hammered out and signed a constitution, and confiscated the hoarded wealth of whichever nobles remained too recalcitrant to accept the accords. One old bear nearly clawed Nabik in half when he collected the gold, and a goose duchess swallowed several fortunes in diamonds to hide them. But with Kolznechia's treasury full, the nation could build roads, sewers, and railways in the modern fashion—and build a future that would benefit all, for the new constitution banned any use of soul-engines on Kolznechian land.

Nabik sat down next to his sister in the balcony overlooking the parliamentary chamber, which was truly just a ballroom packed with a mismatching mélange of chairs and benches. Beneath them, Nivni and the delegation from Stakte laid out how they would manage the sustainability of their silver mine, and a beaverfolk elder negotiated with a wolf pack to trade farmland for protection from poachers.

The curse had broken. Most pines and fields again were green. But the beastfolk remained beastfolk, for Winter had transformed the curse itself. Anyone touched by its power could control how deeply their animal aspects manifested. Now, some in the palace went about growling on all fours, while others wore their beast only as a green flash in their eyes, and others still changed their shape with each new dawn. As for himself, Nabik remained small and fine-featured, a two-legged winter fox—but he'd threaded silver hoops all down his ears. The chaos of shapes was as grand and messy as a nation finding its own way.

"How do you want this to go?" Nabik asked his sister. "Being friends?"

A spot of machine grease dotted her cheek. All of Fydir's soul-engine arsenal had been brought to Znaditin for salvage, and she'd spent her morning dancing them open. "Are *friends* the sort of thing you need to write a plan for?"

"I've never had many. I wouldn't know."

"Small wonder, if you organize companionship like a cavalry charge."

He laughed and waved his hand. A checkerboard appeared, topped with chocolate coins. The tokens on one side were stamped with foxes; on the other side of the board, they were stamped with swans. "Shall we play?"

"I have nothing better to do," she said. "Winner buys drinks."

"If I go out drinking, I might make more friends. And then what will I do?"

She reached out and ruffled the top of his head. The bells on his hair bands jingled. "I wouldn't worry about it."

As winter's long nights stretched out into spring, changes unfurled through Kolznechia alongside carpets of barley and wildflowers. Traders from across the Great Pole and the Sounding Sea trekked to Znaditin, carrying pelts, lumber, and medicine. • New roads cut straight paths through the city, set with tracks for electric streetcars, and the Whale-Friends nations eagerly offered to sell their wind- and wave-powered engines to modernize Kolznechia's farms. Blue and silver tulips bloomed in the palace courtyard. As Nabik strode past them to meet Zolka, he thought their perfume smelled of changing things.

The snowfae had transformed one of Fydir's war machines into an enormous fountain. From the top tier, six brass pines sprayed water skyward in dazzling arcs. Coins glittered in the pool at its base. Rumor whispered that sipping from its waters inspired ludicrous generosity—after partaking, the head librarian had flung open her doors to host storytelling festivals for the palace children, and the housekeeper had granted the castle maids six weeks' paid leave.

Zolka pensively stirred the sparkling waters with one hand. "The assembly is concluding its business. Have you given any thought to what you'll do next? Winter is free. We're no longer bound to stay in Kolznechia."

"But I want to," Nabik said. "I want to travel and see more of the country." Hidden villages in snowbanks. Towns touched by curses. Winter woodlands and open stars, a country born anew, and a wizard free to find his own way.

Zolka squeezed his hand. "Good. I'll be staying here, for now. The new leaders of this country need my council. There's hundreds of spell-touched children who could use a wizard's aid. And

I should make things right between myself and Genna, while I'm at it."

Nabik nodded. A pack of children ran across the cobblestones, chasing a ball. He waved his hand, tied up their loose shoelaces before they could trip and fall. "I'll miss you. But I'll come back to visit when I may."

"No need to hurry." She gave him a knowing nod. "I know what it is, to be in love."

Three days later, Nabik was back in the courtyard, white-trimmed robe swirling about him as he worked spells for warmth and swift travel into a sleigh. Eugen met him there, dragging a trunk along the icy stone. The former prince wore a coat of deep blue wool and black leather traveler's boots. His beastfolk mark—slender stag antlers—jutted up from his brown curly hair. He stopped every few feet to catch his breath and rub his back, his flesh-and-blood muscles still unused to labor.

"Would you like a hand with that?" Nabik called.

"I won't have you strain a muscle by accident. Not when we'll strain them all a-purpose tonight."

Nabik laughed and waved his hand. The trunk hovered off the ground, skimmed across the courtyard, and landed at his feet. The lid popped open. *Small wonder it would barely budge.* It was full of books: primers on history and grammar, texts on geometry and calculation, ancient ledgers of fairy tales with the letters big and block-printed for beginning readers. "Do you really require this much to read? This will take up half our luggage space."

"It'll take up *my* half," Eugen said, walking up to join him. "And if I need clothes or whatnot, you can summon them."

"Very well." Nabik nodded at the trunk. It closed itself; ropes of pine appeared and lashed it to the sleigh beside his own. "But you'll only get to wear what I decide on. And it won't be much at all. You'll be frigid."

"You'll keep me warm." Eugen grinned. "The books aren't all for me anyway. Folk will need to learn to read and write, if they're to help govern a democratic Kolznechia. And I can teach them our histories, or at least my own, and that of my family. If we're to keep our pains and curses from sprouting up again, we should learn to recognize their roots."

Nabik considered. "You might be more useful to this land than I am."

"Good," Eugen said. "Don't be useful. Be *mine*."

Nabik hovered half a foot off the ground and took Eugen by the lapels. Wind spiraled about them, tossing up snow. Long, clever fingers forked back through his unbound hair as their lips met. The slow, lingering kiss tasted of peppermint and pine. The flavor, Nabik thought, of *forever*.

"I think," Nabik said, nuzzling the brown stubble of Eugen's jaw, "that kissing a teacher may be even finer than kissing a prince. But I'll need to experiment a good while longer to make sure."

Eugen laughed. Nabik let him go, and he climbed into the driver's seat. "Are we calling Rutri and his family back to pull this? A flying sleigh would be fine indeed."

"One day, maybe." Nabik slid into his lap. With a flick of his staff, the sleigh raced toward the golden harp-string gates of the palace. "But I'd like to keep you to myself for now."

Myself. Someone Nabik couldn't wait to discover.

Drakne returned to Malirmatvi to find a great deal of confusion. Archduke Marinus and half the members of Parliament had written Fydir long letters demanding news of his Kolznechian campaign. She had responded with the tragic news that he had fallen in battle before Stakte; his army had scattered, save for the heroic men who had escorted her back south and perished on the journey. When they had written to press for details, she'd forged a man's script and written as a doctor to attest that Drakne Zolkedna could speak no more of such bloody business lest it damage her delicate constitution. And that was that. Fydir was gone and, save for a pending military inquest, forgotten. He'd blazed across the Empire like a shooting star and left nothing but embers in his wake.

Some days, even she didn't think of him.

Eugen had given her a handful of royal antiques to pawn, so she was well provided for at the present. With no husband to claim her, her property was hers to control, and she doubted anyone would challenge her residence at the manor until a new governor arrived. The poor man would have a hard time at the job. The battle-scarred, unruly city grew more anarchic by the day.

Merchants and adventurers from every corner of the world streamed into Malirmatvi, lured by the prospect of Kolznechian trade. Imperial scouting parties sent across the border vanished for months at a time, only to come back and claim their journeys took mere days. The women of the city heard Winter calling them and flocked to pray in the woods; the priests denounced the goddess as a demon. Whispers spread through Rot Hill of how the wizards had undermined the Kolznechian nobility, and while the city's factory workers and fishermen spoke among themselves of how equal prosperity might come to all, the high nobles debated how they might strangle such treasonous talk in the crib.

Archduke Marinus won't give up on conquering Kolznechia that easily. Drakne would need to finish what she'd started with him. But now he had problems of his own. Across the Empire, soul-engines were developing strange attunements to workers who spent too long bound inside them. Like the gun she'd taken from Fydir, these machines would work only at the touch of their bound soul—and the attuned workers were demanding quite large sums for their continued labor. Drakne assessed rumors like a sailor judged the winds, and packed for the south as the time grew near to strike.

And every night, she played checkers with Nabik—each of them using a board he'd enchanted for them to share.

"So Eugen kept the class's attention for three whole hours?" If she had to deal with children that long, she'd leap off a bridge, wings folded.

"He's so patient with them," Nabik said, fangs flashing as he grinned. A smoky image of him hovered, magically projected, at the far side of the board. The scars down his cheek had vanished, spelled away by a snowfae. Drakne wouldn't ever forget the pain she'd caused him. But she didn't need to see it to remember what she'd learned. "It's adorable. If they're stuck, he'll explain over and over how to do it. Always trying to find a way that works, accepting when they can't. It's darling. He'll make such a good father one day."

"Please tell me you haven't been messing with fertility spells."

"I did find some relevant books in the Rat King's library in Stakte." He skipped his checker across the board, clearing three of her tokens in a go. "And speaking of the Rat King, you're about to have a visitor."

Drakne looked back over her shoulder, at the candle glowing in her window. *Three long, seven short.* She'd signaled as soon as the sun had set. "I'm not going to ask how you know that. You wizards love being cryptic."

"We love being right."

A knock echoed through the house. The image of Nabik winked at her and vanished into a puff of smoke. Drakne waved away the housemaid, brushed crumbs off her green satin dress, and opened the door to find a tall, spindly young man in a top hat and tails. No overcoat. Face hidden behind a newspaper.

She took the paper from his hands. "What sort of gentleman caller doesn't meet a lady's eyes?"

"I'm not a gentleman. I'm a rat." He pointed to an article on the back page. "The lead of the royal ballet is retiring. Auditions start in six weeks."

"I know. I've already booked my train ticket." She hesitated. "In fact, I booked two. I felt . . . hopeful."

"Hope. For me?" He laughed. "Now there's a novelty."

She pressed her own hand to his sallow cheek, then reached back and pulled the ribbon from his ponytail. Dark hair blew out on a warm wind that carried with it the first taste of spring. "Novelty keeps life interesting. Whether it's the royal ballet or a disgraced, deposed, vicious wizard-king."

"This king sounds delightful," he said. "Send him my way?"

She hummed a tune and tugged him back into the mansion, bronze flicking at her feet. The halls seemed to warm with his presence.

"Are you sure you want me to come with you?" Ruba said, nervously fiddling with his glasses. "We've both spent a fair amount of time trapped in darkness. Me especially. I confess . . . I'm not quite certain how to live in the light."

"You mean, without a cursed throne, do we still matter to each other?"

"You matter to me," he said. "I know that much. But what do you want, Drakne? Make the wish, and it's yours."

"I want you," Drakne said carefully. Considering. "To make me disgustingly happy."

"Good. Because I want you to give me a chance to win your heart. All of it. Not just your shadows."

Oh. Dizziness seemed to flutter through her head. Her heart flipped over. For a moment, she thought she'd caught the flu. *Joy, fear, and hoping. None of these feelings are mine.*

But perhaps they could be.

Drakne toppled back onto a love seat, pulling him atop her. Their lips met, a kiss that tasted like earth and loam, fuel and fumes, the volatile heart of *forever*. "We have a bargain, Rat King."

"My lady!" gasped the housekeeper from the balcony. "This is most improper—"

Drakne hummed a scale and flicked her foot. Bronze light left the woman hopping and skipping into the servants' quarters. "I'm not a lady," Drakne said, pushing Ruba's head down to her collarbone. "I'm a dancer."

A dancer with a soul of summer and a hunger for revolution.

For a world where no one broke innocent girls for shining too bright. For kisses like fire and forest soil. For whatever glory tomorrow would bring.

~

Drakne met the workers in the yard behind Boris Atvidan's hat factory at sunrise. Dawn light crept across the northern hills, red and pink awakening into cloudy blue. A springtime warmth hung in the air. The enchanted instruments hovering behind her played a lively jig. The reek of chemicals stung her nose and sparked her anger. *When the sun blazes and the days run long, hearts come into conflict and the great powers fight for control* . . .

"I knew he was getting pelts across the border," said an old woman with a ripe bruise on her forehead. "I asked if they were beastfolk, and he beat me bloody."

"Beat all three of us," said a girl young enough to be her great-granddaughter. "We had the strength in numbers, but he's so big."

"I almost quit on the spot," said a woman with her hand in a splint. "I will, now that I know what he's doing. But desperate folk will do desperate things for money. That won't ever change."

"Change yourselves, then," Drakne said. "Malirmatvi's folk were born of old Kolznechia, and you still keep Winter's cheer. The curse is broken. All folk of our blood or custom can wear their beastfolk aspect as they please. Give it a try."

The old woman closed her eyes in concentration. Wiry hair

thickened down her face and back, muscle racing up her arms. The girls changed more hesitantly, brows furrowing as they squeezed their fists and willed, mouthing quiet prayers. *Saints, forgive us.* Fur and claws streaked them all the same.

"No one will ever hurt me again," gasped one, staring in awe at her hands.

The wind shifted, blowing down from the north. It smelled of gingerbread and growing things, of hearth fires and togetherness, of rage, justice, and hope. *Winter stands with us.* A mask of black feathers swam across Drakne's face. She grinned behind her bloodred bill, ruffling out her tutu. "Welcome to the revolution, friends."

On the roof of the factory, Talzne gave the hand signal. *All clear.* Drakne gave her a quick nod. They might not ever be friends, but it didn't take a friendship to start a fire.

Wings unfurling from her shoulders, flanked by screaming catfolk and determined ferretfolk, Drakne strode onto the factory floor. Machines whirled to a clattering halt. Her enchanted horn began to play a strong, determined march. She lifted herself up en pointe, swept her foot in a wide arc, and let a flicker of bronze fly. Soul-engines rattled with her every prancing step.

Atvidan ran from his office, red-faced, puffing—and afraid. "This is a place of business!" he yelled. "Can't you—"

Factory women ringed him on all sides, grinning, their fangs shining. He froze and wailed. The horn played a blast. Soul-sockets burst open. Captive workers tumbled out and leapt to their feet, stomping and clapping as they joined the dance. Ruba ducked in through a side door, along with Talzne's beau, Simon.

They passed water and wool blankets to the laborers as Drakne approached the cowering businessman.

"We claim this factory," she said, "in the name of the common folk of Malirmatvi."

Graceful like a swan, grinning like a victor, she grabbed him by the collar and flung him out into the snow.

Acknowledgments

Every book is a journey, and this has been quite a longer one than most. I'm so grateful to everyone who has been there with me along the way.

Special thanks are due to Deb and Dave Perkins, who held a warm door open for me when I needed one.

I'm so grateful to Kaitlyn Katsoupis, who fiercely advocated for this book every step of the way, and to Mekisha Telfer, for all her detailed feedback and strong editorial eye. The beautiful cover illustration is the work of Allison Reimold, who brought Drakne's anger and determination to life. The rest of the beautiful book is the work of the design and production team, with special thanks due to Sarah Gompper, and the fact that you hold it in your hands is thanks to the marketing, publicity, and sales teams.

To all the friends who helped me get this far—James, Morgan, Becky, Kianna, Aster, Sophie, Kay, Tatiana, Hazel, Sol, Motti, Emilia, Foz, Ally, Layne, Gloria, Sam, Artie, Eldar, Erin, Liz, Jess, Page—your encouragement and enthusiasm means the world to me.

Finally, to the readers, especially Lu, Pasha, and everyone else who supported my debut. It's been an incredible journey and I so look forward to what comes next!